Suddenly
Dating

A LAKE HAVEN NOVEL

Suddenly Dating

JULIA LONDON

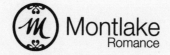

Text copyright © 2016 Dinah Dinwiddie
All rights reserved.

Published by Montlake Romance, Seattle

www.apub.com

Amazon, the Amazon logo, and Montlake Romance are trademarks of Amazon.com, Inc., or its affiliates.

ISBN-13: 9781503937796
ISBN-10: 1503937798

Cover design by Eileen Carey

Printed in the United States of America

Suddenly Dating

One

New York City
April

The first time Melissa broke up with Harry was on a Wednesday night, because Harry had come home later than he'd said he would. Okay, a lot later. *Late*-late. But he couldn't help it—his crew had run into a problem installing a support beam under a bridge and it had taken a colossal effort by dozens of men to right that sinking ship.

When he walked into their little apartment, he knew he was in trouble. Melissa was sitting at the bistro table with an empty wine bottle before her and the dregs of said bottle in her glass. There was a plate of food in Harry's spot: congealed spaghetti and something else he didn't want to examine too closely. "I'm sorry—"

"I don't want to hear it," she snapped with a queenly flick of her wrist. "I'm done."

Done. What did that mean, exactly? For the evening? With him? Harry wanted to ask, but as he was a veteran of this relationship, he knew better than to seek clarification when that much wine obviously had been drunk.

Melissa's blue eyes narrowed; she knew he didn't know what she meant. She came to her feet. Clumsily. And swaying a little when she pushed her long dark hair back over her shoulder. She had on a very short skirt and heels that made her look hot, and, God, Harry wished he'd made it home on time.

"I've had it with you, Harry. You're *always* late. You come in looking like some *Game of Thrones* character with your shaggy hair and your dirty clothes," she said, gesturing wildly in his direction.

"Well . . . I work in bridge construction," he said calmly. "It's kind of a dirty job. I apologize for my hair, but you know that I wear a hard hat most of the day."

"So you can't get a *haircut*?" she cried, and pitched forward, catching herself on the table.

This was the first he knew that his hair was an issue. He dug in his pocket for a hair band and pulled it back into a short tail.

"Oh, yeah, *that* works," she snapped. "Here's the thing, *Harry*. You do whatever you want," she sang, casting her arm wide, "and then you expect me to sit here and wait with a dinner I *slaved* over."

Here they went with the same sort of argument they'd been having a lot lately. "I don't expect you to wait, Melissa. That's why I told you to go ahead without me," he reminded her. "And, to be fair, it's spaghetti."

Fire leapt into her blue eyes.

"Not that I don't appreciate it," he hastily added. Jesus, he didn't want to do this right now. He was tired, he was hungry, and that damn support beam was going to cost him more money he didn't have. "Come on, baby . . . you know what I'm trying to achieve."

"I didn't move in with a *bridge guy*, I moved in with an engineer! A *project manager*," she said, enunciating clearly, as if he didn't recall what he'd been when they'd first met. "A guy on track to be *partner*."

"I'm still an engineer," he pointed out. "And you could say I am the sole partner in my firm."

"You know what I mean," she said dramatically, and tried to dislodge herself from the tight space between the chair and the table, knocking both pieces of furniture out of place and somehow managing to twist the chair around so that she was even more pinned in than before.

"I'm probably using more of my degree now than before," Harry said. "I can honestly say I am more of an engineer now than I was with Michaelson's."

"Don't try to worm your way out of this," she said, pointing at him with such deliberation that she almost fell over the chair. "I don't want to be with you anymore," she said, suddenly tearful.

And now, the waterworks. Drunk waterworks were the worst. "Come here," he said, opening his arms wide. "Let me give you a hug."

"I'm done, I'm done, I'm so *done* with you," she moaned.

Wow, it was that kind of done? Harry was a little surprised. "Come on, Lissa, you're drunk—"

"And whose fault is it that I'm *drunk*? You made me drink the whole thing because you were *late*." The effort she put into the word "late" served the dual purpose of making a point and freeing her from the trap of the chair. It banged into the counter as she stumbled away from the table, teetering on her heels.

"Technically," he said, catching her before she fell right off those stilettos, "I think you did it all on your own. Don't cry, baby. Things will look better in the morning."

"This isn't what I signed up for," she said, slapping his hand away. "You never said anything about building bridges and spending *all* your money on it and then selling the *apartment*."

So that's what was behind this. She'd known about his desire to create his own company since they'd met. But he guessed that she'd assumed he would somehow stay on at Michaelson's in his cushy job with the great salary for the foreseeable future, even though he'd been very clear that he had goals. Big goals. "I need the cash," Harry

3

reminded her. "If I'm going to get this business off the ground, I need to make some investments. Do you know how much those big cranes cost? They're not cheap."

"Why can't you borrow the money? Why do you have to sell our apartment?"

Sometimes, Melissa forgot that it was his apartment. She was quite successful in public relations and owned an apartment that she'd sublet once they'd decided to move in together. "We talked about this, baby." He reached for her again.

Melissa slapped his hand from her.

"You don't even like this apartment. We're downtown, and you want uptown. When I get a couple of contracts under my belt, we'll get a bigger, better apartment on the upper west side, just like you want."

"Nope. Not me," she said, swaying again. "Because I'm done, Harry!"

She lurched away from him. She almost made it to the bedroom door before she rolled off a heel and onto her ankle, and crashed into the door frame. With a wail that should have brought a SWAT team, she managed to catapult herself through the door and slam it shut.

Harry took his hair out of its queue and dragged his fingers through it. She was just drunk. She didn't mean what she'd said—she wasn't really done with him. They'd been together eighteen months now, they were committed. And Harry loved Melissa.

He wished he could make her understand what it was like to have a dream of something, how it drove you, ate at you, made you get up every morning and do something about it. But she didn't get it. She'd fallen into public relations work by chance, and she'd be happy to give it up if something better came along.

In contrast, Harry had always known he wanted to be an engineer. He'd been interested in building things since he was a boy. After graduating with his pricey engineering degree, he'd landed a job at the prestigious Michaelson's, a huge firm out of Pittsburgh with offices in New

York and Chicago. For several years he'd worked designing bridges for big road projects. He loved the design work, but Harry learned he was not cut out for office work. He wanted to build the bridges he designed. He wanted to get his hands dirty and pour the concrete himself.

A year ago, he'd saved enough money and made enough contacts to go out on his own. At first, he got lucky. He won two subcontracting bids for small bridges with a larger road construction firm. Those two contracts had been a blast. He was like a kid with a big erector set; he loved that rough-and-tumble world of big construction. He loved seeing supports poured and beams seated and the bridge going up, piece by piece.

The best part about it was that Harry had done precisely what he'd set out to do when he told his parents he was going to Cornell for an engineering degree. "I want to build bridges and roads," he'd said. His mother had been horrified. "You're too smart and too talented to waste time with labor," she'd said. But Harry was certain of what he'd wanted, and he'd gone after it.

After two successful jobs, Harry's third bid had nearly ended him with unforeseen cost overruns before he could even get started. Both his mother and Melissa had immediately jumped on board the *I-told-you-so* train. "Isn't it time to give up this foolish idea, Harry?" they'd said. "Hasn't this taught you anything, Harry?" they'd asked.

The only thing it taught him was to be careful of the teams he hired and to build in a better contingency. His family and his girlfriend could say whatever they liked, but Harry was single-minded about it. He knew what he wanted and he was willing to work his ass off to get it.

He just had to figure out how to get Melissa to see what he saw in their future and to believe in it, too.

Harry turned back to the bistro table. He picked up the plates, walked into the kitchen, and started cleaning up.

◆ ◆ ◆

Melissa wasn't better in the morning.

Harry had slept badly on the couch and was up at dawn combing through a stack of invoices. The work required to get his firm off the ground was equally grueling on the job site and in paperwork. Someday, he'd have people to do this crap for him. At least that's what he kept telling himself.

He was eating his second bowl of cereal when the door of the bedroom creaked open. Melissa emerged with a very large suitcase. She was wearing yoga pants, running shoes, and a soft jacket. Her hair was in a tight ponytail at the top of her head, and dark circles shadowed her eyes.

Harry slowly lowered his spoon back into his bowl and looked at the suitcase. "What's going on?"

"God, don't shout," she said, pressing her hand to her forehead, and jerked her enormous suitcase through the door.

Harry felt a tic of panic in his chest and slowly stood, staring in disbelief at her suitcase. "Lissa? What's going on?"

She sighed. She stopped trying to move the suitcase, and covered her face with her hands for a moment. And when she dropped them, he could see tears in her eyes. "I'm sorry, Harry. I really am," she said softly.

He strode across the room, but she shook her head and folded her arms across herself. "I don't . . . this is not what I want. You know it's not. I thought when we moved in with each other that we were building toward a future. That we'd get married and have a family—"

"We were. We *are*."

"You are. But I feel completely left out. I hardly see you. You're working so much that we never see our friends any more. And you're losing money and selling the apartment. It just feels like things changed and I didn't get a vote."

"That's not true, Lissa. I was up front with you about what my goals were when we first met. I told you I wasn't fulfilled at my old job. I told you I wasn't a desk guy and I was starting my own company."

"I didn't know that meant that I'd never see you or that we'd be struggling financially. I know what you're going to say—to give it time. Well, I've given it a year, Harry, and it feels like you're clinging to this idea, and you don't see that it's not working, and in the meantime, I'm supposed to wait it out."

"Be patient, Lissa. Have a little faith. This is just a rough patch. Can't you hold out a little longer? I'm this close," he said, holding up his thumb and forefinger an inch apart.

She sighed sadly. "So close that you are selling the apartment. And then what? What will you sell after that?"

When he thought of the future, he didn't think of selling something else. He thought of the bigger, better apartment he would buy for her. Harry was confident that by investing a little he was going to get the break he needed. "Look," he said, moving cautiously forward. "I've had some great contracts with bigger firms. But there's no gain without some risk, baby. I *will* get bigger jobs. But in order to do that, I have to have equipment and manpower."

"You keep talking about this crane," she said. "Where is it even going to go? Where are we going to live?"

He took another step forward. "What about your place?" he suggested.

"My place is a studio. And it's rented."

She did not say that the rent was all hers, too. Hell, she probably had a lot more in the bank than he did. She was a senior account manager at a top New York PR firm.

"Even if we moved there, it wouldn't resolve the bigger issue of us wanting different things," she said.

"Don't you love me?" he asked.

"Oh, Harry," she said, her eyes tearing up again. "Of course I do. But I have to be true to myself, and this isn't working for me. I'm sorry, I really am." A single tear slid down her cheek, and she bowed her head.

"Ah, Lissa," he said soothingly. He hated to see her cry and reached for her elbow. This time, she didn't slap his hand away, so he tugged her forward.

"Melissa." He kissed her neck. "We'll work it out, baby."

"You always say that," she muttered.

"And we always do." He kissed her cheek, then lifted her chin and kissed her lips while he nudged her enormous suitcase away with his boot. "I promise you, I'll make it up to you," he said, and put his hands on her hips and began to move her backward, toward the bedroom.

"I'm not backing down," she said, but her arms went around his neck.

"I know you're not," he agreed as he filled his hand with her breast.

"And you're not forgiven for last night," she said as he managed to get her through the bedroom door.

"I'm on my knees, begging for forgiveness right now," he said, and with his foot, shut the bedroom door behind them.

Two

May

There were five people in the divorce recovery group, three of whom had survived recent, painful divorces from their "soul mates," one in the midst of a nasty and protracted divorce, and one . . . Well, one was Lola Dunne, whose divorce was neither terribly recent nor enduringly painful.

Lola's group mates included John, a balding, overweight, bespectacled man in his fifties who had discovered his wife was having an affair when he walked in and found her with her legs in the air, her panties on the floor, and a much younger man banging away; Betty, a well-dressed, slender woman whose children had grown up and left the nest, at which point she realized she was through raising children, including her husband; and Paul, a big guy who was partial to canvas coats. Paul never said much, but when he did, it was about the bitch who'd taken his money and the best years of his life.

Last but not least was Sara, whose marriage had been suffering death throes for over a year. Sara and Zach Miller had a lot of money,. and neither of them was willing to part with it. Their divorce was so acrimonious that every red cent was being counted, every tit had to match a tat, and not a single memory of the last fifteen years would be allowed to go untarnished.

In comparison, Lola's experience was so mundane, she felt guilty for even mentioning it at group. She wished she had something a little juicier to offer, but alas, her divorce was simple—she and Will had grown apart. No children, no pets—they just walked away from it. Like the six years they'd been married had meant nothing. Which wasn't true, at least not for Lola. But Will? Maybe.

Okay, well, that had all happened more than a year ago, and Lola was embarrassed she'd ever let Sara talk her into coming. She'd met Sara in a yoga class and had been attracted to her sleek, blonde bob, her coordinated Lululemon outfits, and her take-charge-and-kick-some-ass attitude. In contrast, Lola's yoga clothes were Old Navy all-purpose capris with whatever T-shirt she could find. And her attitude was that everything was fine, just fine.

They'd started with an occasional coffee, had bonded over being divorced . . . well, more accurately, they'd bonded over Sara's ongoing divorce. At first, Sara had been sympathetic and outraged for Lola when she'd filled her in on the basics of her split from Will. But Sara's divorce was just beginning. Each week, her split was growing into the Worst Divorce Ever, and Sara refused to let anything or anyone top her drama.

Lola knew this, and she should have known better than to allow Sara to persuade her to tag along with this group, because she didn't have an ax to grind like Sara did. But Sara had begged her, had complained she hated going alone, and Lola . . . Lola was that friend who never said no. To anyone. *Ever.* Even when it was so clearly evident that she should. Present a need, and it was genetically impossible that Lola did not attempt to fix it. It was kind of a problem.

She should have made her exit long before today, but the group was so dang small, and now everyone depended on her to bring the snacks each week. Oh, yes—somehow, Lola had become the donut-wielding smiling face who made sure all of her fellow divorcée snack needs were met.

"You're such a pussy," her younger sister Casey had said when she dropped by Lola's Clinton Hill apartment in Brooklyn and found her sister making a cake. "Just tell them all they're a bunch of whiners and you're never coming back."

"I really should," Lola agreed.

"But you won't," Casey said, quite matter-of-factly. "Because this is what you do, Lola. You take care of everyone else and neglect yourself. Give me a spoon so I don't have to lick the batter bowl."

"I don't neglect myself. And I was planning on licking the bowl."

Casey shrugged and wiped the bowl clean with her finger.

Yep, Lola was definitely a pussy.

She was mulling over all of that in the middle of the group session the next morning. She wasn't thinking about how divorce made her feel, or how Betty was droning on and on about life choices. She was mentally absent from the discussion until Tamira, the counselor, snapped her out of it by asking, "Can we hear from you today, Lola?"

What? *No!* Lola was used to sitting quietly while other people talked, fighting off yawns, wondering about things like whether or not she should take up knitting, or what was up with North Korea, or what the difference was between barley and bulgur as they had both made an appearance in her salads recently. She was *not* used to talking, and was so surprised that it took her a moment to realize everyone was looking at her. She slowly sat up. "Me?"

"Yes, you!" Tamira chirped. "You're so quiet, Lola. But I assume you're in this group for the same reason as everyone else."

"Aah . . ." Jesus, she hoped she didn't have to come up with a good reason for being in this group because she didn't have one. *Sara made me* sounded a little pathetic, even to her.

"By that, I mean, you're divorced, right?" Tamira asked, as if Lola might have forgotten why she'd baked that stupid cake last night.

"Yeah . . . about a year now."

Tamira nodded, and her head of amazing corkscrew curls bounced. She leaned forward, her arm braced on her thigh, absently clicking the end of her pen. "And?"

"And . . . it wasn't very dramatic," Lola said apologetically. "We just grew apart." She lifted her shoulders, let them fall.

"That's what happened to me," Betty said as she studied her nail. "I realized that somewhere along the way Russell and I had gotten on two different ships and they'd gone in different directions. When did you get on your ship, Lola?"

"I, ah . . . I don't know that I got on a *ship*, exactly." Lola hadn't had to think about what went wrong between her and Will in a very long time and was suddenly aware how much she didn't want to think about it now.

"So how did you know you'd grown apart?" Betty asked. "I mean, I had no idea I even felt that way until one morning Russell was eating breakfast." She suddenly leaned forward and looked around the group. "That man ate the same cereal every morning of his damn life. Frosted Mini-Wheats! Can you imagine, every day for fifty years you eat Frosted Mini-Wheats for breakfast? Every morning, the same thing, *munch munch munch munch slurp*." She shook her head. "I was standing there listening to that and it suddenly dawned on me—he and I weren't on the same planet anymore."

Everyone in the circle nodded.

Lola eased back in her metal seat, sure that Betty would take over. But Betty didn't take over. She looked at Lola and asked curiously, "So how did *you* know, Lola?"

"Well, it had nothing to do with Frosted Mini-Wheats," she said, and laughed a little. No one else did. It wasn't anything like that—Will would never go near cereal. He was very careful with his diet. Lola fancied herself an excellent cook, but Will always complained if the meal wasn't a salad and a piece of fish with some flax seed or some bullshit sprinkled on top. Whatever happened to lasagna? When did it become the bad guy?

"So what did it have to do with?" Betty pressed.

Lola swallowed. "I guess it had to do . . . with . . . a text message," she said uneasily, and suddenly wished it had been cereal. How easy that would be! *Will, we're through because I don't like your cereal choices.*

"A text message? For who?" Tamira asked politely.

Lola crossed her legs. "It was a text message to Will from someone named Danielle."

Sara suddenly shifted around in her seat, her focus laser sharp on Lola. "A *text*? You never told me about a text! You never mentioned anyone named Danielle! What'd it say?"

"I don't—"

"What'd it say, what'd it *say*?" Sara demanded.

"It said . . ." Lola really didn't want to repeat it, but she could tell from the way Sara was looming over her like a raptor that she had no choice. "It said, *Babe, I can't stop thinking about last night.*" And boom, just like that, Lola's stomach dropped down to her toes.

She managed to get her foot crossed behind the opposite ankle.

"Wow," Sara said, eying her like some sort of alien. "How did I not know this? What'd you do?"

What does anyone do when they see a text like that? She'd lost it. Just thinking about it made Lola's heart start to pound, and she was suddenly overcome with an overwhelming urge to plant her face in a bucket of ice cream. "I talked to Will about it, of course."

Three or four days later after she'd stopped sobbing hysterically, which was how long it took her to process it—meaning get up off the bathroom floor—she'd decided to confront him. Sara would have picked up a bazooka and fired away if she'd found that text. But Lola didn't know how to use a bazooka, so she'd had to approach it a little more sanely than that.

"And?"

"And . . ." Lola scratched the back of her neck. "Will didn't deny it." Actually, he'd kind of shrugged like she'd found some old sweatshirt he thought he'd lost. *Oh, that.* He'd asked her to sit down like he was the principal and she was the B-average student, and then very calmly told her he thought it was over between them. He'd said he was sick of her family's constant needs and how she couldn't say no to them when *he* had Bigger Needs. He said a bunch of other stuff, too, like how Danielle made him feel alive or some shit like that. "I guess he grew a little further apart from me than I did from him."

"Ya *think*?" Sara snapped, then threw up her hands and fell against the back of her folding chair. "See what I'm up against?" she said to the rest of the group. "This is how she is."

"What do you mean, this is how I am?" Lola demanded.

Sara suddenly sat up again, planted her boots firmly on the ground, and leaned forward to Lola. "You're too *nice* or something. I don't know what it is with you, but you always act like nothing is wrong. Why didn't you tell me this before? And why are you letting him off the hook?"

"I'm *not* letting him off the hook! I divorced him, remember?"

"The man is a dick. Get mad! Call him a dick!"

"Why do I have to call him a name?"

"Because you do!" Sara exclaimed, arms flailing. "He cheated on you! Am I right?" she asked, looking around to the other three divorcées.

John shrugged. "It wouldn't hurt anything to call him a few names. Get it off the chest, you know?"

"Russell definitely called me some names," Betty snorted.

"Everyone, let's remember our rules. No judgments," Tamira reminded the group, and to Sara, she said pointedly, "Please don't project your anger with Zach onto Lola."

"I'm not projecting my anger with Zach onto her," Sara said, mimicking Tamira sarcastically. "I'm projecting my anger with *her* like a missile right into her kisser. She sits here every week and doodles on her notepad like she is so above us."

"That's not true!" Lola objected.

"It's kind of true," Betty said, without rancor. "If you don't have any issues from your divorce, why are you coming?"

"Because!"

Everyone leaned forward, waiting for her to expound.

Because Sara had asked her to? Because she had trouble saying no? Because she hid the truth of her sorry life from everyone and always had because that is how she'd learned to survive? Because she'd buried the pain of Will's betrayal in a hole so deep she couldn't dig it out if she tried?

"Because, Lola, maybe you *do* have some issues you need to deal with, and your subconscious is aware of it," Tamira suggested. She was practically levitating out of her seat with eagerness, as if she'd just led Lola toward some miraculous breakthrough.

"Of *course* she has issues she needs to deal with. You don't get divorced and not have *issues*," Sara said with a roll of her eyes.

The issue right now, Lola realized, was that she'd twisted herself into a human pretzel.

"Well, okay!" Tamira said. "I think we're getting somewhere."

Lola wondered where exactly they were getting, but she knew where she was getting, and that was the hell out of this group.

"Unfortunately, we don't have time to tackle all of Lola's lingering issues today. So next week, we'll talk more about it."

"I don't have lingering issues," Lola insisted.

"In the meantime, I'd like you all to read chapter seven from your handbook for next week," Tamira said, ignoring Lola. "Sorry, but I have to run. Please don't leave empty cups and napkins. There is a Zumba class in here after us, and I've had a few complaints."

Everyone else had left by the time Lola had obediently picked up the room. Sara had left with Betty, talking in low voices with their heads together, probably about Lola. Lola tucked her dirty cake pan under her arm, kicked the door open with her foot, and strode out of the building and into a breezy spring day. She walked across the Brooklyn College campus, headed for Flatbush Avenue and the subway.

She wasn't coming back. She'd have to deal with Sara in yoga class, but Lola had played at this "divorce trauma" long enough, and by God, someone else could make a damn cake—

"Hey! *Hey!*"

Lola whipped around.

Sara was striding for her, with her arms and the fringe on her leather vest swinging with each violent step. "What the hell is the matter with you? Why are you letting your ex off the hook?"

"I didn't let him off the hook!" Lola said angrily. She wasn't angry with Sara, but with herself, because maybe she had let Will off the hook. She was always letting people off that goddamn hook. "Why are you giving me such a hard time about it?"

"Are you kidding me? I have tried to help you—"

"If by helping, you mean having me sit while you talk about *your* divorce—"

"And you sit there week after week, you never say a word, and when you do, you're practically apologizing for having divorced a dickhead who I find out today was cheating on you!"

Lola huffed. She folded her arms around the cake pan and looked away, considering it. "I don't think that's an entirely accurate representation," she sniffed.

"Ah, girl." Sara suddenly linked her arm through Lola's. "Come on, let's get a drink."

"It's only eleven o'clock."

"Fine, have it your way!" Sara exclaimed. "Coffee then." She tugged on Lola to force her to walk with her, dragging her toward the avenue. "Look, I know you don't want to be pushed. I get it. But we need to talk, and even though I've got a million things to do today, and saving you from yourself is not on my agenda, I'm going to be the kind of friend you need."

Lola wasn't sure she needed that kind of friend, but as usual, she went along.

◆ ◆ ◆

At the corner Starbucks, Sara sauntered up to the counter in her skinny jeans and knee-high boots and ordered two lattes without asking Lola what she wanted, then bulldozed her way through the crowded tables to a tiny two-top against a wall. Lola looked down at her jeans and Keds and oversized sweater. Sometimes, she wished she could be like Sara, all sexy and entitled.

"So," Sara said. "You work in a law office. Paralegal, right?"

"Right." Her dream of getting a college degree in creative writing had been derailed by the need to send a few siblings to school. Like, all of them.

"And the ex is a lawyer, right? And this Danielle chick is a lawyer too, right?"

"Um . . . no," Lola said. "Will met her at a law seminar in Miami. She was the hotel concierge."

"Jesus," Sara said. "What, do you just walk up to the concierge and tell her you need dinner reservations and a fuck?"

Lola blanched at that. She didn't want to know what Will had said to Danielle while he was still married to her.

"So listen, Lola. You need a friend," Sara said, tapping her finger on the table.

"I have friends, Sara—"

Sara shook her head. "Not those friends. I'm talking a *friend*."

Lola blinked. "Like one with benefits?" she asked, slightly shocked.

"*No*, I don't mean that," Sara said, and pointed her spoon at Lola. "But that's not a bad idea. You should totally consider it." She put her spoon into her cup and stirred. "The thing is, Lola, you don't stand up for yourself. I'm going to help you do that."

Lola groaned and rolled her eyes. "Look, Sara, I'm sure you mean well. But just because I didn't tell you the nitty-gritty about my divorce doesn't mean I can't stand up for myself."

"Oh yeah? Then why are you still working with your ex?"

"I'm not," Lola said smartly. "I transferred to another part of the company. To a different building."

"Even worse!" Sara cried, throwing up both hands. "You changed *your* life to accommodate *his* affair."

Funny, but Lola's brother Ben had said the same thing one day when he asked her to pick up his son from basketball practice. Lola hadn't been able to fill in for Ben that day because she'd started her new job in Manhattan.

"Manhattan!" Ben had shouted into the phone. *"Why did you change your job? That asshole knows you have family in Brooklyn!"*

Family that needed her to pick up their kids, Lola silently amended. "Actually," she said to Sara, "I transferred when they gave my promotion to the new guy. It really had nothing to do with Will." Except that Lola suspected it had everything to do with Will. She suspected that Will had suggested it to his buddy, Frank Perroni, who just happened to be Lola's boss.

"Tell me something," Sara said, crossing her long legs and adopting a serious mien. "What do you really want to do? If the world was your oyster, what would you do? Where do you see yourself in five years?"

"What is this, a job interview?" Lola asked with a snort.

"If you will get off your high horse for one minute, I actually have a couple of ideas for you," Sara said. "Come on, what do you want to do? And I mean *do*, as in, what in your heart of hearts would fulfill you? If you had no responsibilities, and could do anything Lola Dunne wanted to do, what would that be?"

"I like the idea of no responsibilities," Lola said. "I don't know—date a lot of different guys," she said, tossing that out there.

Sara gave her a withering look. "I'm being serious. If you want to date, get on Tinder. I'm asking what you want to do with your *life*. And if you say be there for your five hundred brothers and sisters, I may punch you in the mouth."

Lola didn't say that, but there was no avoiding her two brothers and two sisters.

"So?" Sara pressed her.

Lola knew what she wanted. She was writing a book. She'd never told anyone but Casey because it seemed so unattainable. Lola squirmed a little, could even feel her cheeks warming as Sara watched her so intently. "It's stupid," she said.

"Is it?" Sara asked, perking up. "I'd like to say nothing is stupid, but we both know that's not true. I'll reserve judgment until you tell me. Come on, Lola, what is it?"

"I don't want to say," Lola demurred.

"Tell me!" Sara cried, and thumped Lola's arm.

"*Ow*. Okay, fine. I'm writing a book. I want to be a writer." There, she'd said it. She'd admitted her dirty little secret to someone.

But Sara looked puzzled, as if she was quite unfamiliar with the concept of writing. "Like . . . a legal book?"

"No! A novel. I would really like to be a novelist."

Sara's eyes lit up. "Now *that* would be cool. Lola, *you* would be cool if you wrote a whole book!" she said happily, as if Lola were uncool now.

"Well, thanks, but cool isn't exactly what I'm going for."

"What are you going for?"

"I don't know . . . fulfillment? It's just in me," she said, gesturing to herself. "I have this need to write. So I do."

"What's the book about?"

"It's about a woman around our age, who is like every woman you'd ever know. She's someone's BFF, and she's a good friend, and a good daughter, but she's just pissed about life and why she never gets the guy. She's also part psycho, and when a guy breaks up with her, she loses it and kills him. And it's so easy, she does it again. And again."

Sara stared at her for a moment. "That is *so* weird, I would read it," she said thoughtfully. "Can I read it?"

Lola laughed. "I haven't finished it. You asked what I want to do, and that's it. I want to finish this book. And write a bunch more."

"So finish it already," Sara said with a shrug.

"It's not that easy! I work full time and I have a lot of obligations."

"You mean you have a lot of siblings that always need something," Sara scoffed.

That was true, but in the absence of parents, Lola was all they had. "I'm just saying, there are only so many hours in the day. I'm working on it, but it takes time and concentration." And she was stuck. She'd written ten chapters and she was frozen with indecision about which way to go with her book. She kept fantasizing about spending a week on a beach with nothing to do but think.

"You can find the time if you really want to do it," Sara said confidently. "What about this weekend? Can you work on it this weekend?"

"Not *this* weekend," Lola said, as if that were a preposterous suggestion. "I've got too much to do." She couldn't even begin to name all the things that she had promised her siblings. For one, there was her nephew Braden's basketball game. *"You have to come, Aunt Lola!"* Two, her brother Ty needed some help cleaning out his flowerbed because his wife refused. *"I make the babies around here. The least he can do is clean out the flowerbed,"* Jaycee had said. Three, Casey needed the zipper in her favorite jeans fixed, and, four, of course her youngest sister Kennedy needed a ride to Ikea for some bookshelves. None of that included checking in on her mom at the home, either.

Sara frowned, studying her. "You know what? You need to quit your job and commit to your dream."

Lola laughed. "While I live on the streets?"

Sara suddenly grinned. "What if I told you I have a great place? What if I said it's on a lake and you could live there all summer, *rent free*? What if I told you that all you had to do was feed yourself and write your book?"

"I'd say, sign me up," Lola said cheerfully.

"I'm not kidding, Lola. Have you ever heard of East Beach?"

Of course Lola had heard of East Beach. Everyone had heard of East Beach. It was about an hour or so train ride from the city on the shores of Lake Haven, a place where the rich and famous escaped in the summer. "Don't make me laugh," she said, and sipped her coffee.

"I'm serious," Sara said. "I have a lake house that no one is using. Technically, it's on the list of things Zach and I can't touch until the divorce is final. So it's just sitting there, collecting dust. It's perfect for writing books, Lola. I mean, it would have to be our little secret, but no one would ever know."

"What? How can no one know?"

"You *have* to keep it a secret," Sara said, as if that were a perfectly normal condition. "Because Zach and I are both banned from going since we had that big fight—" She waved her hand. "Never mind that. I can't go, but you can. It's a *great* place. The renovations cost us a half-million dollars. Are you interested?"

"*No*, I'm not interested," Lola said. But she was interested, more than interested. She thought she might actually be drooling. Forget the beach—she had a sudden image of herself sitting in some swank house on Lake Haven, pounding away at the keyboard in the throes of writing her novel. "This sounds absolutely nuts, this no-one-can-know thing, Sara. But . . . tell me more," she said, leaning forward.

Three

May

Melissa broke up with Harry for the last time on a Thursday night.

He was supposed to be at a huge event she'd orchestrated for a cosmetics firm that was launching a new line of products. She'd worked hard on it. "Everyone in New York who is anyone is going to be there," she'd gushed to him a few days before. "Some of the New York housewives, and the *Today Show* people, and you know, just everyone."

Harry had every intention of being there. He'd even told his foreman he was knocking off early. But then the scaffolding under a section of his bridge had collapsed, which meant the long braces couldn't go up. The project had already been delayed and was costing him thousands of dollars, so he couldn't very well walk off and leave that situation. He'd texted her, told her he'd meet her there.

This is really important to me, she'd texted back.

I know. I'll be there.

But he wasn't there. He'd tried, God, how he'd tried. There was just no way he could get to the event in time.

He was waiting for her at half past ten when she came home.

"You smell like . . . body odor," she said, wrinkling her nose as she dropped her purse on the table.

"How'd it go?" he asked.

"Great," she said with an insouciant shrug. "Fabulous. Bella Cosmetics was very happy, and my boss says I'm going to start getting bigger accounts." She glanced at her watch. "I'm beat," she said, and started for the bedroom.

"Lissa, I am so sorry," Harry said, coming to his feet, intercepting her. "You wouldn't believe what—"

She held up her hand to stop him. "Don't even try, because you always say that." She put her hand on his arm. "Harry? I need to tell you something. I'm moving in with Lexi for a little while. I think we both need to take a break and reassess where we're going with this relationship. We're just not headed in the same direction anymore."

Harry's chest tightened with anxiety. He didn't want to lose her, but he knew he'd really blown it. He rubbed his gritty face with his hands, trying to think. "I don't know how to make you understand," he said helplessly. "I'm committed to you, baby. I'm committed to *us*. I want to give you the kind of life you deserve, but I need time to get my company off the ground, and unfortunately, there are going to be days like this."

"I think you're kidding yourself," she said softly. "There are so many days like this that I'm not sure if you have any money left at all."

"I don't," he agreed. "But I got an offer on the apartment this week. We'll find a place that will work temporarily—"

"*No.*" She sighed, and pressed her fingertips to her temples. "Look, it's not that you're always late or smell like a gym half the time. It's not even that you're trying to build this construction company. It's that I want something different than you. It's really not you—it's me."

"Come on, Melissa," he said, and brushed her cheek. "You really didn't just say that, did you?"

"If the shoe fits," she said, shrugging a little. "I need some time to think about what I really want. And I can't do that being mad at you all the time, you know? It's not fair to either one of us."

Now Harry really panicked. She sounded sane and reasonable. Not furious, as he would have expected. She'd really thought this through.

"I'm going to Lexi's for now," she said, and started for the bedroom.

"Please don't do that. Please stay. We can work through this. Just hang in there. Be patient."

"I've been patient." She disappeared into the bedroom.

Harry stared at the bedroom door as his whole body deflated. He'd been trying to keep it all together for months now—go after his dream, be the man Melissa wanted him to be—and suddenly it felt as if it was all falling apart. He followed her into the bedroom. His mind was racing so fast he couldn't even think of what to say.

She already had a bag open on the bed. "I'm not officially breaking up," she said, as if that helped anything. "I just need some time to think, you know? I'll come back for my things this weekend."

"You can't go tomorrow?" he asked incredulously, gesturing to the bag on the bed.

"No. Because you will start to kiss me, and I'll be weak and we'll have sex, and I'll love you all over again, and then tomorrow, when I wake up, you will be gone back to that . . . *job*," she said, sounding disgusted, "and I'll be in the same place I am right now."

Harry tried to reason with her as she packed a few things. He tried to explain it all again—that he couldn't quit now, that he'd sunk everything into it, and he had to make it work.

But in the end, Melissa hoisted her bag over her shoulder and walked out.

◆ ◆ ◆

The next morning, Harry awoke to steady rain. Figured. It went on all day, washing out any hope of getting some work done on his current job. He paced like a wild animal, ran his numbers again, and worried about how he was going to pay the crews. He would lose his shirt if this weather kept up.

He kept walking back to the closet to look at all of Melissa's things. He toyed with the idea of boxing up her stuff, then toyed harder with the idea of going over to Lexi's to talk to her. But he decided maybe he needed to give her the space she wanted.

It rained the next day, too. And the next.

Harry was beside himself with restless worry and inactivity and eagerness to do something other than sit around and think. He was working out every day for two or three hours. He was meeting friends here and there, but he couldn't keep his mind on the conversations. The gym was the only place that gave him a brief respite from thoughts of Melissa and the need for a million bucks in the bank.

He'd finished up a long workout with heavy weights and was about to head home when the skies opened up. With a groan, Harry retreated from the exit and slipped into the gym's juice bar. He ordered a drink, then sat down near the window to wait out the deluge.

"Westbrook! Is that *you*?"

Harry looked up to see Zach Miller sauntering toward him. Zach was a partner at Michaelson's, and he and Harry had worked together on a couple of projects. Harry liked Zach—he was gregarious, always good for a beer and sports talk. His gray muscle shirt was soaked with sweat, and his gym bag, which banged against his knee as he strode toward Harry's table, had definitely seen better days.

"Dude, what's up?" Zach asked cheerfully. He fell into a chair, his legs splayed wide, then dropped his gym bag.

"Hey, Zach," Harry said. "Good to see you. What's new with you? How are things at Michaelson's?"

"Same old," Zach said. "We won the bid on the new highway outside of Philadelphia."

"That's fantastic," Harry said.

"Yep. Going to be making some *bank*," Zach said with a knock on the table. "So how's it going with you, man? Life treating you well?"

"Fairly well," Harry said. "I've had a few bumps, but, you know, life goes on."

"Oh yeah?" Zach's smile turned serious. "Bumps in your company? What kind of bumps?" Zach never had any compunction about asking nosy questions.

"That, and . . . Lissa and I are taking a break." It was the first time Harry had said it out loud. It felt weird. It was supposed to be Harry and Melissa from here on out.

Zach gasped. "No *way*," he said, wincing. "I thought you guys were headed for the altar."

"I thought we were, too," Harry said with a rueful smile. "But she's not into bridge construction."

"I feel your pain, man. I'm *still* trying to divorce Sara."

Harry wasn't surprised. Zach's divorce was legendary, the cautionary tale to all the single men in the office: *Look what women can do when they are pissed.* Harry had heard through the grapevine that the Millers were counting every penny in the penny jar and arguing over each one. "I'm really sorry to hear that," Harry said sincerely.

"Anh," Zach said with a flick of his wrist. "It will happen eventually. But I've moved on," he said with a wink. "Been seeing this girl who is a cheerleader for the Knicks. Just graduated college." He made a crude gesture with his hand, apparently to explain his attraction to her.

"That's . . . great," Harry said uncertainly.

"So okay, we could talk about women all day long. What's going on with the Westbrook company?" he asked, punching Harry lightly on the arm. "I heard you got a piece of the new bridge over Paxton rail yard."

"Yep. I'm about to wrap that up," he said, deciding not to tell Zach how much he was losing on that project. "I'm hoping to take the next step and bid on my own. No more subcontracting. I've heard that Connecticut is going to build a new toll road. I'd like to get in on that."

"Awesome," Zach said, and sounded genuinely happy for him. "What's stopping you?"

Harry laughed. "Cash flow, man. As in, I don't have any. In fact, I accepted an offer on my apartment." He filled Zach in on his immediate plans for the future, and why he needed a fat bank account.

Zach, of course, understood Harry's needs and his ambition. He agreed that selling the apartment was a way to get the cash without going into debt. "So where are you going to live?" he asked curiously.

"That's a good question," Harry said. "I'm sure I could live with my folks for a while, but dude, I'm about to be thirty-four. I think I'd kill myself."

Zach laughed. And then he got serious, drumming his fingers on the table, studying Harry as if he were privately debating something.

"What?"

"I might have a solution for you."

Harry laughed. "Are you inviting me to take up the guest room?"

"Sort of. Do you need to be in Manhattan?"

Harry thought about it a moment. "Nope. Most of my work right now is upstate. Why?"

A big showy grin spread across Zach's face. "Dude, I've got the perfect place for you. Have you ever heard of Lake Haven?"

"Sure," Harry said.

"I've got a lake house there, about a half mile outside of East Beach. Well . . . that's not entirely accurate. I *had* a lake house there. Now it's part of the divorce, and of course, Sara is contesting it, so it's off-limits to us both until a judge can decide. In the meantime, it's sitting there unused. And it will sit there at least until fall, when our divorce goes to court. You could live there, Harry. Stay there through the summer and get your business off the ground. All you'd have to pay is the utilities. Interested?"

Harry stared at him. It almost didn't seem real. "Are you serious? Of *course* I'm interested."

"I'm serious," Zach said. "It's a great place and it's being wasted. I'd be happy if someone was there keeping an eye on things. The caretaker is some friend of Sara's, so who knows what's going on out there. Give me the word and I'll tell him to take a hike and get you a key."

It was a miracle, a solution dropped right in Harry's lap. It was almost too good to be true. He thought about Melissa. And his work. And how he was so relieved right now that he could kiss Zach.

Four

June

At first, Lola couldn't even find the lake house, not even after driving up and down Juneberry Road twice in search of it.

She'd rented a car in Brooklyn and had stuffed it full of her things. She'd put the address in the map app, but she was not a frequent driver and, therefore, not a good one. Still, she'd managed to follow directions to East Beach, so she knew she was in the right area.

She could see why East Beach was so popular. It was a pretty little village on a gorgeous lake. There were old Georgian- and Federalist-style houses on the main streets of the village, with pointed roofs and gables, big windows, and porches. There was a post office and a couple of bistros, too, and a coffee shop with a large outdoor deck that looked inviting. A row of boutique shops lined the cobblestone street down to the lake, most of them with summer dresses, kites, and fishing gear waving in a soft breeze on the walkway just outside their display windows.

Lola followed the directions out of East Beach to where the homes turned to mansions dotting the hills around the lake. She turned onto Juneberry Road, drove past a hardware store, and motored all the way to the top, to an old stone gate that said *Ross*. Behind the gate, she could see the roof of a massive house.

She turned the car around and went back down for a third time.

It was impossible to see the house addresses. First, the road was windy. Second, the houses here were behind gates and down long drives, and apparently everyone out here liked to display their house numbers in artsy swirls of iron and colorful ceramic mosaics.

Lola was growing concerned. What was she going to do if she couldn't find Sara's house? Her rental car was stuffed full of her clothes and toiletries, her books and her espresso coffeemaker, which, according to Flavorwire, was essential to any real writer. She had a brand-new laptop, because how ironic would it be to quit her job to finish a book and have her old laptop die on her? And the gift from her siblings—a town bike attached to the trunk.

The car was due back at five, and Lola was beginning to believe there was more than one Juneberry Road. Maybe she needed Juneberry Avenue or something. And if she ever did find this lake house, this windy road and gate business was going to be a royal pain in the ass.

Maybe her siblings were right. This was a ridiculous thing for a thirty-one-year-old woman to do. "You don't just quit your *job*," Casey had said. "That's what alcoholics and millennials do. That's something *Mom* would have done if she'd ever had a job. You're so not Mom, Lola."

Lola could see Casey's point, which was why it had taken her a few weeks to get up the nerve to do it.

Ultimately, it was Will who convinced her, however unwittingly, to go for it.

Her ex had called her out of the blue and asked if they could meet at what once had been their favorite coffee shop. It was next to a little park and had outdoor seating. They used to go there on Sunday mornings and watch kids playing across the street.

Will wouldn't say why he needed to meet. He said he was in a place where he couldn't really talk, but he really needed to see her and would explain when they met.

Of course Lola's imagination had run wild. There were very few reasons an ex-husband would want to meet his ex-wife, as she had pointed out to the ever-pessimistic Casey. Either he was going to hit her up for her half of a tax bill or something, or . . . he wanted to reconcile. "Maybe," Lola said, trying to sound casual and uncaring, "maybe his adorable little concierge fuck-buddy turned out to be all wrong for him." And if that were the case, Lola would try very hard not to deliver a smug, *told you so.*

"He wants something," Casey said flatly. "No way is he thinking of anyone but himself."

"He's not *all* bad," Lola had tried.

Casey had thrown up her hand between them. "Don't even," she'd warned her sister. "After what he did to you, I can't even talk about him. If I were you, I'd tell him if he has something to say, he can say it over the phone."

Lola got where Casey was coming from—but Lola also knew there was a different side to Will, and she wouldn't be surprised if he confessed he'd made a mistake. She had no intention of taking him back . . . at least she didn't think she did . . . but she wouldn't mind hearing a little groveling.

She'd dressed carefully for the occasion, determined to give off the I-have-*flourished*-since-you-dumped-me vibe. She chose a very short, dark-blue dress that Lonnie McIlroy, a guy from work, had said was "smoking hot." She wore tall navy pumps and some hosiery that cost almost as much as her electric bill. She casually draped a sweater around her shoulders, donned the pearls that she had scavenged from her grandmother's things before everything had been sold, and tucked a tote bag under one arm. She was the cosmopolitan city girl, dashing by to humor her ex on her way to some place important. She was not the woman who slogged every day to work in a coat two sizes too big for her, carrying her lunch in one hand, and a canvas shopping bag with her laptop, office shoes, and files in the other.

On the afternoon she was to meet Will, Lola had marched confidently down the street with the absolute certainty that she looked so good, she was going to knock his socks off . . . but when she saw Will, it was her heart that had melted. It was him, the same man she'd met her second day on the job at the law firm. He of the broad shoulders and carefully tousled blond hair that was helped along with a lot of product each morning. He was wearing a suit, his tie loose at the collar. He smiled when he saw her, and he sort of lifted his hand halfway as if to catch her eye.

He caught her eye all right. Lola had felt a little fluttery. She hadn't seen him in months, because stalking him on Facebook didn't really count. He was here, in the flesh, smiling at her, and . . . and he was holding the leash of a fluffy brown dog about the size of a cat. It was sniffing intently around a tree.

"Hey, Lola," he said, and put his arm around her, drawing her into his chest, kissing her cheek as if they had never fought and argued and hurt each other as badly as they had.

"Hi." Lola didn't know what to do with herself. He smelled like Will, he felt like Will. Jesus, she'd been so certain of what she was doing and now, suddenly, she had no idea what she was doing. She only wanted to lay her cheek against his chest, close her eyes, and pretend they were still married.

"How are you?" he asked, stepping back.

"I'm good," she said cautiously. He didn't look terribly upset. He didn't look as if he was about to make some grand announcement that he'd been wrong.

A wet snout on her ankle caused Lola to look down. "You got a dog?"

"It's Dani's dog," he said without looking at the dog. *Dani*, short for Danielle. Apparently, Will was living with two bitches now.

Will put his hand on Lola's arm and drew her towards a scattering of tables on the sidewalk outside the coffee house. "Seriously, Lola, are you all right? You seem kind of . . . weird."

He had to be kidding—she seemed *weird*? Like she found it easy to casually meet up with the man who had crushed her heart? And why did he have to know her so well? Lola *did* feel a little weird sometimes, like her life was spinning and turning and going nowhere fast, like she was stuck in an endless public transportation loop between work, and picking up and dropping off nieces and nephews, and then on weekends taking the train out to Long Island to check in on her mother because God knew none of her siblings would do it consistently. *"Weird?"* she repeated, a bit miffed. "I'm fine!" And probably, she was a little too prickly in her response, because it had never seemed fair that Will was living this great life in the middle of Manhattan with a beautiful woman, and now, a cute little dog, while Lola was *still* recovering from the gaping wound he'd left behind.

"I didn't mean anything by it," he said apologetically, and pulled out a chair at one of the empty tables for her. "I'm just concerned." He sat down across from her and frowned thoughtfully at her.

"Will you stop looking at me like that?" she asked, and self-consciously tucked a strand of hair behind her ear. He was supposed to say, *God, you look fantastic,* or *Wow, I really messed up.*

The dog barked at another dog passing by, then scampered under the table. Will didn't seem to notice—he reached across the table for Lola's hand. "Listen . . . I know this is hard. And if I haven't said it before, I want to say it now. I am really sorry for breaking your heart. I mean that sincerely. If I could take it all back, I would."

Even now, driving up and down Juneberry Road, Lola could remember how she'd felt when he'd said those words. She'd stared into his hazel eyes, a little sick, a little hopeful. It was exactly what she'd hoped he would say so she could tell him to fuck off, but instead, she'd said, "You would?" and had sounded pathetically needy.

"Yeah, of course," he'd said, and had squeezed her hand before letting go and settling back in his chair.

Beneath the table, the dog jumped up and pawed at her knee, and she'd had the fleeting thought that the little bugger had probably snagged her expensive hosiery.

"I never ever wanted to hurt you," Will said.

Wait, what? What was happening right then? The right words were coming out of his mouth, but the body language had been all wrong. Too casual, too easy. "What are you saying, Will?"

Will had looked at her blankly a moment. But then his eyes rounded. "Wait . . . you don't think . . ." He sighed, bowed his head a moment, as if he was trying to think how to say what he meant in a way she would understand. "Please don't misunderstand, Lola. I still would have left, no matter what."

No matter what?

"We weren't working out. What I'm trying to say, and badly, it would seem, is that in hindsight, I would have ended it differently."

And just like that, everything had twisted. Lola had felt ridiculous in her navy dress and sweater and was unreasonably furious with herself for having dressed for him at all. She'd been absolutely livid that there was some part of her that believed Will could be a different man, could still love her, and that she'd *wanted* him to love her. But no, he thought that she would somehow feel better if he'd *ended it* differently. What a rotten sonofabitch. And Jesus, Casey was right *again*.

"Is that why you asked me to meet you?" she said, her voice icy to even her own ears. "To tell me there was a better way to break up our marriage?"

"*No,*" he'd said, looking appalled by that accusation. "Why do you have to get so hostile?"

"I'm not hostile, asshole. I'm *furious*."

"What has happened to you?" he asked, throwing his arms open like the forever put-upon male in a romantic comedy. "You looked a little down, that's all. I just meant to help, Lola. I didn't think you'd get all dressed up and get so . . . *hopeful*," he'd said, looking for the right word.

Lola had wanted to kill him. She'd wanted to reach down his throat for his penis and yank it out. "What do you want?" she'd asked sharply and grabbed her purse and stood up.

"Keep your voice down," he said, his eyes darting around them. "I don't know what's gotten into you. I've never seen you act like this."

"Because I was too damn nice to you. Answer the question. What the fuck do you *want*, Will?"

"To see if you wanted the puppy!" he shouted, sounding angry, too. She'd gaped at him. Then at the dog. "What are you talking about?"

Will leapt to his feet and towered over her. "Will you keep your voice down? Everyone is staring. I'm talking about a goddamn dog, okay? Some guy gave it to Dani and we don't have room for it or the time for it. I thought maybe—"

Lola never knew what he thought *maybe* because she'd slammed her hands into his chest and had shoved with all her might. The dog started barking as she marched away. She made it to the corner before she looked down and saw the terrible hole in her hosiery. Tears of absolute fury had begun to stream down her face, and she ran across the street, almost colliding with a taxi, whose driver laid on the horn. Lola flipped him off and kept running until her hose were bagging at the knees.

Thinking back on the afternoon now as she inched her way back down Juneberry Road, Lola muttered, "Thanks, Will. You actually gave me the balls to do this." Because when she'd reached her apartment, she'd called Sara and accepted her offer.

Lola had remained furious for days. With Will, for asking her to take the dog. But mostly with herself, for having become the person who everyone assumed would take care of their problems. And for having hope, no matter how small. When would she learn that hope was for pussies? How many times would her smallest of hopes be crushed by someone like her mother or Will?

And still, even on that day of abject fury, Lola had taken care of Will's problem. She couldn't stand the thought of that little dog anywhere near such a heartless bastard, so she'd called a pet sitter she knew, who in turn called Will. A day later, Lola saw on Facebook that the dog had found a happy home.

"So yeah, Will, this is all because of you," she said loudly. "You are the reason I am driving around like an old woman with dementia looking for a house that clearly does not exist—" She suddenly gasped. There it was, the house number she was looking for—*4450*.

Lola yanked the wheel right and turned into the drive, almost slamming into the pretty wrought iron gate. She rolled down her window, punched in the code Sara had given her, and watched the gate jerk and then slowly begin to retract. "This is *it!*" she said excitedly and, gripping the steering wheel, she pulled through the gate. She paused inside, just to make sure the gate closed behind her, then sent the rental puttering down a winding drive, through stately oak trees and blooming rhododendrons. It was beautiful, like a lovely country lane from a picture book.

Then she rounded a bend in the road. "Holy shit," Lola muttered to herself.

This was a capital L, capital H lake house. It was timber and stone and glass, with decks off the sides and back of the house, and the lake glistening below. It was the sort of house HGTV showcased and then gave away every year. The sort of house that showed up in romantic comedy movies with sets designed by Nancy Meyers. It was fabulous, and Lola could hardly believe she was *here*. That she was going to live here, in this house, for an entire summer while she finished her book.

She pulled to a halt at the front door and gleefully hopped out of the car. Sara said there would be a key under the big flat rock next to the front porch. "You can't miss it—it looks like a flying saucer," Sara had said, and had sketched the rock onto the napkin when she and Lola had met for lunch last week.

There was only one big flat rock, and Lola practically skipped to it, giggling . . .

But there was no key.

She stood up, dusted off her hands, and looked around.

There was no other flying saucer, but there were a few rocks. She looked under every one of them. No key. She stood on the porch with her hands on her waist. "Now what?" she muttered to herself. Maybe the caretaker had left the front door open.

"Oh, by the way, I emailed the caretaker and fired him," Sara had said in passing as they were leaving the coffee shop.

"Why?" Lola asked.

"Why? Because you're going to be there. You can skim the pool and haul the trash up to the road as well as he can. And besides, he's a snitch."

Lola wondered what he would have to snitch about, but she thought it best not to ask Sara, who had a lot of conspiracy theories in general.

She tried the handle of the front door. Locked. Apparently, the fired caretaker wasn't so mad about losing his job that he'd left the door open. She cupped her hands around her eyes and peered in through the sidelight. She could see a sunken living area just ahead, and wow, a stunning view of the lake through some big plate-glass windows and doors.

Okay, there had to be a way in. Lola walked around the house, picking her way through the garden on the south side, climbing over the small retaining wall, and jumping the couple of feet down to the terrace. Here, there was upholstered lawn furniture, and just below the main terrace, one of those fancy pools with water that looked as if it were spilling over the edge and into the lake. "Oh. My. *God*," Lola said beneath her breath. "How did you luck into this?"

She put her face to the first window she reached and peered in. It was a bedroom. The bed was made, and there were some clothes neatly folded and stacked on a chair near the bathroom door.

Lola moved on to the big sliding glass doors, and gave one a half-hearted tug. Amazingly, the thing slid open like it was on bacon grease. "Oh, hey!" she said. She stepped cautiously into the house, pausing just over the threshold to take it all in.

The living room was *amazing*. The floors were handscraped walnut. An enormous, thick shag rug was anchored by two white couches and a low marble coffee table. A pair of rocking chairs sat side by side at the window, a glass end table between them. A large stone fireplace dominated one wall, and on the other end of the room was a gleaming kitchen with stainless appliances, quartz countertops, and shiny white cabinets with glass pulls. The lights that dangled over the bar separating the kitchen from the living space looked like old lanterns. A small fireplace with a brick hearth for sitting anchored the kitchen.

It was amazing. It was *beautiful*. And it was so far above any of the rundown, dilapidated two-bedroom apartments Lola had grown up in that she felt as if she ought to get a sheet and carry it around with her to sit on, just in case any of the grime of her life still lingered.

She wandered down a hallway painted pristine white with built-in bookshelves. She found two more bedrooms, each with their own baths, glass showers, and claw-foot tubs. There was an office, which, she noted, looked as if the caretaker had recently used it, judging by the stack of papers and the fact that the printer was blinking.

Lola wandered back through the fabulous living room, and down another corridor that led to the master bedroom, the same one she'd seen through the window. She walked to the middle of the room, and turned a full circle as she took in the fireplace, the expensive modern art, and the bookcases. The closet was insanely huge, and still had a few of the caretaker's clothes hanging in it. She walked into the bathroom, and admired the view from the enormous garden tub. She could picture herself in that tub, with that view, and a stack of books nearby.

Lola returned to the bedroom and, with a squeal of delight, she fell back onto the bed, her arms splayed wide, and kicked her feet like a little kid.

Was this for real? This was exactly what she'd dreamed it would be! She suddenly sat up and looked at her watch. Okay, first things first. Clear out the last of the caretaker's things. Bring her stuff in, turn in the car, and get a cab back. And tomorrow? Tomorrow, she would become the writer she'd always dreamed of being.

Five

For ten days, Harry had been living in a roadside motel that smelled like dog and cigarette smoke, and going from one meeting to the next, trying to line up his subcontractors for his first solo bid for a full bridge project. It was a small job, an elevated pedestrian walkway. But bidding on the whole project was a lot more work than he'd anticipated, and he was already worried if he had enough money in the bank.

But he was back in East Beach, headed up Juneberry Road, exhausted, wanting a beer and to dive into the pool and just chill before sleeping in a soft bed with clean sheets. He pulled up to the gate of the lake house, punched in the code, and waited as the gate slid open.

The lake house was too good to be true. Harry would never be able to thank Zach enough for this opportunity, which he'd told him profusely three weeks ago when he'd moved in.

"It's all good, dude," Zach had said.

It was better than good. The house was an amazing high-end show-case of modern conveniences and luxuries. Everything was automated and digitized. One only had to push this button or flip that switch, and entire glass doors slid quietly away so that you were practically living outdoors.

It was a dream to come home to after a hard day's work—especially after ten days. It was great to unwind by walking down to the lake and throwing in a fishing line. Harry felt at peace here. He could put his worries in his back pocket for a few hours. He could put Melissa out of his mind here, too. He thought about her a lot, missed having someone to come home to every night . . . but he'd been so busy and so focused that he hadn't dwelled on it. In all honesty, he was happy not to have to justify himself on a daily basis.

He definitely missed the sex. It had been such a regular part of his life that now he felt as if something was off, like the feeling he'd had when he cut back on sugar a few years ago. Like if he allowed himself, he'd sprinkle a whole five-pound bag on a bowl of cereal—it was that kind of feeling.

Harry tried not to think about it.

At the end of the drive he got out of his truck and looked at the house. As great as this space was, and as lucky as he was to have landed here, Harry did feel a bit like an intruder, given the situation with Zach's divorce. He kept expecting a constable or someone to show up and tell him to get out. He was careful not to leave his mark on the house, careful not to get too comfortable.

But today? Today he was going to leave his mark all over the place, starting with the pool. Harry grabbed his bag and briefcase and walked up to the entry as he sorted through his keys looking for the one that would open the front door. Through the door's wavy glass, he could see the sunlight shining in through the enormous sliding glass doors that opened onto the terrace.

Harry unlocked the door, stepped inside, and put his things down at the threshold. He suddenly noticed the smell of something that confused him. He paused, looking around. What was that? It smelled like lasagna. What was lasagna doing in his house? Harry cautiously took a step forward and scanned the sunken living room, and then the adjacent kitchen. He let out a tiny breath of surprise—things had been moved in that kitchen, new things added.

He stood there, hands on hips, completely disoriented. Had he somehow walked into the wrong house by mistake? Of course not—he'd come in through the same gate he always used. So whose laptop was that on the dining table, or the notebook beside it? And was that a *bra* hanging off the back of the barstool? Why were there dirty dishes piled high in the sink? It was as if someone had come in to party while he'd been gone.

He suddenly noticed a woman rise up out of the pool. She was wearing oversized sunglasses, a two-piece bathing suit that wasn't exactly a bikini, but was definitely sexy. Jesus, it wasn't Zach's wife, was it? Harry's belly did a funny little flip—the last thing he wanted was to get involved in a domestic fight over this property. The woman paused on the pool step to wring water out of her strawberry-blonde hair, then stepped out of the pool, picked up a towel from a lounge chair, and wrapped it around her. She bent down to pick up what looked like an e-reader and a big bottle of water and started for the house.

Harry had met Zach's wife only once, and he remembered her as tall and willowy with platinum hair. Zach's wife did not have curves. This woman had nice, healthy curves that had not been whittled away by an overzealous diet. So who was she?

He was a little mesmerized, a little shocked, and a little stumped. He watched the woman walk right up to one of the sliding doors and open it, then walk into the house like she owned it.

She stepped inside, dropped her e-reader on the dining room table, and looked up, her gaze landing on Harry. It seemed like a very long moment passed before she made a sound that wasn't as big as a scream, but not as small as a shriek, either. It was a squeal of surprise, and frankly, he yelped, too, startled by her squeal.

"You scared the hell out of me!" she cried accusingly. "What are you doing here?"

"*Me?*"

"Sara said she fired you!"

"*Fired* me? She can't fire me."

"Why not? Because of the restraining order?"

The *restraining* order? What the hell was she talking about? Was she some random crazy woman on the loose, or was she part of Sara's posse? More importantly, did she not realize she was dripping all over expensive walnut wood floors that clearly did not belong to her? "Are you Sara's sister?" he asked.

"No!" She took off her sunglasses and squinted pale-blue eyes at him. "Aren't you the guy?"

"The *guy*? What guy? Who *are* you?" he demanded.

She snorted. "I think *you* should tell *me* who *you* are. If you're not the caretaker, then who are you?"

"I'm a friend of Zach's," Harry said. "Harry Westbrook."

"Harry Westbrook," she repeated, as if trying to call that name up from her memory.

"Believe me, we don't know each other. Your turn. Who are you?"

"I'm Lola Dunne, and I'm *supposed* to be here."

Her tone implied that she thought he was the one doing the trespassing. "Well so am I, cupcake. My permission comes from Zach Miller, who happens to own this house."

"Oh yeah? My permission comes from *Sara* Miller, who also happens to own this house."

Harry suddenly realized what had happened. So did this Lola Dunne person, judging by the way her eyes widened with shock. For several moments, the two of them stared at each other. His thoughts were racing with lightning speed, and he quickly deduced that while he didn't know what to do about this, he had no other place to go. "I was here first," he said, voicing the first errant thought to make it to his mouth.

"Then apparently," she said, folding her arms, "that was your left-over crap I threw into the spare bedroom?"

"You moved my things?" he said, incredulous. "What the hell gives you the right? Listen," he said, pointing at her. "You can't stay here."

The woman settled her weight onto one hip. "*You* can't stay here."

"Like hell I can't," he said, and pulled his phone from his pocket. "I've been here a little more than three weeks. I have squatter's rights. I'm going to just give Zach a call and see what he says."

"Go ahead. I've been here over a week. I'll just give Sara a call, too. I am sure she'll be *delighted* to know what Zach is up to." She grabbed her phone from the dining room table.

They stood there, both wielding a phone.

Harry was suddenly reminded of Zach's warning: *"This is on the down-low,"* he'd said. *"You can't imagine the shit show if Sara finds out. There's an injunction against both of us from using this house until the court decides who gets it."*

Jesus, what the hell was he going to do? Harry warily eyed his adversary. He noticed she had not dialed her phone, either, and was glaring at him just as warily.

She threw down the first gauntlet. "I'm not leaving."

Harry didn't say anything.

"I sublet my apartment for the summer because Sara said I could stay here."

"Yeah, well, I sold my apartment, and I've got stuff in the works here. So I'm sure as hell not leaving."

Her lovely blue eyes narrowed on him. "We can't *both* stay here," she said, unnecessarily. "I don't even *know* you."

"I don't know you, either, but I'm definitely not leaving."

"You can't intimidate me! *I'm* not leaving!"

"How am I intimidating you?" Harry exclaimed. "I'm just stating the facts, lady. I've been here longer than you, and when I arrived, you most definitely were not swimming in my pool. I have permission to be here, I am working here, and I'm not going anywhere. If that intimidates you, that's your problem."

"My problem is you," she said, folding her arms. "Because I have permission to be here, I am likewise not going anywhere, and I get the master bedroom."

Harry laughed darkly. "Oh, I don't think so. I've already taken the master."

"And I've already moved you out," she said pertly. "I moved all your caretaker-looking things to the mother-in-law suite."

"My caretaker-looking things?" he repeated, indignant.

"How was I supposed to know? I assumed all those boots and flannel shirts belonged to the caretaker that Sara fired! Anyway, I'm all moved in now, all my clothes are in the closet, and my *shoes*—"

"Okay," he said, throwing up a hand in surrender. He was not going to argue about a bedroom in the middle of this fiasco. "But I'm not going to put up with that kind of a mess," he added, nodding toward the kitchen.

"What mess?"

"Are you kidding me right now? *That* mess," he said, pointing to the kitchen.

She looked, too, as if she hadn't seen the dishes piled there.

"Please clean that up," he snapped. He snatched up his bags and started down the hall to the mother-in-law suite. He swore he heard her mutter something unflattering under her breath and he halted, jerking back around to look at her.

She was still standing there, dripping all over the floors. And then she had the audacity to smile at him as if she'd won an arm wrestling contest.

Harry stomped onward.

In the smaller master, he threw his bags on the bed, sat on the end of it, and dragged his fingers through his hair. This was a disaster. Ridiculous! There had to be a way out of it. He needed some time to think about what to do with her, and decided that thinking would best be done in the pool, with a beer. Or five.

All he had to do was find his "caretaker-looking" things and his swim trunks. Jesus.

Six

Through the window of the master bedroom, Lola watched Zach's friend dive into the pool, then come up, breaking the surface like a dolphin and shaking his head to sling the water out of his hair.

Good God, but that man was good-looking. Intimidatingly handsome. He was all muscled shoulders and arms, and hello, those *legs*. Lola felt a little warm. Warm as in acutely aware of her shortcomings compared to a man like him, and yet still turned on beyond what was even reasonable. She moved away from the window and marched to the bathroom.

"Okay," she said to her reflection in the mirror. She noticed the new freckles, thanks to her forgetting to apply sunscreen; the frizzy hair, thanks to forgetting to apply product; the swimming suit top that should have been retired five years ago. "This can't happen. This *cannot* happen." How was she supposed to write a book with a guy like that hanging around? She was having a hard enough time as it was. Funny, but the words did not magically flow from her fingertips in her little patch of paradise as she had expected them to. She'd stared at a blank page all afternoon. Speaking of which—she just realized she'd left her laptop on the dining room table, along with a notebook full of her ideas. She'd chosen the table over the office because of the spectacular lake view and the fact that the doors actually slid open so that it was like she was sitting outside when she wasn't. Ingenious.

First things first, she had to change and do something about her hair. She looked around at the clothes strewn all over the master bedroom—jeans and skirts, T-shirts and linen sweaters. She suddenly remembered the neat stack of clothing she'd moved. Boxer shorts folded into squares. T-shirts folded in the way clothing stores stacked them for display. Two pairs of cargo pants, identical. Honestly? She thought someone had either forgotten their purchases from one of the trendy little stores on Main Street, or the caretaker's mother had brought his laundry to him. Who folded their clothes like that?

Lola tiptoed back to the window, and peeked out. He was floating on his back now. On the side of the pool, there were two beer bottles. That explained all the beer in the fridge in the garage, which she had assumed had been left after a party.

Nope, this was not going to work. She was going to have to think of something to get him out of here. Contagious disease? No. She didn't really want him to associate *ick* with her. Structural damage to the house? That one had potential.

She headed to the bath to think about it.

She lingered in the ginormous tub, floating amid a million bubbles, stewing about this sudden derailment of what was going to be a perfect summer and finding no immediate solution. Eventually, Lola had to get out of the tub—she was hungry as she was wont to be, and she was shriveling up. She'd had leftover lasagna for lunch. Maybe she should have saved that. She began a mental catalog of items in the Sub-Zero fridge. She had the ingredients for moussaka with the leftover eggplant she'd bought at the farmer's market yesterday. She had some red wine. She had ingredients for a salad.

Lola used some of the lotion she'd bought at the little perfumery, donned her bathrobe, and padded out to the closet to have a look at her things. She was generally a yoga pants and T-shirt kind of girl, but today she looked at the few dresses she'd brought. She chose a vintage red one that cinched at her waist and had a little chain of white strawberries marching across the hem. She conditioned her shoulder-length hair and combed it out. And, for the first time in days, she dabbed on a little blush and mascara.

As Lola came out of the master bedroom, she heard a lot of banging around in the kitchen. She rounded the corner and saw Handsome Harry hard at work, his arms in the sink up to his elbows. He'd pulled his hair into a little tail at his nape and he wasn't wearing a shirt, but he'd wrapped a towel around his waist and over his swim trunks.

Lola had to take a moment—he had the body of an athlete. Hard and firm and sexy, and geez, she sort of wished he'd put on a shirt.

Now, he was shoving dishes into the dishwasher, where he'd managed to arrange the bowls she'd used to cook in a tight line on the bottom rack. She was lucky to get three bowls in the bottom rack—he'd put in six with room to spare.

"Umm . . . what are you doing?" she asked.

His head came up and his gaze flicked over her, lingering for a split second on the strawberries. "I am cleaning up this mess," he said crisply. "I'm a little curious—how did you get tomato sauce on the cabinet doors?" He pointed to a spray of it across one of the upper cabinet doors.

Like she was supposed to remember how that had happened. "You don't need to do that. I'll clean it up."

He held her gaze as he picked up a wet rag, lifted his arm and connected with the cabinet at the very spot of the sauce, wiping it away without even looking.

Ooh, a little kitchen-shaming, huh? Lola walked up to him, and without looking, groped around for his hand until she found it, then took the rag and yanked it free. "I wasn't exactly expecting company."

"Neither was I."

His eyes, Lola noticed, were the color of the silver leaf maples up and down Juneberry Road. Silvery green. "Will you please move?" she asked. "You are blocking my way to the dishwasher."

He didn't move. He stared down at her, his gaze zeroing in on her eyes. "I'm not into dirty kitchens," he said.

"Great. I'll make a note of that," she said, and squeezed past him, her breast brushing against his chest, which, for the record, was as firm as it looked. She reached into the sink for a plate and stuffed it into the dishwasher.

Her roommate relinquished control and stepped away as she stuck another plate in the rack. "You can get more in if you have some order," he pointed out.

"Thanks. I'll be sure to add that notation under the one about how you like your kitchens." She heard him mutter under his breath but ignored him and finished loading the dishwasher, shoving in utensils and dishes beside his neat stack. When she'd finished, she turned around—but he'd left the kitchen.

Well that was interesting. Lola had never known a man—or anyone, for that matter—to get their nose out of joint over loading the dishwasher, but she wasn't going to spend any time thinking about him pouting on the other side of the house.

She went to the gourmet fridge with the wine cooler built into one panel—so *fancy*—and began to pull out the things she would need for her dish. A half hour later she had the moussaka in the oven, a healthy glass of wine at her elbow, and was tossing a salad when her surprise roommate reappeared in the living area. His hair was wet and tucked back behind his ears. He was wearing a clean T-shirt that fit tightly across his chest tucked into jeans that rode low on his hips. He walked up to the bar that separated the chef's kitchen from the living area, braced his hands against it, and looked around at the mixing bowls and various *accoutrement* Lola had pulled from the cabinets.

"*What* are you doing?" he asked.

"Are you serious? Isn't it obvious? I'm cooking my dinner. I made moussaka. It's a Greek eggplant dish. With some mashed potatoes. Sort of a moussaka shepherd's pie."

He stared at her.

"It's really good," she assured him, taking his silent stare as doubt.

"Did it require using every pot and bowl in the kitchen to make?"

She snorted at his ignorance. "No. Not even half." This happened to be one of the most well-stocked kitchens she'd ever seen. She'd have to make a double batch of moussaka to use *every* pot and bowl.

He sighed a little, bent his head, and rubbed his nape for a moment. When he lifted his head again, he tried to smile. Sort of like she imagined the runner-up in a beauty contest would try to smile. "It's Lola, right?" he said amicably. "I once had a dog with the name."

Her eyes narrowed. "Good for you." She picked up a knife and moved to his left to chop chives on the cutting board.

"Look . . ." he said, trying that loser's smile again. "I'm hoping we can talk about this."

His hair was dark brown, like coffee. He hadn't shaved; today's whiskers shadowed his jaw. Of all the men to pop into her fantasy summer to ruin it, it would be a guy who looked as sexy as he did. Handsome Harry. Lola had to look away. She pretended to be looking for an ingredient in the little spice boxes from Williams-Sonoma. Kennedy would call this kismet. Kennedy was studying psychology and had a name for everything. She often liked to diagnose her siblings around the dinner table. *You know what you are, Ty? You're borderline ridiculous. Jesus, Casey, how many more brief psychotic breaks are you going to have tonight?*

The thought of Kennedy diagnosing this guy made Lola suddenly giggle.

"Something funny?" he asked.

"What?" She glanced over her shoulder.

He was frowning. "I guess I don't see what's even remotely amusing about this. We have a disaster on our hands."

"A disaster? That seems a little dramatic." She wasn't going to allow an Adonis to drop in and tell her that her perfect summer was a disaster. This was her one chance to do something for herself. So Lola reached for her wine, took a long sip, and said, "It's actually kind of amusing."

He looked surprised. His gaze slid over her again, this time lingering a little too long on her chest. "It's not funny to me," he said flatly. "I have some very important work I'm doing here, and this is a complication I didn't expect."

"Oh, and I don't have important work I'm doing here?"

He hesitated. "I didn't say that," he said carefully. "I obviously don't know what you're doing here. But I will point out again that I was here first, and I'm trying to achieve something."

Now Handsome Harry was beginning to annoy her. Why did men always assume what they were doing was far more important than what a woman was doing? "So am I," she said curtly. She put her wine glass down, threw the chives into her salad, and tossed again.

"Okay," he said nodding. "Let's talk about that. What are you doing at Lake Haven?"

"None of your beeswax," Lola said instantly. She did not want to tell him she was writing a book, for fear she'd get the reaction she got from her brothers. *A book?* Followed by loud laughter. Not to mention she hadn't been exactly hitting it out of the ballpark on the writing front.

Her response made Handsome Harry look a little too smug, as if he was congratulating himself on being right—his work was more important than hers. "You don't want to talk? That's cool. I don't really care what you're up to."

"Ditto," she said.

"Great," he said, his gaze piercing hers. "Neither of us cares. Nevertheless, it's pretty obvious we're both a little stuck here. If Zach and/or Sara find out, we're probably both out, agreed?"

"Agreed."

"So we're going to have to make the best of it."

Why did he have to sound so condescending? Like he was the one who was clearly going to have to strive to make the best of it? "Alrighty then," she said, and smiled. She swiped up her wine glass. "Here's me, making the best of it." She took a nice long swig, set the glass aside, and began to make her salad dressing.

"I think we should establish some ground rules."

"Sure," she said gregariously. "Like what?"

"Like . . . this is my half of the house," he said, turning partially and gesturing to the living room and the hallway that led to the two guest rooms. "And you have the master, which frankly, is almost as big as this. We can work out a sharing arrangement for the living room and kitchen."

"And the pool," she added, lest he think they were going to halve that, too.

"And the pool. You can have the living room during the day, and I can have it during the afternoon and evening."

Leave it to a man to assign himself prime time. "So I'm supposed to stay in my room at night?"

He shrugged. "Why not?"

"Because I don't want to be confined to my room like I've been grounded. I like to watch TV at night."

Handsome Harry's brows dipped disapprovingly. "You watch TV?"

Lola stopped her whisking. "Oh, I'm sorry, does that make me a troglodyte?"

"I wouldn't know. I don't have time for TV."

How anyone could not have time for *Scandal* or *Game of Thrones* was beyond Lola, but boy, didn't Handsome Harry look a little superior right now. "I'm not giving up the only TV in the house," she said, and turned around so she didn't have to see his fat smug face. She shoved oven mitts on her hands and opened the oven door.

"Something smells good," he said.

"You must mean this," she said, holding up her pan. "Moussaka, party of one."

Interestingly, Smug Handsome Harry looked very longingly at her pan. He wasn't so superior now, was he? Lola made sure to put the pan on the trivets just beneath his nose. "When will you be doing *your* cooking?" she asked. "Just so I know the *ground rules*," she added, making air quotes.

"I don't cook."

"No TV. No cooking. Wow, you must have the most fun ever. So what do you do with yourself? Open up cans of soup and then whittle all evening?"

"Trust me, I have plenty to do," he said, as if she couldn't possibly understand how important and complex his life was.

That could very well be, but this was a hungry man staring at her. So Lola scraped off a dollop of mashed potatoes from her dish, put it in her mouth, and with a moan, closed her eyes. "Oh my God, I think this is some of the best moussaka I've ever made." She opened her eyes and smiled.

"Funny," he said. He looked like he was working very hard not to lick his lips. "Anyway, back to our arrangement. You can have the evening in the living room if that's what you want. But I get the office."

Perfect. The office was in the far corner of the house, as far from her as he could possibly be. She hoped he spent all his time in there. "Knock yourself out," she said.

"One last thing," he said. "I think we should respect each other's space by, you know . . . tidying up after ourselves."

Lola picked up a spatula, holding it for a moment for full effect before she shoved it into the moussaka. "Whatever you say, Harry."

His eyes narrowed slightly with her even slighter sarcastic tone. *"Thanks."*

He watched as she heaped a generous serving of the moussaka onto a plate. She pretended to ignore him as she heaped salad onto the plate, too. She picked up her plate and her wine, looked at him, and asked, "Anything else? Maybe we could stick a corkboard up by the front door to leave each other messages. Sort of like a dorm room."

He gave her a withering look. "I think I'll just tell you whatever I need to tell you. *If* I need to tell you anything."

"Okay. Well, if that's all, roomie, I guess it's my time in the kitchen right now."

He looked startled. And a little sad as he looked at her moussaka. "Have at it," he said as he slid off the stool. He padded back across the living area.

She was going to have at it, all right. Lola put her plate on the dining room table, grabbed a fork and her phone, and sat down to eat. Her phone lit up as she was deciding if she'd put too much nutmeg in the dish. It was a text from Casey.

How is life in the land of snobby rich people?

Lola put her fork down and texted back: *Who said all rich people are snobby? Anyhoo, so far so good. You wouldn't believe how sweet this lake house is. Very high-end. But a recent sign of vermin.*

Vermin! Call an exterminator. But call me first. Right now. I have news.

Lola punched in her sister's number. "Whaddup?" she asked through a mouth full of moussaka when Casey answered.

"I got a great assignment. I'm doing a story on this twenty-five-year-old teacher without any legs. She's teaching inner-city middle school."

Casey was a journalist for a Brooklyn magazine, and somehow always ended up with the most interesting stories. Lola ate while Casey talked excitedly about her piece. Of all her siblings, Casey was the go-getter and always had been—which was why Lola had put off her own college so Casey could go. When they were kids, five of them splitting a can of Chef Boyardee, Casey was dreaming up ways to make them rich. Lola had always known Casey would *do* something. Something big. Lola had never had that confidence. The only thing she'd wanted to do as a girl and a teenager was write weepy love stories. So when it came time for college, Lola had saved the money they had from their grandparents and had deferred college so Casey could go. And Ben. And Ty. And Kennedy.

"Anyway, I went to check on Mr. Bagatti today," Casey said.

Lola stopped shoveling food onto her fork. Mr. Bagatti was the old man who lived below Lola's little walk-up studio in the Clinton Hill neighborhood of Brooklyn. He had no one, and she'd worried about him once she decided to take Sara up on her offer. Who would check in on him? Who would make sure he had what he needed, was taking his meds, was eating? "Casey, *thank* you!"

"I told you I would." Her sister bit into something. "He has a new honey," she said with her mouth full.

"A what?"

"A honey. Girlfriend."

"You're kidding," Lola said flatly. Mr. Bagatti never left his apartment.

"Nope, not kidding. She's the mother of the guy who runs the corner store. She was there when I stopped by. She'd brought him some candy and he was very happy. I told you he would be."

"You never said that. What you said was that he should be in a home where they would at least wash his undershirts. And that coming to Lake Haven was crazy."

"That was before I knew how hip it is to be on Lake Haven. My boss has a house there. And that, dear sister, is why I'm calling."

"Because your boss has a house here?"

"No, because she told me that her house is next door to Birta Hoffman's."

Lola gasped and dropped her fork. Birta Hoffman, the German author and winner of the Man Booker Prize for her novel, *Incomplete*, was Lola's all-time favorite author. "She has a house in the *States*?" Lola all but shouted into the phone. She'd thought Birta lived in the Black Forest in Germany. Maybe she'd romanticized that part, but it just fit with her books.

"Apparently so. And get this—she's going on a big book tour in the fall with her new novel. So she'll be in East Beach all summer. I guess you were right, Lola—everyone who is everyone is in East Beach this summer."

Lola's heart was racing. To think she could run into *Birta Hoffman* in this tiny little hamlet! She was almost hyperventilating just thinking about it.

"Oh, and I almost forgot," Casey continued after taking a bite of something. "Apparently she hangs out at the coffee shop there most mornings, working on her book. So pick up that fancy new laptop, girl, and start hanging out at the coffee shop."

"Ohmigod, I can't believe she is *here*," Lola said dreamily.

"You should totally go and meet her," Casey said.

"Right. As if one could simply walk up to Birta Hoffman and say hello. I would never impose—"

"Jesus, you never want to impose!" Casey said loudly before Lola could finish. "Lola, for God's sake, you've been taking care of everyone else for so long, including the douche bag you married—"

"Don't bring up Will," Lola said sharply. But it was too late—she could feel herself coloring at the truth in what Casey said. She *had* taken care of Will's every need. She'd subjugated all her wants and needs to his.

"Fine. But you get my point. Dad died and Mom turned into a full-time crack whore, and you took care of me and Kennedy and Ty and Ben *and* you kept child services off our doorstep. You never rocked the boat, you just kept up this facade that everything was okay so that people would leave us alone. But Lola, child services isn't coming for us anymore, and yet, you're still acting like everything's A-OK. Will left, and you were all, 'sure, if that's what you need,' instead of taking him to the cleaners like you could have done. You got booted to that job in Manhattan. You never went to college so that we could go. You're too *nice*, Lola. You're too giving, too generous, too helpful."

"My God, I'm a monster," Lola said with a roll of her eyes and picked up her fork.

"What I'm trying to say is that finally, you're doing something for *you*. You deserve it! So don't let any opportunity pass you up. You took this chance on, now explore it to its full advantage. For once in your freaking life, go for broke, will you?"

Lola was set to argue, but something clicked in her brain. Casey was right. She was *so* right. Lola had hidden grief and fear and uncertainty behind a wall of shame and placidity all her life. "How'd you get so smart, Casey?"

Casey snorted. "I had the best big sister in the history of the universe, and she taught me to go for broke while she kept up a front. Remember?"

"No," Lola said with a laugh. "What I remember is trying to get through each day with some food and some heat. But you know what? I'm going to do it, Casey. I'm going to meet Birta Hoffman. Because I love her books and it's all about me."

"Yes!" Casey crowed. "But maybe first, take care of the rat problem."

Lola's thoughts were full of images of her and Birta Hoffman having coffee. "What?"

"You said you had vermin. Get rid of the rats."

"Oh, that." Lola glanced across the house. She could see a light in the hallway that led to the extra bedrooms. "Yep. I'm going to handle that, too, not to worry."

They chatted a little more and hung up. Lola polished off her dinner as more images of Birta filled her head. And then, after she "tidied up," as requested by the most Humorless Harry, Lola was so entranced by the idea of being besties with a famous author that she settled down with her laptop and notes to work on her book.

But that blank page continued to stare at her.

Seven

At 6:00 a.m., Harry emerged from his new bedroom at the northern end of the house with the smaller bathroom, the stiffer bed, the non-lake view, and he was starving. He hadn't eaten last night as he'd stewed about this newest complication in his life. He'd waited around, hoping she'd go to bed, at which point he intended to raid the damn kitchen—assuming, of course, that she'd left him anything to eat. But he hadn't felt comfortable entering the kitchen while she was there, looking around for something to nosh on while she dined on that dish that had smelled so damn delicious.

But did the roommate from hell give him the space he needed? No. She had talked on the phone. Then he'd heard her typing away at something. Another phone call, this one with a lot of cackling. And then banging around in the kitchen. He'd fallen asleep sometime after he heard the TV power up and Jimmy Fallon begin to do his monologue.

To say Harry was in something of a sour mood was an understatement. To say that his blood pressure skyrocketed when he turned on the kitchen light was also an understatement. The kitchen was in a shambles. *Unbelievable.* What about their chat last night? Had he not been clear about picking up after herself? Apparently not, because once again, dishes were piled in the sink, there were crumbs on the counter, and the cutting board had not been cleaned. Not only that, her lacy bra was still hanging off the back of the bar stool, a bright slash of pink against dark leather.

Harry picked up that dainty piece of underwear and marched to the master bedroom. The door was ajar; he pushed it open and stepped over the threshold.

The mess was worse in here. There were clothes everywhere, shoes scattered across the floor, a pile of books stacked haphazardly on the hearth. He made a move toward the bed to wake her, but stepped on something that crunched under his boot. He looked down to see a mangled red plastic Solo cup.

The sound startled Sleeping Beauty awake—she shot up, her hair a wreck, and blinked at him. "What are you doing?"

"Returning this to you," he said, and tossed the bra at her.

It landed on her shoulder. She removed it, held it up to see what it was. "Where did you get my *bra*?" she exclaimed, as if he'd snuck in here and taken it off of her while she was sleeping.

"Oh, I don't know—where I get most bras. Hanging off the back of a barstool in the kitchen."

She blinked. "Oh yeah," she said, nodding, as if it all made sense now.

"I hope I don't have to explain that a kitchen bar stool is not the place to hang your bras. Or that you should clean up the kitchen after you use it."

"What?" She tossed the bra onto the floor and fell back against a mound of pillows. "I *did* clean up the kitchen."

That left Harry speechless for a moment. "If you call that clean, we're gonna have a problem. This isn't your house, Lola. None of this belongs to you," he said, making a circular motion with his hand. "The least you can do is keep it clean." He turned on his heel, crunching the Solo cup again, and walked out.

"Hey, just a damn minute!" she shouted after him.

He heard the bed squeak, heard her pounding across the bedroom floor. When he looked over his shoulder, kitchen lady was marching toward him wearing nothing but a T-shirt and panties. He wondered if she even realized it. Or maybe she'd left her pants in some weird place, too, like, say, the garage.

"You can't talk to me like that!" she said hotly.

"Like what?"

"Bossy!"

"Says who?"

"Me! I say!"

Harry slowly turned to face her, and folded his arms across his chest. "And *I* say you can't trash someone else's house."

"It's not *trashed*. It's a little cluttered. And besides, it was late!"

"What has that got to do with anything? You could have put the dishes in the dishwasher while you were cackling at everything Jimmy Fallon said."

Her eyes widened. "First of all, I do not *cackle*. And second, he is really funny! Just because *you're* some sort of obsessive-compulsive neatnik is no excuse to talk to me like I'm your kid."

Half of her hair was hanging over her face. Didn't that bother her? He wanted to push it out of her face. "I'm not obsessive-compulsive. But I do have basic standards."

"Oh yeah? So did you work in a department store at some point, or have you always folded your T-shirts and boxers to a uniform size?"

"What's wrong with being neat?" he exclaimed.

She opened her mouth, but he cut her off. "It was a rhetorical question. I'm not going to take clothes-folding tips from a woman who looks like she's been on a hell of a bender."

She gasped. "I beg your pardon," she said grandly, speaking like some lady from *Downton Abbey,* the show Melissa used to watch.

"I'm just saying, you look a little rough, so if it's all the same to you, I'd rather stick with my folded shirts than go with your method of storing clothes all over the bedroom floor. Now, if you will excuse me, I have to go to work."

"Thank *God*," she said, and turned around, marching back to her room.

Harry meant to march off, too, but he couldn't make himself while that very nice bottom bounced away from him in skimpy black polka dot panties. Yes, the woman definitely had some very appealing junk in that trunk. So appealing that he had trouble thinking clearly about how mad he was.

Harry went out, locked the front door behind him, got in his truck, and drove far too fast down Juneberry Road into East Beach, fuming the entire way. He pulled to the curb outside the Green Bean Coffee Shop and turned off the ignition.

This roommate thing was not going to work. It has been less than twelve hours and already they were butting heads. He would have to do something different. But what? Unfortunately, Harry had run out of money and, therefore, options. It was either East Beach, which was fairly close to his current job and the bigger job he was trying to land, or it was his parents' apartment on the Upper East Side.

"Someone shoot me now," he muttered.

The last time he'd seen Jack and Beth Westbrook had been the week after he and Melissa had split up. He'd joined his family for their standing Sunday lunch to deliver the news.

He'd been feeling adrift, still wondering what he could do to make it right for Melissa. He'd tried to call her, but she wouldn't answer the phone and had finally texted him, asking him to give her some space. So Harry had dressed in dark slacks and the cashmere sweater Melissa had given him for his last birthday, shaved his week-old beard, and combed his hair back as best he could. With all the emotional turmoil of that week, he hadn't made it to the barbershop. He'd fully expected his mother to make a remark about the length of his hair, and of course, she did not disappoint.

"You should really trim it, Harry," she'd said, reaching up to tuck more of it behind his ears when he'd arrived at home.

"I'll get on that, Mom."

The contents of his mother's cocktail glass had tipped to the right along with her, and had come dangerously close to spilling on the expensive Persian carpet. For as long as Harry could remember, his mother never touched a drop of alcohol . . . until Sunday. On Sundays, she would start in the morning and go until Dad poured her into bed in the evening.

"Where is our girl?" she'd asked, looking around him.

"She's not coming, Mom," he'd said. "We, ah . . . we're taking a break."

He had then endured his mother's wailing as if she'd just heard for the first time that the Titanic had sunk. Over the course of a horrible luncheon, he'd told his family—his mom and dad and his sister Hazel—what had happened.

Harry thought back to the bright spring Sunday. His family had been shocked and wounded by the split, naturally, because they'd all assumed Melissa would be part of the family, and had come to think of her as one of their own. It had been tough for Harry to listen to their sorrow. Especially when he was feeling that same sorrow and hadn't really processed it.

He'd been sad, and wounded, and despondent . . . but there also had been a tiny part of him that had felt the tiniest bit of relief. He had goals in life, and he'd begun to feel smothered by Melissa's expectations, his parents' expectations, and the growing demand that he somehow fit everyone's idea of what he ought to be when none of it matched what he wanted to be.

He'd explained to his family that the relationship had been complicated, and that there was no one "thing" that had done it.

"Oh, Harry!" his mother had groaned when he'd said all he could say, her drink sloshing around again. "I can't believe you broke *up*! Is it the apartment? I know it's that apartment. *Dosia!* Dosia, are you going to serve any time soon?" she'd shouted at the family's long-time maid.

Dosia had appeared from the kitchen with a platter of chicken breasts, her long gray hair in a bun on top of her head, and her wide hips covered in the gray shift of a maid's uniform. "Hello, Mr. Harry."

"Hello, Dosia." Dosia had a little room behind the kitchen where she watched reality TV and knitted sweaters for her grandkids in Poland. Once a year, over the Christmas holiday, his parents paid for her trip back home. He had fond memories of lying on Dosia's bed when he was a boy, watching television with her on the many nights his parents were out.

"I'm very sorry, Mr. Harry," she'd said.

"Thank you."

"Well?" his mother had demanded. "*Is* it the apartment?"

"Mom, come on." He had felt suddenly exhausted in that moment. "It's a lot of things," he'd said.

"Can we eat?" Hazel had asked, consulting her watch. "I have to make rounds this afternoon." His sister had a residency in psychiatry at Mount Sinai. She was two years older than Harry and rarely dated that he knew of. She'd often said she was married to her job. She had dark corkscrew curls and deep blue eyes. Harry had never understood why men didn't fall at her feet, but if they did, Hazel kept quiet about it. Maybe she was just a lot smarter than he was.

"Yes, let's eat," Harry's dad had said, reaching for the chicken. Dosia had appeared again, this time with asparagus and some sort of potato dish. She'd set them down and then very quietly removed the setting that had been laid for Melissa.

Harry's mother poured wine into her glass, which she'd placed beside her noon cocktail, and passed the bottle to Harry. "I know it's the apartment," she'd said again. Her cheeks were flushed, her eyes brightened by the alcohol. "I told you this would happen when you decided to quit your job. I *told* you it would all go to hell, all that you'd worked for."

Actually, what she'd said when Harry quit his job was that she and Dad had wanted him to become partner at his engineering firm and join them in country club memberships, fundraisers for important causes, and Upper East Side living. "That's why we sent you to a good school," she'd said then.

"Beth," his dad said at the lunch table. "Don't be so hard on him. Harry has accomplished a lot."

His mother had snorted. "He's doing *manual labor*, Jack. That's not what we raised our son to do. We raised him to be a great man. And Melissa wants a good life," she'd said as she helped herself to a tiny spoonful of scalloped potatoes. "She deserves that."

"I would give her a good life," Harry had said defensively.

But his mother had rolled her eyes. "She is the *perfect* girl for you, Harry, and if you can't see that, there is no hope for you."

"I know it's hard for you, Mom. But I want something different than Lissa wants. And I'm selling the apartment to buy a crane."

"Well," his father had said as Dosia returned with a plate of fruits and cheeses, "maybe we should reconsider loaning him the money, Beth, so he doesn't have to sell the apartment."

"Oh, Jack." His mother had sighed with the perpetual disappointment she held for Harry's father. "You know that's not possible. Harry would have been partner now if he'd stayed at Michaelson's. And you want to buy him a crane?"

"He wants something different," his father had said patiently. "He's told us that more than once. It's his life."

"It's okay, Dad," Harry had said. "The apartment is already sold." He'd not been willing to have that argument again, not that day, not when he was feeling so down. He'd had the same argument with his mother many times, had told her how he hated the idea that he had to have some fancy title in order to gain her approval. That he was pursuing the vision of his life he'd had since he was a kid.

"But what he wants is not something that will put a decent roof over his head," his mother had said, and had lifted her wine glass to her lips. "He'll end up living in some awful part of Long Island."

"You don't know that," Harry had said, bristling. "You know what, Mom? You wanted me to be partner. Well, I'm the sole partner in Westbrook Bridge Design and Construction. If that's not good enough for you, I'm sorry."

"And I'm sorry that we really can't support that, Harry," his mother had said in an incredibly patronizing tone. "We didn't send you to Cornell University so you could build bridges."

"What the hell did you think a degree in civil engineering was about?" he'd asked incredulously.

"I thought it was about a *partnership* in a prestigious firm!"

Harry had looked helplessly to his father, but his father had lowered his gaze, his focus on his food. There had been no point in even pretending that his dad could help him out. Jack Westbrook, a robust, healthy, sixty-five-year-old man, was a complete slave to his wife. That's because he'd married a woman with a lot of money and she'd controlled the purse strings all of their marriage. For all of Harry's life, his dad had played second fiddle to his wife.

But what had really riled Harry was that neither of them could encourage the monumental effort he was making to become a self-made man. "Yeah, okay," he'd said. He'd lost his appetite and his patience, and he was not going to sit there and take his mother's disdain or his father's impotence on top of losing Melissa. So he'd put aside his linen napkin and had stood up.

"Sit down, Harry," his mother had said.

"No thanks, Mom. Have a good afternoon." He'd started for the door.

"Wait—you're *leaving*?" Hazel exclaimed.

"Yeah, I'm leaving."

"Harry, wait!" Hazel had clambered to her feet.

"For God's sake, Harry, don't run off in a snit," his mother had said impatiently. "We're only trying to help."

"Help?" He'd angrily whirled back around. "You're not helping, Mom, you never help! You want a title? I've got a title for you—"

"Don't say it," Hazel had whispered frantically as she'd reached him. "Beth—"

"Don't tell me to give him the money, Jack," she'd snapped.

"I didn't ask you for money!" Harry had roared. He'd made that mistake only once and he would never make that mistake again. What did they take him for? He'd pivoted about and strode for the door.

"Wait, wait," Hazel had begged him, grabbing his arm as she squeezed out into the hall with him. "Jesus, will you *wait?*"

Harry had huffed. But he'd paused. "What?" he'd snapped.

Hazel had glared at him. "Don't treat me like I'm your mother."

"Sorry. But I'm not staying, Hazel. Don't try to talk me into it. I've had a rough week and I don't want to listen to her—"

"I want to offer you the money," Hazel had blurted.

Harry blinked. "For what?"

"For your crane! I can lend you the money."

Harry hadn't been able to keep from smiling, and had fondly wrapped his arms around her shoulders and hugged her. "Thanks, Hazel. But the last thing I want is to take any money from my big sis. And besides, even though I know you're pulling in some bucks these days, I doubt you have the kind of money I need."

"How much?" she'd asked.

"A million."

Hazel had pushed back from him, her eyes full of shock. "Holy shit! For a *crane?*"

"Not all for a crane," he'd explained. "That's operating costs, heavy equipment, manpower . . . I need that in the bank before I go and bid as a contractor on one of these state projects. I've been subcontracting pieces of the bridge. Now I want the whole thing. That's why I'm selling my apartment."

Hazel had groaned. "Look, don't be mad at Mom. She doesn't want to see you sink your inheritance into a business that might not work out, you know?"

His sister was referring to the money they'd inherited from their grandfather. Harry had used his share to buy his apartment. "I know," he said. "But Grandpa built Carlington Industries from the ground up. I think he'd understand. Actually, I think he would tell me there's no gain without risk and to go for it."

"I miss him. Come on, Harry, come back in. Mom will be passed out in an hour, and you and Dad and I can watch the Mets."

"Nah," he'd said, and had tweaked Hazel's nose. "I'm gonna run."

"Please don't tell me you're going to drown your sorrows in beer."

"No," Harry had scoffed as he started for the elevators, punching the down button. "I've got the kind of sorrows only a single malt whiskey can touch." He'd winked at Hazel and stepped into the elevator car.

He did have a couple of whiskies that night. They did nothing to ease the hurt in him.

He hadn't been back to see his parents since.

He damn sure wasn't going back now with his tail between his legs, leaking money and still trying to win a bid on his own, all because a woman with less-than-stellar housekeeping skills had barged uninvited into his life. He could imagine how that conversation would go. *No, I couldn't stay at my friend's house because this woman stacks dishes in the sink and leaves them there.*

No way, man. He was too strong for this. He would make this work somehow. He'd treat it like boot camp—keep his nose down, do his work, and ignore her.

Harry got out of his truck and slammed the door, suddenly determined. He'd go to work, eat out, and never come out of that mother-in-law suite. He didn't need a kitchen or a pool. He just needed a place to sleep.

Eight

Lola figured she might as well get to the coffee shop, seeing as how her roommate had rudely awakened her and made her so mad she couldn't go back to sleep. She didn't know what she was going to do with him yet—ignore him? Annoy him to death? Turn him in? One thing was certain—she wasn't going to let him interfere with her plans to meet Birta Hoffman.

Determined to forget his awful personality, which totally ruined his super-sexy physique, she hopped on her bike at half past eight. The drivers on Juneberry Road were in such a hurry to get to work, and whipped around her so fast that twice she almost lost her balance.

On Main Street, Lola locked her bike to a rack beneath a maple tree, removed her tote bag with her laptop from the bike's basket, and entered the Green Bean Coffee Shop, where she discovered the drivers who'd almost mowed her down were now standing in line for coffee. She took her place at the end, wedging herself between the door and the creamer station.

As the line inched along toward the barista, Lola scanned the crowded tables in search of Birta Hoffman. She had no doubt she'd recognize her—in all of Birta's author photos, she had signature long black hair with a thick streak of white that framed her face. She *looked* like an author. On the book jacket of her latest novel, *Inconsequential*, she was wearing a strand of mala beads around her neck. She held a pair of glasses as if she'd just taken them off to speak to the viewer. She wore leather and silver bracelets on her wrist and stared at the camera with a contemplative gaze, as though she were willing to discuss the meaning of life with you.

There was no such woman in this coffee house. Maybe Birta knew about the morning rush and preferred to wait it out. Well, Lola had brought her laptop so she could work. If Birta didn't show up today, Lola would come again tomorrow.

When it was finally her turn, Lola ordered a caramel latte.

The young man behind the counter didn't acknowledge that he'd even heard her. He said nothing at all, just scratched around his nose ring before he took her debit card and ran it, then placed a paper cup in line with others. She spent another five minutes crowded against the wall before her drink appeared. She gratefully accepted it and sipped.

And winced.

That was no caramel latte. She didn't know what it was, but she didn't like it. She made a move toward the counter to tell them, but a man in a business suit behind her sighed loudly, as if she were intentionally trying to annoy him by not getting out of the way. So she reflexively stepped away from the counter with the drink that was not hers, for which she'd paid five dollars, thank you very much. It wasn't even sweet.

The tables were completely full, but she spotted one across the room tucked up against the wall with a pair of coffee cups and two empty pastry plates. Lola began to weave her way through the tables for it, holding her bag aloft so as not to bonk anyone in the head with it. And just as she was about to break free of the obstacle course of human bodies, wooden chairs, and people's bags on the floor, a girl wearing floral tights and a very short skirt appeared from nowhere and plunked her computer bag down on the table.

Lola gaped at the girl, who was now texting on her phone. She spared Lola a glance. "Sorry," she said.

Lola was going to stand up for herself and demand this table, but the girl took a phone call, and Lola's resolve deflated. She turned around in defeat, and in doing so, her bag bumped against a table. She heard the cups rattle and grabbed the edge of the table. "I'm so sorry."

"Don't apologize! It's super crowded in here. It's a wonder tables and cups aren't flying."

Lola looked at the woman who had said those words. She looked to be Lola's age. She had a book in one hand, a plate with the crumbs of her breakfast at her elbow. She had frizzy brown hair, was pleasingly plump, and wore a silver chain around her neck from which dangled a silver candy wrapper charm. Lola liked her dancing brown eyes and snowy white teeth.

"You can sit here if you like," she said, indicating the empty chair.

"Would you mind?" Lola asked gratefully.

"Not at all. Better you than that guy," she said, nodding toward a man with dreadlocks who looked as if he'd been sleeping on the beach. "I'm Mallory Cantrell, by the way." She pushed the extra chair out for Lola.

"Hi," Lola said, and juggled her coffee and her bag so she could extend her hand. "I'm Lola Dunne."

"Nice to meet you, Lola Dunne! Pretty name. My cousin had a dog named Lola," Mallory said, reaching for Lola's cup.

"Yeah . . . I get that a lot," Lola said, and gratefully relinquished her cup, plopped onto the empty chair, and dropped her bag by her feet with a sigh of relief.

"Are you new to town?" Mallory asked.

Lola had thought about this question and what her response would be if asked, and said confidently, "I'm staying at my friend's house."

"Oh, where's that, on the lake? It's gorgeous right now, isn't it? Everything is blooming."

"Yep, on the lake. Out on Juneberry Road," Lola added absently.

"Hey, my aunt lives on Juneberry. Small world, huh? So who's your friend? I probably know her. I'm a year-rounder."

"A what?"

Mallory laughed. "That's what we locals call ourselves. Year-rounders. Who did you say your friend was?" she asked again.

"Sa . . ." Lola thought twice about what she was about to say, and at the last moment, changed that S sound to a Z. "Zach Miller." That would be safer, she thought. According to Sara, Zach hadn't been a regular at the lake in a few years.

But Mallory gasped with delight and said loudly, "Zach Miller! Well *hello,* Lola Dunne! *Very* nice to meet Zach's friend."

Shit. Shitshitshit. "You know him?"

"I don't really *know* him," Mallory said to Lola's great relief. "Not well, anyway. But we've met a couple of times at different functions. He's very generous to the Lake Haven Foster Kids' Project. But you know how generous he is."

Zach Miller? Lola tried not to look shocked and glanced down just in case her expression gave her away, because the man Sara had so vividly described was a narcissist dickhead who rarely showed his face in East Beach. Not a generous man contributing to a charity for foster kids.

"He's modest," Mallory said, mistaking Lola's reaction. "Is he in town? I'd love to say hello."

"No, no," Lola said quickly. "No, I don't think he'll be out this summer. Lots going on, you know." She glanced away guiltily. She wondered what Humorless Harry said when people asked him where he was living. Oh, right—he was so charming he probably didn't have any friends.

"Oh. Okay. So what do you do?"

"Ah, well," Lola said, and shifted a little. *Just say it!* Casey's voice shouted in her head. *What are you afraid of?* "I, ah . . . I write. I'm writing a book," she blurted.

"Really? How fun!" Mallory Cantrell said. "I love to read. What's it about?"

Lola filled her in on what she had so far, and then their talk turned to books and the authors whose work they enjoyed.

"Actually," Lola said, "My favorite author of all time is Birta Hoffman. My sister told me she has a house on Lake Haven and comes to East Beach to write at a coffee shop every morning. I'll be honest—I came here this morning hoping I might meet her," Lola said, and laughed at her own foolishness.

"Your sister is right, she is in East Beach," Mallory said. "But she doesn't come to the coffee shop every day. I'd say it's more like once a week. If she does come, I'd be happy to introduce you."

"You *know* her?"

"Sure," Mallory said with a slight shrug. "Everyone in East Beach knows everyone."

Lola could hardly contain her excitement. "So what's she like?"

"She's kind of intense," Mallory said. "But you'll see when you meet her. Guess what I do? Never mind, you can't guess. I own a candy shop."

Lola blinked. "Of course! Mallory's Candies and Curiosities! I've seen that shop."

"You want to come have a look?" Mallory asked.

"I would *love* to see your candy shop. I'm a huge fan. *Huge.* Me and candy go way back."

When Lola had finished her coffee, they packed up their things and went out. Mallory pushed open the coffee house door. "Look at this day, will you?'" she proclaimed, and went out into a crisp, sun-splashed world.

Lola would later think about the chance meeting and how a great friendship had sprung from it. She and Mallory hit it off—they wandered around Main Street, then ended up having lunch. They chatted like old acquaintances as they strolled along the shore of Lake Haven. Mallory invited Lola to join her at yoga the next morning and even offered to come and pick her up. And Lola didn't think about Humorless Harry more than twice. All right, fine—she thought of him three times. Maybe four.

It was midafternoon before Lola returned to the lake house, carrying a basket full of fresh produce purchased at Donovan Farms, which Mallory had told her about. Lola was happy. In spite of the weird roommate situation with Harry, she was beginning to feel like this was the place she was supposed to be, doing exactly what she was doing at this point in her life. In fact, when she sat down with her book, and stared at the same blank page that had been staring back at her for days, she had a breakthrough. Just walking away from the book had helped to clear her head. She realized that her main character was too nice. She was supposed to be a little psychotic, but Lola had written her too weakly. Frankly, she was too much like Lola—her boyfriend had just broken up with her, and she was taking the high road like a boss.

Lola didn't want her to take it like a boss. She wrote: *Sherri killed Brad with a hammer. It happened to be the first thing she could put her hands on when he said, "I'm sorry, Sher, but I'm just not feeling it." "Feel this, asshole," she said, and swung before he even looked up . . .*

That was it. That was exactly what her book needed—a little *oomph* before the detective showed up and began to put the pressure on Sherri. For the first time in days, words were flowing again.

Lola worked into the evening, until her stomach began to rumble. She made a vegetable frittata for dinner. Maybe it was the splendor of the day or the organic vegetables, but Lola was fairly certain it was the best frittata she'd ever made.

After dinner, she worked more on her book, then turned in to read.

Sometime after ten, she heard her roommate return, his work boots crunching on the gravel drive. She heard him again, in the kitchen now—which, she hoped he noted, had been cleaned to his OCD standards—and heard him opening and shutting cabinets and the fridge. The microwave dinged, which caused Lola to wrinkle her nose. What did people cook in microwaves, really? Other than frozen dinners, that was. Ugh.

After that, there was only silence.

She didn't hear him again that night, or early the next morning. She had gotten herself out of bed and ready for yoga, and was standing on the drive at the appointed time with a mat strung across her back. Lola heard her ride turn off the road, heard the pause as the driver punched in the code Lola had given Mallory. The vehicle started down the drive at the same moment she heard the front door open and those work boots crunching the gravel again. She glanced over her shoulder. "Good morning!" she said brightly.

Harry had his head down, his gaze on his phone, and was clearly startled by her, and did a bit of a backward hop. He was dressed in worn, faded jeans and a white collared shirt today. He'd brushed his hair behind his ears, had donned a ballcap with the bill at the back of his head. Apparently he'd run out of time to shave. He looked tired. But he also looked so manly and hot that Lola had to look at her feet and quickly remind herself that he wanted to kick her out of her fantastic deal.

"Morning," he said curiously, taking her in. "Are you looking for a ride? Because I'm running late—"

"A ride!" Lola laughed as if that were ridiculous. "Ask *you*? Oh no, no, no, I would *never.*"

The car—a black sedan, just like the ones she saw dropping people at the airport—coasted into the drive. Harry looked puzzled as the car came into view and rolled to a stop. Lola was puzzled, too, when a driver got out, walked around to the passenger side, and opened the back door. "Good morning, Miss Dunne."

Mallory had failed to mention that "picking her up" meant having a chauffeur. "Good morning," she said, and leaned to her left to look inside. Mallory was there, talking on her phone.

Lola glanced sidelong at Harry, who was staring in disbelief at the car. *That's right, pal, I have a car and a driver, so suck it!* She took a step toward the open car door, then paused and looked back at him. "I'm sorry, did you say something?" she asked, cupping her hand around her ear.

"Nope," he said briskly. "Not a word."

She smiled. "I didn't think so. Oh, by the way, I noticed that you left some papers or something on the end of the kitchen bar. You might want to tidy that up."

He looked surprised. Then annoyed. "Huh," he said. "I'm surprised you noticed one flyer through the stack of wine glasses you seem to be collecting on the bar."

"For your information, the wine glass rack is broken," she said.

"Uh-huh. And how'd that happen?" he asked suspiciously.

"How should I know?" she lied. She hadn't meant to bump into it. "Have a great day in your freshly ironed shirt." And with that, she put herself in that car, practically giggling.

"Who was that?" Mallory asked, her gaze on her phone.

"The pool guy," Lola said. She waved at Harry, who was still standing in the same spot as the car pulled around. Lola really didn't know him at all, but she could not be more delighted that the smug bastard was on hand to see her being picked up in a private car.

◆ ◆ ◆

After that morning, Lola didn't see Harry for a few days. But she heard from him. Oh boy, did she hear from him. He began to leave her notes. *The spray of oatmeal on the stove should be cleaned up before it cements there for all eternity.*

Lola responded with, *Did you leave the towels on the top of the washing machine because you need them washed? You must have me confused with your mother.*

He shot back, *When the trash starts to pile over onto the floor, it's probably time to take it out.*

To which Lola responded with, *Perhaps your sense of smell has been compromised by all the dirt you seem to roll in, but your boots stink. Please leave them outside.*

That was met with a *You left the TV on. I like Jimmy Fallon, too, but I don't need to be blasted by him when I come through the door.*

To which Lola wrote, *Are you deliberately revving your truck in the morning? Because if not, you might need to get that looked at.*

In addition to receiving his notes, Lola also heard Harry. Generally late at night, when his heavy boots would crunch that gravel like a military parade. She heard the water pipes banging to life when he got up before dawn to shower. She saw neatly stacked mail on the entry console, or a plate and cup washed and left in the drainboard to dry.

But she didn't see him. Not that she wanted to see Hardhearted Harry, or cared what he was doing. Nope, she was too busy hanging out with her new friend Mallory.

Lola loved this woman. Theirs was a friendship made in heaven as far as she was concerned. They had so much in common—failed relationships, a love of reality television, the desire to do something new and different with their lives, an unhealthy obsession with shoes. And best of all, they had so much *fun* together. Mallory introduced Lola to her friends. Her two closest friends were Natalie Baker, a fortysomething real estate agent, and Nolan Tipton, a slender, doe-eyed blond man who wore loafers without socks, sleek dress slacks, and a shirt opened at the collar. He was a bartender at a swank little supper club. He was obviously a man who preferred the company of other men, but he seemed genuinely interested in Lola. He wanted to hear about her book. He said she had pretty eyes and he loved her smile. Compliments from a gay man, but Lola would happily take them.

She liked him so much that she invited him out to the lake house for a swim one afternoon when Mallory was busy. Nolan showed up with wine coolers, two pink straw hats, and a Speedo.

They spent the afternoon floating around the pool and sipping the drinks he'd brought. Maybe one too many, because when Harry unexpectedly appeared on the terrace, his weight on one hip, his hands on his waist, Lola was feeling a little tipsy.

"Well, hello," Nolan said, and swam to the side of the pool so that he could smile up at Harry. "What's your name?"

Harry looked from Nolan to Lola. "Lola? Could I speak to you a moment?"

"Sure," she said.

Harry looked at Nolan again. "Inside," he said, and turned around and walked back into the house.

"Who *is* that?" Nolan hissed.

"No one," Lola whispered, and paddled with one arm to the side, then sort of half-climbed and half-rolled out of the pool with a little push from Nolan.

She grabbed a towel and walked inside. Harry was standing at the kitchen bar, his arms crossed across his chest. "You're dripping," he said immediately, and abruptly took her by the arm and pulled her into the utility room.

The utility room was small, however, and Lola was between the washer and dryer and him, suddenly standing so close that she could smell his musky, manly-man scent. It had been so long since Lola had been this close to a man that she'd forgotten how arousing that scent could be.

"Why are your eyes closed?" he demanded.

"Hmm?" She opened her eyes.

"Who is that?" he asked, jerking his thumb over his shoulder.

"Nolan."

Harry's eyes narrowed. "Do you really think it's a good idea?"

"What, having friends? You should try it."

"Bringing him here," Harry said, obviously irritated. He looked like he was about to give her a tongue-lashing, but something behind her caught his attention, and he squinted.

"What?" Lola asked, and tried to turn around.

"Are those *wet clothes* just sitting in the washer?"

That's right, she'd started laundry earlier today. "Ah . . . probably," she said.

He gaped at her. "Good God, Lola, don't you know they will mildew?" He reached around her, forcing Lola up against the machine so that he could close the lid and start it again. When he did, he looked at her and frowned. "Why are you looking at me like that?"

"Like what?" she asked, and bit her lip so she wouldn't smile.

"What's the matter, do I smell?" he asked gruffly.

"Sort of," she admitted.

"Yeah, well, I work hard for a living. And you smell like chlorine."

His arm, she noticed, was still on the washing machine, still blocking her in. "You're kind of touchy," she said, as if she found that curious. "Bad day?"

"I thought you were here to do important work," he said.

"I am! Does that mean I can't have a good time? Does that mean when someone offers me a wine cooler on a gorgeous day like this, I should say no?" She smiled.

"I don't know," Harry said, his brows dipping into a frown. He braced his other hand on the other side of her, so now she was trapped between him and the washing machine again. "Why don't you call Sara and ask her how she feels about your little party at her lake house?"

"Ooh, you're going to go there, huh?" Lola said. "For your information, I can't call Sara. She happens to be in Thailand with some friends right now."

Harry leaned closer, his brows dipping into a deeper frown. "Then I'll tell you for her—*no guests*."

Lola's pulse was beginning to tick with one part thrill and two parts pure irritation. She jutted out her chin, staring him in the eye. They were so close they could have kissed if he wasn't being such a jerk right now. "Who declared you king of the lake house, Horrible Harry? I can do what I want."

"No, you can't," he said, and his gaze fell to her mouth.

"Who's going to stop me?"

Harry's frown turned into a devilish smile, and he said to her mouth, "You want to try me, you little lunatic? Go right ahead."

"Lola? Are you in here?" Nolan called from the kitchen.

"That's your swim buddy," he said low, and Lola felt something very warm and very dangerous wiggling down her spine. She pushed away from Horrible Harry and ducked under his arm, slipping on the tile floor where she'd dripped and catching herself on the door frame. She shot Harry a look over her shoulder before she went out.

"There you are," Nolan said. "I have to run and open the bar, because those rich bitches will be wanting their cocktails soon. Hey, you want to come to a party with me tonight? It's on the south end of the lake, down by that big resort," he said as he wiggled into some jeans that were too tight.

"Oh, I don't know," Lola said as Harry walked around her and down the hall.

Nolan watched him go. "He's not very friendly."

"He's just . . . passing through," she said, and waved a hand dismissively. "Thanks for the invitation, but I really should work."

"Celebrities will be there, you know."

"Like who?" Lola asked.

"Like . . . supposedly, Amy Schumer. Her folks have a house up here. She's usually around in the summer."

Amy Schumer? Lola's skin began to tingle with excitement. She said, very calmly, "Well . . . okay." She shrugged. But inside, she was shrieking with delight.

"Great. I'll pick you up at eight."

She walked Nolan out to his car, waved as he went around the drive.

Amy Schumer!

Casey was right! At long last, she was living the kind of life she'd wanted. She was officially hanging out with the cool kids of East Beach, and stodgy, uptight, laundry obsessors could go fold some boxer shorts.

Nine

Harry had endured a very long week, filled with many headaches and late nights. He'd lost a crane operator to a DUI and had to scramble to find another one. His crew had uncovered some bones, which of course brought everything to a grinding halt while authorities determined what sort of bones they were. It turned out they were large animal bones, and his crew was cleared to continue the work—but the three days lost to working on that section of the bridge had put them behind schedule.

He was losing money again, and it felt like it was pouring through his pockets. Not only that, he had some legwork to do in preparing to bid on another subcontracting job, but it was work he had to do after ten to twelve hours on the job.

Today, however, he'd left his job site early, because he'd heard that the newest state project was sixty-two miles of toll roads with three bridge spans, and the main contract had gone to Horizons Enterprises.

He planned to do some research tonight—he wanted to know everything there was to know about Horizons Enterprises. When that company sent out specs for the bridges, he was determined to aggressively pursue it. He wanted at least one of those bridges, but he was gunning for all three.

He had been looking forward to an inflatable raft, a beer, and a pool overlooking Lake Haven. He wanted a little down time before he cranked up his computer. But of course, his crazy roommate was on hand to blow that idea out of the water.

He sat in his office now, staring at his email inbox. He didn't really see the messages there, because his head was filled with images of Lola's glittering blue eyes, her pert little smile, the droplets of water on her skin. He didn't know where she went after her friend left. He heard a door slam somewhere and ignored it. After another quarter of an hour of staring at a computer screen and seeing nothing but her, he got in his truck, and went to look for something to eat.

He didn't have much luck. East Beach did not attract the sort of people who ate at McDonald's. There were probably more private chefs than grill masters in this village, and after driving aimlessly, he couldn't find anything that didn't require a reservation. He finally decided he'd have to make do with the few groceries they kept on the shelves at Eckland's Hardware and General Store at the bottom of Juneberry Road.

He perused the aisles before settling on some chips and dip. This weekend, he would make it a point to visit a real grocery store. Tonight, he would dine like a frat boy.

Harry parked in front of the house and, holding the bag of chips between his teeth, dug in his pocket for the house key as he walked to the front door.

He'd hardly cracked the door before he smelled something so savory that his stomach instantly began to grumble. He started for the kitchen, but hesitated mid-stride, startled by the big mess. It didn't seem as if she'd even had time to do this. Pots and pans, measuring cups, and various dishes were scattered across the bar top. A carton of cream was sitting open on the counter.

Not only was the kitchen a mess, but he noticed things he hadn't noticed earlier—such as the stuffed beach bag on the couch. Two pairs of sandals looked as if they'd been kicked off her feet near the door and had scudded across the wood floor. And on the dining table, papers and books covered the entire surface.

A small tornado had torn through this house.

Harry didn't see the tornado or hear her rattling around. He walked into the kitchen and dropped his chips on the only empty space on the counter, shaking his head in disbelief. That delectable smell was coming from the oven. He opened the fridge. She'd stuffed real food—fruits and vegetables, juices and yogurts—in and around the fast food containers he'd left through the week. Harry had to move aside several things to reach his beers, which, unsurprisingly, had been shoved to the back.

With a beer in hand, he wandered through the kitchen to the dining room and looked out at the gold and pink shimmer of sunset on the lake's surface. The hills around the lake had turned into dark greens and purples with the setting sun, and lights were beginning to twinkle in them.

Harry took a swig of his beer. Now that the pool had been cleared of the little lunatic and her pal, he intended to go outside and soak in some of that sunset. But he happened to look down at the mess she'd left on the dining room table. A stack of typewritten papers caught his eye, the text marked up with pencil. Words had been lined through, others written above it. What was this? He picked up a page from the pile and read:

> *Sherri hadn't thought about the first man she'd killed in a long time. There was no point to it, really—she'd always believed that people who looked back were unnecessarily sentimental. Conner had died, his death was ruled a suicide, and that was that.*
>
> *She wanted to watch Sam die like she'd watched Connor die. That ass should never have ignored her texts. His death was going to be painful.*

She was on her way to the little hardware store on 9th Avenue for plastic sheeting. They still did everything on paper there—untraceable—and bonus, there were no surveillance cameras. The knives and the acid would be bought in other old-school mom-and-pop shops that hadn't upgraded their point of sale systems. Why were people so cheap, anyway? Wasn't it fascinating that in a world where the United States could listen in on phone calls of world leaders, there were still stores that wrote receipts by hand? Idiots.

Sherri strode toward the subway entrance, but before she could reach it, her phone rang. She dug it out of her purse. "Hello?"

"Sherri?"

Her heart surged to her throat. Sam. She slowed her step and ducked to one side to avoid the sidewalk traffic. "Hey," she said. Her heart was suddenly jackhammering in her chest, and for a tiny moment, she had the fear that Sam somehow knew what she was planning. "What's up?"

"Are you okay?" he asked. "You sound a little winded."

"Oh! I, ah . . . I was running."

"Running?" He sounded confused. As well he should be, as Sherri had never run in her life.

"Yep. I've taken up running. Trying to drop a few LB's." For all she knew, he'd called the cops, and they were closing in on her now. She looked wildly about.

"You don't need to lose any weight," he said. "You look great, Sherri."

Sherri's breath caught; she slouched back against the brick wall. She thought she might love him all over again. "Sam, thank you," she said, grinning now. She'd been so hasty in her decision to kill him! Maybe the woman she'd seen going into his apartment with him was just a friend. A consultant. A cousin. A landlord—

"I was calling to see if you want to get a drink sometime this week."

"Ah . . . sure!" Sherri said. Of course she wanted to get a drink. She wanted to marry him, have his babies, never let him leave her sight. "When did you have in mind?"

"Tuesday? I've a got a late meeting but I could meet you at that bar you like in Astor Place."

She didn't like the bar at Astor Place. It wasn't exactly a happening location. She'd only gone there because he'd asked her. But Sherri wasn't going to let location ruin it, at least not this time. Sam was calling her and asking her out. She had misjudged everything! She could work with him, help him see what he did was wrong. And then she wouldn't have to kill him.

Harry's eyes felt like they were bulging out of his head. He didn't know what to make of it—

"Hey!"

Startled, Harry jerked around. He hadn't heard Lola come into the kitchen. She was wearing a short robe, and her wet hair was combed back. She was glaring at him with fire practically leaping out of her eyes as she strode toward him. Harry's pulse jumped a notch and he dropped the pages like a guilty child.

"That's mine!" she said angrily.

"Are you writing a book?" He sounded more incredulous than he felt—what he really wondered was what he intended to do with this . . . story.

"Maybe," she said curtly. "But it's none of your business." She roughly brushed past him, forcing him to take a step back from the dining table. She picked up the pages he'd just read and shoved them into a file. With another glare, she whirled around and returned to the kitchen, pulled the oven open and removed a dish of what looked like macaroni and cheese. She placed it on a hot pad and began to spoon through it, distributing the heat. She glanced up at him, still frowning. "What?"

"What is that?" he asked.

"What does it look like? It's lobster mac and cheese."

Jesus, just cut his throat already—it would be far less painful than watching her devour it while his stomach rumbled helplessly. What did he have in the freezer, anyway—another Hungry-Man dinner?

A smile slowly took the place of her frown. "Would you like some lobster mac and cheese, Harry Westbrook?"

"No," he said instantly. How did she kill the guys in the book anyway? Poison? But he couldn't take his gaze from the dish, especially when she lifted the spoon and thick strands of cheese stretched up with it, tantalizing him.

"Are you sure? Because you can ask anyone—I make the *best* lobster mac and cheese around. And there's plenty."

"You made that for you," he said, sounding as weak as he felt. "And for all I know, that's how you kill guys who don't respond to your texts."

She smiled wickedly. "I would never kill a guy with poison. Too iffy and too obvious. I made this because I had the ingredients to make it. I like to cook, what can I say? Besides, I'm not eating any of it tonight."

"Why not?"

"Because I'm going to a swanky party with Nolan." She beamed at him, leaned across the bar, and whispered, "Amy Schumer might be there."

Her eyes were shining with delight, and Harry was reminded of those charged moments in the utility room. But his stomach was far more interested in the mac and cheese than he was in sex or celebrity at the moment. "You're sure you don't mind?"

"I don't mind at all." She slid the pan closer, smiling as if people practically face-planted in a pan of something she made every day. "See? I'm not such a bad roommate." She took a plate out of a cabinet behind

87

her, heaped a pile of the casserole onto a plate, then set it before him on the bar. She fetched a spoon from a drawer and held it out to him. "Go to town, big guy."

Harry's stomach rumbled loudly in response, embarrassing him. He reluctantly accepted the spoon she offered him, slid onto a bar stool, and pulled the plate closer. He spooned an obscenely large amount of mac and cheese, said "Thank you," and stuffed it into his mouth.

The moment that mac and cheese met his taste buds, Harry almost slid off the barstool with ecstasy. It was so damn good that he inadvertently moaned, then flushed slightly when she giggled with delight.

"You're welcome," she said. She opened the fridge, studied the contents. She apparently didn't find what she wanted, because she shut the door and picked up an apple from a wooden bowl and bit into it.

Harry had, embarrassingly, devoured his food in the time it took her to do this.

With her apple in one hand, Lola dipped the serving spoon into the dish and heaped more onto his plate, leaving a trail of half-moon macaroni soaked in cheese between the pan and his plate.

"No, I couldn't," he said unconvincingly, his hand on his belly.

"Sure you could," she chirped.

Harry didn't even draw a breath before diving back in. It was a feast for a king after the crap he'd been eating all week.

She leaned back against the counter, watching him lap up her food as she munched on her apple. Her scrutiny made him feel conspicuous; he slowed the shoveling. "So. You're here to write a book," he said, taking a breath. "The mystery has been solved."

"Yep." Her sunny smile was completely incongruent with the pages he'd read.

"Are you a published author?" he asked, wondering if he ought to know who she was. Not that he would know—he rarely read fiction. His reading consisted of magazines and manuals.

"Not yet. I'm trying to be. Sara offered me the place to see if I could do it."

"You're definitely doing it," he said, glancing uneasily at the mess on the dining room table. "I wouldn't have guessed writer." The last part sort of slipped out before he realized it.

"Oh no? What would you have guessed?"

Harry shrugged. "I don't know . . . maybe a teacher," he said unconvincingly.

Lola blinked. And then she laughed. "Why? Because women are supposed to be teachers and nurses?"

"No. Just because." Because he could picture her in front of a group of kids, in a cute dress with strawberries on the hem, handing out cookies. So sue him.

"I am *so* not a teacher. Now you have to tell me why you're here."

"I'm trying to get a bridge construction firm off the ground." Lola had very thick, dark-brown lashes, he noticed, that framed pool-blue eyes. Which, incidentally, sat above a slight smattering of freckles across her cheeks.

"You're like a builder or something?"

"Or something. I'm a civil engineer," he said. "I sold my apartment in New York so I could buy the heavy equipment I need to make bids. Zach offered me a place to stay until I could get the business off the ground."

"Wow," she said, nodding as if she were impressed, and Harry's Y chromosomes puffed up a little. "What kind of bridges are we talking?"

"You know, bridges that attach roads over water or rail yards or what have you."

"Huh." She tilted her head to one side. "That's not what I would have guessed, either."

He put down his spoon, leaned back. "Okay, I'll bite. What would you have guessed?"

"Oh, I don't know. Maybe laundry operator?"

He smiled. "Interesting," he said, nodding. "While it is true I like clean, folded clothes, I'm not sure what I'd be doing at a lake house if my business was laundry."

"Maybe because you intend to open a laundry facility around here," she suggested. "A big Laundromat with posters around the walls warning customers of the dangers of mildew."

Harry's smile widened. "There's already a laundry facility. I pass it every day on my way out of town. I doubt East Beach could support two."

"Oh, is there?" she said breezily. "I wouldn't know. I've been too busy writing a book."

"The freckles on your face would argue that you've been hanging out at the pool. But okay, someone wrote the pages about a woman who's going to kill some guy because he didn't answer her text."

"Oh come on, Harry," she said airily. "Admit it—you don't like it either when you text someone and they don't answer right away."

She was enjoying this conversation. And he was enjoying looking at her. She was prettier than he'd given her credit for in the beginning. She was a little quirky, definitely a hot mess, the author of a very strange book, and definitely, definitely pretty. "I admit it," he said. "But would I kill them? No."

"That's why I'm not writing a book about you, Humdrum Harry."

"Very funny," he said, smiling. His gaze strayed, down the lapels of her bathrobe.

Lola took another bite of her apple. "Well, okay then, now that we've confessed our true occupations, I have to get ready for the party. By the way, I want to be a good roommate and formally acknowledge that I know you will totally flip out if I leave the kitchen like this," she said, and pressed her hand to her heart and bowed. "There is no need to leave me a note. I promise to do it when I get home—"

"Don't worry about it," he said. "You fed me, and for that I am very grateful. I'll clean up."

"Really? You don't mind?"

He shook his head.

"*Yes!*" she said, making a victory pump. "Thank you! I hate cleanup."

One corner of his mouth tipped up. "No kidding."

"Do yourself a favor," she said as she started out of the kitchen. "You really don't have to stack all the plates according to color and size, you know."

"Yes, you do!" he called after her, and heard her laugh as she shut her door.

He looked at the mess he was going to have to clean up. That's when he noticed the half-eaten apple she'd left on the counter. *Lord.*

◆ ◆ ◆

An hour later, Harry had finally finished the kitchen and was sitting on the terrace, his feet up on a stool, a half-empty beer dangling from his hands. The window for working had passed; his brain had checked out for the day. He was idly thinking of throwing some wood onto the fire pit when he heard the click of heels behind him. He turned his head with as little effort as he could manage, but Lola made him sit up and look again.

Her shoulder length hair was all waves, and bangs brushed across her forehead in a very sultry way. She was wearing a buttery yellow halter dress made from silk or something like it. It had a bit of flounce in the hem just above her knee. And her legs . . . well, now, he hadn't really paid them enough attention before now. She had some very shapely legs that disappeared under that skirt and just soared right on up. They looked especially good in the pair of shiny gold high heels she wore. She looked fantastic, utterly delectable, about as hot as a girl could be, and the male in him was taking notice.

He slowly gained his feet. He tried not to be a pig, tried not to look her up and down, but he couldn't help himself. He shoved one hand into his jeans pocket. "Nice," he said, nodding approvingly.

She flashed a dubious look as she draped a sweater over her arm. "Seriously?"

"Yes. Seriously." More than seriously. He hadn't been this . . . *attracted* to a woman since Melissa. There was something about the yellow dress and the way it fit her that caused the pistons in him to crank.

"Would you mind?" she asked, and presented her bare back to him. The dress was zipped halfway up. "It's a little tight and I can't get it all the way."

Harry looked at her back, the smooth skin. He could see her spine, her shoulder blades. He had a sudden and insane urge to kiss her back.

Lola glanced over her shoulder. "What's wrong?"

"Nothing," he said, and zipped her up, trying not to make actual contact. But it was impossible; his fingers brushed against the middle of her back, and a tiny little shiver went shooting up his fingertips.

"Thank you." She turned back around, and ran her palm over her belly to smooth her dress. "I never know what to wear to a party. Do you? I mean what if I show up in a dress and everyone is sitting around in shorts and Tevas?" She paused, thinking, and bit her lower lip. "Maybe I should put on some something more casual—"

"No."

Lola looked at him, surprised.

"You look great, Lola. Really . . . great," he said, shoving his hands into his pockets again. "If you're going to a party with people in shorts and sandals, you're out of their league."

A smile of pleasure lit her face, and it occurred to Harry he'd not seen Melissa smile like that in a very long time. Had he neglected to tell her she was beautiful?

"Why, thank you, Harry Westbrook. That might be the nicest thing a guy has ever said to me. It's amazing what a little mac and cheese can do for someone's mood." She was still smiling as she opened her tiny purse, took out a lipstick, and dabbed some on using her shadowy reflection in the glass door. "I'm going to go wait outside for my ride. Have a good night!"

"You, too." He watched her walk into the house and across the living room, jogging up the two steps to the door. When the front door closed behind her, Harry shook his head. This roommate situation was highly precarious for a guy like him. When a woman cooked like she did *and* looked like that, it made him think of all the things a guy wasn't supposed to think about his roommate.

With Lola gone, Harry moved into the living room and watched some baseball. And he kept watching baseball, long after the game had ceased to be interesting. He was bone-tired, yet he remained on the couch. Harry didn't want to admit it to himself, but he was sort of waiting up for her. He wanted to see her in that yellow dress again.

What was he even thinking, anyway? He hardly knew her. He'd talked to her three or four times, and most of it had been a little infuriating. He just really liked that dress.

And that mac and cheese.

At half past eleven, he gave in to his body's need for rest. He had a lot to do the next morning. Harry was dreaming about bridges and a crane that was rolling away from him when the distant ringing of a phone startled him awake.

He sat up, confused, and rubbed his face with his fingers. His cell phone was on the nightstand—whose phone was ringing? He got up, stumbled toward the sound of the phone wearing nothing but his boxers, and finally located it in the small office alcove off the kitchen. "Hello?" he said with gruff curiosity.

"Harry? Thank God! Harry, it's me!"

"Me," he repeated uncertainly. "Who is me?"

"Lola! Your roommate!"

Harry winced. "Jesus, Lola, it's two in the morning—"

"I know, I know, and I am so, so sorry, Harry. Please don't hang up—I didn't know who else to call!"

"Why are you calling anyone at this time of night?" he asked irritably, and rubbed his eye. "Look, I've got to get some sleep."

"Harry, please—I need your help," she said frantically, and when she did, he heard that unmistakable crack in her voice—the sound of a woman about to cry.

He mentally shook the sleep off his brain. "What's wrong?"

"You'll think it's so stupid. I can't even—"

"We can discuss how stupid it is when the sun is shining. What's going on?"

"Can you please come get me?" she asked weakly. "I was going to walk all the way, but . . . well, did you see my shoes? My feet are killing me! I'm not Bear Grylls. I can't *do* this."

She was definitely not the survivalist Bear Grylls. "Why are you walking home? What happened to your ride?"

"I had to get out of there, Harry. I didn't know it was *that* kind of party."

"What kind?"

"*You* know."

No, he didn't know, but whatever it was, he didn't like the sound of it. *Dammit. Damsel in distress.* It was guy code—you couldn't turn your back on women or children or animals when they needed help. "Okay. Where are you?"

"Thank you, *thank* you. I'm at the hardware store at the bottom of Juneberry Road. The one with all the pinwheels."

"The what?"

"The pinwheels. You put them in your yard—"

"Right, yeah, pinwheels." He would have said it was the place with all the riding mowers out front. "All right. I'll be there in about ten minutes."

"Thank you *so* much, Harry! I really owe—"

"Hold tight," he said impatiently. He hung up the phone and went in search of pants.

Ten

Well, this was super embarrassing.

Lola was sitting on a riding lawn mower, her feet propped up on the steering wheel, and her shoes, her fabulous, way-too-expensive shoes, on the ground beside the mower. How could shoes that cute be that lethal?

When she saw headlights coming down Juneberry Road, she knew it was Harry. She watched as his silver truck coasted to a stop into the parking lot, the headlights pointed at her. She leaned down to pick up her traitorous shoes and stood up on the running board of the mower. The headlights blinded her—she couldn't see the truck or Harry. She gave a weak wave.

That wave was followed by the sound of a truck door closing, and then, like a spirit in a ghost movie, Harry emerged from the blinding light of the head beams. He was wearing a hoodie, sandals, and shorts, his hands in his pockets. He walked to the mower and looked her up and down as she stood on the runner. "Are you okay?"

No, she was not okay. She'd been through a harrowing night, and if she hadn't thought he'd recoil or think her weird, she'd have thrown her arms around him for coming to her rescue. Instead, she shrugged sheepishly. "I'm okay."

"That's good." He yawned. "Let's get out of here."

"I can never thank you enough, Harry. I mean that."

"Okay." He gestured toward the truck. "Let's go."

She clutched her bitchy shoes to her chest. "I never have to ask for help. Usually, I'm the one picking people up in the middle of the night."

One of his brows rose above the other.

"I don't mean . . ." She shook her head and pressed a palm to her forehead. "Forget it. I don't know what I mean."

"It's okay, Lola. Come on." He looked at her shoes. He extended his hand, palm up, and gestured for them. She put the implements of torture in his hand, then stepped gingerly off the mower.

She followed him to the truck, hopping on bare feet across the lot. She went around to the passenger side of the truck, but Harry said, "Over here."

"Huh?"

"I've got some tools on that side. Over here."

She went around the front of the truck to the driver's side. He was holding the door open. "Get in," he said, nodding.

Lola ducked under his arm and slid in, pausing underneath the steering wheel. The passenger seat was full of papers, blueprints, a metal box, a leather tool belt. The back seat had what looked like a bunch of rebar iron. "I don't—"

"Console," he said. "I would have moved stuff around but I was too tired. Move over."

Lola slid on top of the closed console. There was no place to put her feet, really, and her dress was sliding up her thigh, but she managed to perch on top of it. Harry got in and shut the door. She was pressed against him now, her thigh wedged between his side and the console, and her bare arm against his shoulder. He was warm. Hot. A furnace that was going to blister her skin every place they touched.

He reached over her to deposit her shoes on the passenger seat, his arm brushing against her chest. "Sorry," he muttered. He smelled clean—spicy soap clean. An image of him in a shower, rubbing some man soap all over his naked body, popped uninvited into her head.

Great. Now her cheeks were flaming. She glanced down . . . at the rolled up blueprints, and the Green Bean coffee cup she was straddling in the cup holder.

Harry put the truck in gear, his arm moving against her bare thigh—no matter what she did, she couldn't keep her dress from sliding. He started a slow turnaround and said, "You wanna tell me what happened?"

He sounded brotherly, and Lola suddenly wished for Ty or Ben to magically appear and threaten to kill someone on her behalf. "No, I don't want to tell you what happened, because you'll think I'm an idiot if you don't already. But I feel like I owe you an explanation since you so graciously came to get me, and I thank you so much—"

"You said. What happened?"

"Okay, I'll tell you—it was a *swinger* party."

Harry jerked his gaze to her. And then he laughed. Quite roundly, too, as if that was the funniest thing he'd ever heard. His head fell back and the cab of that truck filled with uproarious laughter.

"It's not funny."

"Of course it is," he said jovially. "Are you kidding me?"

"I'm not kidding!" she insisted. "Maybe technically it wasn't a swinger party, but it was definitely a sex party. Everyone was there to hook up! Men and men, and women and women, and men and women. Or any combination thereof."

"Seriously?" he asked.

"Well, I don't know about all the combinations, but yes, everyone was there to hook up. And there was a *lot* of cocaine."

"Yikes," he said as he pulled onto Juneberry Road.

"Yeah, yikes," she said, catching herself on his shoulder when he gave the truck a little gas, so that she wouldn't fall backward into the rebar. "I'm not into that," she said flatly. "I thought cocaine went out with big hair and the eighties."

"I don't think so," Harry said, smiling as if he found that amusing.

Lola was very serious. She could not think of a single person she knew who ever did cocaine. "And then there was this guy who thought I should want to hook up with him. He got super handsy."

Harry's smile faded. "Not cool."

"*So* not cool. You want to know what's really sad? I didn't even get it at first. People were floating off to bedrooms, and I thought, okay, they're going off to talk. But then this guy said, 'Looks like it's you and me, sweetheart,'" she said, mimicking his voice, "And then started getting pretty adamant about it. Asshole."

He'd been more than adamant—he was a pushy drunk and Lola was still shaking a little. He'd been a big man, too, almost as big as Harry, and he'd put his hands on her, groping, trying to convince her with his whiskey-soaked breath that he could *definitely* show her a good time, as if that qualifier would be the magic that would cause her to consent to his clumsy advances. He'd scared her. She'd wanted only to get out of there, but the first mistake she'd made was not knowing quite where she was, thanks to her gleeful chatter with Nolan all the way there.

"So what'd you do?" Harry asked.

"Well, first I panicked. And then I almost hyperventilated when I couldn't find Nolan. But then I found him—on the lap of a man." Relief had washed over her nonetheless . . . until Nolan opened his mouth to speak. "Unfortunately, Nolan had partaken in whatever was being passed around, because when I asked him to take me home, he tried to answer, and he started giggling, and he could hardly slur two words together. And when he started looking around for his keys, I realized he was the last person I would get into a car with. So I just . . . I just walked out," she said. "I walked right out the back door and down the street." She'd thought it couldn't be very far. Maybe four or five miles at most? "But I didn't know quite where I was, and after a couple of blocks, my super cute shoes turned into machetes and started hacking away at my feet."

Harry didn't say anything. She looked at him in the darkness of the truck cab, trying to read his expression. "For what it's worth, I did try to get a cab," she added. "But get this—they don't operate after midnight in this stupid little village."

"Good to know," he said.

"And I would have called my friend Mallory, who was supposed to be there by the way, but she lives with her parents. I didn't want to be the girl calling the house at two in the morning, you know?"

Harry slanted a look at her that felt withering even in the darkness. "So you called *me* at two in the morning."

Lola winced. "Okay, I know, I know. I didn't want to be that girl with you at *all*," she said, slashing her hand through the air for emphasis. "But by then I'd made it to Juneberry Road, and I thought, it can't be that far, right? I'm sorry, Harry. I am *so* sorry. I swear it won't happen again. Scout's honor," she said, holding up three fingers.

"I don't think you're allowed to throw the Scout's honor sign if you're not a Scout," he pointed out. "Are you a Scout?"

"Then I'm swearing it on the grave of someone important. You can choose the important person."

He smiled and propped his wrist on the steering wheel. "It's okay this time, roomie," he said congenially, and patted her knee. "Just please don't make a habit of it." The dazzling smile he flashed her after a dismal night made Lola feel a little woozy. See, *that* was how you lured a girl into one of the back bedrooms at a party. There should have been a sign hanging somewhere in that party house—*Don't be gropey, be sexy! Be so sexy that the girl sitting next to you is forced to look out the passenger window or risk drooling all over your shoulder!*

Lola looked out the window.

"Sounds like your night really sucked," Harry said sympathetically.

Lola snorted. "You have no idea."

"I guess the only bright spot was hanging out with Amy Schumer."

Lola shot him a dark look; Harry laughed. "Sorry," he said, holding up a hand. "I couldn't help it."

They reached the lake house a few minutes later. Harry parked, opened the door, and got out.

Lola grabbed her shoes and purse and inched her way across the driver's seat, but Harry was still standing in the open door. "You know how to ride piggyback?"

"Excuse me?"

He pointed to the ground. "It's gravel from here to the door. Unless you want to walk barefoot, you're going to have to hitch a ride."

Lola glanced at the door. He was right; she couldn't bear the thought of her blistered feet on gravel. She scooched over to the opening and stood up on the running board. Harry presented his back.

She put her arms around his neck, then her legs around his waist.

He grabbed onto her thighs and hitched her up her like she were a backpack, and walked across the drive. Lola tried desperately not to think of all the other reasons she might wrap her legs around a guy like him, but she couldn't keep all the ideas from slipping into her thoughts. One would think that after her awful evening, the last thing Lola would do now—exhausted, embarrassed, still a little shaky—would be to imagine this man on top of her. But that was exactly what she was doing. He was so firm and so strong, and he smelled so enticing. Oh yeah, it had been a while. She was thankful the walk across the drive was very short, because she might have done something really stupid to top off this ridiculous night—

"Are you nibbling my *ear*?" he asked incredulously.

"What? Is that your *ear*?"

Lola was suddenly on her feet again. Harry frowned at her as he fit the key into the door. "What is the matter with you?"

"Sorry!" she said, throwing her hands up. "But you smell really good."

"Hmm," he said, and pushed the door open and stepped inside. Well then. Crisis averted.

♦ ♦ ♦

Harry was long gone the next morning when Lola finally roused herself from bed. She padded into the kitchen for a cup of joe, and noticed that the kitchen was as sparkling clean and neat as it had been the first day she'd shown up here and thought the house had been closed for the season.

She made some coffee, found her purse, which she'd fairly thrown across the living room when she'd come in last night, fished out her phone, and called Mallory.

"*Hola!*" Mallory said cheerfully.

"Hey, where were you last night?" Lola asked. "I thought you were going to the party."

"The party? Oh, that's *right*. I forgot to text you. I was going to come, but Dad wanted to go out for dinner and talk about the candy shop. He's all about profit. *Gah,*" she said, as if that were unreasonable. "So how was it? Did you have fun with Nolan? He's so much fun!"

"*No*, I didn't have fun," Lola said grumpily. "It was a big party with a lot of drugs and a *lot* of people pairing off for sex. There was no Amy Schumer! It wasn't even a cool house. And there was a guy who wouldn't leave me alone."

Mallory gasped. "Tell me!"

Lola filled her in on her horrific night. When Lola had finished, Mallory said, "That's so *weird*. I thought Nolan was on the wagon. Didn't I tell you he was on the wagon?"

"Nope. He's not on any wagon, Mallory. In fact, he was run over several times by the wagon last night by the look of things."

"So how did you get home?" Mallory asked. "Cabs stop running after midnight. Did I tell you?"

The list of things Mallory had neglected to tell her was getting quite long. "You didn't, but I discovered it soon enough. I had to a call a friend." And then she'd nibbled his ear like a drunk girl character in a *Saturday Night Live* skit. The sad thing about it was that she hadn't been drunk. Nope, what she'd suffered was just a plain old-fashioned lack of impulse control.

"A *friend*?" Mallory chirped. "Have you been holding out on me, Lola?"

"He's not that kind of friend. He's a guy who's staying here for a few days. Just passing through."

"Ah. Hey, come into East Beach later. I'll buy you a latte to make up for not being there last night."

"Nah," Lola said, casually examining her blistered toes. "I'm going to stay in and work today. But I'll meet you for coffee tomorrow?"

"Great," Mallory said.

When she'd hung up, Lola stretched her arms overhead and decided it was time to get to work.

She'd managed to draft two rough chapters by three o'clock, at which point, she was feeling a little bleary-eyed. Her girl had just ventured into Home Depot to buy some body-cutting tools. That seemed as good a place as any to quit for the day.

Lola wandered into the kitchen and looked around for something to eat. She thought of Harry coming to her rescue. When her gaze landed on a bowl of apples, it occurred to her that she ought to do something nice for him. She was going to make him an apple pie. The man always seemed so hungry! If she wasn't mistaken, she still had some steaks in the freezer, too, courtesy of her brother Ben, who had driven out one day to bring some of her stuff.

It was perfect—she would feed the man to thank him for rescuing her last night.

She hoped he was coming back for the weekend. She did not want to be alone in the house with a full apple pie.

Eleven

Harry pulled into the parking lot of Taco Tornado, but he didn't turn off his truck. He stared at the blinking neon taco dancing on the roof. While it was true that he was so hungry he could eat his arm, he didn't think he was hungry enough to choke down a pink-slime burrito.

He backed out of the parking lot and headed to the lake house. If he could just get through one more night on junk food, he'd make a run to the grocery store tomorrow and treat himself to a really good meal at the Lakeside Bistro. Maybe, if he was lucky, Lola would let him have some more of that mac and cheese.

But Harry grimaced when he stepped out of his truck; even on the drive he could smell something delectable. Surviving on frozen entrees was doable as long as there wasn't any other food in the house. He opened the door and stepped inside, put his briefcase and hardhat down, and looked toward the kitchen. There was the source of the torture, clearly visible from the kitchen bar: a pie.

"Oh hey!"

Harry noticed Lola then. She was standing on a wobbly wicker chair, reaching into a cabinet above the fridge.

"I was beginning to think you weren't coming back tonight. Do you like wine?"

"What?"

"Wine," she said again.

She was wearing a skirt and T-shirt, and her hair was tied in a messy knot at the nape. And as she reached overhead, her breasts were clearly outlined against her shirt. They were the size of oranges.

Damn, even breasts were beginning to remind him of food.

"I prefer red, and I just happen to have this great bottle of wine that my friend Mallory gave me. It's organic. Want some?"

"Ah . . ."

"Oh," she said, before he could answer, "I forgot to mention that I made you dinner. I mean, if you want it. But I wanted to show my gratitude for rescuing me last night, and you always seem so hungry."

He stared at her—or rather her legs, which were now directly in front of him. He was amazed by this stroke of luck. The offer of food, *real* food, and not some processed shit, had drawn him to the kitchen without him even realizing it.

"I'm going to make a mushroom sauce, but the sauté pan is up here. Who puts a *sauté* pan up here?"

Well, he had. He couldn't find another place for it.

Lola reached, and when she did, she hopped a little to reach it, but in doing so, her foot missed the chair. "Careful!" Harry said, and put his hands up to catch her. One accidentally landed on her derriere, which, he couldn't help but notice, was neither too firm nor too soft. It was perfect, pliable yet firm. The ideal ratio of fat to muscle in his non-expert opinion. He wanted to examine it, push his fingers into it.

"God, thank you," she said, glancing down at him. "I could have broken my neck." She withdrew her arm from the cabinet clutching the sauté pan, and Harry withdrew his hand from her ass.

She jumped down from the chair and pushed it a little haphazardly beneath the kitchen desk. With his foot, Harry nudged it completely under. That was the point he noticed she was wearing an apron with the body of Superwoman painted onto it, giving her the illusion of having that figure.

"It's steak," she said.

He glanced up from her cartoon figure. "Huh?"

"Dinner. I'm going to grill steaks. It's grass-fed beef, which is supposed to be better for you. Oh God, you eat beef, don't you? If you don't, I made a salad. Oh, and baked potatoes. You look like a guy who would like baked potatoes. Oh, and guess what else? I made you a pie. See?" She slid past him, dropped the pan onto the stove, then reached across the kitchen island to pick up the pie and show him. The dough was latticed across the top of the pie. "Apple."

"Yes," he said, without thinking. His stomach was already rumbling.

"Yes . . . it's apple?"

"No. I mean, yes, I want whatever you're offering," he said, and added gratefully, "I'll eat anything right now. Because you're right, Lola, I'm hungry. Unfortunately, my options are pretty bleak out there."

Lola beamed. "Great! So yes to the wine?"

"Yes to the wine. I'm just going to clean up," he said, jerking a thumb over his shoulder in the direction of his room.

"Okeydoke," she said, and put down the pie. She turned back to the kitchen, and for once, Harry was not annoyed that there were dishes and condiments scattered about and something oozing out of a pot on the stove. Nope, he wasn't annoyed, because she had made him a fucking *pie*.

He took a quick shower, dressed in some jeans, and managed a quick shave. When he returned to the main living area, he heard voices and realized they were coming from Lola's phone, set to speaker as she worked at the stove.

A young woman was complaining. "He doesn't have the right to tell me what to think or who to hang out with," she said.

"Uh-huh." Lola dropped the lid to the pan on the counter with a clang. "Ty, don't tell her what to think."

"I haven't told her what to think," a man's voice said irritably. "I just said she might be a little more careful about who she hangs out with! The woman was a *Moonie*, Lola."

"I can't stand this!" the girl screeched. "How can you be so narrow-minded, Ty? You hate everyone! You have contempt for anyone different from you!"

"That is not true, Kennedy! The only people I have contempt for are siblings who don't agree with me!"

"Okay, all right," Lola said, her back to Harry. "What do you want me to do about it, Ty? I'm up to my elbows in a mushroom sauce."

"I would kill for some of that," the man said wistfully. "Anyway, you need to come home and talk to her, Lola. No one is looking out for Kennedy, and God knows what she's doing on campus without someone checking up on her."

"I am not a child!" the young woman shrieked.

"I'm not coming home, Ty. You're going to have to deal with it if you're worried about it," Lola said, stirring something in the pan.

"Me! I already have three children, remember?"

"I am right here!" Kennedy said angrily. "I can hear everything you're saying, Ty!"

"Okay, how's this?" Lola said calmly as she whirled back around to the counter. She saw Harry and winced, mouthed an *I'm sorry*, then said, "Kennedy, please call your brother once a week and make sure he knows where you are. Ty, lighten up. Kennedy is twenty-three and, therefore, an adult. You can't dictate her life to her."

"Thanks, Lola, helpful as always," Ty said curtly. "Look, I have to go, I don't have time for this. I'll talk to you both later. Kennedy, I'm coming over tomorrow!"

"Whatever," Kennedy said. "Is he gone?"

"He's gone," Lola confirmed.

The young woman said, "Sometimes I hate him."

"Don't say that. He's your brother."

"I don't *hate* him, hate him. He just makes me so mad. Hey, Lola—do you have any money? I found this sweater at Topshop that I *love*. But I don't get paid until the end of the month."

"How much?"

"Fifty bucks."

Lola groaned. "Okay, fine, I'll PayPal you. But that's it, Kennedy. I'm not working right now, I can't keep you in sweaters."

"I know. Thank you!" the young woman chirped. "You're the best big sister ever."

"And remember, you're going to go see Mom this weekend."

"I will!"

"And I'm going to call you tomorrow to talk about this Moonie business."

"She's not a Moonie," Kennedy said. "I'll talk to you later."

Lola said good-bye, and with a tap of her elbow, ended the call. She smiled sheepishly at Harry. "Sorry about that. Siblings," she said with a shake of her head. She removed the sauté pan from the stovetop, then picked up a rolling pin and began to roll a glob of dough directly onto the kitchen counter.

Harry decided not to say anything because he also noticed two glasses of wine on the bar. "One of these for me?"

"Yes! Please take one. I'm going to join you just as soon as I roll out this extra dough. I'm going to make some extra piecrusts and wedge them into the freezer around your mountain of frozen dinners."

"Yeah, well, I'm pretty sure I got the freezer when we divided things up." He winked at her.

"Ooh, making a joke about it now," she said brightly. "We must be getting somewhere."

"I think we are," Harry agreed. "It's been a couple of weeks and no one has been murdered. I've cleaned your kitchen and rescued you, and you've bit my ear. I'd say we're off and running with this roommate thing." He picked up the wine and slid onto a barstool.

"I apologize for the ear thing. That was a failure of personal impulse control. I promise," she said, pressing her hand to her heart, apparently having forgotten it was covered in dough, "that I won't do that again."

"It's okay." It had surprised the hell out of him, but it hadn't been unpleasant. Quite the opposite, really.

Lola continued working on the dough as Harry sipped the wine.

"So . . . those people were your brother and sister, huh?" he asked, curious about Superwoman now.

"Yep. That was exactly half of the herd. I have two more." She stopped rolling a moment. "You ought to hear all five of us go at it."

He'd rather not. "That's a lot of kids in one house," he said absently.

"Especially in a two bedroom, one bath walk-up. It's a wonder any of us made it to adulthood." She laughed at herself, wiped her hands on Superwoman's bare middle, and picked up her wine, but Harry was mentally taken aback—she'd grown up with four siblings in a two-bedroom walk-up? He and Hazel had had their own bedrooms, a nanny, and so many extracurricular activities that they'd rarely seen each other when they'd been kids.

"Hey," she said, as if a thought just occurred to her. "Let's have a drink on the terrace while the sun sets. It's so gorgeous, every night. I can see why Sara and Zach bought this house. They bought it, right? Or did they build it?"

"I don't know."

"I'll ask Sara next time I talk to her. *If* I talk to her. I got an email from her. Apparently she met a new boy toy at the Thai resort and now she's pretty hard to get hold of," Lola said as she walked out, leaving the dough flattened to the counter top, the rolling pin still on it. "Oops, I probably wasn't supposed to mention that. Promise you won't say anything. But why would you? Zach would wonder how you would know anything about Sara, am I right?"

She stepped outside and began to chatter about the view instead of Sara's love life.

Harry followed her out. Lola set fire to the charcoal and they took up residence in two Adirondack chairs and shared a footstool as they waited for the coals to get hot. Neither one spoke for a few moments as they gazed out at the deepening shadows. Harry was thinking about food. Just the smell of the charcoal in the grill was making him ravenous. But he wouldn't ask when he'd be fed like some impatient clod.

He tried to take his mind off his stomach. He squinted at the lake and a pair of paddleboarders coming back to shore and asked, "Where are you from, Lola?"

"Brooklyn. What about you?"

"Manhattan." He eyed his glass before sipping.

"Upper East Side," she said matter-of-factly.

She said it as if she knew him, and he glanced curiously at her. "How did you know?"

"Easy. You have that look."

"That *look*?"

"You know, a little preppy, a little rich."

"That's ridiculous," he scoffed. "I don't look preppy or rich. I wear hard hats and steel-toed work boots. I don't even have a look."

"Maybe it was the Cornell T-shirt," she said. "I saw it in the laundry. No one in my neighborhood is trying to start a bridge company or wears a Cornell T-shirt. That's really curious to me, by the way."

"That I went to Cornell?" he asked, laughing a little self-consciously.

"No, the wanting to start a bridge construction company. Why not the rest of the road? Why single the bridge out for special treatment?"

He grinned. "Because I like bridges. I like designing them and figuring out how to build them. After working several years in a big civil engineering firm, I discovered that I'm pretty darn good at bridges. So I decided to go for it."

"Cheers!" she said, holding out her wine glass to him.

Harry touched his to hers. "And what about you, Superwoman? When did you decide you wanted to be a writer?"

"Oh, I . . ." She waved her hand and looked out over the lake. "Always. But I never thought I could. That always seemed like one of those jobs you either fall into, or you're born to do, you know? It's not like you can get a creative writing degree and just hang your shingle, right? Not if you want to eat, anyway. My family was really poor, so I went to community college and became a paralegal before I decided to commit to writing." She smiled sheepishly. "That's what my sister Kennedy calls it—committing to a vision. You would not have guessed from that phone call, but she's actually studying psychology. Which she is very good at applying to all of us, but never to herself."

"Small world," Harry said. "My sister is a resident psychiatrist at Mount Sinai."

"No way!" Lola said with delight.

"So you were a paralegal with dreams of becoming a writer."

"Not exactly. I always wanted to write, and I wanted to study creative writing. But Casey and Ty and Ben were all bound for college on scholarships, and there wasn't enough money to cover all the expenses. And Kennedy would need money for school . . . so I bowed out."

She had given up pursuing writing so her siblings could go to college? "Could you have borrowed the money?"

"Oh yeah," she said. "I almost did. But do you know how much it costs to get a degree these days? I would have been paying it back for the rest of my life."

"What about your parents?"

"My parents?" She glanced away. "My dad died when I was young, and my mother is . . . she's not well. Oh, geez, I have to get the steaks on." She popped up and hurried back inside before he could ask her more about it.

It was an interesting difference in life, he thought idly. There had never been any question that he would go to college, and to a good one.

The point of friction between him and his parents had been his field of study and the fact that he'd not wanted to pursue graduate degrees like his sister.

Lola returned a few minutes later with two thick slabs of steak on a plate and put them on the grill. They chatted about the weather until the steaks were ready, and then went inside. Lola pulled out a salad from the fridge, potatoes from the oven. She took off her apron, pulled her hair down from a hair tie and shook it out with her fingers. "Please sit," she said as she found the wine bottle and placed it on the table.

The meal was delicious—the steaks were grilled to perfection and the mushroom sauce reminded Harry of the meals he'd had in five-star restaurants with his family. Lola was animated during the meal, asking how one went about starting a bridge construction company. He told her bits and pieces, how he'd had some setbacks—skimming over how far in the hole he actually was—and that the need for heavy equipment and operating costs had led him to sell his apartment. He told her about the toll road and how he hoped he could get the bridges on that project.

"And then what?" she asked.

"Then, bid on the next job. And the next." He had polished off his steak and was feeling completely renewed. "Like you, right? You finish your book, then start another one, right?"

"That's the plan. If I finish it. And then I have to sell it. It's not easy to get a book published these days. It's going to be a challenge convincing a publisher they ought to buy it."

Harry chuckled. "I can imagine."

"Excuse me?" she asked, looking up. "Why do you say that it like that?"

He looked up with surprise. "I, ah . . . well, the pages I read were . . . different."

Lola laughed. "You clearly don't appreciate *American Psycho* meets *Gone Girl* meets *Bridget Jones's Diary*."

"Huh?"

"See, that is one reason I want to meet Birta Hoffman so badly—how do you explain something as complex as a book? And I want to know how she works, how she plans a book, what her routine is. I want to know everything about her."

Harry had no idea who she was talking about. "Who is Birta Hoffman?"

Lola gasped so suddenly that she almost sent half a potato flying across the dining room table. She gaped at him, wide-eyed, and Harry felt a little foolish for not knowing the name. As if this Birta Whoever was someone everyone would know, like the President of the United States.

"She just happens to be last year's winner of the Man Booker Prize for Fiction, that's all. And she was a finalist for the Pulitzer once."

That meant nothing to Harry; he looked at her blankly.

Lola gasped again at his apparent stupidity. "She is one of the most important writers of our time and I've been dying to meet her for *years*. I love her work, I would love to know how she constructs her novels. Is she a plotter? A pantser? Now do you see?"

What he could see was a very attractive woman whose eyes sparkled when she talked gibberish. "Umm . . . no," he admitted, shoving a hand through his hair.

"Ohmigod, what is happening to our society?" she murmured, and tossed back in her seat, staring off toward the window as if she'd just realized life was hopeless.

"Wow. Surely I'm not the only uncultured male walking around."

"God, definitely not," she said, sitting up again.

Harry was too amused to be offended. "So what about this Bertha, genius of fiction—"

"*Birta*. Birta Hoffman is the genius of fiction. And what about her is that I just found out she lives on Lake Haven!"

"Is she rooming with Amy Schumer?" He laughed at his own joke.

"Hey!" she said, pointing at him. "You can't blame me for hoping to meet Amy Schumer." She grinned and poured more wine into her glass. "But my friend Mallory actually knows Birta." She sipped her wine. "I have this fantasy that she and I will meet, and we'll be friends, and then one day I will casually mention my book, and she'll be all like, 'oh, I must have a look, Lola,'" she said, mimicking some sort of accent that Harry didn't recognize. "And of course I'll let her, and she will love it, and she will want to send it to her agent—he's like one of the best agents in all of New York, by the way—and the next thing you know, they are offering me a million bucks for the book. Does that sound weird?"

"One hundred percent," Harry assured her. "They actually pay a million dollars for a book?"

"What? No!" She laughed as if that was as ridiculous as believing Amy Schumer would attend a party in a village the size of a postage stamp.

This woman confounded Harry, as women often did. But more than that, Harry thought, he was actually having a good time. A surprisingly good time. Lola was a bright light, a fun dinner companion. Maybe it was the second glass of wine—or was it a third? Maybe it was the smell of apple pie. Or maybe it was that the last several times he'd had dinner with a woman, it had been Melissa, and the tensions between them had seemed to permeate even the taste of the food.

Whatever it was, he was beginning to think that as far as roommates went, he'd lucked into a good one. She liked to cook. She had a healthy appetite, silky hair, and pretty eyes. They talked about New York and their favorite spots, about the new resort area at the other end of the lake. They talked about favorite bands and films. She said she liked the Mets.

Harry's opinion was solidified when she served the pie—warm, with ice cream, of course. It was incredible, the perfect complement to their discussion about the possibility of the Mets going all the way.

Harry was sold. If he had to have a roommate, he wanted it to be Lola Dunne.

When he stood up to help with cleanup duty, he was fairly Zen about the mess in the kitchen. Tonight, it seemed amusing that there was dough stuck to the counter and more pots and pans in the sink than in the cabinets. "I'll wash," he offered.

"You know, you are turning out to be nicer than I thought," Lola mused, peering up at him with that sparkle in her eye.

"Don't jump to conclusions," he warned her. "I'm drunk."

She laughed. "Then my nefarious plan has worked." She cleaned up around him, but apparently she'd had enough wine to make her a little wobbly. She kept brushing against him or bumping into him. "Sorry," she muttered when she'd done it a third time.

"Are you trying to get my attention?" he asked over his shoulder.

"No. It's a very small kitchen."

He looked around them; it was one of the biggest kitchens he'd ever seen. When he turned back to make that point, she was standing at his elbow, holding a butcher knife. Maybe Harry was a little too drunk, but he flinched.

"What?" she asked innocently, then dropped the knife into the sudsy water.

"How does someone as cute as you write a book like that?" he asked.

She smiled, clearly pleased. "I have a very vivid imagination."

"I always heard writers were supposed to write what they know," he said.

"I don't think you have to worry . . . yet," she said, and tilted her head back, looking up at him. "But if I were you, I'd keep up the good work just in case." She slapped his butt like a coach, brushed past him again, and poured more wine into their glasses. Harry had lost track, but he thought maybe a second bottle had been opened.

"Seriously? From what little I read, that is some dark stuff," he said, curious about her book.

"Well yeah, because she's a cute psycho. Looks can be so deceiving, don't you think?"

Harry stopped washing and looked at her. Lola burst out laughing. "I'm teasing you!" she said as he dried his hands on a towel and turned toward her. "It's one hundred percent fiction. Haven't you seen *Gone Girl*?"

"No," he said.

"Well, don't," she said, frowning a little. "It might alarm you." She laughed as she tossed down the dishtowel, then removed her super-woman apron. She put her hands on her hips, tilted her head to one side and smiled at him. "You know what, Hardhat Harry? This has been fun."

"It has," he agreed. "You're an excellent cook." He could see the pie tin behind her, and his hazy thoughts wandered toward a second piece.

Lola followed his gaze, then looked back at him. "And you're the perfect dinner companion. You eat everything on your plate."

"I have a long history of being a perfect dinner companion then. I'd have to say the same of you, Lola. Not every woman out there is into the Mets." That reminded him—there was a game on tonight. He said, "I think I know the perfect end to this delightful evening."

"Wait . . . are you thinking what *I'm* thinking?"

"I think so."

Lola laughed. So did Harry. But he didn't get it at first, didn't see it coming until Lola put her hands on his chest and rose up on her toes and pressed her soft, warm lips against his. It shocked him—he was not used to women planting one on him, and in that moment, he froze, his head frantically trying to decide what to do while his heart was totally into it. The rest of his body got in line behind his heart when her tongue began to tease his stunned mouth, and then, somehow, his hand was on her breast. And then he was moving. He was lifting her up without any thought at all and putting her on the counter. He shoved his hand into her hair, cupping the back of her head as he pulled her into his body, pressing against her. She had lit a flame in him, and desire was suddenly burning him up, turning his inside to ashes.

Lola drew her knees up around him; her skirt had slid down her thighs, baring them to him. He took hold of one, kneading her flesh as he kissed her. His body was reacting, powering up, ready to launch . . . but then something pierced his wine-fogged brain. *What the hell was he doing? Where was he going with this?*

Harry managed to corral the rest of himself and stopped what he was doing. He pressed his forehead to hers, wiped her bottom lip with the pad of his thumb. "That should not have happened," he said roughly.

"Uh-huh," she said dreamily.

"We're roommates," he reminded her.

Lola opened her eyes. "Temporary roommates at that," she said and let go of his wrist, which he hadn't realized she was holding until that moment. She pushed him back, then slid off the counter, straightening her skirt, shoving her fingers through the wild mess of her hair.

"I'm sorry—" he started.

"No, you can't," she said firmly, putting her hand over his mouth. "I can't stand it when a guy apologizes for touching."

He pulled her hand away from his mouth. "I'm damn sure not sorry for that," he said. "I'm sorry for having crossed a boundary."

"Well don't be," she said, and picked up the dishtowel. "I'm the one who crossed it." She began to polish the countertop. "We're grownups, Harry. We can kiss if we want."

"Right," he said uncertainly. Kissing was not a game to him. Kissing was a door that opened onto a whole other landscape.

"But I think we both agree the night got away from us," she said as her polishing intensified.

Now she sounded like some middle school teacher. "Yes," he said obediently.

"And I know you're just really grateful because my apple pie kicks ass."

He smiled. "It does."

"Okay," she said, and tossed the dishtowel across the kitchen to land near the sink. "I'm going to bed now."

Harry shoved his hands in his pockets, unsure what to say.

Lola didn't seem to need him to say anything. She started out of the kitchen but paused before she reached the hallway and glanced back. "Just out of curiosity, what were you thinking?"

"Just now?" he asked, confused.

"No—you said you knew the perfect end to this evening, and I asked if you were thinking what I was thinking, and you said yes. What were *you* thinking?"

He felt like an idiot now, a man with no game. "Ah . . . I was thinking we could watch the Met's game."

Lola's eyes narrowed. "Huh," she said, nodding a little as she looked him over. Probably assessing his sexual orientation.

"We still could," he said clumsily, pointing to the television.

"You go ahead." Her voice was full of that false politeness that women used when they were not happy. She disappeared into the hallway, and Harry shook his head, both confused and pissed at himself.

He turned on the Mets and fell into a slight funk, the result of having drunk too much wine and having played a moment so wrong. The game went extra innings, most of which Harry did not see, as he had fallen asleep on the couch. He wasn't sure what time it was when he finally wandered off to bed, but he was very much aware that when he closed his eyes, his head was spinning with images of Lola.

She was dancing with a slice of apple pie.

Twelve

Usually, on the morning following an encounter with a member of the male species, Lola would call Casey and vent about her lack of finesse and understanding of men. But Lola wasn't going to do that this morning because she didn't need anyone agreeing that she was such an idiot.

Granted, she'd been a bit lit last night, but that didn't excuse mishandling that moment in the kitchen as badly as she had. She'd made that bold move because she'd been taught by umpteen romantic movies that a highly charged moment ended with an electrifying kiss. Apparently, it was only in the movies, because while she was thinking of kissing him, he was thinking of baseball.

Baseball.

It had been a huge hand-to-forehead moment for Lola, and she either needed to up her game or forget it. She was pissed about it. Furious with herself, of course, for reading him all wrong, but also furious with Harry for being so damn handsome and charming and engaging that she could even think of kissing him. Oh yeah, he definitely bore a big chunk of responsibility for her blunder.

She'd been so annoyed and mortified with herself that she hadn't slept very well. She was up at six o'clock, wiping down the kitchen, polishing silverware, and rubbing water spots off the glasses that had come out of the dishwasher. Lola didn't like to clean, but when she did, she was awesome.

By eight-thirty, she'd showered and dressed, and slipped out of the house. Handsome Harry was still in bed. She wasn't surprised—she'd heard the TV blaring until sometime after one.

In town, Lola parked and locked her bike just outside the Green Bean and entered the coffee shop.

Mallory was there, an empty plate and enormous coffee cup before her, her hair a giant, untamed ball of frizz this morning.

Lola took off her sunglasses and fell into a chair across from her.

"You look like you got whacked by a whack-a-mole mallet," Mallory said.

"I did. What happened to your hair?"

"Huh?" Mallory put her hand to her head then said, "Oh yeah. I tried to give myself a perm, but I forgot what I was doing and left it on too long. I'm going to see Christa at the salon a little later. You have to meet her! She's great, and she can fix *anything*. So why do you look like that?" Mallory asked, nodding at her.

Lola looked down at her shorts and T-shirt and red Keds. "Like what?"

"Not your clothes, silly. Your face."

"My face?" Lola asked, pressing her fingertips to her cheeks.

"You know what I mean. It looks like you were up way too late."

"Oh, that," Lola said. "I had a bit too much of that excellent organic wine you gave me."

"Isn't it good?" Mallory said sunnily. "But please don't tell me you were drinking alone. You should have called me! Friends never let friends drink alone."

"No, no," Lola said, squirming a little. "I had drinks with my friend."

"Your friend? What friend?" Mallory asked.

"My friend who is passing through?"

"Oh, right, right," Mallory said, nodding. "So who is he?"

"No one. I'm starving," Lola said. She was not starving, because she'd helped herself to a banana and a fistful of chocolates this morning. But she hastily picked up a menu and buried her blooming cheeks behind it in the hope she could change the subject.

"Oh, you should try the oatmeal. It's *fabulous*," Mallory said. "And you need some coffee. I'm going to get you a coffee." Mallory stood up before Lola could even reach for her tote bag.

She returned with oatmeal and a latte for Lola, then chatted about the candy shop and some new items she wanted to stock as Lola ate.

"Oh, I almost forgot!" Mallory said brightly as Lola finished the oatmeal. "Lillian and Albert are having a party tonight." Mallory had a strange habit of referring to her parents by their first names. "You have to come!"

"A party?" Lola said.

"I forgot to tell you—it's been on my list of things to do. Thank goodness I remembered! Anyway, it's a cocktail party, with a buffet. Dancing on the lawn, too. Albert had a three-piece jazz band come in from the city."

"That sounds like a big deal," Lola said. "I don't want to crash—"

"You're not crashing! Albert reminded me this morning to invite you. Oh, and guess who's coming?" Mallory asked, sitting up, her eyes sparkling now.

"Let me guess . . . Amy Schumer," Lola said drily.

"No. But someone just as good as that."

Lola was interested now. "Lena Dunham?"

"Lena Dunham!" Mallory repeated, laughing.

"Hello."

The deep male voice startled Lola and Mallory, and they both jerked around at the sound of Harry's voice. He had materialized right behind Lola, looking pretty darn fabulous. *Again.* He had on shorts that came to his knees, the Cornell T-shirt, and sandals. His hair was still damp from showering, bound at his nape, and his face rough with the shadow of a beard.

"Oh," Lola said. "Hi."

One of Harry's brows quirked up.

"Hello? Excuse me?" Mallory demanded. She was practically levitating out of her seat as she feasted on Handsome Harry.

"I'm sorry. This . . . this is my friend," Lola said carefully.

Mallory was listening with only one ear. "I'm Mallory Cantrell," she said, offering up a hand, coming halfway out of her chair to reach him.

Harry shook it. "Nice to meet you, Mallory. Harry Westbrook."

"Sit, sit, Harry! Want a coffee? Let me get you a coffee. Black coffee?"

"I can—" Harry tried, but Mallory was already halfway to the counter.

"Stephen, can we get a coffee?"

"You still haven't paid for the oatmeal!" the barista said. "You know you're supposed to come to the counter and pay up front."

"Please, sit. I'll go," Harry tried.

But Mallory had already banged into the guy sitting at the table next to them in her haste to be a good hostess. "Don't worry," she said to Harry. "It's just a lot of red tape you have to go through to get a coffee here, that's all." She shoved past the next table on her way to the counter.

"That makes no sense," Harry muttered. Then he fixed his gaze on Lola. "Mind telling me why you're acting like I'm the grim reaper all of a sudden?"

"I'm not!" Lola protested.

"Yes, you are. Look, Lola, don't be embarrassed. It wasn't a big deal."

She gaped at him in disbelief. She couldn't believe that one, that he would just confront it head on, and two, that he didn't get what a big deal it was to her. "I am *not* embarrassed," she blustered. But she could feel the heat of the truth rising up in her cheeks. She was mortified.

"Okay," he said, shrugging, his amusement clearly evident in his eyes. "If you say so."

"Stop looking so smug," she muttered as Mallory reappeared with a cup of coffee.

Mallory handed the mug to Harry, then reviewed the full list of creamers and sugars and whatnot available to put in his coffee. It took some doing before Mallory would accept that he liked his coffee black, but she sat at last and smiled coyly at Lola. "So this is your *friend*," she said. She planted her forearms on the table and leaned over them, locking her gaze on Harry. "Does *Zach* know about your friend?" she asked, making air quotes around the word *friend*.

"I don't . . . probably," Lola said quickly. "I mean, it's no secret," she said, and looked at Harry. God, she hoped he kept his mouth shut.

But Harry looked confused. "I—"

"We haven't seen Zach in a while," Lola said, and reached for Harry's arm. She tried to squeeze it, but Harry was pretty solid.

Harry's look of confusion turned into a frown. He glanced at her hand on his arm—which, she would have to admit, was fairly damp with anxiety—then lifted his gaze to hers again.

"Aha! I *knew* it!" Mallory cried triumphantly. "You're more than friends!"

"Lola?" Harry said. "Don't you want to tell—"

"You have to come to the party, Harry!" Mallory blurted. "I was just telling Lola about it. Everyone in East Beach is going to be there."

"Oh, but he can't!" Lola said cheerfully. "Thanks, but he has to go into the city today."

"Don't say no," Mallory pleaded with Harry. "I live with my parents and it's a *really* nice place, and if you don't come, Albert and Lillian will be very upset. They pretty much think they own East Beach, you know what I mean? And these things are a big deal to Albert especially. He fancies himself quite the host," she said. "Not only that, he would *love* to meet Zach's friends! He and Zach are like that," she said, and held up two crossed fingers to indicate just how close.

Lola noticed that Harry was staring at Mallory just as intently as she was. He was probably trying to think of some excuse, too. "Thanks, Mallory, but we have plans—"

Mallory suddenly gasped. "Lola, I forgot to tell you! Guess who's going to be there? *Birta Hoffman.* And she's bringing her agent, too. What's his name? I forget—"

"Cyrus Bernstein!" Lola all but shouted in her excitement. She knew all about Mr. Bernstein. He was one of the top literary agents in New York. To think that both Birta and her agent would be at this party was almost too much for her to bear. It felt a little like winning the literary lottery.

She made the mistake of looking at Harry, who was staring at Mallory as if he knew her from somewhere but couldn't place her. "Still, I don't think we can come," Lola said apologetically, and felt herself deflate.

"*Nooo,*" Mallory moaned. "You *have* to come. What am I going to tell Albert and Lillian?"

"I'm sorry . . . Albert is your dad?" Harry asked. "Your dad is Albert Cantrell?"

"That's him," Mallory said. "Why, do you know him?"

"No," Harry said, glancing at Lola. She tried to beg him with her gaze. *Please don't blow it, please don't blow it, please don't blow it.*

He was going to blow it.

"But I've heard of him," Harry said and shifted his gaze back to Mallory. "He builds roads, right?"

"That's right! Wow, I never knew my dad was a celebrity. Would you like to meet him? Lola, say you will come and bring your delicious boyfriend."

"Oh-ho, wait a minute," Lola said, laughing nervously. "He is *not* my boyfriend."

"Oh, please," Mallory scoffed. "You have lovebug written all over you."

Lola could feel her face burning. "We're *friends*. He's just passing through—"

"We'd love to come," Harry said, and stretched back, put his arm across the back of Lola's chair, his hand on her shoulder, and gave her something that felt like the Vulcan death grip.

She turned her body around to face him. "I'm *sure* you don't have time for a party. Don't you have to be in the city? You said you'd be gone *all weekend*."

"No," he said breezily, and playfully tweaked her nose, like a boyfriend. "Whatever gave you that idea? And why do you keep trying to convince poor Mallory here that I'm only passing through?"

"I *knew* it," Mallory said, slapping her hand against the table and rattling all the cups.

Lola didn't know what game he was playing, but she was having none of it. She narrowed her gaze. So did Harry.

"Why didn't you tell me, Lola?" Mallory gushed.

She was going to kill him. She was going to kill him Sherri-style, with a claw hammer or something like it. Cut him into pieces and feed him to some fish at the bottom of Lake Haven.

"She's shy," Harry said. "And it just sort of happened. Lola can be very cautious when it comes to her heart," he said, and smiled devilishly as he reached for his coffee. He did not seem the least bit bothered by the heat-seeking missiles Lola was launching at him with her eyes.

"Well of course! That's totally understandable," Mallory said. "I would be, too, if I were divorced."

Harry choked on his sip of coffee.

"Be careful!" Mallory warned him. "It's super hot coffee around here."

Harry looked at Lola, his gaze even narrower.

"I'm not that shy," Lola said. "It's just really complicated. Isn't it?" she said to Harry, and kicked him under the table.

He jumped a little. "It does seem to be getting more complicated by the second," he agreed.

"These things have a way of working themselves out," Mallory said sagely. "Lola, you have to get back in the game. You can't let that divorce hold you back. So will you come to the party?"

"You bet," Harry said at the exact same moment Lola said, "No."

He grabbed Lola's hand and squeezed tight. "*Absolutely*. Thanks for the coffee, Mallory. I hope you won't mind if I steal Lola away. We have a trip planned to the big supermarket in Black Springs today."

"No we don't," Lola said.

"Sure—oh, God, look at the time!" Mallory suddenly blurted. "I promised Albert I would open the candy shop on time today. He went on and on about having to make sure that shops on prime Main Street real estate are open every day in the summer months and *blaaaah*," she said, fluttering her hands. "The party starts at seven! We're the big white house on Hackberry Road," she said. She stood up, and so did Harry. Mallory impulsively hugged him. "So nice to meet you, Harry!" She gathered her things.

"Pleasure to meet you too, Mallory."

"See you two tonight!" Mallory sang out as she headed for the door.

"Wait! Which white house?" Lola called after her.

"There's only one house on Hackberry Road," Mallory said, and called a good-bye to Stephen behind the counter as she exited the shop. Stephen sighed wearily.

Lola slowly turned her gaze from the door through which Mallory had disappeared and glared at Harry.

Surprisingly, given the mess he'd just made of things, he was glaring at her, too. "Are you crazy?" he asked.

"Me?" she exclaimed, astonished. "What do you think you're doing, Harry? You can't go to that party!"

"Oh yes I can, and so can you. Why did you tell her you were a friend of Zach's for Chrissakes?" he asked, holding out his hand to pull her to her feet.

"Obviously, given my promise to Sara, I thought it best not to mention her name," she snapped, and bent down to pick up her tote. "A better question is why did you make it sound like we're together?" she demanded as he presumptuously put his hand on her elbow and steered her through the labyrinth of tables.

"Because I want to go to that party, that's why." He shoved the door of the Green Bean open, holding it so that Lola could sail through.

"Why?"

"Because I need to meet Albert Cantrell in the worst possible way," he said, striding a step ahead of her toward his truck. "He is the CEO of Horizons Enterprises, and they just landed that giant toll road contract with the three bridges that I want to build. Un-fucking-believable! How small is this planet, anyway?" He pointed his key fob at his truck to unlock it, then opened the passenger door and grandly gestured for her to enter.

He didn't honestly think he could just gesture and she would hurry over and hop in his truck, did he?

"Get in," he said, as if she were so dumb she didn't know what all the waving was supposed to mean.

"No!"

He sighed impatiently. "We're going to the grocery store, remember?"

"I'm not going to any grocery store." She folded her arms.

Harry stared at her. He braced his arm against the door. "It will be okay," he said gently. "We have some things we should probably discuss. And as long as you promise not to throw yourself at me, we ought to be just fine."

Lola gaped. Her cheeks flamed. "Oh, I don't think you have to worry about that, Buster," she said. "Cold day in hell and all that."

Harry smiled. "Baby, you would never make it to that cold day if I didn't want you to. Come on, get in."

What a presumptuous, self-satisfied, egotistical being! She lifted her chin and looked away, sniffing lightly. She glanced at Harry sidelong. He was smiling, all too sure of himself. Too bad he was half-crazy and half-jerk, because otherwise, she might be sort of interested to know what his moves were.

"How long are you going to stand there?" he asked.

"I'm not riding on the console."

"I cleaned it out."

"What about my bike? If I leave it here, it might be stolen."

"Oh, right—East Beach is a hotbed of thieving and robbery," he said. "Where is it?"

She pointed to the rack.

Harry squinted in that direction. "Key?"

Was she really going to do this? Had she not humiliated herself enough as it was? Not quite, apparently, because she very coolly retrieved her key and pressed it into his open palm. "Be careful with it. It's an antique."

She heard him mutter something under his breath as she climbed into his truck.

Thirteen

Harry tried not to lecture her, but he couldn't help himself. "Of all the reckless things you could have done," he said as he sped down the road to Black Springs. "Claiming to be Zach's friend? All it would take was a question or two to figure out you don't know him at all. You can't talk about the house, Lola."

"You think I don't know that?" she shot back. She was sitting with her legs crossed, her arms folded tightly over her middle. "What I am supposed to say when someone asks where I'm living? Sara said they never used the lake house once things got bad between them and that no one was there but some caretaker. It never crossed my mind that Mallory would actually *know* Zach Miller. And by the way, you're one to talk! Mallory knows everyone in town, so now everyone in town is going to know that Zach's friend, who would be *me*," she said, jabbing herself in the chest, "is shacking up in Zach's house with some random dude."

"How did I become a random dude?" Harry repeated, not liking the sound of that.

"Because that's what you were before you opened your big fat mouth," Lola said pertly. "What was all that business about draping your arm over the back of my seat?" she asked, and squirmed, as if she were trying to shake off his invisible arm.

As Harry didn't know why exactly he'd gone down that road, he changed the subject. "How did you manage to meet Albert Cantrell's daughter anyway?" he asked, still amazed by the coincidence.

"I didn't know that she was Albert Cantrell's daughter. Is it really that big of a deal?"

"Yes. *Huge.* You have no idea. Where did you meet her?"

"At the Green Bean. I went in there looking for Birta Hoffman, but there were no seats, and she offered me a seat at her table. We hit it off. "

"Okay, right back at you—is Birta Hoffman really a big deal?"

Lola turned her head and gave him a look that suggested he was dense. "It could only make my career as a writer, that's all. So yeah."

"Well same here, cupcake. Are we agreed? We're going to that damn party if we like it or not?"

"I'm thinking about it," Lola said coyly. "I wasn't prepared for this. And I have nothing to wear."

Why was it that women with closets full of clothes always said they had nothing to wear? "You could try sifting through some of the clothes on the floor of your room."

"Very funny, Bob the Builder. I don't expect you to understand. I know it must be super easy for you, what with your never-changing look of hard boots and harder hats."

"My clothes are functional. I didn't come to East Beach to win a beauty contest," he said as he pulled into the grocery store lot. "Those are clothes I wear to work, Lola. That's why they're called work clothes."

"Has it even occurred to you that we could meet someone who knows Zach or Sara at this party and blow our sweet deal with that lake house?" she demanded.

Harry looked out his window a moment. She was right about that— it would only take one person to know either Zach or Sara to get the ball rolling toward disaster. "Yes," he said. "I thought about it and I'll be thinking about it all day. But for me, it's worth it." He shifted his gaze to her once more. "I guess I need to know if the risk is worth it to you."

"I don't know," she said, and opened her door.

They got out of the truck at the same moment and marched in sync to the door of the grocery. Cool air and piped-in elevator music hit them squarely in the face as the glass doors slid open.

Harry grabbed a basket and started for the frozen food section. But Lola caught the front of the basket and forced it around, toward the fresh produce section. She grabbed a bag of spinach and put it in his cart.

"What are you doing?" he asked, staring at the package of baby leaf spinach. "I won't eat that."

"Spinach? You won't eat spinach? What kind of Neanderthal are you, anyway?" She added a purple cabbage.

Had he ever eaten purple cabbage? It had probably appeared in some restaurant dish in his life, but he would never consciously pick that thing. Harry let it go—at the moment, he had bigger fish to fry. "Okay, Lola, let's dissect this. We both want to meet people who could be very important to our careers at this party."

"Apparently," she said as she picked up two apples and examined them.

"Then let's just do the date thing, and who knows, maybe even have a good time. Once I meet Albert, we can go back to this," he said, gesturing between them.

Lola looked up from her apples. "This? What's this?"

"The temporary roommate thing."

Lola chewed on the inside of her cheek as if she were mulling that over. She put the two apples back on the pile and picked up two new ones, put them into his cart, then moved down the aisle, picking up a big, dark-green and oddly shaped thing.

"What is that?" he asked.

"Acorn squash. When you say *do the date thing*, what exactly do you mean?" She put the squash in his cart.

"You know . . . pretend we're on a date."

"I'm not very good at pretending." She walked on.

And what did *that* mean? That she wouldn't go along with it? Well, she had to—Harry was determined. He might never get an opportunity like this again, and he was fast running out of options. He followed her, tossing in some cheese sticks, bananas, and something that looked like donuts into his cart. He rounded the corner and followed Lola into the next aisle, where she had stopped to peruse the coffee selections.

Harry was momentarily distracted from his cause by her sexy-as-hell legs. He'd never really considered himself a leg man, but Lola was making him reconsider.

She happened to glance up and catch him checking her out. She rolled her eyes.

"Can't help it," he said with a shrug. "I'm a guy. So what's the verdict?"

"You're definitely a guy," she said.

"I mean, are you going to the party with me?"

"That depends," she said. "I want to meet Birta Hoffman and her agent. If I help you meet Mr. Cantrell, which I am obviously doing, as you wouldn't be invited if it weren't for me," she said, smiling devilishly at that, "then you have to help me meet Birta Hoffman, or no deal."

"Deal," he said easily. How hard could that be? "So we're doing this? We'll do this as a favor to each other and get it done?"

She picked up a bag of coffee and added it to the cart, braced her hands on either side, and said, "I'm still wondering about this date business. When you say *date*, what exactly do you mean?"

Damn it, she was determined to make him work for it. "Like . . . two people on a date," he said. "You've been on a date, right?"

Her eyes narrowed. "Plenty. Have you?"

He snorted.

"So then you know we have to establish a story. Are we a couple?"

"Ah . . . I guess," he said, uncomfortable with applying that word. In some ways, he hadn't completely uncoupled from the idea that he was with Melissa. And besides, this was a favor. Why did they have to put a lot of labels on it?

"You *guess*? Are we a couple, or did we just meet over spinach and sort of show up at the same place?"

Harry sighed. He dragged his fingers through his hair. "Why are you making this so hard?"

"Couples have to know each other, Harry. They talk to each other, they are *together*. And I don't know anything about you."

"You're right," he said, nodding. "I don't know anything about you, either. I didn't know you were divorced. Maybe you could start by telling me if there are any other surprises lurking. That would help. Know any other people in East Beach? Any other thing about you that might pop up?"

He hadn't meant it as it apparently sounded, because Lola's gaze suddenly hardened. "I just remembered I need some kale." She brushed past him, walking quickly back to the produce section.

For the love of God, if there was one thing that drove Harry insane, it was having to darken the door of a grocery store. If there was anything worse than that, it was backtracking in a grocery store. But he felt like an ass at that moment and dutifully turned his cart around, going against traffic, and followed her back to the produce section.

She was standing under a sign that said Organic Produce picking up bunches of kale. Harry was familiar with kale—Melissa had deemed it her diet food. He had personally eaten pounds of it in the last year. "I'm sorry," he said. "I should be more sensitive."

"Don't mention it," she said, her eyes fixed on the kale as if studying a new plant species. "It's no big deal."

Bullshit. Divorce was always a big deal. Just ask Zach and Sara. Just ask him. The breakup of any relationship was, by its very definition, a big deal. "Do you mind if I ask what happened?"

She glanced up from her kale. "The usual."

What was the usual when it came to divorce? He stared at her blankly.

Lola sighed. "Infidelity?" she said, as if the answer were obvious.

Harry blinked with surprise. "You had an affair?"

"Not *me*," she said, hitting him in the chest with the kale before adding it to the cart. "*Him.*"

"Oh. Yeah, of course." Of course? Was it a foregone conclusion that the man in any couple equation would have the affair? There were lots of women out there who got their jollies outside the bounds of holy matrimony, too. "How long have you been divorced?"

"Fifteen months. Not that I'm counting. What about you?"

"I haven't been divorced," he said quickly. Perhaps too quickly, judging by her slight frown. He hadn't meant it as a criticism. It was just that for him, if he ever did take that walk down the aisle, he wanted it to be permanent. Which, his astute sister had once pointed out, was why he never really settled with anyone. He hadn't been convinced of anything permanent with his girlfriends until Melissa had come along.

"Ah, so you're a *bachelor*," Lola said, nodding sagely.

"I'm not a *bachelor*," he protested. "I just ended a long-term relationship, if you must know."

"Oh really? Let me guess . . . afraid to commit?" She tossed an onion at him. Harry caught it with one hand and put it in the basket as Lola walked past him, once again going in the opposite direction of his cart.

Harry turned the damn thing around. "That wasn't it."

"That's what they all say," she tossed over her shoulder. She was now in front of the yogurt case. But she wasn't looking at the yogurts with fruit or honey on the bottom. She was looking at a giant tub of plain, fat-free Greek yogurt.

Harry was irritated now. Maybe because there was some truth in her accusation. "Just because I'm not married doesn't mean I'm some player, you know."

"I wouldn't know what it means because I don't know any men as old as you who aren't married. What are you, forty?"

Harry's jaw dropped. "I'm just shy of thirty-four! And don't look at me like that," he said, pointing a finger. "You're not exactly fresh out of college, either."

Lola gasped.

"Am I wrong?"

"No, you're not *wrong*, but you're not supposed to say it!"

"Do you not hear yourself? *You* just said it to me. How old are you, Lola?"

Her eyes were dancing with amusement now. She picked up the biggest bucket of plain Greek yogurt in the display case and put it in his cart. "I just turned thirty-one. And now, you're probably doubly shocked that someone my age is already divorced."

"Wrong again. Because I don't have any preconceived ideas about divorced people. I wasn't even thinking about your divorce."

"Then what were you thinking about? Baseball?"

He was thinking that her eyes, pale blue and crystalline, were the aquamarine color of their pool—he was not thinking about his major gaffe last night. "Not that," he growled.

"Mm-hmm. We need some ground rules."

"Some what?" he asked, confused by her non sequitur.

"*Ground* rules." She walked on, to a frozen-food case. She opened it and a bag of something frozen went flying into his cart. Harry glanced down; it was edamame. He opened the case next to hers and pulled out two Hungry-Man dinners.

"What are you doing?" she cried. "You can't keep buying that stuff."

"Why not? Has there been a recall? Because if there hasn't, I'm getting about ten of these puppies."

"No! It's not good for you, Harry. How did you ever graduate from Cornell? Those things are full of preservatives and dyes."

"Too bad," he said, settling the boxes into his cart. "I have to eat."

"*I'll* cook," she said.

"I don't want you to cook for me." He didn't want to be beholden to her for anything. Even if he did find her meals to be excellent.

"That's good, because I am not cooking for *you*," she said, as if he was being ridiculous. "I cook because I like it. I'm going to cook no matter what." She leaned over and picked up the boxes from the cart. "And I can't, in good conscience, let you continue to eat these things. They are *so* not healthy."

"Really? Because as fantastic as your food is, I must point out that the mac and cheese wasn't exactly healthy."

She rolled her eyes. "I *know* that, Harry. I was just showing off. Mostly, I cook healthy food." She opened the freezer and returned the frozen dinners to their place. She shut the door and dusted off her hands. "You're not going to win this one. You made me come to this grocery store, so now you're going to have to humor me." She arched a brow at him, daring him to argue.

"Fine," he said, and threw up his hands in surrender. He wasn't sorry at all. He was relieved—he honestly didn't know how many more frozen dinners of some sort of meat product and frozen peas he could take.

"This means I'm going to need more kale." She walked past him, in the opposite direction. Harry whimpered helplessly and turned the cart around, following her back to the produce section.

Lola had already picked up more kale and some garlic by the time he reached her. She deposited them in his cart, looked up, and asked, "How long have we been together?"

Harry shrugged. "A month?"

"A *month*? And we're already living together? No way."

"Okay, three months, then," he said.

"Wow. I hope you don't really jump into relationships that quickly, pal. Six months at least."

Yes, he did jump that quickly. It was a lot easier to have sex on a routine basis if the object of his desire was routinely in bed with him. "All right, six months."

She smiled, clearly pleased with her powers of negotiation. "Where did we meet?"

"The city."

"In a bar? In the park? In the produce section?"

"Tinder," he said. Lola instantly shot him a look, and Harry laughed. "Kidding."

"No, wait . . . I like it," she said, nodding. "*Tinder*. That way, when we break up, no one will be surprised."

"Good point. So it's a go? I want to hear you say it."

Lola puffed out her cheeks. "Fine. All right. We're doing it."

He smiled at her.

"We need meat," she said, and strode away again.

After a prolonged battle over frozen taquitos, which Harry won, and a discussion about the best salsa, they took their cart to the register.

When Harry had loaded a cooler in the truck bed with the groceries, he pulled onto the main road that would take them back to East Beach.

"Wait!" Lola said, startling him.

"What?"

"We have to go into Black Springs."

"Why?"

"Because there is a dress shop there—"

"*No,*" Harry said instantly, before she could say what he knew she was going to say.

"*Yes,*" she said, and put her hand on his forearm, squeezing a little. "I have to go, Harry. I have nothing to wear tonight and I am not showing up at the Cantrells' in a sundress."

"What about the yellow one?" he argued. "You were pretty damn hot in that dress."

Her eyes widened with surprise, and Harry realized that what he'd been thinking actually had come out of his mouth. "I'm just saying, if it was good enough for a sex party, it's good enough for cocktails."

She was smiling now, her eyes sparkling. "Why *thank* you, Temporary Boyfriend. But I can't wear that dress again. What if some of the same people who were at the sex party are at the Cantrells' tonight?"

"Oh yeah, that would be a disaster," he mockingly agreed.

"Turn right. I won't be long."

He sighed. "Do you promise?"

"I promise," she said sweetly.

Harry turned right.

On the main street of Black Springs, a village slightly larger than East Beach thanks to the presence of a train station, Harry followed Lola's instructions and pulled up in front of MelAnn's Boutique. There were three mannequins in the window displaying dresses like the sort he'd seen Lola wear.

Lola hopped out and walked around the front of the truck, stepping onto the curb. She paused there and looked back at Harry. He waved. She gestured for him to roll down the window.

He punched the window button. "What?"

"What are you doing?"

"Me?" He looked around him. "Waiting."

She clucked her tongue. "Come on, you have to go in."

Harry shook his head. "I'm not going in to the dress shop, Lola. I'll wait out here."

"You can't wait!" she cried, flinging her arms open. "You have to help me!"

"Lola, no. If we were really a couple, I wouldn't be doing this," he said. "I spent a few afternoons following Lissa around from one Soho store to the next, and thought I was going to lose my mind."

Her hands found her hips. "Are you my boyfriend or not?" she demanded. "Do you want to go to the party?"

Harry was beginning to realize that this one-day agreement between them could have unanticipated consequences. He dropped his head against the steering wheel, closed his eyes, and prayed for patience.

"Come on, we're wasting time."

Harry opened his eyes and started; she was standing at his window now, her hands shoved into her back pockets. And she was smiling, damn her, because she knew before he did that he was going to give in.

Harry turned off the ignition and pointed at her. "You're trying my patience, woman."

"*Am* I?" she asked with feigned surprise as she stepped back to give him room to open the door. "Because the way I see it, you owe me big time." She quirked a brow above her smile.

Harry groaned and followed her inside.

Lola pushed open the door to the boutique and a little bell tingled over Harry's head. He had to dip down to step inside. The shop was stuffed with clothing, shoes, and handbags. He was surrounded by lace and silk, could hardly take a step without brushing up against something frilly.

"Hello!" A stout woman appeared from the back wearing black pants and a colorful patchwork jacket, a scarf tied artfully around her neck. "May I help you?"

"Yes, please. I need a cocktail dress," Lola said.

"We have some great new pieces on the back wall. If hubby would like, he can sit here," the woman said, gesturing to a chair so small and so spindly that Harry doubted it could hold him.

"Hubby would like," Lola said gaily, and with a smile of great amusement, she followed the woman to the back of the shop.

Harry arranged his suddenly enormous ass onto that little chair and began to count the minutes he would be forced to wait for his improbable, one-day-only girlfriend.

Fourteen

Over the course of the next half-hour, Lola tried on every dress the woman brought her. She hadn't had much luck, and she was down to the last one: a pale-green silk dress with a vine of tiny embroidered pink roses meandering around the bodice and down to the hem. It dipped quite low in the back, just above the small of her back, and the bodice scarcely covered her breasts. Frankly, Lola was afraid if she turned suddenly or even laughed, one of them would pop out. But she stepped out of the dressing room all the same, her dismissal of the gown already forming on her lips.

She did not expect Harry's reaction. So far he'd said, "It's fine," and "Hurry up," and "That one looks good, but so did the last fifty." But this time, his expression made her think twice about rejecting the green dress. His Adam's apple moved with a deep swallow, and his gaze slowly slid down the length of her body, and back up. When his eyes met hers, he looked the tiniest bit hungry. Like he could down a nice, juicy cheeseburger at that very moment.

It was enough that Lola chose the dress. And it helped that she had some adorable pink sandals to wear with it. "This is it," she said.

"Thank God," Harry said with great relief.

She paid for the dress, then listened to Harry grouse about how long it had taken to choose it as they drove out of town. He continued to grouse about the detours she was making him take when she convinced him they should grab some lunch, and then he insisted on picking up the tab. When they finally arrived back at the lake house, he disappeared into his room with the excuse of having a lot of work to do.

That was just as well with Lola—she had to think what she was going to say to Birta Hoffman and get her game face on. So she hung her dress up, found a bathing suit on the floor of her room and put it on, and headed for the pool. She walked down the few steps and hopped on to an enormous float made to resemble the yellow duckies that populated toddler baths across the nation.

Once she was comfortably ensconced in her ducky, she paddled back to the edge of the pool and retrieved her phone, then pushed off again with a toe. The ducky twirled off in big, lazy circles to the deep end. Lola was just dosing off when her phone rang. She opened one eye and looked at the caller ID.

"What's up?" Casey asked when Lola answered. "What are you doing?"

"Right now? I'm floating in a giant rubber ducky. What are you doing?"

"Deciding what to wear. You should come to the city tonight. We're all going to hear Ty's friend, Mark, play with his band in that little club on Flatbush. You know which one I'm talking about?"

"I can't come. I'm going to a party here in East Beach. I think I'm finally going to get to meet Birta Hoffman."

"No way!" Casey squealed. "For real? How? Are you going with the woman you met?"

"Mallory. The party is at her house. But I'm going with . . ." Lola hesitated and squinted toward the living room. The big sliders were open, and she could see through to the front door.

"Who?"

"No one you know," Lola said.

"Who," Casey said sternly.

"A guy—"

"A *guy?*—"

"Who happens to be my roommate. Don't get too excited."

Lola's announcement was met with a long moment of stunned silence. *"What* roommate?" Casey shouted. "You have not mentioned a roommate all month! I thought it was just you in that house."

"It was! I mean, at first it was. He was completely unexpected. But it's turned into the weirdest thing," she said, and filled her sister in on the events leading up to that very afternoon.

Casey took it all in, punctuating Lola's tale with a lot of exclamations. But when Lola finished, she said, "Well? What's he look like? Is he hot?"

"Casey!" Lola said laughingly.

"Oh. He's ugly."

"He's not ugly! I'm just saying, looks have nothing to do with this situation."

"Of course they do! On a scale of one to ten—"

"Stop it! Are you, a young woman who hates being objectified by men, really asking me to objectify a man I hardly know? Are you *really* asking me to tell you that on a scale of one to ten, he's a nine?"

"Yes!" Casey shrieked. "A nine! Lola, you *have* to take advantage of that!"

Lola wasn't about to confess that she'd tried to take advantage and had failed. So she took the path of least resistance. "I can't. I'm sharing a house with him! It would be so awkward."

"I'm not saying you have to date him, for God's sake. Whatever you do, don't do *that*."

As usual, Casey was all over the map. "Why not date him? What are you saying, I should just have sex with him one day and then we go back to being reluctant roommates? That is not the way I raised you, Casey."

"Remember Dustin?" Casey asked, dredging up a boy from high school she'd been in love with. "You told me not to get involved with him because he had so much baggage and you were right."

"What's that got to do with anything? You were fifteen and he was nineteen. Hardly the same thing."

"So how old is this guy?" Casey asked.

"He said he was closing in on thirty-four," Lola said, trailing her fingers over the water.

"Thirty-four!" Casey shouted. "Red flags are popping up all over the place."

Lola laughed at her silly sister.

"I'm serious. You have to ask yourself why a nine is single at the age of thirty-four. He's probably a tool."

"No, he's not. He just ended a relationship. It's a pretty common thing."

"Yeah, when you're twenty-four. At thirty-four, you have to assume there is something wrong with him that he can't commit. Trust me, at that age, men are generally desperate for someone to do their cooking or they are afraid to commit."

Lola tried to ignore the little niggle of guilt—she'd already accused him of that. "Could you maybe tone down the sweeping generalizations? What do you know, anyway? You haven't been in a relationship since Jonah," Lola reminded her. That was another of Casey's boyfriends who had turned out to be bad news. Casey was definitely attracted to the bad boys of Brooklyn.

"Yeah, but I date, Lola. A *lot*. And you don't. And your one time up at bat was a foul tip or whatever."

"Your metaphor doesn't make sense."

"I'm just saying, have fun, but be careful."

Lola sighed skyward. "Okay, all right already. How's Mom?"

"The same," Casey said without emotion. "Kvetching about this and that. Why no one comes to see her. How everyone has forgotten her. Her kids don't care if she lives or dies. You know, the usual."

"I need to go see her—"

"No you don't," Casey said firmly. "I had a huge fight with Ben about it, but we agree—we've got it covered. You deserve this, Lola. Go get you some of that thirty-four-year-old man meat and forget about Mom for once."

"You are horrible," Lola said. But she was laughing.

"You can thank me later. Okay, I gotta jet. Have fun tonight!" she said, and clicked off.

Lola paddled lazily with her feet back to the edge of the pool and tossed her phone onto a beach towel.

She wished she could take Casey's advice and forget about Mom for a change, but Lola did worry about her mother. She'd been worrying about her since she was five or six years old. Her mother lived in a state-run house for the infirm out on Long Island. She had a chronic and debilitating lung condition that kept her from working or caring for herself, the result of years of substance abuse. The same substance abuse that had kept them in that rundown, two-bedroom apartment. How her mother had managed to hang on to it at all without a job was something of a mystery to Lola now. She'd never worked that Lola could remember, and what money she did come by was split between feeding her kids and whatever drug she was abusing at that point.

Even at six years old, when her father was still stumbling home at the end of the day, exhausted from his work in the shipyards, Lola was taking care of Ben and Casey. Then Ty and Kennedy had come along, and their father had died, and Lola had become the de facto head of their tragic little family while her mother had coughed and moaned and slammed the door of the back bedroom. Lola had kept it together, had made sure her sisters and brothers were fed and that they got up for school. When social workers came around, which they would from time to time when a neighbor complained, Lola smiled and said, *Mom just ran out to the store.* Or, *Mom's at work.* Or, *Mom's asleep. We're just watching TV.*

Was her mother grateful that Lola had stepped in to take care of her siblings, even before she knew what she was doing? Not for a moment. Lola's mother was the sort of person who felt as if the world had turned on her. Her sorry life, her many children, her horrible disease of addiction—all of it someone else's fault. And still, Lola went every week to visit her mother and listen to her litany of complaints—most of which seemed to center on her children, all of whom, in her mother's estimation, had it "better" than her.

It was impossibly hard to go, and yet, Lola kept going. The woman had no one in the world but her children, and if Lola didn't go, who else would look after that bitter old woman? In the back of her mind, Lola had the idea that if she actually managed to sell her book, she could perhaps move her mother to a better place. Maybe her mother would perk up a little if she was in a nicer place with a private room.

Well, never mind that—Lola had been given a reprieve by her siblings for a few months, and right now, she had a party to go to. A very important party that could get dicey very fast if they weren't careful.

◆　◆　◆

It was half past seven, and Lola was putting the finishing touches on her hair for the evening. She'd seen no sign of Handsome Harry all afternoon, but apparently, he'd roused himself, because he was knocking on her bedroom door. "What?" she shouted.

"What is taking you so long?" he shouted back. "It's time to go!"

"I'm coming!" She did one last twirl before the mirror and then walked to the door, adjusting the bodice of her dress as she opened it. "Hold your horses, pal. It takes a lot of work to—" Lola's words trailed off, because Hardhat Harry looked like a GQ model. He was wearing a dark blue suit that was formfitting . . . *form*fitting . . . and a creamy white shirt open at the collar. He'd brushed his hair back behind his ears and he'd shaved. Lola couldn't help but stare, so astonished was she by the transformation.

He waited for her to finish her sentence. When she didn't, he cocked his head to one side. "Are you checking me out?"

"Yes," she admitted, still slightly dumbfounded.

Harry slipped his thumb under her chin and pushed it up to meet her upper jaw. "What, were you expecting a hard hat?"

"Yes! I mean *no,* of course not. Okay, maybe I was a little. I sure wasn't expecting *this*," she said, gesturing to the full length of him. "I mean . . . this is completely surprising."

Harry chuckled. "I'm not sure how to take your utter surprise. But I guess you approve. And by the way, you look fantastic, Lola."

"What?" She glanced down, then smiled at him. "Are you buttering me up?"

"You're my date, aren't you?" He grinned, put his hand on her shoulder, and dipped down to look her directly in the eye. "Are you as ready as I am to get this over with?"

She wouldn't have put it precisely like that, but she said, *"Yes,"* as if this party ranked right up there with trips to the dentist.

The funny thing was, she suddenly wasn't worried about how dicey the party could get if they weren't careful. She was suddenly looking forward to it.

Fifteen

Mallory was right—there was only one house on Hackberry Road, and it was the biggest house Lola had ever seen.

A valet had divested Harry of his key, and the truck was already inching along a very crowded drive, back up to the road, where cars were being parked along the shoulder. This was no small party; there had to be one hundred cars parked in and around the property.

Lola looked up at the sprawling mansion. She had guessed that Mallory came from money, but this was insane.

"Nice," Harry said.

"It looks like a hospital," Lola said.

"I don't think it's going to look like one inside." Harry casually put his hand to the small of her back, ushering her to the front door.

It was opened by a uniformed man who pointed them in the direction of booze and food—straight through a very crowded living room. The room itself was the size of a hotel lobby, and was dressed in white furnishings. In the corner, a man played a baby grand piano. Waiters in black waistcoats sailed through the crowd with trays held high above their heads. And the people! There were dozens of them, women milling about, dazzled with jewels and expensive designer sheaths, and men dressed like Harry. Lola was intimidated by all the finery. She felt out of place in her little green cocktail dress.

"Would you like a drink?" Harry asked.

"Not yet," Lola said. Her palms were damp, and she resisted the urge to wipe them on her dress. Somewhere in this crowd, Birta Hoffman was lurking, and Lola could feel all of her well-rehearsed lines rapidly fading from her brain. She was out of place. She didn't belong at a fancy party like this. Where the hell was Mallory?

"Let's go have a look outside," Harry suggested, and once again, steered her along with that giant hand to the small of her back. But this time, his thumb was singeing a tiny patch of her skin, and Lola was acutely aware of its heat. She was aware of the glances from women as they passed, too, checking out the hunk that was Harry. A few of the glances raked over her, too. No one had to tell her she wasn't supposed to be with a guy like him.

Outside, the view of the lake was spectacular. There were multiple levels of decks, all of them festooned with lights and flowers, all of them joining to create a giant staircase down to a grassy lawn, which swept down and bled into a white sand beach. There was a double boat dock, and even that had been dressed for the party.

Scores of people milled about here, too. Two levels down from the house, a three-piece string ensemble played lovely, lilting tunes that seemed to Lola to drift up into the night air. And on the boat dock, a duo sang popular songs from the Billboard charts.

Lola and Harry had wandered through the entire party, neither of them seeing anyone they knew. "I don't know how we are ever going to find your friend in this crowd," Harry said.

"I know," Lola agreed. "I had no idea about . . . this," she said, gesturing to the big fancy house and its many decks, the glittering people.

"It's a much bigger event than a party," Harry said. He frowned slightly at Lola. "What's the matter?"

Lola turned toward the bar, putting her back to the tony people walking past. "I feel out of place," she said low, glancing around her. "I shouldn't have come. I can't meet Birta Hoffman in a place like this. I should wait until I run into her at the coffee shop. I—"

"Hey, hey," Harry said, and caressed her arm. "*Relax*. It's a party." He snatched a glass of champagne off the tray of a waiter walking through the crowd and handed it to her. "Drink it. Calm down. You're not out of place any more than anyone else here tonight. Who the hell are these people? No one," he said, looking around him, apparently unbothered by the crush of bodies.

Lola drank from the champagne, then set it down. "I need a napkin."

Harry shifted to his left, leaned across a temporary bar and asked the bartender for a martini, and handed Lola a napkin.

"See?" Lola said as she wiped her palms. "*Martini*. That's what all of these people probably drink," she said, noticing the number of highball glasses people were holding. "I've never known anyone who drinks martinis, and I worked in a law firm."

"Am I maybe misreading the situation?" Harry asked curiously, making a swirling motion at Lola's face. "Because you seem on the verge of losing your shit."

"Yes!" Lola whispered loudly. "Completely on the verge!"

"Hmm," Harry said. He turned back to the bartender. "Make it two."

"*No!*" Lola hissed, glancing around her to see if anyone had heard. "I cannot get blotto before I meet Birta Hoffman."

"You're not going to get blotto from one drink," he scoffed.

"You don't know me, Harry. I'm a super lightweight."

He suddenly grinned and tucked a strand of her hair behind her ear. "You didn't look so lightweight to me when you were putting down the nachos today."

"Hey! That was different! I had to if I was going to get any of them, because you were going to eat them all! Why are you always so hungry, anyway?"

"Baby, I'm a grown man with a grown man's appetite," he said, and winked at her as he accepted the drinks from the bartender. He handed her one of them. "Just sip it, nice and easy. It's not water." He touched his glass to hers, then tasted the concoction, and nodded approvingly.

Lola peered down at the clear drink with the little row of olives floating serenely on top. She hesitantly tasted it and immediately wrinkled her nose. It tasted like kerosene. But it also left a trail of warmth in her that she liked. She sipped again.

"Easy," Harry reminded her.

"Lola!"

Harry and Lola both jerked around at the sound of Mallory's voice, suddenly close and loud. She was standing right behind them, grinning gleefully. "Check it out," she said, holding her arms wide. "Lillian hired a stylist to doll me up."

"*Wow,*" Lola said with true astonishment. Mallory was a knockout. Her crazy hair had been tamed back into an artful chignon. She was wearing a formfitting dress that hugged all her curves. Diamond earrings dangled from her ears that matched the tennis bracelet around her wrist. "Mallory, you're . . ."

"Go ahead and say it. I'm gorgeous."

"You're gorgeous!"

"I know, right?" Mallory twirled around. "Lillian doesn't trust me. And with good reason!" She laughed at her own joke. "Lola, you look so cute! I love that dress."

"Thank you," Lola said. Cute. That's what she was in this sea of designer togs and gorgeous women.

"And *you*, New Boyfriend," Mallory continued, looking Harry up and down. "Hubba-hubba."

Harry laughed. "Thanks, Mallory." He caught her elbow, leaned forward, and in a very polished and easy move, kissed her cheek.

"You are definitely here with the best-looking guy in town," Mallory said, jovially elbowing Lola.

Harry slipped his arm around Lola's waist. "Did you hear that?" he asked. "Mallory thinks I've got it going on."

Lola glanced hesitantly at Mallory, who was clearly waiting for her to agree. "You *do*," she said.

"Aw, that's sweet," he said, and bussed her temple, startling her.

"Oh, I almost forgot!" Mallory said. "Have you met Birta?"

"Is she here?" Lola asked, a little panic-stricken. "How do you know? There are so many people here!"

"She's here. Come on, I'll introduce you." She grabbed Lola's martini out of her hand and put it on the bar. "Don't look so forlorn! We'll get you another one just as soon as you say hello. She's just down there."

Mallory pointed through a throng. Lola didn't know where "just down there" was, but her heart seized all the same. She stared with wide-eyed horror at Harry.

He smiled, picked up her drink from the bar. "Take another sip. No more than two."

Lola did as he suggested without hesitation. She felt the burn slide down her throat and land squarely in her belly.

"Come on, lovebirds," Mallory said, and began to sashay through the crowd.

"Better follow her," Harry said and, with a little effort, wrenched the drink from Lola's hand, turned her around, and nudged her in Mallory's direction.

She and Harry followed Mallory down onto the lawn, where Adirondack chairs had been scattered around to face the lake. Most of them were filled, and people were standing about in clusters of three and four. Lola didn't see Birta at first, but then caught sight of her standing beneath a tree, talking to a short, round man. Good God, could that be her agent? Was she really going to be so lucky to meet Birta Hoffman *and* Cyrus Bernstein in one fell swoop?

Lola's heart abruptly began to pound in her chest. She grabbed Mallory's arm. "She's talking to someone," she said frantically, trying to slow Mallory down.

"She's talking to Bob Gottenhoff. They're neighbors. She won't mind." She shook off Lola's hand and continued on, apparently eager to make the introduction.

Lola could not shake Birta's hand, not with palms practically dripping sweat. She turned wildly to Harry and took his arm. He looked confused until she wiped her palm on the sleeve of his jacket.

Harry stared down at his jacket. "You seriously didn't just do that."

"Lola!"

Lola whirled around; Mallory was already in Birta's presence, gesturing for to come over. Birta was leaning to her right, peering directly at Lola.

Harry leaned over her shoulder. "*Go*, scaredy-cat," he said, and gave her a pat on her rump. It was enough of a surprise to make Lola's feet move.

So many emotions were churning through her in those few feet—excitement, uncertainty, shock that she was so nervous. But here she was now, standing before the Great Birta Hoffman. Just like in her jacket photo, Birta's long, dark hair lay like silk around her shoulders. She was wearing a satin kimono with an intricate pattern of birds and trees that made Lola's little string of roses look like a child's work. Two enormous turquoise rings covered the fingers on her left hand and matched the squash blossom turquoise necklace she wore around her neck.

"Lola, I'd like to introduce you to Birta Hoffman," Mallory said, suddenly quite formal.

Birta smiled kindly. "Hallo, Lola."

"It is . . . it's *such* a pleasure to meet you," Lola said, her voice almost shaking with anxiety. She extended her hand; Birta slipped her very limp one into it.

"Thank you," she said.

"I've been a huge fan of your work since forever."

"Have you?" Birta asked, with only a hint of an accent. "Which book did you like?"

"The *Unforgiven* series, of course," Lola said, trying not to gush at the seminal works that had put Birta on the literary map. "I adored the *Tobias Chronicle*. And I think I might have been first in line to buy *Inconsequential*."

"My, you've read quite a lot of them," Birta said, chuckling. "Did you enjoy my newest?"

"Of course!" Lola said, beaming. In truth, she hadn't liked it as well as she had the others, but she loved Birta so much she would overlook one less-than-stellar book out of ten.

Birta pulled her hand free of Lola's, because apparently, Lola was still holding it. She turned her sultry smile to Harry.

"I'm so sorry!" Mallory said. "This is Lola's boyfriend, Harry Westbrook."

"Well hallo, Harry," Birta said.

"Ms. Hoffman, it's a pleasure," he said.

"But I have to say that my favorite is *Incomplete*," Lola added, suddenly remembering. "It was so masterful. The complexity of your plot just blew me away, and all that emotion—"

"Do *you* read, Harry?" Birta asked, cutting Lola off.

"Sports Illustrated," he said.

Lola gasped with horror—how could he say such a thing? But Birta was not offended. She laughed, clearly amused.

"Actually, I love anything Lola writes," Harry said. "She's writing a book, too."

"Oh?" Birta shifted her gaze to Lola. "What's it about?"

Here it was, her big moment. Lola's tongue felt thick in her head, and all the words, the carefully rehearsed words, had deserted her. "Ah . . ."

"Don't be shy. Tell her about it, baby," Harry said, and put his arm around her waist, pulling her close to him.

Birta stood, waiting expectantly, her gaze razor sharp.

"Ummm . . ." Lola couldn't remember what she was writing. It seemed impossible, but in that moment, she could not find her book in her muddled thoughts.

Harry laughed warmly. "She's so shy," he said and pulled her tighter, even pinching her waist a little to shake her head out of the clouds. That was hardly necessary—it wasn't as if Lola wasn't painfully aware she was panicking and forgetting everything. "You know how writers are," Harry said. "Such introverts."

"We are, that's true," Birta said, her gaze on Harry again, the smile returned to her face.

"So I'll tell you," Harry said. "Because it's great. It's about this woman who is a psychopath. If a guy doesn't respond to her texts, she kills him."

Yes! Yes, yes, that was it!

Birta's eyes widened with surprise, and she looked at Lola. *"Really."*

"Yep," Harry continued. "It's *American Psycho* meets *The Wedding Planner*—"

"Actually, it's *American Psycho* meets *Gone Girl*, meets *Bridget Jones's Diary*," Lola heard herself say.

"Oh my, that's quite ambitious," Birta said, and laughed. "And yet, it sounds somewhat intriguing."

"And while Lola would never ask you in a million years, I think she would love it if you could take a look," Harry said easily.

"What?" Lola cried, panicking all over again. That was not how these things were done! One did not walk up to a very famous author and ask her to read a manuscript! Harry clearly had no idea how many people must ask Birta Hoffman to read their book every week!

"I'd be pleased to do so," Birta said, shocking Lola to her core. "It does sound interesting, Lily."

"Lola," Harry said.

"Pardon, Lola. I'll tell you what," she said, smiling at Harry. "I'm having a dinner party a week from Sunday. Why don't you two come? It's a small group, just a few of my close friends and colleagues coming up from the city. Several of them are here tonight, but it's so crowded that I should like to have them back for something a little more intimate."

"We wouldn't dream of imposing—" Lola started, feeling sick at the mention of a dinner party with Birta.

"But we will," Harry said, as if agreeing to something as mundane as wanting whipped cream on his coffee drink. Lola shot him a desperate look, hoping he could read the serious *shut up* signals in her eyes. But Harry wasn't looking at her. He was looking at Birta in a sexy, devilish way that confused Lola. What the hell was happening? Was he *attracted* to Birta? She might be an exotic creature, but she had to be twenty years his senior.

"Then it's a date," Birta said, smiling back at him. "Oh, and you too, Mallory, if you're available."

"Sure," Mallory said, and Lola remembered that her friend who had arranged this meeting was still standing beside her.

"And Bob," Birta said with a much thinner smile, "you know I'd invite you as well, but you're going back to the city, aren't you?"

Bob looked around everyone assembled under that tree. "I could change my plans—"

"But you shouldn't," Birta said. "It's a small affair, and I've just enough seats at the table as it is." She turned her smile back to Harry, ignoring the look of stunned dejection on Bob's face. "Mallory can tell you where I live. Sunday at eight o'clock. Is that convenient?"

"Absolutely," Harry said. "Thank you. We'll be there."

"Yes, thank you," Lola added.

Not that Birta noticed; she had locked her sultry gaze on Harry. "I'm looking forward to it very much," she purred. "Now you must excuse me, I see the editor from the *Hudson River Valley Review* is here, and I have a bit of a bone to pick with him."

She sailed out of their midst, Bob hopping along behind her.

Lola slowly turned her gaze to Harry. He was smiling like a fat-ass cat, obviously pleased with himself.

"Mallory?" Lola said, glaring at her so-called boyfriend. "Harry is dying to meet your dad."

"He is?" Mallory asked, surprised.

"I am," Harry said, his gaze similarly locked on Lola's.

"I haven't seen him. Stay right here. I'll be back in a jiff."

Harry waited until she was out of earshot before he frowned and asked, "Why are you looking at me like you'd like to claw my eyes out?"

"I don't know. Maybe because I'm like two seconds away from doing it?" she snapped. "What were you doing?" she cried, gesturing behind her.

"With Birta?"

"*Yes*, with Birta Hoffman! Famous, *famous* author! Are you *attracted* to her?"

Harry laughed in disbelief. "Of course not! What the hell is the matter with you, Lola? Didn't you notice that she was totally into *me*?"

Lola gaped at him. No, it couldn't be . . . Good God, of course it could! Birta had kept her gaze on Harry and had practically licked her lips. Lola could be so stupidly blind at times.

"What I was doing was helping you out, because *you* turned into a zombie."

"Oh my God," she said, slapping her hand to her forehead.

"What happened?" he asked.

"I don't know!" Lola moaned, bending backward with the weight of her folly. "I was nervous and flustered, and I couldn't *think*."

"Well, that was obvious," Harry said. He slung his arm around her shoulder and gave her a collegial shake. "You're going to have to buck up, you little lunatic. Birta Hoffman is going to take a look at your book and invite you into her inner circle, just like you wanted. And now, if all goes well, I am going to meet Albert Cantrell, and then we can really enjoy ourselves at this party."

Lola waved him off. "I need a drink. I'm a wreck!"

"Harry!"

They glanced up. Mallory was standing on the deck, gesturing for Harry to come.

Lola sighed. "I suppose you need me to come with you in case you forget what it is you want to say, right?" she asked drily.

"I think I can handle it. Get yourself a drink and I'll find you." He started to walk away but paused and looked back at her. "My advice? If you see Birta again, walk the other way. I'm afraid of what might happen if I'm not around to talk for you." He grinned.

"Ha ha," Lola said, and shooed him off. Then, feeling like an idiot, she went in search of the bar and her new favorite drink, the martini, so that she could properly drown her humiliation.

She walked down to the dock with that goal, but the line at the bar was really long. Lola carried on, wondering if there might be another bar, but the dock turned a corner, and with the exception of a bench overlooking the water, there was nothing.

A woman with sleek, dark hair was sitting on the bench. Lola glanced back at the crowded dock and the line at the bar, then at the bench. She took a few steps forward. "Would you mind if I joined you?" she asked.

The woman looked up. Her blue eyes popped in the heavy makeup she wore. She smiled. "Not at all." She scooted over.

Lola sat down. "This party is insane," she said.

"A zoo," the woman agreed, and sipped daintily from a flute of champagne.

"Are you waiting for someone?" Lola asked.

"No. I'm hiding," she said, and smiled a little. "I'm here with some people from work." She leaned forward and squinted around Lola, as if looking for them. "One of them is a little too interested in me, if you know what I mean. I'm avoiding him."

"Ah." Lola nodded.

"What about you?" the woman asked. "Hiding? Or waiting?"

"I'm taking a break," Lola said. From herself, if possible. She couldn't believe she might have blown her big chance. "This house belongs to my friend's parents, and when she invited me, she didn't mention how many people were coming. I thought it was going to be a much smaller affair. I'm trying to get my crowd face on."

The woman laughed. "If you figure out how to do it, let me know. It's a mob scene—I'll bet there are two hundred people here. I'm Melissa, by the way."

"Hi," Lola said. "I'm Lola."

"Lola!" Melissa said. "My sister has a dog named Lola. A little pug."

Lola suppressed a sigh.

"Oh God, there's Andy," Melissa said, and leaned back, so that Lola's body shielded any view of her. Lola looked around; there were several people gathering at the bar.

"Is anyone looking at us?" Melissa asked.

"I don't think so," Lola said uncertainly.

Melissa sighed. "I'm being silly. He's really not so bad—I'm just not in a partying mood."

"Everything okay?"

"Yeah, yeah," Melissa said, nodding. "It's . . ." She looked off a moment. "I broke up with my boyfriend a couple of months ago. It was all my doing . . . but nights like tonight make me realize how much I miss him."

"Oh, I'm sorry," Lola said sympathetically. "I know how that is."

"You do?"

"Well . . . the breaking up was done to me," Lola said. "But yeah . . . every party, every cocktail hour, every dinner with friends, I was reminded of him and how much I missed him. Sometimes, I still am."

"Exactly," Melissa said.

"Why'd you break up?" Lola asked curiously.

"I don't really even know anymore. We wanted different things. Classic story of it's not you, it's me," she said, in a mockingly high voice.

She rolled her eyes. "Can you believe I actually said that? But lately I've been thinking it really was all me. He was a great guy. Really great," she said with a wince of sadness. "And I was impatient." Melissa shook her head. "God, look at me, the proverbial wet blanket."

"No you're not," Lola said, laughing.

"I am! I'm awful." She smiled again, and Lola thought she was really pretty when she smiled. Maybelline pretty.

"I love your dress," Melissa said. "Where'd you get it?"

"This? A little dress shop in Black Springs."

"Do you ever get to the city? Because there is this great shop on Lex, in the fifties, I forget which . . . but they have designer clothes for more than half off."

"Really?" Lola asked. Not that she could afford designer clothes even at more than fifty percent off. But she wouldn't mind having a look.

Melissa told her about the shop, and had moved onto shoes when a man walked up to them. "There you are," he said, and smiled at the two of them.

"Oh. Hi, Andy," Melissa said. "This is Lola."

"Hi, Lola." He looked at Melissa. "Ready to get out of here? I need to get back to the city."

"Sure," Melissa said. She stood up and smiled at Lola. "Really great talking to you, Lola."

"You, too, Melissa."

"Too bad you're not in the city," Melissa said. "We could check out that dress shop."

"Rain check," Lola said, pointing at her, then waved as Melissa walked away with Andy in super-high heels and a super-short dress. When they had disappeared into the crowd, Lola noticed the line at the bar had eased somewhat. Time for that martini.

Sixteen

Albert Cantrell was not where Mallory had left him, which was with her mother on a terrace at the back of the house. As Harry stood by awkwardly, the two women argued about when, exactly, Mr. Cantrell had wandered off to look at a friend's boat. In the course of the argument, Mrs. Cantrell glared up at Harry and said, "Will you please sit. I don't like people towering over me."

Startled, Harry sat in the chair next to her.

Lillian Cantrell was the opposite of her daughter—tiny and perfectly put together. Her face had been surgically enhanced, so she looked much younger than she could possibly be. Harry guessed she had to be around sixty.

Mrs. Cantrell held out her hand with an empty glass in it; a waiter appeared from nowhere to take it as Mallory and her mother argued. Harry sat, caught like a bunny rabbit in this dysfunctional family trap.

Just as the waiter returned with the drink, Mallory huffed away, incensed by something her mother had said, leaving Harry there. "Well," he said. "I should—"

"Stay right there," Mrs. Cantrell commanded, then paused to sip her drink. "Too sweet," she said, and held it out to the waiter.

It was forty-five minutes before Harry could extract himself from Mrs. Cantrell, who was determined to relate her recent experience at bridge club, at which Debra Pressley had condescended to the entire group by explaining how to play. *To women who had been playing for forty years.* Mrs. Cantrell had emphasized that more than once. Harry was desperately trying to think of a polite way out of this, but fortunately, the little dog beside her was apparently real, because it suddenly leapt up, barking and racing for something in the woods, and in the course of doing so, knocked Mrs. Cantrell's glass from the arm of her throne, which resulted in a flurry of activity that gave him the means of escape.

He headed down the decks two steps at a time, looking for Lola and a drink, but not finding her anywhere in the crowd. He must have wandered around for another quarter of an hour before he spotted a flash of green and silky strawberry blonde hair on the dock. She was dancing with the man Harry had met in his pool. Roland? Nolan? They were holding each other loosely, sort of swaying this way and that. Lola's shoes had come off, and she was still slightly taller than her partner.

Harry strolled along the edge of the dock, stepping over her shoes, and pausing only a few feet from her. Her dance partner was laughing, and suddenly twirled her around so that Lola spotted him.

"Oh, hey," she said. She tapped her partner on the shoulder.

"What?" he said, and looked in the direction Lola was looking. Nolan's gaze did a quick up and down over Harry's body, and he smiled.

Harry frowned.

Lola dislodged herself from his grip. "You remember Nolan—the guy who took me to the party?"

Harry looked at the itsy-bitsy man again. "I remember," he said curtly. He didn't like this guy, especially after what had happened to Lola that night.

"Girl, wherever did you meet this man?" Nolan cooed, and dipped Lola backward.

"Tinder," Harry said. "I swiped right."

"What?" Lola said, her eyes wide as Nolan lifted her up. "No, no, that's not how it went. *I* swiped right." She laughed nervously, as if that were some great joke between the three of them.

"I'm pretty sure it was the other way around," Harry said, for no other reason than she was so adamant that she had done the choosing. He leaned down and picked up her shoes.

"Well I'm definitely going to have to give Tinder another try if this is the selection," Nolan said saucily as he brazenly looked Harry up and down again.

"All right, that's enough of that," Harry said, and held out Lola's shoes to her on one finger.

Lola patted her partner on the chest and dislodged herself from his arms. "Great to see you again, Nolan." She took her shoes from Harry, then grabbed onto his arm for balance as she leaned down and bent one leg at a time to slip her shoes back on her feet.

"Wait—that's it?" Nolan exclaimed. "What about our dance?"

"She's dancing with me now," Harry said.

"Well," Nolan sniffed. "Lucky for me you're not the only beard at this party, Lola. Now where is Mallory when I need her?" he asked petulantly, and toddled off . . . but not before giving Harry one last smug little smile.

Harry was yanked off balance by a strong tug on his sleeve. "We have to get this Tinder story straight, pal," Lola said.

"We just did."

"Oh no," she said, shaking her head. "*You* pinged *me*. Anyone who knows me knows I would never ping you."

Harry snorted. "Because men fall at your feet?"

"No!" she said, swatting his arm. "Because you're too good-looking."

That surprised him, and Harry smiled with delight. "Ms. Dunne, did you just say what I think you said?"

"Deflate that ginormous head of yours and don't take it so literally," she said, her cheeks blooming. "I'm talking about the psychology of dating apps."

"I don't know anything about the psychology of dating apps. But now I know that you think I'm hot." He was suddenly feeling jovial and pulled her to his side.

"I didn't say *hot*," she said into his chest.

"Yeah, baby, you did," he said.

"Don't call me that," she said, lifting her head. "I'm not your baby, I'm not your boo, I'm just your roommate."

Harry grinned into the pale-blue eyes glittering up at him under the party lights strung along the edge of the dock. "Call it whatever you want," he said, pulling her into a full embrace and settling his hands on her hips.

"What are you doing now?"

"I'm dancing. And it would be a lot easier if you put your arms around my neck."

"If you read my Tinder profile before you swiped right," she said with mock sarcasm, "you'd know that I'm a horrible dancer."

"I had an inkling when I saw you dancing with Nolan. Put your arms around my neck."

Lola groaned as if he was pestering her, but she put her arms around his neck. "Well you're in a fine mood. I guess it went really well for you with Mr. Cantrell, huh?"

"It didn't go at all. He left to go look at a boat before I could meet him."

"You're kidding!"

"I wish I was."

"What are you going to do?"

Harry shrugged. He'd been so desperate to escape Mrs. Cantrell that he hadn't really thought about it. "Not sure. Maybe talk to Mallory about it. In the meantime, I'll focus on turning things around for you. With some coaching, I think I can get you ready for Birta in a week."

Lola snorted. "There's not enough time in the world."

"Yes there is," Harry said, and teased a strand of her hair from draping over her eye. "With my expert people skills, Birta might actually learn to like you. And if that doesn't work, there's always me."

"Shut up," Lola said, trying not to laugh.

"Impossible," Harry said, and pulled Lola's hand free and twirled her out of his embrace, and then back again, and anchored his arm around her waist. Tightly.

Lola frowned at him. "I can't breathe."

Harry bent his head and murmured into her ear, "Are you afraid to be close to handsome me?"

"Yes, as a matter of fact. I'm afraid your ego will suck up all the oxygen in the area and I'll suffocate."

She smelled so fresh. She reminded him of the way the air smelled in spring—crisp and fragrant. "If you're going to date me, baby, you have to be close. A man likes to know his sex appeal is appreciated by the opposite sex."

Lola smiled, lifted their clasped hands to her mouth, and bit him. "Stop calling me baby," she said as he yelped. "You don't need me to appreciate your sex appeal—you seem to be doing a fine job for everyone."

"Your dating skills are awful, you know that?"

"That's no surprise," she said cheerfully. "I don't really date."

"What do you mean you don't date? You've been divorced more than a year."

"And your point?"

"Surely you've dated in the last year."

Lola sniffed and shifted her gaze away from him. "Why is everyone always so concerned about who is dating who?"

Harry stopped their gentle swaying. "Lola, no way," he said incredulously. "You're not dating?" A dancing couple bumped into them at that moment, pushing Lola into him. He steadied her and cupped her face. "Seriously?" he asked.

"What's the big deal?"

"The big deal is that it's a very long time to go without . . . having your, uh . . ." He tried to think of how to say it. "Your needs met."

Lola's brows dipped into a vee. "My *needs* met?"

"You know. *Needs*," he said. Harry didn't trust himself to say more. But he was fascinated by the idea Lola hadn't had sex in a year, and glanced down without meaning to. His gaze landed on her breasts.

Lola punched him on the arm. "Well *that's* kind of personal."

"I'm sorry," he said instantly. "I'm just surprised. I can't imagine going a year without it."

She clucked her tongue at him. "Who said I was without?"

Harry arched a brow.

Lola managed to worm her way out of his embrace. "So I guess you just jumped right into the sack the minute you cut your ex loose, is that it?"

"First of all, I didn't cut Lissa loose. She dumped me. And second, it hasn't been that long. I can go a couple of months before I start climbing the walls."

"Well that's just *great*," she said, and tugged at her earlobe before folding her arms across her body.

They stared at each other. Harry's gaze inadvertently drifted to her mouth. Those were lush lips, and he was reminded of that surprisingly sexy little kiss in the kitchen of the lake house. "You know," he said, lifting his gaze to hers, "we could consider—"

"Don't even say it," she interjected, pointing at him.

"What?"

She gave him a withering look. "I know exactly where you are going with this. You are going to suggest we become friends with benefits."

That was absolutely what Harry had been about to suggest, but he wouldn't admit it now. "I was going to say maybe we could consider putting you on Tinder for real. I could help you find the right guy. But if you'd rather just jump straight to friends with benefits, I'm okay with that, too."

"I didn't say that! Seriously, isn't it time to go?" she asked, looking around.

Harry caught her hand, pulling her toward him.

"Leave me alone, Harry Westbrook," she said, but she didn't resist him pulling her into his embrace once more. He caught her face between his hands and touched his lips to hers. Gently. Sweetly. It was amazing how such a small and simple kiss could set him on fire, but it did—another conflagration, courtesy of Lola Dunne. Maybe because he felt her soften into him. Maybe because she tasted sweet. Maybe because he really liked this girl with her strange novel and messy cooking.

He lifted his head and murmured, "Just think about it."

Lola didn't move; her gaze, crystal clear, locked on his. Harry didn't move, either. He felt a different kind of spark as she peered into his eyes, as if she were trying to read him. He had that feeling there actually might be something there to read, something that had sprung up out of nowhere. Not two months ago, he was devastated that he'd lost the woman he thought he would marry. How could he be feeling the kernel of desire and affection take root in him now?

Harry tried unsuccessfully to figure out what was happening in him until he began to worry that she would read how horny he was. So he kissed her again.

Only not as gently.

This time, he kissed her like he meant it. At first, Lola stood stiffly, and he thought he was the only one feeling this thing between them. He was about to let her go, to stop teasing her, but Lola abruptly relented. Her body sagged into his and he had to slip an arm around her to keep her from sliding to the dock. She reached for his hand that cupped her face, curling her fingers around his wrist as she opened her mouth to his.

Whoa. Lola was suddenly kissing him on turbo mode, like a woman who hadn't been with a man in a year, and it was stoking a rush of desire and affection in Harry that surprised and confused him. He had not felt this electric, this charged—

Lola suddenly jerked back. *"Dammit,"* she said with a shake of her head. "I swore to myself I would not make that mistake again."

"That was not a mistake," he said, buzzing from the charge in that kiss.

"Well hands off, Hardhat Harry," she said, batting his hands away from her.

"Lola," he said, reaching for her, but she batted at him again. "Fine," he said, and lifted his hands in surrender. "Whatever you say."

"Hey! *You're* the one who came up with the ground rules, remember?"

"What's going on with you two?"

Mallory had reappeared.

"Nothing!" Lola said too quickly and too loudly.

Some of the wine in Mallory's goblet sloshed onto the dock, but she didn't notice. "Is this a great party or *what?*" she shouted, swaying forward like one of those car dealership air dancers. "Hey, a bunch of us are going for a moonlight boat ride. Want to come?"

"Yes," Lola said.

Harry did not want to let go of Lola just yet.

"Follow me," Mallory said, and began to sway and slosh her way down to the boat.

Lola and Harry fell in behind her. Harry unthinkingly took Lola's hand. "Are you holding my hand?" she asked, as if she were unfamiliar with the experience.

Harry looked down. "I guess so."

"Honestly!" Lola exclaimed, as if she was exasperated . . . but she didn't take her hand from his.

Seventeen

The boat—or what Lola thought might be a small yacht, but didn't want to be the bumpkin from the group to ask—was crowded with drunks in expensive clothing. She and Harry mutually agreed they needed air and pushed through to the upper deck as the captain piloted slowly out onto the lake. They accepted champagne from a waiter who was passing them out in plastic flutes, and stood at the railing, looking at all the lights twinkling back at them from million-dollar lake houses on the shore.

But as they moved into deeper waters, Lola began to shiver in her barely-there dress. "Here," Harry said, shrugging out of his suit jacket.

"No, you keep it," she said. "I'm fine."

"Sure you are," he said, and draped it across her shoulders anyway. It smelled like man—spicy and fresh, with a twinge of cigar smoke. She was grateful for the warmth and pulled it closer around her body and smiled sheepishly. "You keep surprising me with how *nice* you can be."

"Gee, thanks," he said, chuckling a little. He braced his forearms against the railing and looked out at their surroundings.

Lola studied him. She took a sip of her champagne and then, because she couldn't help herself after that kiss and the longing that was starting to bake in her, she blurted, "Why did your ex dump you?"

"Sorry?" he asked, shifting his gaze to her.

Lola swallowed more champagne. *Shut up, Lola. Shut up, shut up.* "Just curious as to why you, ah . . . broke up."

Harry groaned. "I prefer not to think of that right now, if you don't mind. It's a long, complicated story."

"Fine," Lola said.

He sighed. "Let's just say she didn't share my vision of our future. She didn't understand that there would be failures along the way . . ." He paused and shook his head. "Maybe she was right about that," he said ruefully. "There have been more failures than I anticipated, that's for sure. But there have been victories, too. It requires a lot of patience and fortitude."

"I can relate," Lola muttered under her breath. Had Will ever really wanted what she wanted?

"I can't really blame her," Harry said. "But I couldn't work for someone else all my life. I need to make my own way."

Lola puffed out her cheeks at that. "Working for others is highly overrated," she agreed.

One corner of his mouth tipped up. "You'd be surprised how many people believe security is the goal."

"I used to think I could work for someone else," Lola said. "I thought it would be okay to give up goals I had because others depended on me. To be fair, I also thought my job was a depot stop until Will and I started a family. But . . ." Lola winced, reminded of the disappointment and heartbreak again. "Here I am." She looked up at the moon. "Funny how things go, isn't it?"

"Yep," Harry said. But he was looking at her.

What was funny was that she and Handsome Harry had more in common than she would have thought.

The boat ride turned out to be the best part of the party for her, really, floating around on the lake with Harry's coat on her shoulders and the fizzy feel of champagne and martinis in her head, and the memory of a super-hot kiss still tingling on her lips. Her humiliation in front of Birta Hoffman quietly receded.

When the boat docked, Harry said, "Ready to go? I've a lot of paperwork to do tomorrow."

She wasn't really ready, but she nodded, swung his coat off her shoulders, and handed it back to him.

"You sure?" he asked.

"I'm fine," she said automatically, and smiled. But she wasn't fine. If she'd had her druthers, she would have stayed wrapped in that warm wool piece of him all night. It was an old habit, a trait she'd learned as a little girl—say you're fine and smile. Never let them see how you really feel, or they might take you away. Will had once accused her of being emotionally closed off. Lola wondered if that problem wasn't bigger than she'd ever allowed herself to see.

She and Harry walked down the little gangplank and across the dock. He was holding her hand again, but Lola didn't say anything, because she really liked the feel of his big, rough hand surrounding hers.

They said good night to Mallory and made their way to the drive and waited silently for the valet to bring Harry's truck around. Neither of them said much on the drive back to the lake house, either.

When they finally reached home, Lola felt slightly nervous. She wasn't sure how to end this evening. So she went to her comfort place—the fridge—and took out a plate of cheese and grapes. She set it on the bar and popped two grapes into her mouth.

Harry divested himself of his coat and stood across from her, his hands on his hips, his expression inscrutable.

"That was insane, right?" Lola said, popping more grapes into her mouth. "There is so much money up on that road."

"Yes. The whole evening was insane."

She wondered what parts he was referring to, and stuffed two more grapes into her mouth. "Thank you," she said with her mouth full.

One of his brows rose above the other. "For . . . ?"

Lola swallowed. "For helping me. For being there when I couldn't find my tongue. And for agreeing to go to dinner next week. I would never have said yes if you hadn't." Apparently, standing up for herself and seizing opportunities was going to require a lot of work.

Harry smiled. "I figured that out. I've never seen anyone quite as starstruck."

Lola reached for another grape, but Harry caught her hand and held it. For a brief second, she thought he was concerned with how many grapes she was eating. But instead, he turned her hand over, and lifted it up to kiss her palm. "I had a good time," he said. "Really good. You?"

God, he was *killing* her. Something that felt strong and magnetic was flowing between them, and frankly, Lola didn't know what to do with it. Part of her wanted to leap headlong into it; part of her wanted to retreat and protect her heart from expanding too far beyond its borders.

Harry kissed her wrist. "You won't change your mind about your roommate benefits?"

His gaze was smoldering. Lola had a strange sensation when he looked at her like that, almost as if she were swimming in deep water, her head only barely above the surface. She shook her head. She wanted to suggest it was a bad idea. What if he didn't like her in bed? She would still be here tomorrow. She wanted to analyze the offer and ask what *friends with benefits* really meant, what happened tomorrow, and the day after that . . .

Harry chuckled softly, squeezed her hand, and let it go. "Just my luck," he said. "My sexy roommate is locked up like Fort Knox. All right, go to bed," he said. He tapped his knuckles against the bar and turned, swiping up his coat on the way back to his room.

What had just happened? *Jesus Lola, you blew it before anything happened.* "Good night!" she called to him.

From down the hallway, she heard, "Good night, you little lunatic." And then she heard his door close.

Lost in thought about her incredible knack for blowing great chances—two in one night!—Lola absently ate more grapes until she realized what she was doing, and put the plate away. She walked to the picture windows and looked out at the moon again, then absently made her way to the couch and sank down, kicked off her shoes, and propped her feet on the big leather ottoman, leaning back into the cushions. She closed her eyes, folded her arms over her middle.

All she could see in her mind's eye was Harry. She could imagine him taking off his clothes, getting ready for bed. She could still feel his mouth on the skin of her wrist. *What was the matter with her? What red-blooded woman turned down an offer like that?*

This was exactly the sort of opportunity Casey would challenge her to take. Why not? Lola hadn't had sex in forever—so long that sometimes she believed she might truly die without ever having sex again. She liked Harry—*really* liked him—so what was holding her back?

She was afraid of being hurt again, of being rejected. *Aha, so there it was* . . . an unconscious thought that had turned into an ugly blob of truth, tossed out of her subconscious and onto her lap. She was afraid of any sort of relationship for that matter, for fear of another mortal wound to her heart. That fear went even deeper with the whole friends-with-benefits idea. She understood the *idea*—a casual, no strings attached hookup—but she didn't understand the emotions of it. Sex with men had never been so simple for her. With sex came feelings. How was she supposed to turn that off? How was she to hide them when he wanted only a friendly encounter?

You have to get over yourself, came one of her thoughts, uttered in the voice of a very persuasive and very smug younger sister. *Are you going to die with cobwebs in your va-jay-jay?*

God, Casey was right, even in absentia. Lola was thirty-one and divorced. It wasn't as if she was meeting a lot of single men. Her opportunities for good old-fashioned, wall-banging copulation were not great. For all the drama in her head over men and betrayals and feelings she didn't want to face or experience, there was another, awfully persistent thought pushing in right alongside: *Do me, Handsome Harry. Do me in the shower, on the bed, in the kitchen, in the back seat of the car.*

It was that voice, fueled by a little alcohol and a lot of libido, that won out over all the other Nervous Nellie thoughts in her head. "Okay, all right, Casey. You win," Lola whispered. She slowly stood up. She smoothed her hair down and adjusted her dress. She started walking toward Harry's room . . . but then abruptly changed course, darted back to the kitchen, and uncorked an open bottle of wine. She took a sip of liquid courage, corked it up, washed her hands and her mouth, smoothed her dress once more—

"For God's sake, I'll die first at this rate," she chastised herself.

She breathed in, breathed out, squared her shoulders, and walked down the hall to Harry's door.

There was no light peeking out from beneath his door, and Lola couldn't hear anything inside when she rudely pressed her ear to the door. She tapped lightly. Nothing.

Normally, this would be the point Lola would scurry like a mouse back to her room. But the new Lola, the Lola who was going to be a writer and live life to the fullest, was going to go for it. She turned the handle of the door and cracked it open.

Nothing! Not a sound, not a light. She slipped inside and stood beside the door. She could see Harry in his bed now, his body illuminated by moonlight coming in through his open window. He was asleep, lying on his back with one arm slung over his eyes, and bare-chested.

A heart-pounding sight, that.

Lola loudly cleared her throat.

Harry suddenly shot up and blinked at the door. "What's wrong?" he asked, and moved as if he meant to get out of bed.

"No, no, don't get up," she said, waving both hands at him.

"What's happening?" he asked, rightly confused.

Lola drew a deep breath. "You were right."

"Huh?"

"You were *right*, Harry. It really has been a very, *very* long time—"

He threw the covers off the other side of the bed so quickly that it startled Lola. "C'mere," he said.

"Are you sure? Because I really don't get the roommates with benefits thing."

"Come *here*," he said insistently.

So Lola walked to the side of the bed. Harry reached for her—grabbed her, really—and pulled her hard to him, twisting and bearing her down on to the bed in one super-sexy athletic move. "What took you so long?" he asked.

"I had to think about it."

"You think too much," he said, his gaze skimming over her features.

"I don't know what the rules are," she tried to explain.

"Rules," he repeated, and kissed her cheek, her temple. "No rules."

"We have to have ground rules," she said breathlessly, as each touch of his lips sent a jolt through her.

"Okay," he said, and slid his hand inside her dress, kneading her breast. "How's this for a rule: We act first, talk later."

"But what if—"

Harry kissed her, silencing her question. When he lifted his head, he kissed the bridge of her nose and said, "Don't overthink it. Just relax, and let it happen."

Let it happen. Okay, Lola was going to let it happen. In fact, she was going to do him one better and make it happen. She was going to take charge, go for broke, and not overthink it.

She had to get her bearings first, because Harry was kissing her fully, all minty fresh and soft and wet, his tongue dipping between her lips, his touch warm and heavy. She pushed against him, trying to roll him onto his back. Harry grunted and his kiss intensified. Lola leveraged him with her knee, finally succeeding in getting him on his back and then trying, unsuccessfully, to sort of slide up onto him.

"What are you doing?" Harry asked.

"I'm going for it," Lola said.

"Okay," he said uncertainly, and when Lola leaned down to kiss him, he took her head in his hands and resumed kissing her in a way that made her turn to jelly.

She was sinking and tumbling down the rabbit hole, and began to grope for her back to remove her dress, but she was off balance, and slid off the side of him with an *oof*.

Harry's arms fell away from her. "*Now* what are you doing?" he asked, his voice a little ragged. "I was thoroughly enjoying myself."

"I can't reach my zipper," she said breathlessly.

"Are you always this clumsy?" he asked as he reached behind her and in one fell swoop unzipped her dress.

"I don't think so," she said as he sat up and pulled the dress off of her. He tossed it aside and cupped her breasts. Thank God she'd worn a good bra tonight, and not one that was stretched out of shape.

"Okay, are we set?" he asked, and kissed her neck, at the point where it curved into her shoulder.

Sparks were flying through her now. Thousands of glittery sparks, firing and pinging throughout her body. "We're set. Just lie back," she said, and shoved at his chest. This time, she managed to get on top of him, her body pressed to the hard length of him. "Wait . . . you're still wearing pajama bottoms." She tried to slide off to push them down, but her knee hit him in the groin.

Harry came up with a hiss. "Look," he said, and reached behind her and unhooked her bra. "I really appreciate your willingness to take charge here . . . but how about you let me worry about clothes and logistics," he said. He was moving, kicking. And then his hand was in her panties. "Think you can do that?" he asked as he slipped his fingers in between her legs.

Lola closed her eyes. "I really wanted to take the lead, but if you insist."

He leaned down and whispered in her ear, *"I insist."* He rolled them again, putting her on her back once more and coming over her, and that was it. Lola had fallen all the way down the rabbit hole. Her body was floating in a sea of pure sensation as his lips followed the trail of his hands, sliding down her body. It was a heady, frothy concoction of skin and lips and desire all mixing into one utterly surreal experience. Lola had forgotten how delicious this could be, how satisfying, how earthy. They swam along in that sea, both of them reaching and stroking, kissing and sliding. It was foreplay like Lola had never experienced—twinkly and fiery, tender and rough all at the same time. She was rocked by the physical sensations and the emotions that were mixing and churning in her.

Harry suddenly sat up and groped around the nightstand next to the bed, producing a condom. A moment later, he pulled her into his body as he slipped in between her legs. He paused, braced above her, and brushed away a strand of hair that draped across her face. "You're really beautiful, Lola," he said. "Sexy as hell," he added, and entered her.

Lola gasped sharply at the feel of his body in hers. She pitched forward into it, pressing into his body and every bit of masculine physique she could reach or touch, giving over completely to the sensations he was arousing in her. He caressed her as he moved, slow and fluid at first, his mouth on hers in one long, stupefyingly seductive kiss. He took his time, unwilling to rush it. It was passionate agony, and Lola's pulse was pounding so hard in her veins, her body straining for his, her thoughts so focused on her arousal that it was a wonder she didn't implode. He began to quicken his stroke, and all was a blur of pure sensation—of touch and smell, of length and breadth.

She felt wild beneath him, an animal unleashed from its tether. She bit lightly into his shoulder, kissed his mouth, rocked against him in time to his own movements. It had been an eternity since she'd been ignited like this, a lifetime since she'd felt the power of sexual release building in her. Harry muttered something incomprehensible, grabbed one of her hands and laced his fingers with hers, pressing it into the bed.

He was moving quickly now, the tempo maddening until Lola let herself go with a cry of release as the tsunami of sexual gratification crashed through her, washing out months and months of pent-up desire.

Harry gave in, too, thrusting powerfully into her one last time with a moan against her shoulder.

Lola was stunned by the sensation of it all and utterly incapable of movement for a long moment. Harry's voice woke her from the fog. "God, Lola." He lifted his head and gazed at her with an unfathomable expression in his eyes that made her heart leap. Lola could see so many things in his eyes. Definitely satisfaction. Maybe a bit of surprise and curiosity. And, she thought, perhaps even a little affection. Whatever that look was, she was feeling the same way. She was mystified, bewitched, and confused.

"Rule number one," he said, and stroked her cheek. "If you're going to turn me on like that, we're going to have to bring in some supplies, because I may not let you out of this bedroom."

Lola smiled. "Rule number two: No judgment on how often we exercise our benefits in a twenty-four-hour period."

Harry laughed. He dislodged himself from her body, gathered her in his arms, and rolled onto his back, bringing her along to nestle in his side. "That was definitely worth all the begging you made me do," he said.

Lola giggled into his chest, then propped herself up on her elbows. She felt exhilarated and happy. She felt like a sex goddess. This gorgeous man was telling her that she turned him on, and she could not recall ever feeling as vibrant and sexy as she did now.

Harry's smile deepened as he looked at her, and he chuckled softly.

"What?" she asked, knowing full well that he was seeing the sex kitten.

"I'm smiling because you're beautiful, Lola. In your own, unique way, you are real . . . and beautiful. A little clumsy in the seduction department, but I like that."

She laughed and shook her head, and imagined her hair tossing silkily around her shoulders. "Oh, please, I'm just ordinary. But you can go on if you like."

He smiled, cupped her chin. "The truth? You are taking my breath away even now."

Impossibly, her grin grew bigger. "Such a charmer," she teased him, and pushed herself up to her knees and inched toward the edge of the bed.

"Where are you going?"

"Bathroom," she said.

"Come back, gorgeous. Right back here," he said, pointing to the spot she'd vacated.

Lola giggled. She felt like a supermodel. She was six feet tall and built like a brick house, a total knockout. She was that girl who didn't get how appealing she was until a moment like this, when a drop-dead sexy man took one look at her rosy cheeks and artfully tousled hair and told her she turned him on and she was gorgeous.

"I'll be right back," she promised, and slipped into the bathroom.

She was smiling when she turned on the light. She was smiling when she turned on the faucet. But she cried out with alarm when she lifted her gaze to the mirror and saw the bird's nest that was her hair and the streaks of make-up that ran down both cheeks. She looked like she'd pulled an all-night drunk fest, had a bar fight, and just woke up in an alley somewhere. "You said I was beautiful!" she shouted at him.

She heard Harry howl with laughter. "You are to me!"

Lola threw open the bathroom door and raced to the bed, pouncing on him. "How long were you going to let me go like this?" she demanded.

Harry laughed and rolled with her, pinning her beneath him. "Come here, you sexy little lunatic," he said, as he roughly cupped her face and kissed her.

Lola sank into him. She might look like she'd been on a bender, but in that moment, she was insanely happy.

Eighteen

Harry felt the nudge to his back and a whisper, *"Are you hungry?"*

He was groggy, feeling heavy with the sleep that comes on the heels of great sex. "Mmm," he said.

She clasped his shoulder, shook it, and propped her chin on his shoulder. "I'm starving."

Harry opened his eyes to find Lola peering down at him. She had a towel wrapped around her. Her hair was wet, and her face was scrubbed clean of the clown mask she'd managed to give herself last night. He opened both eyes and rolled onto his back, blinking up at her. "Did you take a shower?"

"Yes."

"In my bathroom?"

"Yep."

"And you didn't invite me?" he asked, yawning.

"Trust me, I did you a favor. My look was even more frightening by the light of day."

Harry reached for the towel between finger and thumb, and pulled it down over her breast a bit. "I like this look," he said.

Lola pulled the towel back up, then hopped off the bed. "I'm think-ing French toast and sausage."

"Are you kidding?"

She looked at him strangely. "Why would I kid about something like that?'

It occurred to him that Melissa never made breakfast for him—or Harry for her, in fairness. They had busy lives, both of them always run-ning somewhere. He tried to remember the last lazy Sunday they'd had. Whenever it was, he couldn't recall it—he'd worked so many weekends over the last year. "Where will this breakfast be served? In bed?" he asked hopefully.

"On the terrace. It's a beautiful morning," Lola said. "I'll meet you out there!" she called over her shoulder, and disappeared into the hall.

Harry got out of bed. He showered and shaved, then meandered out to the living area, feeling like a fatted calf—content and sated. It was more than a little surprising how much he'd enjoyed himself last night. Lola was . . . well, she wasn't the kind of woman he generally went for. She was different—very different. And that was both refresh-ing and a little disconcerting.

Lola was pouring orange juice in the kitchen. She'd put her hair up in a ponytail, and had dressed in short shorts and a halter top. Harry brushed past her on the way to the coffee pot, pausing to touch her shoulders and kiss her neck. "Something smells great," he said.

"I make the best French toast, if I do say so myself. Everyone loves it."

"I meant you," he said, patting her hip as he passed her. He grabbed a cup of coffee and went outside. Lola was right; it was a beautiful morning, the air crystal clear, the light brilliant and warm. Just like his mood.

Lola had already set the outdoor table, and appeared moments later with a plate of sausage, and another platter piled high with French toast.

"Are you expecting company?" Harry asked laughingly.

"I told you—I'm starving. I probably burned five thousand calories last night," she said with a saucy smile.

"I am available to help with calorie burn any time you like," he said, and dug in, eating with gusto, unaware until this moment just how hungry he was.

Lola also ate with gusto. He liked that, liked a woman who would eat. She sat cross-legged in the chair and poured maple syrup onto her French toast without any apparent concern for diabetes. The two of them ate in silence for a moment, until Lola pointed a fork at him and said, "Okay. What are the rules for friends with benefits?"

"You seem very concerned about rules for once. That's so unlike you."

"Shut up," she said, grinning.

"Okay, how about this one—you keep cooking, and I'll keep worshipping at your altar."

She nodded, as if mulling that over. "So . . . casual cooking for casual sex? Are we talking every day, or . . . ?"

Harry's brilliantly warm mood was beginning to cool. He knew the sound of trouble brewing and the words *casual sex* set off alarm bells in his brain. He was suddenly uncertain about things. He was *never* uncertain, but he'd had a great time last night. He'd had fun with her at the party, and then in his bed, she'd really blown the lid off things. He had been very turned on by her no-holds-barred response to him. But this felt oddly reminiscent—a woman wanting answers from him that he didn't have. This thing between them was new and, he would admit, powerful. What he was going to do with it, Harry couldn't say. Why did it have to be defined and categorized? Why couldn't they just go with it and see where they went?

"Lola," he said. He put down his fork and reached for her hand. "This is what it is," he said, gesturing between the two of them. "We're enjoying each other's company. That's all." He squeezed her hand and let go, and picked up his fork again.

He noticed Lola didn't resume her meal right away. She propped her chin on her hand and stared at him as he ate.

"What?" Harry asked, bracing himself for an interrogation.

"What if Channing Tatum walked in here tomorrow and swept me off my feet?"

"You should definitely be swept."

"But what about our arrangement?"

"I would be grateful for the time I had and probably go to work."

Lola's brows sank, and Harry realized how cold that sounded. And it wasn't really what he was feeling this morning. The truth was that he would be one very unhappy camper. "I mean, what else could I do if Channing Tatum swept you off your feet?"

"Well, then. If Jennifer Lawrence walks in, you too, are free to go."

Harry laughed. "Thanks, but no thanks."

Lola's jaw dropped. "You'd say *no* to Jennifer Lawrence?"

"Right now, one friend with benefits is enough for me. I've got too much going on."

"Wow. I think maybe I should be flattered that you would choose me over Jennifer Lawrence for your casual, no-strings-attached sex. But I'm not sure," she said, watching him shrewdly.

"What are you saying?" he asked cautiously. "Is this more than casual for you?"

Lola stiffened. She glanced down at her plate. "I'm not saying that. I'm not exactly looking for any complications right now, you know?"

Harry wanted to believe her. "Lola, I don't want to—"

He was about to tell her that he didn't want to set up any false expectations. That he liked her, but he didn't know where he was with relationships in general. That this had begun as a mutual desire for sex, and maybe it was more, yet wasn't it too early to tell?—but Lola's phone rang.

"Sorry, I need to get this," she said, and she picked it up. "Hey Ben, what's up?" She listened a moment and then suddenly sat up. "When?" she asked, and pressed her hand to her heart. "Is she okay?"

More information was relayed on the other end, Harry assumed, because Lola hopped up from her seat and went into the kitchen. *"Shit,"* he heard her say. "I can get the twelve o'clock train—I don't have a car, Ben. I can't get there any faster."

This sounded serious; concerned, Harry got up, too, following her into the kitchen.

"What do you want me to do?" Lola was saying with frustration.

"Where do you need to go?" Harry asked.

She jerked her gaze to him. "Long Island. My mom."

He said, without hesitation, "I'll take you."

"No! You said you have paperwork—A friend," she said into the phone.

"I don't have to do anything today," Harry said. "Let me take you, Lola."

"Really?" she asked, wincing a little. "It's a long way."

"Two hours. You won't get there any faster by train."

Lola stared at him, obviously debating his offer. She suddenly said, "All *right*, Ben! I hear you—I'll be there by noon. Let me know if you hear anything." She clicked off and smiled nervously. "Thank you."

"What's going on?" Harry asked.

"She's sick," she said, and looked away. "In more ways than one," she added darkly. "They took her to a hospital this morning."

"What for?"

"I'm not sure," she said. "Ben was on his way to the hospital and didn't know for sure, either."

"Get dressed," Harry said. "I'll pick up the table outside. We'll worry about the kitchen later." He started putting the many pots and pans into the sink.

"God," Lola groaned and raked her fingers through her damp hair. "Thank you *again*, Harry. Thank you so much. You keep bailing me out."

"It's what friends do," he said, but when he looked up, Lola had already darted to her room.

◆　◆　◆

Lola stared out the window for the first part of the drive, saying very little, clutching the bottle of water she'd brought, but not drinking from it. Harry didn't like to see her worried. He preferred the buoyant, slightly irreverent Lola. He wanted to know if this was a matter of life or death so he could be prepared for what they would find in Long Island. He finally asked what was wrong with her mother.

Lola looked startled, as if she'd just remembered he was driving. "My mom?" She frowned a little. "Wow, where to begin. You know what's funny? If we were actually dating, I would make up some sugarcoated version of the truth so I wouldn't scare you off. But since we're not, I'll tell you the truth. Are you ready?"

What the hell? Did her mother have Ebola or something?

"My mother has chronic obstructive pulmonary disease. COPD. It's a lung disease that makes it hard to breathe and, eventually, it will kill her."

Harry didn't get why that would necessitate any sugarcoating. "Did she smoke or something?"

Lola laughed bitterly. "Yeah, she smoked all right, all her life. Pretty much anything she could put into a pipe."

Whoa. That was stunning, and Harry didn't know what to say to it. He'd never known anyone with a serious drug problem. "Wow, Lola. I'm so sorry."

"Yeah, well. It is what it is," she said low. "I didn't have a normal childhood, obviously. It was pretty damn hard, to tell you the truth."

That was a lot more information than Harry thought he wanted to have. It astounded him on some level. Lola was charmingly carefree from what he'd seen, and it pained him to think of her in that kind of environment. "What about your dad?" he asked.

"He was great," Lola said, and glanced down at her hands. "But he died when I was twelve. And when he was alive, he worked all day trying to keep a roof over our heads. Mom just couldn't stay away from drugs, you know? And after Dad's car accident, she really went downhill and got really sick. Now she lives in one of those care homes that take in people like her and lives off my dad's pension."

Harry was horrified. Lola had, what, three or four siblings? "Wow," he said sincerely.

"Shocking, huh? But we did okay in spite of it. We had grandparents who were there for us as much as they could be. Unfortunately, they lived in North Carolina, so they never really saw how bad it was."

"Why is she in the hospital today?" he asked.

"That's the million-dollar question. In addition to being an addict, my mother is also a chronic complainer. There's always something wrong, you know? Sometimes she truly is in a bad way, like her breathing is really bad. But she also has been known to complain of illnesses or pains that don't really exist for the attention. She likes the ones that require a trip to the hospital, because she can boss those nurses around."

Harry looked at her, confused.

Lola smiled sadly. "I wish I was kidding."

Harry's mother could be a royal pain, and God knew she tied one on every Sunday, but for the most part, he'd had a stable, happy, privileged childhood. He couldn't imagine the sort of life Lola must have lived.

He turned his gaze to the road, and silently reached across the cab of his truck and took Lola's hand. She hesitated, then curled her fingers around his.

An hour later they arrived at the hospital in a part of Long Island so dingy that Harry was more than a little nervous to leave his truck. He pulled into the parking slot, sliding in between an old Buick and a Toyota pickup truck jacked up on super tires.

Lola opened her purse, found a comb, and pulled it through her hair. "What are you going to do while I'm inside?" she asked.

"I'm coming in with you," Harry said.

Lola stopped combing. She looked slightly panicked. "You don't have to come in with me. My brothers and sisters are here."

Harry frowned. "Are you ashamed of them? Or me?"

"Neither! You don't know them, Harry. They will be all over you, asking questions."

"I think I can handle it," he said confidently. "But if the news is not good, you're going to need someone, Lola."

She gave him a dubious look. "Are you certain? Because this has the potential to make you reconsider all of our benefits and maybe try to take some back."

Harry laughed. "I'm certain about everything I do, baby." He winked. "Let's go see about your mother."

◆ ◆ ◆

The nurse at the front station directed them to the Intensive Care Unit on the third floor. Just off the elevator was a waiting room full of people. And the moment Lola walked into the waiting room, all of them stood up. Harry was startled—apparently all of these people belonged to Lola.

"Lola!" cried one young woman. "I thought you'd never get here!"

"Is it that serious?"

"It looks bad," a man said, and looked at Harry. "Who is that?"

"He is my friend." Lola grabbed Harry's arm and pulled him forward. "He gave me a ride. Harry, this is my brother Ben and his wife, Tasha," she said.

Ben, tall and handsome with curly dark hair, eyed Harry suspiciously, but offered his hand. His wife was tall and slender, too, with big doe eyes.

"And this is my other brother Ty," she said of the blond man, slightly shorter than his brother. "Where's Jaycee?" Lola asked.

"Home with the kids." He extended his hand. "Hey, man."

"Hi," Harry said, shaking his hand. "Harry Westbrook."

"This is my sister Casey," Lola said, pointing to a woman who resembled Lola the most with her blonde hair and big blue eyes. "And the youngest, Kennedy, and her boyfriend, Mario."

Kennedy was cute, with hair the color of Ben's and expressive green eyes. "Since when is he your friend?" she asked as Mario shook Harry's hand.

"That is so rude, Kennedy," Casey said, chastising her. "He's her roommate."

"Her *roommate*?" Kennedy said loudly and disbelievingly. "Since when do you have a roommate, Lola?"

"Since recently. Can we discuss it later?" Lola asked, and hugged Kennedy, who refused to uncross her arms, as if Lola had somehow offended her by failing to report a roommate. "I need to see Mom right now."

"I'll warn you, she's in rare form," Casey said, and smiled sympathetically at Harry. Casey was beautiful, and Harry suspected she knew it. "You might want to leave your roommate with me for safekeeping," she added.

"Do you mind?" Lola asked Harry. "I'll be back in a few minutes. They never let you stay long."

"Not at all. Do what you need to do," Harry urged her.

"She's right there," Casey said, pointing to a door across from them.

Lola walked to the room and cracked open the door, sticking her head in. "Mom?"

"Where the fuck have *you* been?" was the wet, raspy reply.

Lola stepped inside and closed the door.

Harry glanced uneasily at the others. The rest of the Dunne clan, or whatever their names were, stared at him. He shoved his hands in his pockets. This was one of the more awkward moments he'd endured in recent memory, and he tried to think of something to say. He made the mistake of glancing at Kennedy, who took the opportunity to lead the charge.

"So are you two *dating*?" she asked accusingly.

"Nope. Just friends," Harry said, and ignored the tiny tingle of guilt in his chest.

"Do not start giving him the first degree," Casey warned Kennedy. "All of you, quit staring at him like you've never seen a man before. He's going to think we're all idiots."

"Half of us are idiots," Ty said, shooting a look at Kennedy. "But I want to know if they are dating, too. Lola never said anything about a roommate."

"Maybe because she knew you and Kennedy would act like this," Casey said, pointing at the two of them.

"How long?" Ben asked, directing the question at Harry.

"Excuse me?"

"How long have you been *roommates*?" Ben asked, making invisible quotes with his fingers.

"Ben!" Casey sighed, clearly annoyed.

"Not long," Harry said. "Close to a month."

"And she's bringing you to Mom's bedside?" Ben asked. "She didn't bring Will around until they'd been dating for like a year."

"Maybe because she was *dating* Will and she's not dating Harry," his wife Tasha pointed out. "If you're dating, you don't want to spring this on your guy. No offense, Harry," she said apologetically.

"None taken. Look, I gave her a ride. It seemed really serious and she was freaking out a little, so I—"

"Like, what do you do?" Kennedy interrupted.

"I build bridges."

"Bridges!" Kennedy looked at Mario. "How are you her roommate? I thought she had a friend with a fancy house up at Lake Haven."

Harry was beginning to understand why Lola thought he should stay in the truck. "We have the same friend," he said. "He's letting us both use the lake house"

"He?" Ben said. "I thought it was a she."

"Yeah, it was definitely a she," Ty agreed, nodding. "Sara someone."

They all stared at him, expecting him to explain that.

Harry decided his best course of action was to say nothing at all, and fortunately, Casey was there to help him.

"Can you guys please leave the poor man alone? He gave Lola a *ride*, for God's sake. Jesus, we're like a herd of vultures, ready to swoop in."

"Actually," said Mario, "it's a venue."

Now all the Dunne eyes turned toward that poor man with the collared shirt and rectangular glasses. "What?" Kennedy snapped, seemingly annoyed with him, too.

"A group of vultures is called a venue. Or, sometimes, a committee. Or, if they're in flight, a kettle."

"Mario, stop talking," said Ty, throwing up his hand. "Venue, kettle, whatever, yeah, we are protective of Lola, because the last guy pretty much destroyed her," he said, his voice accusing, as if somehow Harry had been in on that.

"Hey!" Casey interjected, throwing her arm up. "That's Lola's story to tell him, not yours, Ty!" She suddenly lunged forward and grabbed Harry's arm. "Let's go wait in the cafeteria," she said, and shot a dark look at her siblings as she pulled him out of the waiting room.

"I'm coming, too!" Kennedy said.

"No you're not! You need to sit with Mom when Lola comes out."

"Seriously?" Kennedy said, and groaned toward the ceiling. "I already had to see her once!"

Harry gladly allowed Casey to pull him out of that room.

"I am so sorry," she said, when they were out of earshot. "We really are super protective of Lola."

"So I gathered."

"It's just that . . . well, it's weird, but she was more of a mom to us than Mom ever was, you know?" She stopped at a vending machine and opened her purse and pulled out a dollar. "I'm sure she hasn't told you about Mom, because Lola never tells anyone anything. Keeps it all very close to the vest. But Mom was never around, and when she was, she was up to no good. So Lola took care of us." She fed the dollar into the bill slot, then punched a button. Nothing fell.

"And then Will dazzled her but turned out to be such a *dick*—" She gave the machine a shake. "Lola didn't deserve that. She was so good to that asshole—" Casey kicked the machine. "What the hell? I want some M&M'S!" she said loudly.

Harry reached around her and punched the second button required for candy to drop. The packaged twirled forward and fell into the slot.

"Oh. Thanks," she said. She picked up the candy and started walking again. "The thing about Lola is that she is super nice, and people take advantage of her. They just walk all over her because they know she won't say anything, and she will accommodate whatever they want, and so yeah, we're protective of her because she protected us."

They continued on into the cafeteria, where Harry picked up two coffees for them. His tasted as if it had been sitting on the burner for a week. Casey talked a lot. She talked about what brought her mother to the hospital—she couldn't breathe, she said, and passed out, but as of yet, the doctors weren't sure why.

She talked about her job as a journalist. She talked about her dream to become an editor at a periodical, and how promising that looked for her right now. She talked about how the man who had lived downstairs from Lola in Brooklyn didn't look so well the last time she saw him.

Harry's head was spinning by the time Lola found them, and frankly, Lola didn't look much better.

"What's going on?" Casey asked.

Lola frowned. "The doctor came in while I was there. He said they are going to keep her another few hours, then probably send her back. He said they couldn't find any reason she might have passed out."

Casey sighed. "Again?"

"Apparently." Lola shrugged. "He said she's not well, and these things are to be expected."

"Oh, it's expected all right," Casey said.

"She's getting worse, Casey."

"Yeah, I know," Casey said softly. She glanced at her watch. "How long do we have to stay? I'm supposed to meet Junie and Farouk for drinks tonight."

That seemed a little callous to Harry, but he didn't want to judge. This was obviously a frequent occurrence, and they'd obviously been through a lot with their mother.

"You guys go on," Lola said. "I'll stay with her and get her back to the home."

"But how are you going to get back to Lake Haven?" Casey asked.

"I'll take the train."

"Are you sure?" Casey asked, but she was already standing, already looping her purse over her shoulder.

"I'm sure. Come on, let's go tell the others."

Harry followed along because he wasn't sure what else he ought to do. They'd all forgotten about him when Lola announced she would stay and they were free to go. Just like Casey, they all asked if Lola was sure as they backed toward the door, all of them, down to a man, fleeing that hospital and leaving Lola to handle things.

"Nice meeting you, Harry," Ben said as he ushered Tasha out.

"Come to Brooklyn sometime," Ty added, the last one to crowd into the elevator.

The door slid shut. They could hear Kennedy say something, and a collective cry of disagreement went up as the elevator sank down.

Lola looked tired and worried. Privately, he was indignant for her. Not one of her siblings had offered to come and spot her, or even to bring her food. They'd left her to care for the woman no one wanted anymore.

When Lola noticed he was looking at her, she instantly forced a smile. "Thanks so much, Harry, but you should go, too. I'll take the train from here. If it's too late, I'll crash at Casey's."

"I don't want to leave you here alone," he said flatly. He didn't want to leave her here at all.

"It's okay!" she assured him. "There is absolutely nothing to do but wait. Trust me, I've been through this a few times. Please, will you go? I would feel awful knowing you're hanging around because of me."

"Okay," he said uncertainly. It was true that there were a million things he could be doing this afternoon. Still, he felt sorry for Lola. He had the sense that this scene, of Lola batting clean-up behind her siblings, was a common one.

"Really. Get out of here," she said, and punched the down button.

"Okay, I'll go," Harry agreed. "But don't leave me hanging, roomie. Let me know, okay? You have my cell."

"Yep." She punched the down button again.

When the elevator door opened, Harry stepped in, but as the doors were sliding shut, he braced his hands against them to keep them from closing. "Look, I'm going into the city to see my parents," he said. "I'm going to text you their address, just in case. I'll be there until about eight o'clock, all right? You can catch a ride with me if you make it back by then. Okay, Lola?"

Lola's smile brightened. "That's really nice, Harry. Thank you. I don't know if I would be so nice if you'd forced me to drive you to Long Island."

"It was worth it just to meet the other Dunne lunatics."

Her smile deepened. "Thanks, Harry. Oh, by the way . . . I didn't get the chance to tell you that the benefits last night were just . . ." She sighed toward the ceiling, but when she lowered her gaze, her eyes were shining. *"Surreal."*

She said it with such soft earnestness that it touched him. Harry thought of himself sitting on the terrace, ready to tell her that this was nothing but casual sex. He was strangely glad that the call from her brother had interrupted his speech. He touched her face. "Better than surreal," he said, and bent his head to kiss her.

Lola moaned softly, then pushed him, forcing him to let go of the elevator door. She waved as the door closed.

Dammit. Harry sighed. He ran his hands over his crown, linking his fingers behind his neck. She was getting to him.

Nineteen

"None of you kids care about me at all. I'm already a corpse to you."

Lola and her mother were in the transport her care facility had sent to collect her. Lola stared out the window, trying to ignore her mother.

"After all I sacrificed for you kids, this is the way you all treat me. Like I'm *nothing*." The force with which she spoke resulted in a spasm of wet, phlegmy coughing.

Lola closed her eyes and pretended her mother wasn't there. She knew her mother's attitude was due, in part, to her debilitating illness. But her mother had always been an unpleasant person. How had she produced five likable children? What had Dad seen in her? If Lola could have one day of her father's life back, she would pose that question to him. A very simple, *what the hell, Dad?*

The coughing grew worse. Lola grabbed her mother's hand. "Mom?"

Her mother's eyes were closed, and she squeezed Lola's hand, as if holding on for dear life. Her mother was only fifty-four, but she looked as if she were seventy-four. The coughing finally subsided, leaving her mother to wince in pain. "You were the only one who ever cared about me, Lola," she said hoarsely. "How come you don't come out and see me like you used to? That's all I have to look forward to, seeing my kids."

Julia London

"I told you Mom. I'm taking a couple of months off to write a book, remember? I'm staying at Lake Haven and it's hard to get here from there."

"A book," her mother said disdainfully. "Everyone thinks they can be a writer, don't they. So you write a book, and then what? How are you going to feed yourself?"

"Well, I hope to sell it."

"Don't be naive, Lola," her mother said. "I can't believe you quit a good job to go off and do something stupid. And after Will went to the trouble to get you that job."

Lola gaped at her. How old would she be before her mother's words would stop wounding her? "Will didn't get me the job," she said tightly. "I transferred jobs to get away from him. Because he *cheated* on me, Mom. He was having an affair."

"Please. He's a muckety-muck in that firm. He arranged it so he could pork his girlfriend on your desk. That's what I think."

Her mother's disloyalty and insensitivity were often staggering. No matter how many times Lola had been exposed to it, she never got used to it.

They arrived at the awful place where her mother was forced to live. The paint was peeling from the walls, and in the front salon, blinds were missing from one window. The furnishings were standard-issue institutional metal and plastic.

An attendant wheeled her mother into her room. A healthcare worker, tall and broad, shuffled in behind the attendant, reaching into her pocket to produce some pills. "Well, Lois, I guess you ain't dead yet," she said.

"Can't get rid of me that easy," Lola's mother said, and laughed, then coughed. "I know you wish I had."

"You have no idea," the woman said, and tapped the pills into a little cup, which she handed to Lola's mother. She tossed the pills down her throat and swallowed them dry.

After the attendant had put her mother in her bed, Lola arranged her pillows behind her while her mother glared disdainfully at her roommate, Mrs. Porelli, an elderly woman with dementia.

"There she is, that empty old bucket."

"Mom," Lola said softly.

"She don't know what I'm saying. She's a zombie. She doesn't do shit but watch *Wheel of Fortune* all fucking day."

"Language, Lois," the healthcare worker said.

"Shut up, Roberta. Lola, pull those covers up to my lap," she said, and sank back into the pillows with a heavy sigh. "I'm exhausted," she said, and closed her eyes. The healthcare worker went out of the room.

Lola started to gather her things, but she heard her mother chuckle and glanced around.

"They hire shit-for-brains here," she said. She smiled, extended her hand, and opened her fist. In her palm were two blue tablets.

"What's that?" Lola asked.

"Painkillers," her mother said, and popped them in her mouth, swallowing them dry, too.

"Mom! Where did you get those?"

"Where do you think, genius? At the hospital." She laughed that thick, wet laugh that was beginning to make Lola nauseous. "Don't look at me like that," her mother said, gesturing for some water. "You'd do the same if you had to live with the zombie in this dump."

Lola probably would have killed herself by now. But tonight, she had to get out of here before she did something very wrong, like strangle her very ill mother. Visits with her always ended with Lola feeling miserable on so many levels. A rush of old, dusty emotions would come crawling up from the crypt to torment her. Fear and revulsion, resentment and uncertainty. Duty. Responsibility. The need to make sure everything appeared fine, just fine. "Are you comfortable?" she asked curtly.

"Hell no, I'm not comfortable. Look around you—I live in a shit hole."

Lola put her hand on her mother's arm. "You know what, Mom? When I finish my book, if I can sell it, I'm going to find you a new place."

"Oh, sure," her mother said, chuckling. "You're going to come to the rescue. Another empty promise, that's all I need. My whole life has been empty promises," she said, and closed her eyes. She was fading.

Lola knew a little something about empty promises, too, courtesy of the woman in this bed. She picked up her purse. "Good-bye, Mother."

Her mother didn't answer.

Lola's mother was a hateful, bitter woman, and she deserved no sympathy from any of her children. But dammit if Lola could quit her. She was driven by that sense of duty and compassion, and every single time, she was slapped in the face for it. In the space of a few hours, her mother had insulted her, had derided her desire to be writer, and to add insult to injury, had taken so long to be discharged from the hospital that Lola was stuck in a bad part of town with several blocks to walk to the subway in the dark.

She was spent. Her mother drained her spirit from her.

On the way to Manhattan, Lola pulled out her phone and looked at the text Harry had sent her. The address was on East 72nd. She debated asking him for that ride. She'd relied too much on him in the last few days. She didn't want to be a burden, or the kind of woman who couldn't handle the slightest bit of drama. But Lola was also emotionally exhausted, and it was already six o'clock. She'd have to change trains twice, and then there was the problem of getting a ride from Black Springs to the lake house. Harry was going the same way—was it really such an imposition?

Or was the truth that she could use a bit of his strength and a shoulder to lean on right now? Was that one of the allowed benefits? Should she even go down that road? Last night had left her feeling so . . . *right.* Now what was she going to do with that feeling and with him? She didn't know . . . but catching a ride wasn't going to change anything.

With her doubts raging, Lola got off the train at Grand Central and grabbed a cab uptown. In the cab, she texted Harry. *Offer still good?*

He answered almost immediately. *You bet.*

I'm in your hood.

Close?

A few blocks away.

Come up.

Don't want to disturb your family.

?! Come up, you little lunatic.

Lola smiled. She directed the driver to let her off at the corner of 72nd and Madison, where the buildings had doormen and stone carvings for window casings. In fact, when she reached Harry's building, the doorman surprised the hell out of her by greeting her by name. "Good evening, Miss Dunne," he said.

"Oh. Wow. Good evening," she said with surprise.

The doorman escorted her to the elevator banks and pushed the button to send her up to the fourteenth floor. The doors slid silently shut, and Lola saw her hazy reflection in their highly polished fronts. She tried to comb her hair with her fingers as best she could in that blurry reflection. She was standing as close as she could to examine her face when the car stopped and the doors slid open.

She jumped back. And then stepped out gingerly onto thick carpet. And a mirror, thank God, a mirror! Well, not a mirror, exactly, but a painting behind glass, and if Lola stood a certain way, she could just make out her reflection. She groped around the bottom of her bag for a lipstick. She had a red one. It was too red for someone who had come from her mother's bedside in intensive care, she figured. And besides, she couldn't even see if her mascara was smudged beneath her eyes, much less manage to get lipstick on straight. Her normal face would just have to do.

"Stop acting like he's your boyfriend," she muttered under her breath. She didn't have to impress him.

At apartment C, Lola knocked.

Harry was the one who opened the door. His gaze swept over her, top to bottom, and then he smiled so warmly that Lola's heart did a little pitter-patter.

"Rough day?"

"Oh, it was *great*," she said sarcastically.

"How's your mom?"

"She's okay for now," she said, and looked past him, unwilling to speak of Lois Dunne.

"Come in," Harry said, and stepped aside so that Lola could step into luxury.

She didn't know what she'd expected, exactly, but she couldn't have imagined this. Obviously, she knew his parents wouldn't be living in a shack on the Upper East Side—but this was opulence. She was walking into an apartment that could be showcased on any realty show. The entry was marble tile, with crown molding and a crystal chandelier overhead, and striped wallpaper above wainscoting. Lola followed Harry into a living room that was huge by New York standards, trying not to gape at the bank of windows that overlooked the carefully landscaped rooftop terraces. Her feet, encased in some old Converse Chuck Taylor high-tops, sank into thick pile carpet. "This is spectacular," she said, her voice full of awe.

"Yeah, I guess," Harry said.

Lola was so entranced by the apartment that she didn't notice the man who had appeared, drink in hand, until Harry said, "Dad, this is my friend, Lola Dunne."

Harry's father was tall and broad-shouldered like his son. He had full head of salt-and-pepper hair and was wearing tan slacks and a pink collared shirt. He was barefoot. "Hello," she said.

"Lola Dunne!" he said bombastically, extending his hand. "That's a very dramatic name, miss. It would look good on a Broadway marquee. Would you like a drink?"

"Sure she would," Harry said before Lola could decline. He winked at her. "She's just discovered a liking for martinis."

"Martini! A civilized, imperative drink for all of mankind. Allow me to mix one, Lola. I'll join you."

What was he going to do with the drink he was holding? "Ah . . . thank you," she said, and watched with surprise as he downed the drink in his hand and wandered to the bar.

"My mother has gone to bed," Harry said as his father stepped behind the bar. "It's just me, Dad, and Dosia. She's here somewhere."

"Your sister?" she asked, confused.

"Dosia is the family maid. Or, as Dad puts it, the person who sails this ship."

"Ah, *Dosia*," Mr. Westbrook said, as if about to launch into song. "She's been with us since Harry was learning to walk. She's retired for the night, probably in her room watching those god-awful soap operas her family sends her."

"Who are you talking to?"

That question, posed by a woman, was followed by the sound of the front door slamming shut.

"Your brother's friend!" Mr. Westbrook shouted back. "Her name is Lola Dunne, star of stage and screen."

"What?" A pixie of a woman appeared. She had a full head of dark curls, and was dressed stylishly in jeans that rode low on her hips and a boxy sweater over a button-down shirt. She came to a halt at the entrance to the living area and stared at Lola. "Jesus, Harry, you didn't say you were seeing someone new!" she exclaimed, and marched forward, headed for Lola. "I'm Hazel," she said. "Lola, right? So you and Harry, huh?"

"No, it's not like that," Lola hastened to assure her. She could just imagine what his family must think of her in old, faded jeans, a T-shirt and denim jacket, and her hair held back with a bandana she'd rolled up and tied around her head like a hair band.

"It's not?" Hazel asked, peering at Harry with shrewd brown eyes.

"Wow, is that how you greet my friends these days, Hazel?" Harry asked. "Nice."

Hazel responded with a bear hug for her brother. "Sorry. But I was going to be really mad at you if you had a new girlfriend and I didn't know about it."

"I didn't get a new girlfriend," Harry said.

Heat prickled at Lola's nape. He sounded as if he was going to get a new girlfriend, it definitely would not be Lola.

"Listen up, people," Harry said. "I gave Lola a ride today, and I'm going to give her one home. No need to interrogate her or me, okay?"

"Okay!" Hazel said, and saluted. She whirled around, practically skipped to her father's side, and kissed him on the cheek. "Hi, Dad. I'll take one of those. Where's Mom?"

"Oh you know your mom," Mr. Westbrook said as he studied the many liquor bottles on the bar. "She's in bed."

That seemed a little odd to Lola, seeing as how it was only half past six. It occurred to her that Harry's mom might be sick. She didn't know anything about his family. She didn't know anything about *him*.

"Lola, would you like to sit?" Harry asked.

No, she would not. The pink-and-white couches looked like they were upholstered in very expensive silk, and she'd been on a commuter train. Who knew what biohazard might be lurking on her jeans.

But Harry flopped onto one of the couches and gestured for her to do the same. She sat gingerly beside him.

"Do you live in East Beach, Lola?" Mr. Westbrook asked. He was holding the silver shaker above his shoulder, swaying side to side as he shook the contents.

"Um . . . yeah," she said, sounding as if she didn't know where she lived. "For the time being."

"Uh-huh. And what do you do for a living?"

"Oh, I ah . . . I was a paralegal—I mean I *am* a paralegal, but just not right now."

"She's writing a book," Harry said, and looked pointedly at Lola, shaking his head a little, as if he didn't understand her.

"A writer! Now that's a talent I admire," Mr. Westbrook said, as he poured the liquor into four martini glasses. "I've long thought I wanted to write a book," he added.

"You should totally do it, Dad," said Hazel. She had perched on the arm of the couch and was studying nails that looked freshly manicured. "People who pursue their passions are the happiest."

"Well, I think the time to pursue my passion has run out for me," Mr. Westbrook said jovially, and handed his daughter a drink, then brought one to Lola. It was so full she was certain she couldn't take it from him without spilling some of it on the Oriental rug at her feet.

"What do you write, Lola?" Hazel asked.

"Fiction. Women's fiction," she said.

"Wait," said Hazel, lifting her gaze from the study of her nails to eye Lola again. "You two met in East Beach?"

Lola nodded.

"Wow. And here I thought Harry was so busy working he didn't have time to hang out with friends. Certainly not his family. We haven't seen you in a month, Harry! Oh God, that reminds me—guess who I ran into the other day?"

"Who?" he asked.

"Your ex," she said, and her mouth gaped open, as if that news surprised even her.

Lola wasn't looking at Harry, but sitting next to him, and she could feel him tensing. She reached for that martini.

"Oh yeah? How was she?"

Did she detect some emotion in his voice? Reluctance? Sadness? Maybe she hadn't heard anything at all. Maybe her overactive imagination was overreacting.

"She seemed good. Glam, as usual," Hazel said. "She asked a lot of questions about *you*," she said, pointing at Harry. "Oh, I'm sorry, Lola. Has Harry mentioned his ex?"

"Um . . . yeah," Lola said, and risked a look at Harry. "He mentioned he'd ended a relationship recently."

"Boy, did he ever," Hazel said, and Mr. Westbrook laughed.

Harry didn't. He was staring at his sister. "What'd you say, Hazel?"

"Well of course I told her you were doing *great*," she said as Lola took a sip. "I told her you were working out of East Beach. Just so she'd know you hadn't had to move to some pit in Brooklyn."

Lola coughed.

"Careful there, cowgirl," Mr. Westbrook said.

"Nothing wrong with Brooklyn," Harry said evenly.

"Maybe not. But I wouldn't want to live there. I swear we get more of our patients from Brooklyn than any other borough. Anyway, I thought it was interesting she was asking about you," Hazel said. "You know what I think? I think the grass wasn't so green on the other side, and now she realizes she had it better with you after all."

"Very astute observation," Mr. Westbrook said. "You may be on to something, Hazel."

"She said you two were taking a break," Hazel said. "That gives her an entry back, you know? Anyway, I'm having lunch with her next week. Maybe I can ask her." She winked at Harry.

"Mind if we save the analysis of my former girlfriend for a time when I don't have a friend sitting right next to me?" Harry asked. "I'm sure Lola doesn't want to hear all the details of my relationship."

Au contraire, Lola very much wanted to hear all the details, every last one. But now everyone was looking at her.

"Anyone here a Mets fan?" she suddenly chirped, recognizing the moment the words flew out of her mouth that it was the weirdest of segues.

"Yankees!" Mr. Westbrook said emphatically. "Lola, don't ruin your life rooting for the Mets."

That prompted a lively discussion of the Mets' chances this year, and some friendly arguing between father and son about the New York teams. Lola had sipped half her drink when Harry stretched his arms overhead and said, "Lola and I should probably get going."

"You're not going to stay until Mom wakes up?" Hazel asked.

Harry gave his sister a look that seemed to suggest she knew better than to ask. "I have to work tomorrow. Who knows when she'll wake up?"

Hazel looked down the long hallway where Lola presumed the bedrooms were situated.

Harry stood up. "Are you ready, Lola?"

"Yes." She stood up. "Very nice to meet you. And thank you for the drink."

"You are more than welcome, my dear," said Mr. Westbrook. "You come back any time, will you? We love to meet Harry's friends, and I love making martinis. It's a win-win."

"See you, bro," Hazel said, and playfully punched Harry in the belly. "It better not be a month before you show up at Sunday dinner. You know I can't handle the Old People on my own."

"Hey, I think I resemble that remark," Mr. Westbrook said, miming Groucho Marx as he headed back to the bar.

◆ ◆ ◆

Harry didn't say much as he drove out of the city. He remarked on the traffic twice, and mentioned how much he loved Dosia and her pancakes. Lola tried to read him, tried to detect if his sister's news had affected him at all. She was making herself crazy with it and finally asked, "Is your mother okay?"

"My mom?" he asked, glancing at her. "Yeah. Why?"

"I don't know. She was in bed early, and there was that talk of her getting up."

"Right." Harry sighed. He scratched his chin. "She's okay. If I were actually dating you, I'd sugarcoat it," he said, using her words. "The truth is that my mom gets pissing drunk every Sunday."

Lola laughed.

"I'm not kidding," he said seriously. "Looks like we have more in common than you know."

"You're joking," she said. If Harry's family had been living in a rundown, two-bedroom apartment like she and her family had, she'd believe it. But the apartment she'd seen this evening didn't look like it could possibly be the home of a drunk. People who lived in homes like that never had the problems of people who lived hand-to-mouth. Or so she'd always believed.

"I wish I was joking," he said. "We've all gotten used to it. It's weird—she doesn't drink a drop through the week. But on Sunday, she starts drinking early and she goes until she just about passes out."

"But *why*?" Lola asked, confused.

"Why?" Harry shook his head. "Why did your mom do drugs? What makes anyone abuse alcohol or drugs?"

That was a question Lola had pondered many times in her life. "I wish I knew." She looked out the window at the passing lights, silent.

"What are you thinking?" Harry asked.

"That I really don't know you," she said honestly. "I don't know if you have more than one sister, or what your dad does for a living, or if you've lived on the Upper East Side all your life."

"Well you're all kinds of curious tonight," he said. "Let's see—Hazel is my only sibling. I grew up in the apartment you saw. And my Dad? He doesn't do anything. He married my mother's money and he's been a stay-at-home dad all my life. Anything else?"

She could hardly process that information, but yes, there was something else. "Do you miss your ex-girlfriend?"

Harry looked at her, his brows dipping in a vee of confusion. Or irritation. Lola wasn't certain which. "What?" he asked, as if he hadn't heard her correctly.

"Sorry," she said, holding up a hand. "It's none of my business."

"No, it's okay," he said. "I was expecting you to ask where my mother's money came from. Banking, by the way. And yes, I miss her sometimes. But not all the time."

"So . . . are you over it?" She picked at a fraying hole in the knee of her jeans, dreading his answer.

"Man," he said. "Twenty questions, huh?" He laughed ruefully, as if he was gearing up to grin and bear something unpleasant. "I loved her, Lola. I still do in a way. But when something doesn't work, it doesn't work. I'm sure you know what I mean."

"Boy, do I ever," she said with a snort. "Were you together a long time?"

"A little over a year," he said. "We were living together. I'll let you in on a secret. I thought she was the one. But . . ." He shrugged it off and didn't elaborate.

Lola didn't press him, either. She was sorry she'd asked. She didn't want to hear about the girl Harry had thought was "the one." And now, even though he was staring ahead, she had the sense he was seeing anything but the road. It made her feel strangely at odds—like she'd misbuttoned herself and was all lopsided now. She didn't need Kennedy's budding psychology degree to point out that as hours clicked by in Harry's company, she understood less and less what to think about the gorgeous man beside her, this roommate slash casual-sex partner.

What Lola did understand were the rules—she didn't have the right to feel strange that he had feelings for another woman. That's not how friends-with-benefits worked. She had the right to have fun, and nothing else. She wasn't allowed to care. Unfortunately, she did care. She cared a lot. Maybe too much.

The jury was in—Lola did casual sex about as well as she bowled: terribly.

When they arrived at the lake house, Lola walked into the living room, dropped her purse beside some clothes on the couch that she hadn't finished folding, and turned toward the kitchen. She sagged when she saw it. It was a wreck. "I forgot all about it."

"Come on," Harry said behind her, and put his hand on her shoulder. "Let's knock it out."

She much preferred to knock out a bucket of wine—that was her go-to response after a day with her mother—but Lola followed Harry into the kitchen and started in on the cleanup.

It didn't take much time with two of them, and there was only a bit of washing left to do. Harry picked up a towel. She handed him a pot, and Harry asked, "What about Will?"

"Will?" she asked, startled.

"That's his name, right?" Harry asked. "Your ex? Are you over him?"

Lola stared down at the soapy water, recalling the day they'd met at the café. "I am *so* over him."

Harry put the dry pan down and picked up the second. "How do you know? What's the cosmic sign that says, I am over this guy, or this relationship has changed and it's not what I thought it was?"

Lola could feel the shame in her cheeks rising up at just the memory of how hopeful she'd felt the last time she'd seen Will. She snorted.

"What's funny?" Harry was smiling, as if he expected a joke.

"Nothing, trust me. That is unless you find total naïveté funny. You want to know how things have definitely changed, Harry? That you don't feel the way you used to? When the puppy appears—that's how."

He smiled with confusion. "You'll have to elaborate."

Lola told him about the last time she'd seen Will. It was something she'd tell a friend like Mallory, or Casey. But telling Harry made her feel ridiculous. It made her *look* ridiculous. She wasn't even sure why she told him, other than she felt like unloading. And there was something about Harry that she trusted on an almost primal level. She must, because she told him the whole ugly truth. About getting dressed up, about thinking this was it, that Will had asked to meet her to apologize. She told him how she hoped he would ask her to take him back, because part of her really wanted to be Will and Lola again. "But what he wanted was for me to take a puppy."

Harry's expression of sheer horror reaffirmed what Lola's siblings had said—Will was the worst. "The sad thing is, if he'd apologized, I probably would have taken the puppy," she said, trying to make a joke of it.

Harry didn't laugh.

Well, of course not. Lola was very good about laughing off her deep hurts, pretending to the world that they weren't so deep, that she was okay—it was hard for her to let other people see her pain. She never felt entitled to it. Yet even she could recognize the puppy story was god-awful, a glimpse into a relationship that had gotten terribly unbalanced along the way.

"Are you okay?" Harry asked, and put his hand on her back. "I didn't mean to dredge up bad memories."

"I'm fine," she said. "I'm over it, I really am. I learned a lot from my marriage, like how you never really see all sides of a person. I mean, you can believe you know someone so well, inside and out, and then suddenly a new facet pops up from nowhere, and you never saw any hint of it. And you're so confused how you might have missed that side, how you could sleep with someone and never see that side, and the next thing you know, you're trying to make sense of the whole fucking world." She threw the washcloth into the water and braced her hands against the sink. "It just makes me so furious that I fell for it. That I let my hope convince me it was something it wasn't. Hope is for idiots."

Harry gingerly stroked her head. "Maybe that's part of making sense of the world."

She nodded. "You're right!" She pulled the towel free of his hold and dried her hands. "Just look at me now, Harry Westbrook. I'm in East Beach, living illegally in someone's house, writing a book like I know what I'm doing, and sharing benefits with a roommate who wasn't even supposed to be here. See? The world is making sense again."

Harry grinned. He pulled the towel from her hand, tossed it onto the counter, and then settled his hands onto her waist. "You know what I don't get? How a man could be such an asshole to you."

Harry didn't put any particular emotion in those words—it was just an observation. Nonetheless, those words moved like rockets through Lola's heart. "That is very kind of you to say right now," she said, smiling lopsidedly. "But in fairness, it takes two, and I—"

"Don't say another word," he said, touching his finger to her lips. "I like my fantasy of rooming with the world's most perfect little lunatic. Don't spoil it for me." He kissed her.

"What are you doing?" she muttered against his mouth.

"Collecting my roommate benefit," he muttered back. "You owe me."

"I do?" Lola closed her eyes and sank into his kiss.

"Yes, absolutely. I helped you clean up this mess. I've never seen anyone treat a kitchen like you do. There ought to be a kitchen support group."

Lola slid her hands around his neck. "Did it ever occur to you that maybe you owe me?"

"Oh yeah? For what?"

"Give me a minute," she said, and smiled. "Okay, I've got nothing. I just want you to owe me so I can collect." She rose up on her toes and pressed her lips to his, very lightly, very softly.

Harry drew a deep breath, cupped her head, and kissed her with a little more urgency. That kiss struck Lola like a bolt of lightning. A million thoughts of why casual sex was really a bad idea in so many ways flitted about her brain like butterflies, but a big net of sheer want swept them up and deposited them in some dark corner.

Lola caught Harry's collar in her fist and pulled him closer, pressing her lips to his, trying to pull him down, right there on the floor, so that she could have her way with him.

"I thought we agreed—I do the choreography," he said into her hair, and suddenly lifted her up and put her on the countertop and moved between her legs, bracing his arms on either side of her.

"Did we agree? Because I have some moves, too." She took his face in her hands and angled her head, kissing him thoroughly, exploring him with her tongue. Harry grabbed her hips and yanked her into his body; she could feel his erection, hard and insistent against her.

She moved her mouth to his ear and nibbled his earlobe.

A groan rumbled in the back of Harry's throat; he picked her up, and Lola locked her legs around his back. Somewhere, a pan and something metal clattered to the floor as Harry twirled her around and pushed her up against the fridge. He was kissing her wildly, devouring her. Lola sank her fingers into his shoulders to hold on. She was overwhelmed with his touch and his scent, and so quickly turned on that she was beginning to pant. She forgot about everything, forgot they were roommates, and her mother, and the novel she was writing. She forgot about everything in the world except this man holding her, biting her nipple through her shirt. This man wanted her, and she wanted him back in the most desperate way.

"Couch," she said breathlessly.

"Bed," Harry countered, and still holding her wrapped around his waist, moved in the direction of her room as he continued to kiss her. They slammed into the door frame—Lola's head took the brunt of it—and then stumbled over something on her floor. He tossed her down onto her unmade bed, and with one sweep of his arm, sent most everything on top of the bed—shoes, her purse, some papers and a notebook—onto the floor.

She was going to regret this, Lola thought as he yanked at her jeans, pulling them off her body. Tomorrow, she would be confused and wondering if they were a thing now. But it was too late—she'd dived in with all her emotions and yearnings and pheromones firing left and right and pinging off the walls. She assisted when he lifted her up to remove her shirt and bra. She closed her eyes as her hands wandered his chest, now wonderfully bare. She could feel her lips stretch in one very happy smile as he kicked his pants off, felt her smile grow wider when he planted his lips on her abdomen.

There was no going back to roommates, Lola thought dreamily as Harry took her breast into his mouth. This was too good, and it went too deep. She felt like she was shimmering as Harry's hands ran wild over her body, her bare breast, her thighs . . . and then deeper, into the folds of her body.

She mindlessly scraped her fingers down his arms and chest, over his hips.

Harry suddenly came up for air and touched his damp forehead to hers. "This can't be right."

"What?" she asked, suddenly frantic that he was going to stop. "Because you can't do casual sex, either?"

"Huh? No! Because it shouldn't be this freaking *hot*."

"Do you want me to open a window?"

"I am talking about you, Lola. *Us*." He rolled over, pulling her to straddle him. "You're killing me." He put his hands on her hips and lifted her up, and Lola's heart fluttered wildly. She slid her hands down his slate of an abdomen and took him in hand.

"Do you have a condom in the cyclone debris?" he asked roughly.

She reached for her cosmetics bag, still on the bed, and frantically dumped the contents beside them. Lipsticks and mascara rolled down to nestle in Harry's side. A tube of ChapStick, a mint she'd picked up at some restaurant, a Fitbit she could never remember to latch onto her waistband, and a tampon scattered across the sheet. She dug into a small interior pocket and produced a condom whose wrapper was turning brittle with time and held it up triumphantly.

"Give me that thing," he said, grabbing it from her hand, and in a flurry of sheets and flying tubes of lipstick, he slipped it on, then grabbed Lola's head between his big hands and kissed her again. But this kiss was different; it was slower. Deeper. It wasn't the frenzy with which they'd started this beneficial meeting, but much more reverent. As if it *meant* something.

Oh, God, her heart was pounding now—did it mean something to him? He returned his attention to her breasts, and Lola lifted herself up and slid down onto him.

"Damn," he groaned as she began to move on him. Harry put his hands on her thighs, anchoring her, and began to move with her. When he looked into her eyes, Lola saw the same fire that burned deep inside of her, beneath all her baggage. She began to move faster, and the spark in Harry's eyes seemed to grow brighter and brighter as she slipped closer and closer to release.

He suddenly flipped them over, onto her back, and began to push deeper into her. His gaze was locked on hers, and he didn't look away, didn't lose himself in the throes of ecstasy. He kept looking at her eyes.

Why did everything suddenly seem so serious? So fraught with meaning? All of the emotions she had been careful not to let loose were clamoring to get out of her, to envelop this man.

Lola closed her eyes, tried not to let feelings of tenderness and affection interfere with a really good orgasm. But it was too late—Harry rocked into her, pushing her over the edge, and Lola cried out with her release and with all the unattended desires she had promised herself to never let see the light of day.

Harry growled and thrust into her once more, joining her beneath her blanket of bliss.

Lola had nothing left; she was jelly. She wrapped her arms around his head, sighing with great contentment.

"God . . . you *slay* me," he muttered against her breast.

At least that's what Lola thought she heard. "What?"

"Nothing, never mind," he said, and lifted his head. "I have an idea—let's go skinny dipping."

She wanted to ask him what that meant, that she slayed him. She wanted to attach the proper gravitas to it without going overboard as she was wont to do, so she could remember it again and again. But Harry was already moving. "Come on, don't you want to?"

Lola wanted so many things in that moment. She wanted love, she wanted babies, she wanted stability and someone to love her and a life to look forward to, and more sex like this, a *lot* of sex like this, and a new lipstick because she was pretty sure that tube was now smeared on her sheets—but she was at a loss to say any of those things.

Harry looked at her, expecting an answer, and she was too afraid to say she wanted more, too afraid of the rejection, the look of impatience on his face and the *listen, we need to talk* denouement of their fling. "Are you reading my mind?" she blurted. "I swear I was just thinking the same thing."

He grinned. "What, then, do I need to get the wheelbarrow to get you out there?" He hopped off the bed.

Lola hopped off, too.

Whatever she was feeling, she would bury. She was a pro at that.

Twenty

Harry didn't see much of Lola the week after that mind-blowing Sunday. He left early and arrived home late, having run into another obstacle when his crew accidentally cut through a main water line.

She left him notes. *There's a hunk of lasagna in the fridge for a hunk.* And *Mallory and friends are coming over tomorrow for yoga on the terrace. Bring an open mind and your mala beads.*

He responded. *Thanks so much for the hunk of lasagna. You might have saved me from extinction.* And *As much as I would love to watch you doing yoga, I have no idea what mala beads are. Plus, I have to repair a water line.*

He didn't see much of her . . . but they managed to find their way into each other's bed at night. "Where have you been?" she asked him one night when he slipped in between her sheets.

"I've been in water main hell," he said. "*Ouch*—what is that?" he asked when something sharp dug into his hip.

"Hey, don't break my flash drive," she said, sliding her hand under him.

"I've got a flash drive for you, baby," he said, and gathered her up in his arms.

The sex between them was fantastic. Harry was too tired to analyze why it was so fantastic, but he knew innately that the spark between them was not anything he'd experienced before. At least not as sharply or intensely as this.

One night he came home to a dark house. Lola was not at home, and after he showered, he collapsed into bed. He was awakened by the pleasantly soothing sensation of a caress. "You're snoring," she said softly. "What are we going to do about that?"

"Have any ideas?" he asked groggily.

"One or two," she said, and slid down his body and took him in her mouth.

On yet another night, he arrived home very late—half past midnight—and found her in the kitchen, sleepily tapping away at her laptop.

"Wow," she said, taking in his grimy shirt, his soiled jeans, his caked work boots. "Were you working in the dark?"

"Site lights," he said. Another expense he hadn't counted on.

"You should take a dip in the pool," she said. "The water is really warm."

"That sounds like a great idea. Will you join me?" he asked, holding out his arm.

Lola grinned and stood up. She opened her bathrobe to reveal a new, very sexy bathing suit. "I thought you'd never ask."

It was a warm, humid night, and they ended up at the side of the pool, their arms folded over the pool's lip while the rest of their bodies floated. They gazed out at the lights on Lake Haven. They talked companionably—Lola had hit a rough patch on her book, and wasn't sure if Sherri was going to kill again before Lola allowed the detective to figure a few things out. Harry told her about the nightmare of the water main, and how it was draining his bank account. It felt nice to talk about it without a debate over whether or not he was doing the right thing by starting this company.

And yet, a tiny part of Harry had begun to wonder if he was doing the right thing. It seemed as if every step forward was met with two blows to knock him back.

When Harry wasn't with Lola, he thought of her. A *lot*. At weird times, too, like he was a fourteen-year-old all over again. When one of his subcontractors was reviewing the blueprints with him, Harry was thinking of Lola. When the drainage pipe repair cracked within twenty-four hours, he thought of Lola. On the long drive to and from work, he made himself crazy by reliving those nocturnal moments in her arms.

If he could trust himself to be objective about this sudden dating thing, he would say there was something happening within him that he hadn't quite plumbed. He was intrigued by that notion in some ways, confused in others. It felt a little like he was turning over on himself; old notions about life and goals were suddenly on shaky ground, and new *what-if* scenarios were popping up in his head. He didn't fully understand these thoughts, and moreover, he didn't want or need the entanglement of a relationship or relationship angst right now . . .

Wasn't that exactly what had happened with Melissa? Hadn't putting his career first cost him the woman he meant to marry? Didn't he need the time now to get his company off the ground, and then think about issues like life and marriage? Yes, he needed that time. And yet, he couldn't stop thinking about Lola.

He couldn't stop thinking about her so much that he'd stopped noticing the state of the lake house. One day it was tidied up, the next day a wreck. She even washed two of his shirts and said in the note she left that they'd mysteriously appeared in her laundry basket. He could only imagine how that had happened in the way she tossed clothes around, then gathered them up. But in return for her thoughtfulness, he picked up the kitchen one night and made sure he programmed the coffee machine before he left.

He worked Saturday with his crew. The general contractor on the project was breathing down his neck about all the delays. Harry had calculated that what he would make on this job—assuming it was clear sailing here on out—would barely cover what he'd put into it. For the first time since embarking on a career in civil engineering, Harry's doubts were growing. He had yet to make any money building bridges and had done nothing but pour money into it. If he didn't get a shot at contracting soon, he wasn't sure where he was going to end up.

Lola wasn't home when he finally arrived, exhausted and filthy, on Saturday night. But he awoke on Sunday to the sound of feminine chatter in the living room. He stumbled out, desperate for coffee and a couple of aspirin. Lola and Mallory were in the living room, and there were several dresses draped over the back of the couch. Lola was wearing a red one that was sexy as hell, turning this way and that for Mallory.

"There he is! What do you think, Harry?" Mallory chirped when she saw him. She gestured grandly to Lola. "Which should Lola wear to Birta's dinner party tonight? The one she is wearing? Or this one?" she asked, and held up a long blue dress that looked to have rhinestones glued to it.

"Ah . . ."

Lola twirled around for him; the skirt on the red dress flared out, giving him glimpse of her excellent legs.

"That one," he said, pointing at her. "Hands down."

"Ooh, hands *down*," Mallory said, nodding in agreement.

"I knew you were going to say that," Lola said with a sigh.

"Don't listen to her, Harry," Mallory said. "I found this dress in the city yesterday and I thought Lola would look *fabulous* in it, so I brought it back with the rest of these."

"Don't you like it?" Harry asked curiously.

"I *love* it," Lola said, then whispered loudly, "But it's *six hundred* dollars." As if Mallory didn't know how much she'd paid for it.

"Wear it tonight, return it tomorrow," Mallory said with a shrug.

"No!" Lola said, aghast.

"Then I'll loan you the money," Mallory said. She fell onto one of the couches and propped her feet up on the ottoman.

"*No*, Mallory."

"Then it's a gift!" Mallory exclaimed. "You have to wear it, Lola. You look fantastic. Doesn't she look fantastic, Harry?"

"She does," he said. He was ogling her, he realized. She was gorgeous, really, and he had to be honest—highly fuckable—which is exactly where his male mind went. Kudos for Mallory; she couldn't seem to dress herself, but she had picked out a perfect dress for Lola.

"That good, huh?" Lola said.

"That good. You look beautiful, Lola."

She glanced down, considering it. "Okay," she said. "Okay, okay, I'll take it. But I'm not borrowing money and you're not giving it to me. I'll buy it. Somehow."

"Yippee!" Mallory said, clapping her hands. She didn't seem to understand Lola's reluctance, which was really unsurprising given that Mallory had obviously been raised in crazy wealth. Like him, Mallory probably didn't understand crazy poverty.

"Now Harry, I didn't bring anything for you," Mallory said as she twirled a tassel on her shirt around her finger. "Do you have something to wear to Birta's tonight?"

"I do," he said as he headed for the kitchen. "Do you?"

"Yes, I do," Mallory said. "Lola, we better get going."

"I'll just change," Lola said.

"Going where?" Harry asked, feeling mildly disappointed that she wasn't going to be around on his day off.

"Baby shower," Mallory said. "I made Lola promise she'd go with me. I hate baby showers. All those rattles and diapers." She shuddered, as if these were reprehensible things.

♦ ♦ ♦

Lola returned later that afternoon carrying a plate with tiny baby bottles glued to it. Harry stopped constructing his sandwich and looked at the thing with all due suspicion.

"I knew the most baby trivia," Lola said. "And this is my prize." She put it down on the kitchen bar and shook her head, too, as if she couldn't make it out. "Harry! We're leaving in an hour for a dinner party. Are you going to eat that sandwich now?"

"I am," he said, and took a healthy bite. He held it out to her.

Lola rose up on the toes and took a bite. "God, that's good," she said, her mouth full. "I can't watch you eat that," she said. "I might pass out from hunger. I'm going to get ready. We can't be late, Harry!"

"We won't be late," he assured her, and true to his word, an hour later, he was sitting in the living room when Lola emerged from her bedroom in the red dress. She had on red heels, too, and a long gold chain with a gold heart charm that draped down her front, the heart dangling above her waist.

Harry stood up, taking her in. It was amazing to him that she could transform from someone covered in cake batter to this. "Gorgeous," he said.

"And you," she said, pointing at him. "That's a fine suit, Handsome Harry."

"Only the best for Birta Hoffman. Are you ready? Have you rehearsed your lines?" he asked.

"Very funny. I'm ready. I think," she said, and laughed nervously.

They arrived at Birta Hoffman's summer residence ten minutes late, having driven up Hackberry Road to pick up Mallory. They had not factored in how long it took for someone to walk from a room in the Cantrell mansion all the way to the drive.

But now the three of them stood staring at the Hoffman residence as the valet drove Harry's truck away—everyone on Lake Haven had a valet, apparently.

Lola cocked her head to one side, studying it. "It's not as fancy as I thought it would be," she mused.

"It's a rental," Mallory said. She had chosen to wear what Harry thought was a muumuu, complete with several long necklaces that reminded him a little of what a fortune-teller would wear. "Property is hard to come by out here," she added. "Deed restrictions and all that. You two are so lucky Zach is letting you use his lake house."

Harry didn't look at Lola, and he was certain she didn't look at him. "Shall we?" he asked, and put his hand on Lola's back, guiding her to the door.

Mallory didn't knock; she opened the door and crooned, *"Hello!"* before sailing inside. Harry and Lola exchanged a look before following her.

The house was very modern, all glass and chrome and shiny white. The kitchen was to the right and looked out over an expansive dining area and living room. The kitchen island stretched the full length of the kitchen and was laden with plates of finger foods. Soft jazz played in the background, and a man in a chef's coat and apron was busy at the stove. Two uniformed waiters bowed and held out trays of wine.

"Ah, look who has come!" they heard Birta trill. She stepped through the sliding glass door that opened onto the deck. Her long black hair looked like silk tonight, and she had bangs that hung down almost over her eyes. She was wearing a black, floor-length dress, and around her neck, another monstrous turquoise arrangement. "Hallo, darling," she said to Mallory, exchanging a couple of air kisses with her. She walked up the steps from the sunken living room. "Lisa, right?" she said to Lola, holding out her hand.

"Lola," Lola said, and awkwardly clasped Birta's hand and gave it a shake.

"Yes, yes, Lola, of course. I should remember that—my brother's cat is named Lola. My apologies." Birta turned to Harry. "Hallo, Harry," she said, and presented her cheek to be kissed. Her hand, Harry noticed, landed on his sleeve.

"Lovely place you've got here."

"Oh, thank you. I can't take any of the credit," she said, her voice silky and a bit more accented than Harry recalled. "My agent found it for me."

"Oh, is he here?" Lola asked lightly.

"Cyrus?" Birta laughed. "Heavens, no. Cyrus wouldn't be caught dead at Lake Haven. It's not the Hamptons, darling," she said, as if Lola were a precocious child.

Harry didn't know what to make of this famous author, but was fairly certain he didn't much like her.

"Come, now, have some wine," Birta said. "My good friend Mr. Rothschild sent it from Napa just for tonight. And Chef Donatelli has graciously agreed to prepare our meal tonight. I'm sure you've heard of his restaurant in New York, Harry. Aro?"

Harry knew about Aro. Reservations were booked a month out. He wondered idly what the chef was doing here on a Sunday night instead of cooking at his restaurant.

"This setting is ideal for writing," Lola said to Birta. "You must be inspired by the view."

"The view inspires me to nothing but procrastination," Birta said. "You should see the boat my neighbor Bob had delivered just this week. Come, Harry, and I'll show you. Lola, darling, you should introduce yourself to Mallory's friends."

What the hell? Harry reached for Lola's hand, but she had glanced away toward Mallory, and Birta had linked her arm in his and tugged him away before he could get Lola's attention.

Harry allowed Birta to escort him out onto the deck, and looked down at a boat that didn't seem particularly noteworthy to him. He was determined to curtail her interest in him, and managed to detach himself from her grip. "That's a great boat," he said just to get it over and done. "You may not be inspired by this view, but I know Lola has been very inspired." He looked at Birta. "I hope you meant what you said at the Cantrell party and will look at her book when she's ready."

"Ah, yes, the *book*," Birta said, as if annoyed by it. "If I take a look, what will be my prize?" she asked, putting her back to the water so that she might prop her elbows on the railing and gaze up into his face.

"My undying gratitude."

"Is that all? You seem a savvy man to me." Her gaze flicked over him. "I'm sure you know that the odds of any one person actually seeing a book published are astronomical. And I'm talking about writers who have talent. We've not yet determined if your girlfriend has that essential ingredient."

"There is only one way to find out," he said, smiling. "Read it."

"Oh, I'll read it," she said smoothly, and pursed her lips. "But it's going to cost you, love."

Women had come on to Harry, but in all honesty, he'd never met one so bold about it. "You're barking up the wrong tree, Birta."

"Am I?" She stepped closer. "She's just a girl, Harry. But you? You're a man." She touched his shirt and trailed her finger down his abdomen.

There wasn't enough booze in the world to make him want Birta, especially now. "It's not working," he said.

"No? Just how badly do you want me to read your little girl's book?" she whispered with a sultry smile.

"Ah . . . hi."

Birta sighed and turned away from Harry, because Lola and Mallory were standing one step up. Lola was looking at Harry, her expression one of irritation and confusion.

"Lola, I'm glad you're here," he said, reaching for her, his hand finding hers. "Birta is excited to read your book."

"She is?" Lola asked skeptically.

"I am excited," Birta said unenthusiastically. But then she said suddenly, "I've an idea, darling," and put her arm around Lola's shoulders and drew her companionably into her side. "I could use a bit of help day to day." She fixed her gaze on Harry and said, "What would you think of offering an hour or two each day to apprentice with me? I'll take a look at your pages, and you can mail things for me, or tidy up—whatever I need."

Harry's gaze narrowed on Birta. He wasn't certain of the game she was playing and Birta knew it—she smiled triumphantly at him.

But Lola's eyes widened. "Are you serious?"

"Of course!"

God help him. "What about your book, Lola?" Harry asked. "You really don't have the time—"

"Oh, I could definitely carve out a couple of hours each day," she said excitedly.

"You don't have a car," he reminded her. "How would you get up here?"

Lola shot him a look that he read as a warning not to ruin this for her. "I have a bike. I'll figure it out."

"Then it's settled," Birta said brightly. "All right, then," she said, slipping her arm through Harry's again. "Shall we go and see what the chef is preparing?"

It was another quarter of an hour before Harry could put some space between him and Birta and join Lola. She was with Mallory, who had introduced them to her friends, amazingly the legendary rock star Everett Alden, and his girlfriend, Mia Lassiter. Harry hadn't expected any celebrity sightings tonight, and he was a little starstruck. He also noticed that Mia was wearing the most interesting conglomeration of fabrics he'd seen on a woman.

As much as he wanted nothing more than to hang out with Everett Alden, there was something more important. Harry excused himself and Lola and pulled her away.

"What are you doing?" Lola moaned. "That is *Everett Alden*."

"Yeah, I know. I'm a huge fan of his. But he doesn't look like he's going anywhere, and I need to talk to you."

"About what?"

"About Birta, Lola. She is asking you to be her assistant, or whatever, because of me."

Lola blinked. And then she laughed. "Okay, Harry. You're a good-looking guy, but you don't honestly believe that."

"Yes, I do—"

Lola laughed again. "Stop!" she playfully protested, pushing against him.

"Listen to me—"

"I mean *stop*," she said, and her smile faded. "I'm not blind. But just because she is hot to trot for you doesn't mean I don't need her help. If she will look at my book and give me some feedback, it's totally worth it. Seize the moment, right?"

"Even if she is using you?" he asked.

"My eyes are open," she said, and smiled. "Just think about what a great opportunity it is!"

Harry didn't think it was a true opportunity at all, but there was a sudden flurry of activity at the door, and he and Lola turned with everyone else to see who had come in.

"Well it's bloody well time, Andy," Birta said, sailing across the living room to the door to greet a man. He was tall and lean, like a swimmer. "You know how I feel about tardiness."

"I know, and I'm sorry," the man said. "The traffic from the city is horrible."

"Everyone, this is the Andy Carson, the man who handles my publicity," Birta said. "And this lovely young woman will be taking over for him this fall. Melissa Fulton."

Shocked, Harry stared at the brunette with the long dark hair and the skin-tight gold dress. Her gaze met his, and widened with surprise.

"Melissa!" Lola said.

Before Harry realized what was happening, Lola was walking forward. "Small world, huh?"

"Oh! Hi, Lola," Melissa said, and glanced nervously at Harry.

Harry was staggered—Lola *knew* Melissa? How was that even possible? For a moment he couldn't move, he couldn't speak. The shock of seeing Melissa so unexpectedly—and with Lola—was like a bucket of ice to his brain.

"Fabulous, we are all here," Birta said, clapping her hands. "Now we can dine. Places, everyone! You'll find your names at your seat. Andy, Melissa, you can meet everyone at the table."

They began to move toward the dining room, but Melissa paused before Harry. She looked nervous. Insecure. "Hi," she said.

"Hi."

"Fancy meeting you here," she said.

"What?" Birta asked. "You two know each other?"

"We know each other, all right," Melissa said. "We were almost married."

Harry heard Lola's sharp intake of breath . . . but it was nothing compared to the roar in his head.

Twenty-one

Everyone in the room went quiet for a few seconds, their gazes going from Harry to Melissa. "Well," said Birta stiffly, breaking the awkward silence. "This should make for a very interesting evening."

Interesting was not the word that Lola would have used. Disastrous, maybe. Terrifying. She was still trying to wrap her head around it all. *Melissa. Lissa.* How could the Melissa she'd met—and liked—be Harry's Lissa? How was she here, *now?* Had she known Harry would be here? Did she know he was at the Cantrells' last weekend?

There was no time to make sense of it, or to ask Harry what the hell was happening, because Birta was instructing everyone to take their seats, and he was escorting her to the table. He held her elbow as they began to move toward the table. "Lola—"

"Harry, you're here," Birta said, putting herself in their path and directing Harry to a seat at one end of the table. Apparently, she'd made up place cards, and Lola was sitting at the opposite end of the table from Harry. Harry glanced at Lola as Birta pushed him toward the other end of the table.

Lola was seated between Birta's doctor, Mr. Rosenthal, and Mia Lassiter. At the other end, Harry was between Everett Alden and

Melissa. Talk about adding insult to injury—not only did Harry get the woman he wanted to marry, he got the rock star.

Across from Lola was Andy Carson, seated next to a surprisingly sullen Mallory. Birta sat in the middle of the table, across from Mrs. Rosenthal, so that she could join conversations at both ends.

Lola couldn't keep her mind on the conversation around her. Her thoughts were spinning, and she kept stealing glimpses of Harry, watching him swivel between Everett Alden and Melissa. What were they talking about? What were they saying to each other? More importantly, where did she and Harry stand? Was it over now? Melissa was smiling at him, a soft, intimate smile, and Lola damn sure noticed the way Harry looked at Melissa. It was heart-wrenching.

"I love your dress."

It took Lola a moment to realize Mia was speaking to her. "Oh, *mine*," she said. "Thank you. Yours is really gorgeous."

"Mia is a designer," Mallory said.

"An aspiring designer, anyway," Mia said with a smile. "I haven't seen you around East Beach, Lola. Are you visiting?"

"No, I'm, ah . . . I'm here for a few weeks."

"Visiting friends?"

"Actually, I'm writing a book."

Mia's face lit with delight. "Really? Have you written any books before?"

"This is my first. And it might be my last," she said, stealing another glimpse of Harry. "If I can't get it published, I'll have to get a job."

"I think that's really cool," Mia said. "I love to read."

"Read what?" Birta said loudly, commanding the attention of everyone. The table quieted, and Birta laughed it off. "I beg your pardon, but I hear a mention of books and I can't help but go there."

"I was saying I love to read books," Mia said politely. "I just finished *The Goldfinch*."

"I will not take offense that the book was not mine," Birta said, inclining her head to more polite laughter. "But you do have good taste in books. That was a masterful novel. Did you read it, Lola?"

Lola blinked, startled to be asked. "I did."

"And what did our aspiring writer think?" Birta asked, her smile terribly patronizing.

Everyone was looking at her. This felt like a setup, but Lola couldn't imagine why. She didn't think *The Goldfinch* was masterful. She glanced at Harry, who gave her a small smile of encouragement. "I thought Boris—the Russian friend?—I thought he was more interesting than the protagonist. And the end was unsatisfying for me."

Birta chuckled with amusement and glanced around the table. "I think you missed the point of the book then."

Yep. A setup all right, and now, Lola looked like an idiot.

"Really," Mia said, as if pondering Birta's point. "Well I guess I missed the point, too, because I thought the very same thing."

With that statement, Mia had cemented her place at the top of Lola's adoration list. She could kiss her right now, plant a big smacker right on the lips.

But Birta waved her hand. "I admit that I tend to read with a very technical eye," she said, shrugging it off. "Now then," she said, turning toward Harry. "What are you speaking of so intimately in this corner?"

"Just my idea to give up music and take up fishing," Everett said.

"Oh, God," Mia groaned. "That can't happen, sweetie. You're a *horrible* fisherman." She regaled the table with a story of a fishing excursion they took together when Everett had spent most of the day below deck, green to the gills.

The talk turned to his music and a soundtrack he was creating for a film, which gave Lola the opportunity to sink back in her chair while her mind did gymnastics, trying to understand what was happening between Harry and Melissa, and Harry and her. She needed a bottle of wine, a box of Godivas, and some deep covers to slide under as she made sense of this horrible jolt to her heart.

It was maddening—the company was excellent, and the meal divine, all things Lola would have studied with keen interest under normal circumstances. But her appetite was nonexistent. She couldn't stop glancing down the table at Harry and Melissa, at the way they talked, their heads together, as if they were sharing a secret.

The dessert was served; Lola scarcely noticed it until Mallory said, "Look," and pointed at it. "That's candy from my store," she said, indicating the candies embedded in the icing.

"I thought you closed it!" Mia said. "I went by there Wednesday, and it wasn't open."

"Yeah," Mallory said, and looked at Lola forlornly. "I need an assistant."

Jesus, what was happening? Lola couldn't handle Mallory's mood with all the somersaults her thoughts were doing about Harry and Melissa at the other end of the table. Her imagination was running wild now—she'd already written their love story. They were beautiful people, lovers reunited who had realized, just tonight, that they never should have been apart. Harry was with the woman who, by his own admission, he wasn't quite over, and Melissa . . . well, Lola knew exactly what she wanted.

Lola was already pining for Harry, mourning her loss.

She should never have let her infatuation take root and sink deep into her. She should have kept her distance instead of allowing the last couple of weeks to set up shop in her heart and happily wing visions of blissful futures to her brain. Now, the evening of a lifetime was ruined by her own wants and insecurities, and worse, the inevitable end of her fantasy.

She was startled by the faint sound of her phone buzzing and dug it out of her purse. It was a text from Kennedy: *Call me.* Thank God.

"Excuse me," she said as people devoured their dessert. "I have to take this." She walked outside onto the deck, into quiet, away from the laughing voices, and called her sister.

"Lola! You are never going to believe it," Kennedy squealed when she answered.

"What?"

"I got a paid internship! It's only part-time, but it's going to pay me something, and it's with this really prestigious doctor," she bubbled. "Do you know what this means?"

"No."

"*Everything!*" Kennedy shouted, and launched into a long and winding tale of how she'd landed the post, talking without a breath. As Lola listened to her over-the-moon sister, she heard people coming out behind her and walked down some steps to the dock for privacy. But once on the dock, she made the mistake of looking back, and as Kennedy nattered on, Lola's heart dropped. Harry and Melissa were standing at the railing, side by side, talking in low voices as they gazed out at the lake. Harry didn't see Lola. How could he? He was looking at Melissa with an expression of longing, of regret . . . and desire. As if Melissa were diamonds and whipped cream and sex all in one frothy confection.

It sucked. It *sucked.*

"Why aren't you more excited?" Kennedy demanded.

"I am excited, Kennedy. I'm just having a weird night."

"How come?"

"I don't know. I'm at this party, and I guess I just miss home." Lola turned away from Harry. She did miss home just then. She missed her quiet life, where her emotions were kept at bay. She missed checking on Mr. Bagatti, picking up nieces and nephews, and joining her siblings on Sundays at Ben's apartment. She missed it terribly just then.

"Then come home, Lola. You can write here, too, you know," Kennedy said. "You can stay with me."

Lola smiled. "You live in a room, Kennedy. One room. I'm not staying with you because I'd probably have to kill you."

Kennedy laughed. "If I didn't kill you first. Well okay, if you won't come home, you're going to have to gut out your homesickness. But you can do it. If anyone can, you can."

"Right," Lola agreed. She was always gutting things out, wasn't she? "Thanks, kid. I'm really proud of you, but I need to go," she said.

They said their good-byes and ended the call. Lola made herself look up; Harry and Melissa weren't at the railing anymore, but as Lola started back up the steps, a pair of shapely legs moved into view.

Lola glanced up into Melissa's smiling face. "Hi, Lola," she said.

"Ah . . . hi." Well, this was a pickle. Melissa was blocking her way—there was no stepping around her. Lola would have to address her.

Melissa was holding a drink, and absently combing her silky, long dark hair back with her fingers. "Is there another level down there?" she asked, looking past Lola.

"Just the dock."

Melissa nodded. "Nice evening, isn't it?"

"Very."

Melissa breathed in deeply. "This is weird, isn't it? Meeting each other again?" She bounced back a step so that Lola could step up onto the deck.

"Yeah. Weird," Lola agreed.

Melissa's smile was warm, and even a twinge sympathetic. "So you came with Harry," she said.

Lola stared at her, uncertain how to answer.

"He told me," she said. "What are the odds, do you think?" she asked curiously. "That I would meet this really cool chick at a party, and say too much about my ex, and then run into her again as my ex's date. I'm not sure Harry believed me," she said with a rueful smile. "It's bizarre."

"It's bizarre all right," Lola said. It was more than bizarre. She felt as if something in her had shattered, and she was scrambling to pick up the pieces.

"Look, Lola . . . I'm going to cut through the tension here."

"Tension? I don't—"

"This has been a shock," Melissa said, cutting Lola off before she could deny any tension. "I didn't know Harry had moved on," she said, pressing a hand to her chest. "I had no inkling he was seeing anyone, although I probably should have guessed that a guy like him would be snatched up."

"I didn't snatch him," Lola said.

"I obviously didn't know he was at Lake Haven," she continued. "I was just as shocked as you probably are."

Ah, but she did know. Hadn't Harry's sister said she told her where he was? "We're not really seeing each other," Lola said, in all honesty. "We're roommates." But that didn't sound entirely accurate, either. What the hell were they? They'd had fabulous sex, had enjoyed each other's company. Didn't that mean there was *something* between them? Something deeper, something more meaningful than sharing a pan of mac and cheese and fooling around? Or was she really such an idiot?

"You don't have to try to make me feel better," Melissa said. "Believe me, I know what a big mistake I made."

What was Lola supposed to say? Yes, you did? Your loss is my gain? But Lola didn't say that. This situation was obviously different than what had happened with her and Will, but nevertheless, Lola knew what it was like to be the one on the outside. She knew how Melissa must be feeling right now, how crushing it was to see someone you love with another woman. So she said, "Harry and I are just friends," and the moment the words left her mouth, Lola felt a strange twist in her belly.

Melissa frowned. "Really?"

Stand up for yourself! Tell her how you really feel! But Lola couldn't do it. She kept thinking of the way Harry had looked at Melissa, and vice versa. Of all that history between them, and the time and effort they'd put into their relationship—didn't they deserve another shot? Could she really upend it after only a few weeks when there was nothing really spoken between her and Harry? "Really," she said, and the twist in her gut deepened.

Melissa didn't have to look so relieved. "Wow, that's . . . that's really interesting. It's just that, I don't know . . . I've had some regrets, you know?"

Lola nodded. She was best friends with regret, and she was going to be sleeping with a big fat one when this was all said and done.

"I've had some time to think about it, too, and I . . . I don't know, I'd like to try again."

"Yeah . . . I sort of got that," Lola said. She wished Casey was here. Casey would know how to extract herself from the bomb that was detonating around her right now.

"Well," Melissa said, and smiled sadly. "Thanks, Lola. Thanks for understanding. You seem really nice."

Don't be so fucking nice, Lola, she heard Casey whisper in her ear. "Sure," Lola said. Who thanked her ex-boyfriend's date for listening to how brokenhearted she was?

"Want to get a drink?" Melissa asked, as if now they could be besties.

"Ah . . . I'm going to find Mallory," she said.

"Okay. Talk to you later?"

Lola nodded, and Melissa sashayed over to Harry, who was speaking with the Rosenthals. She watched Melissa put her perfectly manicured hand on his arm and lift her chin up to say something. She watched the way Harry looked down at Melissa and gripped his drink.

Lola's heart sank.

She looked back to the lake. Maybe she should be grateful that her questions were answered now—this was casual sex for him, and he still had feelings for Melissa. Instead of sinking into a pit of despair, maybe she could see this and accept it for what it was. They were friends, and a friend would help Harry get what he wanted. After all, isn't that what Lola did best? Make life easier for people around her so they could have what they wanted while she kept searching?

Bitter much?

◆　◆　◆

The night did not improve, because Mallory was terribly drunk. Mia and Everett had left. So had Melissa and Andy. Lola hadn't seen them leave, because she couldn't bear to see Harry say good-bye to Melissa and had stayed outside with Mallory.

But now it was time to get Mallory out of here. Lola made her way to Harry's side and touched his arm. He smiled down at her. "There you are. Are you ready to go?"

"If you are," Lola said. "We might have to carry Mallory."

Harry winced and nodded. He turned back to Mr. Rosenthal. "I guess we're heading out."

"What's this? You're leaving?"

Birta apparently had a pair of elephant ears on her; she'd been at least ten feet away.

"Birta, thank you for a lovely evening," Harry said smoothly. "But Lola and I both have to work tomorrow."

"We hardly had a moment!" Birta said, pouting like a child.

Lola thought she'd had plenty of moments with Harry. She'd monopolized him for half the evening, so that even Melissa couldn't steal him away.

"I wish you'd stay for a nightcap," Birta said.

"Thank you, but no," Harry said.

"When would you like me to start?" Lola asked Birta before she could beg Harry again.

"What? Oh yes. Come Tuesday, darling. I'll be too exhausted to think tomorrow," she said, as if she'd cooked the meal and waited on her guests, instead of hiring others to do that for her.

Lola said she would, then went to find Mallory. She left Birta with her hand on Harry's arm, shifting closer. Jesus, was there a woman in the northeast who didn't want into the man's pants?

In the meantime, a wobbly Mallory had trapped one of the waiters with some tale that involved a lot of hand gestures. "Come on, Mallory, it's time to go," Lola said, and smiled at the waiter. Or rather, his fleeing back. He made a run for it as soon as Lola showed up.

"Lola?" Mallory said, throwing her arm around her shoulders. "I have been *waaaay* overserved."

"That is an understatement," Lola muttered and managed to get Mallory moving in the direction of the door.

Harry joined Lola to help, putting his arm around Mallory's back, propping her up against him and telling her to use her feet.

"Feet," Mallory said, and laughed. "Where are they?"

They managed to navigate the walk to the drive with Mallory between them, then poured her into the backseat of Harry's truck when the valet brought it around. As they started toward Juneberry Road, Mallory had rolled onto her side in the back seat. "I'm the *worst*," she moaned. "I drank *so much*."

"You seemed kind of down tonight," Lola said. "Is something wrong?"

"No!" Mallory moaned. "I'm just a drunk."

"No you're not," Lola said, exasperated.

Harry put his hand on her knee and rubbed it. "Save your breath. You can't argue with anyone that drunk."

He was right—Lola knew that firsthand from her childhood. Best to hide under the bed and wait for it to pass. She sagged into the passenger seat. "I hate to see her like this. Whatever is going on with her, tying one on is not going to help."

Harry looked in the rearview mirror. "Is she alive?"

"For the moment," Lola said. She stared out the window at the road the headlights illuminated. She was dying to ask Harry all the obvious questions—what did Melissa say, did he know she was coming, how did he *feel*—but she forced herself to keep quiet.

"Lola?" he said softly. "I need to talk to you."

This was it. He'd tell her that he and Melissa were talking. The one thing Lola had feared going into this casual relationship was rejection, and she was quick to head it off at the pass. "Please, not here," she said low. It was one thing to hear him say that the love of his life had come back, trotting into a party when he had least expected her. It was another thing entirely for Mallory to hear it, too, no matter how drunk she was.

Harry didn't say anything. Not a single word. He didn't disagree, he didn't agree.

"You don't want to talk about Birta, right?" Mallory blurted from the back seat. "That's why I am so *mad*, Lola! Why Birta? Why not me? Albert is so upset about the candy shop."

Was one crisis not enough for the evening? Did Mallory have to have one, too? "What are you talking about, Mallory?" Lola asked irritably. "Is your dad mad because you didn't open the shop Wednesday?"

"No!" she said, and surged in between the seats, so that her head was between Harry and Lola. "Sort of! No, no, it's more than that. The books are *horrible*," she said with a little hiccupped sob.

"What books?"

"*My* books," Mallory said, and tried to tap herself on the chest, but missed, and fell forward a little more before righting herself.

"Are you talking about your accounting?" Harry asked, sounding confused.

"Yes. *That*."

"That makes no sense," Lola said, annoyed. "Every time I'm there, it's full of people. You have so many customers!"

"You're not understanding," Mallory said gravely, and latched on to Lola's shoulder, gripping it. "The sales *are* good. But I'm going to tell you a secret."

"Please don't," Lola moaned.

"No, wait. It's not a secret," Mallory said, frowning. "It's not a secret because I am thirty years old and I live with my parents, so how can it be a secret?" She whipped her head to Harry. "Did you hear that, Harry? I'm *thirty* and I live with my *parents*."

"That's your big secret?" Lola asked, increasingly annoyed.

"No! The secret is that I can't do anything on my own because I have brain damage," she said, and tapped her head with her fist.

"Mallory, for God's sake," Lola said. "You may forget a few things, but you're really smart and funny—"

"I am severely . . . *severely* dyslexic," she said, grabbing Lola's shoulder again. "Why do you think Albert set me up in a candy shop? I can't keep a job!" she cried with such verve that she toppled into the back seat again. "Albert is going to close the shop down! He doesn't get dyslexia. He thinks it is something I can shake off. Now I don't know what to do—I love the candy shop, and I love all the kids who come in. But I'm really disorganized, and numbers turn upside down. And I am so *mad* that you are going to help Birta," she said, casting her arm presumably in the direction of Birta but hitting the window with her hand. "And not *me*."

"Jesus," Harry muttered.

"Mallory, I'll help you," Lola said. "Of course I'll help you."

"I don't want you to help me!" Mallory shouted. "I can't pay you!"

"Who said anything about money? I'll help you because you are my friend."

"No you won't," Mallory said, and dissolved into a fit of hiccups and tears as she sank onto her side across the back seat.

"How much did she *drink*?" Harry asked softly.

"Buckets?" Lola whispered back.

By the time they reached the lake house, Mallory had drifted off into la-la land, and it took Lola and Harry's combined strength to maneuver her out of the car and into the house. At the door, Harry grew impatient with Mallory's wobbly legs. He scooped her up in his arms. "Where do I put her?"

"My bed," Lola said, and hurried behind him as he carried a giggling Mallory down the hall into the master suite. He deposited her on the bed, on top of the dresses she'd brought from New York, and shook his head. "She's going to regret this in the morning if she remembers."

They left Mallory on the bed and walked out into the living area, the two of them standing awkwardly at the end of the kitchen bar. Harry seemed to be thinking. Probably how to deliver the bad news.

"Well . . . thanks again," Lola said, folding her arms across her. "For going with me tonight. And for helping me with Mallory."

"I'm glad I was there. I don't think you could have managed her on your own."

Lola nodded. "You keep helping me, Harry. But you don't have to, you know. Seriously, I think I can handle it from here."

Harry gave her a look of bafflement. "Handle what?"

The way he had looked at Melissa kept flashing in her mind's eye; she felt a burn in her belly and glanced down, unwilling to look at him just now.

"Lola?" He touched her face.

Lola held her breath. Maybe now he would say it had been great, but . . . *Melissa*. She almost wanted him to say those things so they could stop pretending that there was really something between them and go back to being temporary roommates.

"We should talk about Lissa."

And now her heart was falling, sinking. She drew a deep breath.

"I know tonight was something of a surprise," he said. "I know that must have come as a big shock to you."

"To me? What about you?"

Harry combed his hair back with his fingers and looked away for a moment. "It was a shock to me, too," he said.

"How do you feel about it?" she asked, and dug her fingernails into her palm as she waited for his answer.

"I honestly don't know," he said. "I thought—"

"She's a great girl, Harry," Lola blurted. "I can see why you love her."

Harry looked at her strangely.

"You should totally get back together. I mean, it's obvious that you still have feelings."

"It is?"

"And Melissa, too," she said, as she mentally tried to wrap steel bands around her fragile heart. She'd lost her footing somewhere tonight, and she had to find it again. She had set herself up for heartbreak and if there was one thing Lola knew how to do, it was to retreat from that. "I mean, I know she does. She told me at the Cantrells' party."

"She did?"

"She was talking about her ex, but yeah . . ." Lola shrugged. She glanced over her shoulder toward her bedroom. "I better keep an eye on Mallory."

"How do *you* feel about it, Lola?" Harry asked, touching her face again.

He looked a little bewildered. But Harry understood the rules of friends with benefits and he knew that emotions weren't supposed to get in the way. "Me?" Lola forced a smile. "Great! It's great! What . . . are you worried about *us*?" She smiled and flicked her wrist dismissively. "Don't be! Everything is cool. This wasn't going to last much longer anyway, right?"

"Come on, you don't mean that," he said, and tried to draw her into his arms, but Lola resisted.

"I *totally* mean it," she said. "You didn't think that I . . . that I was *falling* for you, did you? I've really enjoyed it, and maybe in another place and time, sure. But I never thought this was anything more than friends with benefits. Honestly, once I've finished my book, I'm out of here."

"But I—"

"I'd love to chat about it, but I better make sure Mallory is still breathing."

Harry's hands slid away from her. He clenched his jaw and stared at her, looking slightly annoyed. "Okay," he said, nodding. "Okay. I've got to get out of here early tomorrow. I'll see you tomorrow night?" He sounded uncertain.

"Ah . . . sure," Lola said, sounding just as uncertain.

Lola left him standing there and walked—fled—to her room, where Mallory was snoring like a pack of dogs. Why couldn't she have met him a long time ago? Before Will, before Melissa? Why did it seem she was always one beat behind?

Twenty-two

Harry couldn't sleep. He tossed around, periodically punching his pillow into a shape that never felt right.

At four in the morning, he couldn't take it any longer and sat up, rubbing his face. Too many conflicting thoughts were skating around in his head, crashing into each other. Not the least of which had to do with the extraordinary meeting of the legendary Everett Alden last night. Not only had Harry met him, he'd had dinner with him, laughed with him, talked music and life with him. On any given day, he would have been ecstatic about that, calling up friends to tell them about it.

Unfortunately, that once-in-a-lifetime meeting had been completely overshadowed by the surprise appearance of Melissa.

And on the heels of that, the disappearance of Lola.

She hadn't physically disappeared, but she may as well have. She'd withdrawn from him, clearly avoiding him after Melissa had arrived. It frustrated Harry that he couldn't read Lola. Frankly, that came as no great shock to Harry—he'd always sucked when it came to understanding women. But he'd wanted to address Melissa's surprise appearance with her, and unfortunately, Mallory had chosen this night to drink herself into oblivion. By the time they had wrangled her inside and into bed, Lola was distant and even a little short with Harry. Nothing overt, but noticeable to him.

And then there was Melissa. *Melissa.*

Harry got up and went into the office to work.

He opened his computer, stared at some figures, but what he was seeing was Melissa walking through that door. His heart had hitched a little when he'd seen her. She'd looked fantastic, and he was reminded of the first time he'd met her, likewise at a party, and he'd been bowled over by her beauty.

"How did you know I was here?" he'd asked her when they'd had a moment to talk.

"I didn't know you'd be *here*, obviously. I'm here because I'm taking over Birta's publicity tour."

He frowned with suspicion. "Seems a little too convenient."

"All right, Hazel told me you were in East Beach, and Andy told me who was on the guest list. Please don't judge me, Harry. Is it a crime that I wanted to see you? I wouldn't have come tonight at all if I'd known you'd already moved on."

Had he moved on? The only thing Harry knew was that he'd always been so certain about Melissa . . . but he was terribly uncertain about her now.

Melissa had sensed his reluctance, his distance, and had touched his hand. "I've wanted to call you. I've been thinking a lot about us lately, and I wish . . . I wish we could give it another go, Harry."

"Melissa—"

"If you don't want to, I totally understand. But I really want to try again. I was so wrong about so many things," she said, clasping her hands at her breast. "I want to prove to you that I am more understanding now and I want to help you realize your dreams. I should have been more supportive, I know I should have. I really miss us. Don't you?"

No, he didn't. He hadn't missed Melissa in a few weeks and frankly, he hadn't thought of her at all in the last two weeks. He stood there, gazing at the woman he thought would be his wife, wondering if he'd really moved on so quickly? Had he been so wrong about his feelings for her?

"You don't have to give me an answer right now, obviously," Melissa said. "But I'm asking you to think about it." She lifted her gaze and locked it on his. "Just *think* about it. I love you, Harry."

But Harry didn't love Melissa anymore . . . at least he didn't think he did. After years of doggedly pursuing his company, and failing thus far, all it took was one small plea from Melissa for him to question everything he wanted from life. He realized he'd had some questions he'd been ignoring. Those questions really had nothing to do with Melissa—and they had everything to do with Lola. She was the fresh air in his life.

Jesus. Somehow, some way, his world had been uprooted by a pair of women who were nothing alike.

Harry looked at his ledger again. He was leaking money, and dangerously close to being out completely. It occurred to him that he'd once been so certain of everything in his life—his woman, his business. Now, he was uncertain about everything. If he'd been so wrong about Melissa, maybe he'd been wrong about bridge construction, too.

◆　◆　◆

Harry was in a black mood when he left for work before dawn. He walked quietly down the hall to the kitchen. The lights were out, but he could see Lola's figure on the couch. She didn't rouse in the least as he went into the kitchen and gathered a few things. He made coffee, picked up his things, and tiptoed out.

When Harry arrived home from work that night, Lola wasn't there. She'd left him a covered dish in the fridge. It was labeled *King Ranch Chicken. Help yourself.* It was not the funny little note she typically left.

While Harry was wondering about Lola, Melissa was texting him. *Thinking of you!* she texted, along with a picture of her in one of his old T-shirts. And then, *Remember the time we did this?* and attached a picture of them at a ballgame.

Harry didn't respond to her texts. He felt manipulated by them. Melissa had asked him to think about reconciliation and he didn't think it was fair that she was trying to influence his thinking. Not that it mattered—he had no idea what he was thinking.

Half the week went by before Harry actually saw Lola, mainly because he was racing against the clock to finish his job and staunch the flow of money. That, and he didn't know if he could be in the same house with Lola while Melissa was texting him notes and selfies while out with their mutual friends.

Ah, but Harry missed his roommate. He missed the smell of something delicious wafting through the house when he came home from work. He missed the banter, he missed her charming, dimpled smile, he missed her crazy little notes. By Thursday, Harry had finished his job, had lost money on it, and had nothing lined up.

He was as dejected as he'd ever been when he returned to the lake house.

He perked up when he saw Lola bobbing around in the pool on the big yellow rubber ducky.

"Hey, you," she said when he walked out onto the terrace.

"Long time no see." He squatted next to the pool. "If I didn't know better, I'd think you'd been avoiding me."

"Really? I was thinking the same thing about you."

She sounded like her old self, which was encouraging. "So where have you been?" he asked.

"Everywhere. For your information, I have gone from having no jobs to having two jobs. Well, except for today. Today I went into the city to pick up my nephews from summer day care and ride home with them, and I just got back. Ty was in a bind."

Seemed a long way to go to pick up two kids from summer day care. Harry dipped his hand into the warm pool water. "Mind if I join you?"

He detected a slight hesitation, but Lola smiled brightly. "Sure!"

Harry returned a few minutes later in swim trunks and eased into the water. He swam across the pool and latched onto Lola's ducky. She looked happy and pretty. Those sparkling blue eyes always got to him. "So you've got two jobs, huh?" he asked.

"I do. I've been seeing Birta for a couple of hours every day, and then I go to Mallory's shop for a few more hours. She wasn't kidding about dyslexia," Lola said. "It's really bad. Or, she skipped math altogether. I'm no mathematician, but I can at least add. Mallory? Not so much," she said with a shake of her hand. She took a tumbler from the cup holder and drank through a straw.

"If you're spending time with Birta and Mallory, when do you have time to write your book?" he asked curiously.

"Well," she said, wincing slightly, "I hit a bit of a snag. I'm mulling over Sherri's fate. I can't decide if I want her to get away with it or get caught. Guess what? Birta looked at my pages."

"And?"

"And she liked it! She said they showed real promise. And then, of course, she wanted to know what Hunky Harry thought of them." Lola playfully splashed him. "Harry Westbrook, the object of every woman's desire."

He smiled wryly. "Not every woman."

"Who doesn't drool when you walk by?" she asked cheerfully, and held up a hand. "Birta," she said, folding a finger. "Mallory, Melissa—"

"You don't."

"Me?" She splashed him again. "You've clearly forgotten our arrangement."

"I haven't forgotten a moment of it," he said. "But it seems you have. You've been a little distant this week, Lola."

To her credit, Lola didn't deny it. She sighed and said, "I guess I have."

Her honesty was both surprising and slightly alarming. "Mind if I ask why?"

"Really?" she said, splashing him playfully again. "Maybe because your ex came waltzing back into your life. Don't you get it? I'm trying to give you space to reconnect, Harry," she said grandly, and swept her arm across the surface of the pool.

"Who said I'm reconnecting with my ex?"

"Aren't you?"

"No."

She gave him a skeptical look.

Harry groaned and dragged his hand over his hair. "I'm not."

"Then you're an idiot."

"Thanks. Listen, Lola, I—"

"Don't you dare say it, Harry," she said quickly. "I knew what I was getting in to."

"Say what?"

"We hooked up, that's all," she said flatly.

He did not care for the way that sounded. So . . . impersonal. So mechanical. So meaningless. "Is that really what we were doing? Is that really the way you feel about it?"

"Yes. Absolutely," she said, nodding adamantly. "You and I sat on the terrace right there and you said it, no strings attached."

"Yeah, I did," he admitted. "But I really like you, Lola. A lot."

"Great. Thank you," she said pertly.

"Hey," he said, his voice full of warning.

Lola sighed. She pinched her nose between her fingers, as if staving off a headache. "Here's the thing, Harry. I really like you, too." She dropped her hand. "But if Will had ever once said he wanted me back, I would have been ecstatic. No matter what had happened between us, all the hurts, all the betrayals . . . if he'd wanted me back, I would have gone back to him. So I get it. I understand. There is something about that big love you can never let go."

"You're kidding," Harry said. "After what he did to you?"

"Well, of course, that all changed after the puppy. But Melissa didn't bring you a puppy. She brought you herself. And I saw how you looked at her."

Harry started to shake his head, but Lola kicked away from him. "I don't hold it against you at all, you know. But you don't need the complication of me in making that decision."

"You're not complicating my decision," he argued. "I don't want to go backward, Lola. I would like to see where we go," he said, gesturing between them. "But I want to know what you want."

"I want friends with benefits," she said. "That's all I ever wanted."

He didn't believe her. He could see it in her eyes even now—she was lying, and he didn't understand why. "Why are you saying that? Why can't you admit to your feelings?" he asked softly.

"Why can't you?" she returned. "You can't tell me that a part of you doesn't want to be back with Melissa, in New York, with your friends and the life you built there."

Harry was momentarily stymied by the tiny kernel of truth in that. It wasn't that he wanted Melissa—he didn't. What he wanted was the life. He wanted the picture Lola had just painted. "We could have that life, too, you know."

Lola laughed. "Are you serious? You don't know me, Harry. You think you do, but you don't."

But wasn't that the point of being with someone? To know them?

Lola misunderstood his hesitation. "You'll thank me for it someday. Oh, I almost forgot," she said as the ducky twirled in circles. "Mallory is hosting a barbecue so you can meet Albert Cantrell."

Harry smiled a little lopsidedly. "Thanks, but I think we already tried that."

"No, this is for real. It's part of the deal I made with her. I told her I would help her with the candy shop, but she had to make that meeting between you and her dad happen."

There was something all wrong with this little chat they were having. Lola was being too understanding, too giving. "You did that for me?"

"I owed you. But don't thank me yet," she said lightly. "It's possible that he won't like you at all, you know. You don't have the same effect on men as you do on women, I've noticed. You're too good-looking for guys, I suspect."

"Oh yeah?"

"Definitely. You've got that *Men's Health* thing going. You look like a cover model trying to pretend he's a big bad bridge guy instead of a gym rat. Oh, and Birta is coming. She's been asking about you all week. I thought I should toss her a bone and invite her, too, while I was at it. You're welcome."

"*Thanks,*" Harry said, and splashed her. "I appreciate the barbecue, more than you know," he said. It could possibly be his last-ditch effort to make this company work. "Points off for Birta and the entourage, however."

She giggled. "It was the least I could do. You helped me so many times, and I am returning the favor. And in spite of Birta's social skills, she did give me some great feedback on my book."

"That's great, Lola," Harry said sincerely. He hoped she went far with her wild book.

"Who would have thought that we both might get what we came for in this little town?" Lola asked.

Harry sort of nodded, but he wasn't thinking of bridges. He was thinking of life, and the choices one had to make from time to time. Of the people who swam in and out of his world. Of how things that once seemed so certain were suddenly uncertain, and how relationships formed and then unformed. The why and how of it, what it all meant in the long run. How decisions he made now would determine the course of his life. And how heavy it had felt these last few days. For the first time in his life, he was feeling the weight of real dilemmas.

"What?" Lola asked.

"Nothing. Thank you for arranging it, Lola. It might be my last gasp."

"You can thank me by cleaning the kitchen. I made beef bourguignon."

Harry began to glide through the water toward her. "I saw that disaster area when I came in. I don't think I have the right boots or gloves to go in."

Lola's eyes sparkled with amusement. "Big baby. What's a few pots and pans?" She kicked hard, showering him with water and at the same time sending her giant rubber duck sailing backward, out of his reach.

Harry wanted nothing worse than to haul her off that duck and kiss the brass right out of her. But Lola had already dumped herself off the ducky and was walking up the steps of the pool, water pouring over every ridiculously sexy curve. She looked back at him. It was a brief look, hardly more than a few seconds, but it seemed to Harry that the light in her eyes had changed. She wasn't as okay about any of this as she'd said. If she couldn't or wouldn't admit it, what was he supposed to do? Pin her down and force her to say it?

Lola grabbed a towel and wrapped it around her body. "Are you coming?"

"Yes," he said. "Be right there."

He turned his back to her and looked at the lake and the golden glitter of the sun on its surface as it sank behind the hills. He was at a loss to what to do with her.

Twenty-three

Birta was in fine form the next morning. She was tense, snapping at Lola at every turn. Her tea was too hot. Her papers were not straight. And as Lola worked to format a blog post Birta had been asked to write about the creative process, Birta was hanging over her shoulder, reaching for the mouse. "No, no, that's not how you do it," she said, and made a few clicks, undoing the work Lola had just done.

"Sorry," Lola muttered.

"For God's sake, stop saying you're sorry," Birta snapped. "You have nothing to be sorry for, do you? It's such a weak, girlish thing to always apologize. I can't abide it."

Lola gaped at her, surprised by the admonishment. "Then I'm sorry for being sorry too much."

Birta glared at her.

The woman had no sense of humor. How could one become a famous author with no sense of humor?

Birta turned away from Lola and locked her hands behind her head.

"Is everything okay?" Lola asked, frowning now.

"What?" Birta dropped her hands and looked blankly at Lola. "Fine. Everything is fine. My last book hasn't performed as well as the publisher hoped, that's all. Naturally, they blame me for trying something new."

"Ah." Lola hadn't enjoyed Birta's latest book as much as she had her previous work. It didn't have the same emotional complexity that Lola admired about her writing.

Birta waved it off with her heavily jeweled fingers. "But I am a writer. An artist! I must explore new landscapes or I will *die*. I can't spoon-feed the masses with genre-driven tropes," she said with disgust.

Personally, Lola would feed the masses whatever they wanted if they would only read her books.

"Never mind this. Cyrus and I mean to discuss it when he arrives this weekend."

Lola stopped what she was doing. "Your agent is coming here? I thought you said he would only go to the Hamptons?"

Birta clucked her tongue at that. "I say many things," she said dismissively, as if it were Lola's fault for having believed her. "He is coming here."

"You should bring him to the barbecue at the Cantrells'," Lola suggested.

"Perhaps I will. And your beau?" she asked, glancing slyly at Lola. "He will, in fact, attend this barbecue?"

Lola didn't have a beau, a fact that made her belly do a funny little flip. "Yes, he'll be there."

"Hmm," Birta said. "Perhaps I will have Cyrus accompany me. Now, I must go and write. "And please," she said, as she swanned out of the dining room where Lola was working, "I must once again remind you to have a care how you close the door. I was quite startled by the slam of it yesterday."

Lola had not slammed the door shut yesterday; she had carefully drawn it closed. "Sorry," she said, and smiled inwardly as Birta glowered at her apology.

She left soon after that, headed for Mallory's candy shop. Her new morning routine was to ride her bike into East Beach and meet Mallory for coffee. From there, Lola borrowed Mallory's car and headed to Birta's. After two hours there, she would return to East Beach and tackle Mallory's accounts.

The beauty of it was that Mallory's accounts were in such a mess that Lola could hardly think about anything else. She didn't have to think about Harry, or the things he'd said to her. She didn't have to think about how she was doing him a favor by letting him go. She didn't have to think about how her heart ached every time she saw him. She could only think about numbers.

Speaking of numbers, it was almost as if Mallory had worked at making them a mess. When Lola tried to explain to Mallory what was wrong, Mallory would throw up her hands two seconds in and say, "I can't deal with this. I'm dyslexic!"

It was clear to Lola that Mallory relied on that disability to excuse her from learning.

Nevertheless, Mallory was great in the store. She'd created a wonderful little shop, including a play area for children complete with games and books and a crafting table. The candy bins were built so that they lit up when the lids were opened. Children loved it, and Mallory loved children. Lola hoped she'd be able to convince Mallory to hire an office manager when she'd finished setting up the software system Mallory's father had purchased for her, because this store was perfect for Mallory. But she couldn't continue on like she had.

Lola was working on Mallory's books when Casey called. "You should be in the city today," she chirped when Lola answered. "The weather is *gorg*. I'm at Bryant Park for lunch and honestly, I am thinking of ditching the afternoon and staying right here. Maybe read a book. What are you doing?"

"Helping a friend," Lola said.

"With what?"

"Accounting! How bad is it when I am better at accounting than the friend?" Lola said, and explained to Casey what had happened with Birta and Mallory, and how she had come to be helping them both.

"For free," Casey said disapprovingly.

"No one is paying me money if that's what you mean," Lola said primly. "But it's all great experience."

"Lola, stop helping people!" Casey exclaimed. "You're doing it again! You're putting everyone else before you. Only this time, it's people you don't know that well! You haven't mentioned your book *once*."

"I don't have to mention it, Casey. We're just talking. It's not like I have to report to you what I'm doing."

"Then how is it coming?" Casey snapped.

Lola was too mad to answer that question. "It's not. Birta said she really liked what I had, but I'm stuck. I can't seem to find words."

"Why not?"

"I don't know . . . too much on my mind," Lola said, and threw down a pencil.

"Oh, Lola," Casey said, her disappointment evident in her voice when Lola remained silent.

"Don't, Casey," Lola said sharply.

"Okay," Casey said. "*Fine*. Ruin this opportunity, what do I care? New subject: What's up with Harry?"

And there was the reason that Lola couldn't find words. "Well, his ex came to East Beach and it looks like they are going to give it the old college try once more."

Casey gasped. "Details!" she demanded.

Lola gave them. She told Casey how she'd met Melissa at a party. And about the look she'd seen on Harry's face, and the longing that had seemed to vibrate around those two. When she had finished telling her sister every last horrible detail, Casey said simply, "But what about you?"

"What about me?"

"Don't you want him?"

Lola snorted. "Of course. But I had what, a month with him? Melissa had a year. Melissa was going to *marry* him."

"Not your problem! You have to fight for him, Lola."

Lola rolled her eyes. "I don't want to fight, Casey. It's not like that."

"What do you mean, it's not like that? Who do you think you're talking to? You *like* him. And you two seemed really good together. Need I remind you that you're not going to get a guy that good-looking to come waltzing into your life every day?"

"Well thanks for that. Need I remind you that this was only a casual sex thing? That *you* advocated?"

"And aren't you glad I did? Anyway, casual sex never stays casual. You have to tell him how you feel, Lola. Let him make the decision!"

"Stop directing me, Casey! You're always doing that. I don't know how I feel. It's not like it was a relationship."

It just felt like one.

"Oh for God's sake. If you have any feelings for him, you better say it before it's too late—"

"There is no *late*," Lola snapped. "It's done! It's over!"

Casey groaned. "Lola. I don't want to see you let something really good pass you by because you're too busy burying your feelings and helping others who are going to take advantage of you in the meantime."

"Okay, all right," Lola said. She was beyond angry now. She wanted to argue that Casey was way off base, but Casey knew Lola better than anyone, and she'd seen through her. Lola was hiding behind a wall of being helpful, of filling her thoughts and her time with someone else's problem instead of facing her own. "I have to go," she said curtly. "I promised Mallory I'd help her."

Casey was silent for a moment, and Lola could almost hear her debating with herself. "Okay," she said, giving in. "When are you coming into the city?"

"Not sure. Maybe next week. I have to go," she said, and said good-bye.

She tossed her phone into her purse and stared at the wall of the tiny office in the back of Mallory's store.

She was fine. She was going to be just fine. She always was. This wasn't the end of the world. Frankly, she'd probably dodged a bullet. How long could it have lasted, anyway? A couple of months?

◆ ◆ ◆

Mallory dropped Lola home after swinging by a fish market in Black Springs so Lola could pick up some lobsters.

"Harry is a lucky guy!" Mallory said.

Yes, he was a lucky guy, and as usual, Lola was the one on the outside of luck.

She'd put on a skirt and a T-shirt, donned her *Last Time I Cooked, Hardly Anyone Got Sick* apron, and made a batch of her famous garlic-cheese mashed potatoes. She was boiling the water for lobster when Harry came in from work, looking more disheveled than usual.

"Hey," he said, smiling fondly as he walked into the kitchen.

"Do you like lobster? They were on sale."

He smiled hopefully. "I *love* lobster," he said, leaning over the bar to look at her preparations. "Are you inviting me?"

"I am."

"That's the best news I've heard all week. Thank you. I'll get cleaned up."

As he started for his room, his phone rang. Harry dug it out of his pocket and looked at it. He shoved it back in his pocket.

That call was from Melissa, Lola was certain. Perhaps more than anything, Lola hated being envious of the beautiful Melissa.

Harry returned as Lola was finishing up the lobsters. They sat at the kitchen bar with the paper lobster bibs Lola had found in the utility room. They talked amicably about the day. Harry had to crawl up on a truss to inspect some bolts, which explained how disheveled he'd looked. He reported he'd heard through the grapevine that the bid specs for the toll road bridges would be out soon. "I hope so, because I don't have anything lined up at the moment," he said. "How is your book coming along?"

"Slow," Lola admitted. "I haven't had much time to work on it."

He looked oddly concerned. "Are you overextended? Because you were so into it."

"I'm still into it. I love writing." Lola truly believed it was her calling. But . . . there was something holding her back. She could feel it growing like a vine in her. At first it had been her disappointment about Harry and Melissa. That had morphed into a bigger thing over the last couple of days. She said she was stuck . . . but the truth was that she was petrified of continuing on. She ran her finger around the rim of her wine glass. "My problem is that I have this unnatural fear of disappointment," she said. "And when Birta said she liked it, that it showed promise, I was over the moon. But then . . . I started to panic."

"Why?"

"It's hard to explain. When I was growing up, I was constantly disappointed. It seemed like every time I got my hopes up that things were going to be different or better, or at least bearable, something would happen to crush those hopes and disappoint me. And now, I think I live in fear of it."

Harry stopped eating. "But you can't live in fear of it. Disappointment is part of life. If you're never disappointed, you can't really understand true happiness."

"Oh I know," she said, nodding. "I get that. And still, I can't help it. I know that I work really hard to avoid chances because I have that fear in me," she said. "This book makes that fear worse. Generally, it's people who disappoint me, but my book is all me. It will be *me* disappointing me." She sighed and shook her head. "That must sound completely whacko to you."

"No," Harry said. "I totally get it."

Lola snorted. "You've probably been disappointed like three times in your life."

"Not true. I've been disappointed many times. My big fear is failure."

"It is?" she asked, surprised by his admission.

"Oh yeah," he said with an adamant nod. "My biggest fear is that I will have given up a really great job to go out on my own, and for whatever reason, I can't make it work. If that happens, I'll have to live with myself somehow. But I know me, and I'd be miserable. So the fear of failing drives me. It makes me work that much harder. It makes me take chances."

Lola smiled. "Are you going to tell me I'm not working hard enough?"

"No, I'm going to point out that you're working so hard at not being disappointed, you're already disappointing yourself. I can see it in your eyes, Lola. I just hope you don't wake up one day wondering if you could have sold that book. Or wondering where all those passed chances might have led you." He took her hand in his, stroked her knuckle with his thumb, and looked directly into her eyes. "I know it's not easy to step out on a limb. But I also know if you really want something, you have to do it. You can't cling to the tree. You can do it—you are braver than anyone I know."

Lola smiled a little. "I'm not brave. I can hardly ride a bike."

"Yeah, you are." He held her hand against his knee. "Look at what you did—you raised your siblings even though you were a kid yourself. You have kept your family together under circumstances so difficult that I can't even fathom what it must have been like. This book is a cakewalk in comparison. You've already lived the hardest part of your life. So don't worry about disappointing yourself. Because you won't."

His silver-green eyes were filled with the warmth and light of the setting sun behind her. How had this perfect man walked into her life? "Wow. You're handsome *and* smart."

He grinned. "Nope. I'm just pretty good at knowing the value of things."

God, she wanted to kiss him right now. She wanted to kiss him and make love to him, and *dammit*, why did Melissa have to come to East Beach and ruin it? She thought of Casey's advice, of telling Harry right now all the mixed-up and utterly undeniable things she was feeling. But Lola couldn't bring herself to do it in that moment. Harry's pep talk aside, it was impossible to slough off years of conditioning. She couldn't face the disappointment of losing him. If not today, then in a month, or even two . . . however long it took him to realize he'd made a mistake.

She took a breath so deep that it lifted her chest, and sighed it out. She squeezed his hand. "You really are a good friend, Harry."

The light in Harry's eyes began to dim. He smiled sadly and let go her hand.

"I guess we're both rounding third base, aren't we?" she asked. "One last pretend date tomorrow night?" she asked, referring to the barbecue.

"Yeah," he said, and pushed a strand of her hair from her face. "One last pretend date."

Twenty-four

Harry was crunching some numbers, trying to figure out how long he had before he pulled the plug on Westbrook Bridge Design and Construction when Melissa called. "Hey, you answered!" she said cheerfully.

"Hi, Lissa," he said, rubbing his eyes.

"Guess what? I'm going to be in East Beach tonight."

He dropped his hand, blinking. "You are?"

"Birta's agent is coming out for a barbecue or something, and she wants me to come and meet him. Apparently she wasn't happy with the work Andy did on the publicity for the new book and wants to talk changes."

"Huh," Harry said.

"This account is a big deal for me, Harry."

"Yeah, that's great," he said absently as he tried to collect himself. So she would be there tonight, at the barbecue that had been arranged for him. Great.

"Will I see you at the barbecue? Birta said you'd be there."

Harry tried to think. He desperately needed time with Albert Cantrell, and he didn't need the complication of Melissa interfering with that plan. Not only that, he was taking Lola. And he didn't want Melissa interfering with that, either. "I guess," he said.

"Wow," she said. "You don't sound very excited."

Maybe because he wasn't. "I wasn't expecting this. Lissa . . . I'm taking Lola to the barbecue."

That was met with dead silence for a moment on the other end. "I guess I see where I stand," Melissa said at last.

"Please don't do that," he said wearily, and leaned back in his chair, scraping his hair back from his face. "You left me, remember? Did you think I'd sit around like a monk?"

"You're right," she said, surprisingly contrite. "I know you're right, Harry, but I'm just *so* hoping you will give me another chance. I have always loved you. *Always*. And I think you've always loved me."

This felt so dense on top of everything else on Harry's mind. He didn't want to have this conversation with Melissa right now. "I'll see you tonight, all right?"

Again, the long silence. "Okay," she said, her voice soft. "Please remember that I love you." She clicked off.

Funny, wasn't it, that a few weeks ago, Harry would have been thrilled to hear her say those words, but today they just muddied the waters that seemed to be creeping up to his neck. There had been a part of him that truly had wanted to go back to the way it was with Melissa. To hot nights and fine dining and life in the city. He'd thought he would marry her, would put down roots and grow a family. When exactly had that changed? When had she stopped feeling like a lifemate and had begun to feel like one more thing he had to handle? More than a couple of months ago, he realized.

Harry didn't have time to think of it now. His fledgling company was in dire straits, and he had to focus on what he'd say to Albert Cantrell tonight.

He managed to block out the world for the afternoon until it was time to shower and dress for the evening.

When he emerged from his room, Lola was waiting, sitting on one of the living room couches, her legs stretched before her and propped on the leather ottoman. "Hi, handsome," she said, and stood up and smoothed out her dress. She was wearing the yellow halter dress he really liked. She turned her back to him, glanced over her shoulder and said, "Will you help me?"

Harry remembered the first time he'd zipped her up in this dress, he'd been afraid to touch her. This time, he zipped her up, then impulsively put his hands on her shoulders, dipped his head, and kissed her neck.

"Hello?" she said, and turned around, eyeing him suspiciously. "What was that for?" she asked as she slipped her feet into sandals.

Harry smiled. "You're not the only one who sometimes suffers from lack of impulse control." He did it because she was beautiful and he missed her. Lola was undeniably sexy, but it was more than that—he was drawn like a moth to light by her spirit. "Ready?" he asked.

"I am ready for some ribs, baby," she said, and with a grin, picked up her purse. "I hope they have bibs."

◆　◆　◆

It was another crowded affair at the Cantrells'. The first person Lola and Harry met inside the residence was Mrs. Cantrell, who saw them from across the room and started forward, her arms outstretched. "And here we have the first Handsome Harry admirer of the night," Lola muttered under her breath.

"Stop," Harry warned her with a squeeze to her hand.

"Harry!" Mrs. Cantrell said, and turned her face, presenting her cheek for his kiss, as if she was his aunt. She smelled of expensive perfume and powder.

"Hello, Mrs. Cantrell."

"Is Mallory here?" Lola asked after greeting Mrs. Cantrell.

"Oh, she's here," Mrs. Cantrell said, sounding perturbed. "She's wearing denim shorts! I swear on my life I think she does it on purpose!"

Lola glanced at Harry and mouthed the words, *me too*.

Mrs. Cantrell gestured toward the French doors. "She's out there somewhere."

They headed outside where dozens of guests were soaking up the late-afternoon sun.

"There she is," Lola said—Mallory's frizzy hair could be seen two decks down. She waved; a moment later, Mallory was threading her way through the top deck to them.

"Hello!" she said grandly. She threw her arms around Harry and kissed his cheek, then did the same to Lola.

"I thought you said just a few people," Lola said, looking around them.

"Albert and Lillian never do anything small," Mallory said cheerfully.

"Is your dad here?" Lola asked.

"Yes!" Mallory lightly punched Harry in the arm. "Dude, you must really like roads, like a *lot*. Lola has been after me to introduce you to the road king for two weeks. So let's go meet him!"

"I'm ready," Harry said. He put his hand on Lola's elbow.

"You don't need me," she said, pulling back.

"Well *I* do," Mallory said, and linked her arm through Lola's, then Harry's. "This way, children," she sang, and led them off the deck and back into the house, down a wide staircase to another level of the house. It was a rec room of sorts, and several men were gathered around a pool table.

They followed Mallory to a pair of leather chairs where a man sat alone, chewing on the end of a cigar. "Albert, meet my friends."

"Huh?" He squinted up at her.

Harry could see who Mallory resembled—Albert Cantrell was a barrel-chested man with a mass of gray hair on top of his head that looked a bit like overgrown turf.

"This is my friend, Harry Westbrook. And my other friend, Lola Dunne."

"Lola Dunne," he said, refusing to take the cigar from his mouth. "You're the one who is doing the work Mallory here is supposed to be doing for herself, is that right?"

"I'm helping her," Lola said.

"Don't start, Albert," Mallory said. "Anyway, I want you to meet Harry because he really likes roads."

"How are you, Mr. Cantrell?" Harry said, and extended his hand. "I'm a bridge builder."

"You don't say," the man said. "Have a seat, Harry." He gestured to the empty leather chair. "You like cigars?"

Harry hated cigars. "Sure," he said.

Mr. Cantrell pointed to a box on the table between the chairs. "They're Cuban—knock your socks off. Butkiss! Fix this man a drink!" he shouted hoarsely at a waiter.

"Stop calling him Butkiss," Mallory complained. "His name is John, I've told you."

"Whatever," Mr. Cantrell said and turned back to Harry. "Bridge builder, huh? What firm?"

"A new one," Harry said. "I have started my own. Westbrook Bridge Design and Construction."

"Just starting out," Mr. Cantrell mused. "That's a big gamble in today's economy. You can't do a half-assed job. That's what I keep telling my girl here. Can't do a half-assed job with your own company if you expect to get anywhere. You know what I'm saying? I built my company from scratch, and look what I've got."

"Okay, if you're going to insult me, Lola and I are leaving," Mallory said, clearly annoyed. She grabbed Lola's hand and dragged her away; Lola shot Harry a look of helplessness over her shoulder.

"See that?" Mr. Cantrell said, pointing his cigar stub at Mallory. "That's the face of a coward running away from me right now. She knows what I'm saying is right." He reinserted the soggy cigar into his mouth. "Not many bridge builders running around Lake Haven."

"True. I've wanted to meet you for a while, Mr. Cantrell. I really admire how you've built your company," Harry said. Because he was nothing if not thorough in his research of Albert Cantrell, he told him what he admired about his company. And then he told him about the vision he had for his own company. He told Mr. Cantrell about the four bridges he'd done now as a subcontractor to Ferrigan Industries, including the supports he'd done for a bridge job he'd just completed near Thorson.

"I saw that bridge," Mr. Cantrell said, nodding. "I told Lillian it would take six months to build that thing."

"It took four," Harry said.

He let the conversation meander around to some of Mr. Cantrell's more memorable projects, until he saw the opening to broach the subject of the toll road job Mr. Cantrell had won.

"Ah, so you want to do my bridges, eh?" Mr. Cantrell said.

"I do, sir."

"Can't do that on my own, you know. I've got people that are in charge of bidding out those things."

"I understand. I'm just asking for a shot."

Mr. Cantrell sighed. "You're new, son. My team isn't going to want to hire an untried company."

Harry's pulse began to tick with anxiety. "I'm not untried. I'm good, Mr. Cantrell. Really good. I need the right opportunity to prove what I can do."

Julia London

Mr. Cantrell shook his head. "Old Bill Nelson hates when I do this, but let me call him." He withdrew his phone from his pocket and punched a button, then held it up to his ear. "Bill. You busy? Oh, your son's birthday," he said, and waggled his brows at Harry. "I got someone I want you to meet. Come down to East Beach Monday so I can introduce you." He pointed at Harry and arched his brows in question. Harry nodded.

"Lunch at the Lakeside Bistro. Yeah, okay, one o'clock. See you then." He chatted for a moment about the birthday, then hung up.

"Mr. Cantrell . . . thank you," Harry said. "I appreciate this more than I can say."

"Don't thank me yet," Mr. Cantrell said. "Bill is a tough son of a bitch. He doesn't like newbies, I'll tell you that, so you best come with your game face."

Harry grinned. "Absolutely. Thank you."

Mr. Cantrell began to talk about fishing, as Harry's mind raced ahead to Monday. He kept his seat, but all he wanted to do was run and find Lola to tell her the news.

Twenty-five

Mallory was hungry for barbecue and led Lola down to the lawn where three men were manning pits under a large white canopy. They helped themselves to ribs and potato salad, then sat at a picnic table under an oak tree, devouring the food.

Lola had finished half her plate when she pushed it away. "I can't eat another bite," she said, and put her hand on her belly. "How did you pull off a barbecue this big? Where did those men come from?"

"Girl, when you have money, anything is doable," Mallory said, and licked her fingers one by one. "I'm going back for seconds."

"I'll get us some drinks," Lola offered.

Lola went off in the opposite direction of Mallory to a bar set up on the dock and took her place in line. She looked around for Harry, and as she searched the crowd, she happened to see Birta. A distinguished-looking gentleman was helping her down the stairs. Lola knew immediately that he was Cyrus Bernstein, famed literary agent, and her heart leapt into her throat. He was actually *here*, so close that she would, in a matter of minutes, be able to reach out and touch him. She was so enthralled by the sighting of Cyrus Bernstein that she didn't even see Melissa for several moments.

Oh, but that was Melissa, all right, turning heads as she walked down the deck steps in heels about ten-feet high. *"Shit,"* Lola whispered to herself. What the hell was she doing here?

Birta, Cyrus, and Melissa made their way onto the dock. Lola didn't want to speak to Birta or Melissa, but she was not going to miss the opportunity to meet Mr. Bernstein. She awkwardly stepped into the trio's path. "Hi!"

"Oh!" Birta put a hand to her chest. "Good Lord, Lola, you scared me. You shouldn't sneak up on people."

"I'm sorry, I—"

"What have I told you about *sorry*?" Birta said. "Darling," she said to her agent, "this is Lola. My assistant."

Mr. Bernstein had shining blue eyes, and the skin around them crinkled with his smile. "Your assistant is in New York, Birta. I know her, remember? She's my daughter."

"And a wonderful assistant she is. This is my East Beach assistant," Birta purred. "She's very good at taking out the trash and what not. She's also an aspiring writer."

"Is she?" Mr. Bernstein said, and looked at Lola with renewed interest.

"It's such a pleasure to meet you, Mr. Bernstein," she said. She spared Melissa a quick glance. "Hello again," she said.

"Hello," Melissa said, and her gaze moved over Lola, assessing her.

"What do you write, Lola?" Mr. Bernstein asked, peering at her through stylish lenses.

Birta laughed. "It will be a delight to hear her articulate it," she said gaily.

"Is that the bar?" Mr. Bernstein asked, now looking past Lola.

She hadn't had a chance to tell him yet! "Can I get you a drink?" she offered.

"*May* you get him a drink," Birta corrected her.

"I'll get it," Mr. Bernstein said amicably, and moved to step around her.

"My book is a tale of revenge," Lola blurted, hopping to stay beside him.

"Everyone likes a good revenge book," he said absently, but he was moving quickly, homed in on the bar.

Lola suffered a brief moment of crisis. Was it rude to persist? Or should she let the man get a drink? She realized she was letting the moment slip through her fingers, so she stepped around several people to keep up with Mr. Bernstein as he made his way to the bar. "It's about a psychopathic girl who can't stand it when men dump her. So she kills them."

"Hope that's not autobiographical," he said with a chuckle.

"Not yet," Lola said.

"What?" he said, startled. And then he laughed. "It sounds unusual. Excuse me!" he called to the bartender.

"But it's not all dark," Lola said desperately. "There is some humor in it. I know that sounds strange, but it works."

"Excuse me!" he said again, holding up his hand.

Lola glanced around, saw Nolan behind the bar. *"Nolan!"* she cried, perhaps too sharply, but this was an emergency. She waved at him. *"Nolan!"*

"Do I need to call a paramedic?" Nolan asked as he slid down the bar. He looked at Cyrus Bernstein. "What happened to the hunky hardhat?"

"The what?" Mr. Bernstein asked.

"He's here somewhere," Lola said quickly. "But this is Cyrus Bernstein! He is one of the top literary agents in New York, and he needs a drink."

"Actually, I need three," Cyrus said, and gave Nolan his order. When Nolan went off to make the drinks, Mr. Bernstein smiled at Lola. "Thank you! Birta drove us, and she is a *terrible* driver. I've needed to drink for an hour. And there she is in Germany, not a stone's throw from the autobahn. All right, this book with the psychopathic boyfriend killer—do I have that right?"

"Yes!"

"I read some of your pages this afternoon. You're right, the humor works."

Now Lola's heart stopped beating altogether. "You . . . you read some pages?"

"I did. I saw them lying on Birta's desk and picked them up. I read the part where Sherri is in Home Depot and can't decide between the chain saw or the machete, and she is price-checking them, then arguing with the cashier about whether or not one of them is on sale."

"That's it," Lola said uncertainly.

"Hilarious!" he said, grinning. "I love a good sense of humor. Do you have a full manuscript?"

Was she breathing? Lola couldn't tell if she was breathing. "Not yet. But I'm very close."

"Here you go, doll," Nolan said, setting three drinks before Mr. Bernstein.

"Thanks," said Mr. Bernstein. He reached into his pocket and pulled out a business card, which he handed to Lola. "When you finish the book, send it to me. Remind me that we met at East Beach, and I'll give it a look."

"I can't . . . I am speechless," Lola said as he picked up his drinks. "Thank you so much!"

"No promises, you understand, but one never knows." He smiled and turned around, carrying the drinks back to Birta and Melissa.

Lola's heart was beating so hard now she could hardly make out his card. She couldn't believe it! She had Cyrus Bernstein's card and an invitation to send him the manuscript. This was actually *happening* to her!

"Are you going to drink something or just block the bar all night?" Nolan asked.

"Champagne!" she shouted at him. "Three of them!"

Nolan shook his head, but moved to get the champagne. Lola stared at the card in her hand and began to worry she would lose it. Where was Harry with his pockets? She slipped the card into her barely-there bra and adjusted her dress with one hand just as Nolan returned with the champagne.

"Keep your hands out of your dress, love," he said. "That's what your luscious boyfriend is for."

"Speaking of which," she said gaily, and picked up her champagnes—one for her, one for Mallory, and one for Harry. She couldn't wait to tell him that she'd done it, she'd actually done it—she hadn't let fear keep her from pursuing the opportunity.

She turned around and almost bumped into Mallory.

"Where'd you go?" she asked, taking one of the champagnes from her hand. "I waited so long I ended up eating the rest of yours."

Lola laughed. She laughed too loudly, and too gaily, but she didn't care. "I met Cyrus Bernstein," she said. "He wants me to send my book when I finish."

Mallory's jaw dropped. "That's fantastic!"

"I *know*! I did it, Mallory! I can't believe it—none of this would have happened if I hadn't come to stay in Zach Miller's house!"

"We have to tell Harry," Mallory said.

"I have a glass for him, too," she said, and looked past Mallory, her face nearly breaking open with her smile.

She spotted Harry at once. He was taller than most, and there he was, standing with Melissa, Birta, and Cyrus, while Lola held a flute of champagne for him. She watched Cyrus gesture toward the barbecue tent. Harry glanced around, as if looking for her, but when he didn't see her, he turned back to the group. Melissa reached for his arm for an assist in navigating the next few steps down onto the lawn, with Birta and Cyrus following behind.

"Isn't that Harry?" Mallory asked, following her gaze. "Let's catch up!"

"Ah . . ." Lola's heart was fluttering crazily, on the verge of complete destruction with all the stress of Harry, the excitement about her book. "Let me just . . . this glass feels warm. I'm going to get Nolan to refill it."

"I'll save us a seat," Mallory chirped and went off in the direction Harry and the others had gone.

Lola turned back to the bar, set both glasses down, and braced her hands against it, sucking in her breath. *Okay, get a grip.* She wasn't going to let disappointment win this time. No matter what else, she had Cyrus Bernstein's card. *She had his card.*

Lola snapped out of it. She lifted her head . . . and looked directly into the gaze of the man standing next to her.

"Hello," he said.

"Hi."

He looked to be about forty, with a pronounced paunch and thinning hair. He was leaning on one arm against the bar and nibbling from a little plastic skewer of olives. "Dobbs Harvey," he said.

"Lola." She smiled absently and picked up the champagnes, prepared to make a quick getaway.

"I heard you talking to your friend," he said, and ate another olive. "I could have sworn I heard you say you are staying at Zach Miller's lake house."

No. *Nonono.* This was the last thing she needed tonight. "Do you know him?" she asked, trying to sound casual and unconcerned, even though she was suddenly feeling a little ill.

"Yeah. Zach and I go way back," he said, and ate the last olive on his skewer.

Crap.

"I didn't know he had anyone staying at the house."

"Just temporarily," Lola said. *Everything is fine.* It was amazing how quickly she slipped back into the twelve-year-old girl, smiling and happy so that the social worker wouldn't dig too deep.

"I thought it was off-limits to him and his wife until the divorce is final. Didn't they file an injunction or something?"

She was going to die right here with Cyrus Bernstein's card in her bra. "That's right, they did," she said. "But it's been dragging on for a while, and he . . . well, everyone knows Zach is a generous man," she said, borrowing a line from Mallory.

"He's definitely that," Dobbs agreed. "That's a nice place," he added. "They used to have some wild parties up there. Not as fancy as this," he said, gesturing toward the Cantrell house with his olive skewer. "But boy, they were wild, if you know what I mean." He grinned.

Lola laughed nervously. "I know what you mean." Someone touched her arm and Lola started so badly she spilled some of her drink. She twisted around to find Harry staring at her strangely. "Are you okay?"

"There you are!" she said, her voice sounding breathy with nerves. She glanced back at Dobbs Harvey. "Nice to meet you," she said, and backed into Harry, managing to step on his foot.

"Ouch," he said.

"Yeah, nice meeting you," Dobbs Harvey said distractedly . . . he was looking at Harry. He had a funny expression on his face, too, as if he recognized Harry. "When you see Zach, tell him I said hello, and to get his ass out here so we can play some golf."

"I sure will," Lola said cheerfully and turned away from the bar. "Run," she said low. "At least walk fast."

"Who was he?" Harry asked.

"I don't know!" she said frantically, and shoved one of the glasses into his chest. "But whoever he is, he knows Zach, and he knows that no one is supposed to be at the house."

Harry looked back toward the bar.

"Don't look at him!" Lola cried in a whisper.

"Take a breath," Harry said, caressing her back. "What did you say?"

"The party line." She groaned. "This is a disaster."

"I doubt that," Harry said. He sipped his champagne as he thought about it. "Look, it's going to be okay. Zach won't be out this summer, and that dude is not going to run into him and tell him about you. And even if he does, you'll be long gone by then. Zach's got a new girlfriend. He's not hanging out with the boys, trust me."

"God, I hope you're right," Lola moaned.

"Don't worry," he said, and put his arm around her shoulders. "We're fine." He tapped his glass against hers. "I have some good news. Mr. Cantrell set up a meeting with the guy who is putting out the bridge bids for the toll road project."

Lola momentarily forgot Dobbs Harvey and gasped with delight. "No way!"

"Yep," he said, grinning. "Called him while I was sitting there. I have a good feeling about this Lola, I really do."

"That's amazing," she said. "Guess what? An amazing thing happened to me, too. I met Cyrus Bernstein. He read some of my pages and he wants me to send him the book when I'm finished."

Harry's eyes widened. "Lola . . . that's *fantastic*."

"I know, right?" she said, and impulsively threw one arm around his neck. "How the hell did we manage to pull this off?"

"I have no fucking clue," Harry said laughingly, and kissed her.

It was a celebratory kiss, a New Year's Eve kind of kiss, but it stoked a flame in Lola immediately. All the mixed-up emotions she'd been feeling about Harry began to bubble up, quickly frothing to a head. She and Harry both swayed back from one another; he looked as surprised as she felt.

"Damn it," Lola whispered. The joy began to leak out of her. Here it came, the nauseating swell of disappointment, riding high on the agony of wanting to celebrate this moment with her casual sex partner.

Harry must have been feeling something similar, because they stood there, looking at each other. Harry's gaze moved over her face, his expression pained. For a slender moment, it felt as if there was no one else but her and Harry on that dock, no movement but the longing that was pulling at them. Lola couldn't look into his green eyes without feeling the longing curl around her heart and squeeze.

She was the first to look away. "I should find Mallory."

"Please don't run away from me, Lola."

She wasn't running. *She wasn't running.* She glanced at him from the corner of her eye and smiled. "I'm really happy for you, Harry."

He touched the earring dangling from her ear. "I'm really happy for you, too." But he didn't look happy; he looked sad.

So many thoughts crowded into Lola's head, so many things she wanted to say. *Come on Harry, let's get out of here! Let's go celebrate!* "Hey, what would you say if . . ." A familiar laugh managed to catch her attention. Lola paused and looked to the left. Melissa was coming up behind Harry.

"What would I say to what?"

"Melissa is here," she said.

"I know."

"I mean *here,*" she said as Melissa reached them.

Melissa touched Harry's arm and gave him a dazzling smile. "Hey, you," she said, and then to Lola, "Hi! Wow, another amazing dress, Lola. You look great."

"Thank you," Lola said. But she was looking at Harry.

"So," Melissa asked, leaning into Harry's side. "What's up?"

"I was just telling Lola that I had a great conversation with Albert Cantrell. He was awarded a huge toll road project and will be bidding out the bridges."

"Harry!" Melissa said, turning her full attention to him. "That's wonderful! All your hard work is finally paying off—I am so *proud* of you," Melissa said, and cupped his face. "You're *amazing*."

Jesus, the woman was beautiful and glowing and she loved Harry, and Harry would be a fool not to see it. Lola took a step backward. "I'm going to find Mallory."

Harry reached for her, trying to catch her hand, but Lola shifted slightly so that he couldn't. "Fill her in, Harry!" Lola said gaily. "She's dying to know." With a little wave of her fingers, she turned around and walked away.

If she had paused to look back, she would have seen Harry standing there, watching her go. She would have seen the look of longing on his face, too, and how he didn't seem to see Melissa at all.

But Lola didn't look back.

Twenty-six

Harry was more than ready to go—his mind was racing around all he wanted to do to prepare for the Monday meeting. He wanted to find Lola and get the hell out of there, but instead, he found himself trapped at a picnic table with Birta, Cyrus Bernstein, and Melissa, who had begged him, "*Please* don't leave me alone with Birta. She's so *intense*."

The crowd had seemed to swell, and now there were too many people at the barbecue. Harry could hardly hear the conversation at the table, which was fine with him. He was looking for a flash of yellow dress, listening for that sunny laugh. He wanted to talk with Lola about his meeting with Albert Cantrell, to hear everything Bernstein had said to her. But Lola had disappeared.

He began to wonder if she'd left the party altogether.

Melissa pressed into his side, propped her hand on her chin, and smiled up at him. "What's on your mind, babe? You're kind of quiet tonight."

"I'm just thinking about all I need to do for this meeting Monday."

"Harry!" she said and laughed. "That's so you, thinking about work at a party. What I want to know is, when are you going to think about *us?*" She trailed her fingers up his arm, smiling into his eyes.

There had been a time Harry had not been able to keep his hands from her. He'd been a different man then—a confident, self-assured man who had arranged all his chess pieces. He was a humbler man now who was trying to keep his chess pieces from falling off the board. "There is no *us*, Lissa. All those issues that kept us apart are still there—that hasn't changed."

Melissa blinked. "No, they're not. It was all me, babe. I know what I did, I know how I behaved. I'm so ashamed of it now, but you have to believe me—I've changed. I'm so proud of you and what you've accomplished. You know what? We should have a drink to celebrate. Where did your date get off to, anyway?" she asked, and sat up and looked around.

"Who?" Birta asked, noticing Melissa.

"Your assistant," Melissa said.

"I don't know how you've missed her. She's there," Birta said, and nodded to a point behind Melissa and Harry. "Heavens, will you *look*," she said disapprovingly.

Melissa looked in the direction Birta had indicated. "Oh," she said.

Harry couldn't see around Melissa, so he stood. There was a commotion across the lawn where three people were happily following a fourth, who was teaching them what looked like some sort of hip-hop dance. Those people included Mallory and Lola. Harry moved a step or two away from the picnic table to have a better view, and he smiled as he watched them. God, they were awful. But they were laughing, holding onto each other, and dissolving into fits of laughter when Lola accidentally kicked Mallory.

"Oh, wow . . . she's making a spectacle of herself," Melissa said.

Lola and Mallory grabbed each other's arms and pulled themselves out of the dancing queue. That was when Mallory happened to see Harry and waved. Harry waved back.

"Didn't I tell you?" Birta said. "You ought to read the book. What an unmitigated disaster! The structure is all wrong and the prose is so overwrought. I was absolutely *shocked* when Cyrus said it wasn't bad. I had to point out to him just how bad it was."

"Harry, can you give me a hand?"

Harry glanced back; Cyrus had returned to the table juggling drinks in his hands. Harry took some from Cyrus's hands and set them down on the picnic table before the ladies.

"What did you point out to me?" Cyrus asked.

"My assistant's book!" Birta said. "It was *awful*. Just a train wreck."

Cyrus shrugged. "It could use some work, as all books can. Still, I liked the premise."

Birta laughed incredulously. "You like a book about a psychopath who murders the men who reject her? And with all that alleged humor so tragically woven in?" she added, fluttering her fingers.

"I said it could use some work," Cyrus repeated. "But I see promise."

"I think it would be a publicity nightmare," Melissa offered. "How would you promote a book like that?"

"Oh!" Birta said suddenly, and reached across the table to grab Melissa's hand. "Remember the passage I read you where she changes her clothes at least three times, uncertain what to wear when she stabs her boyfriend, and she's thinking all those ridiculous things—"

"Like if blood would be better disguised by the dark red mini, or the long black halter?" Melissa eagerly added.

"And then she fusses with the shoes!" Birta crowed, and she and Melissa laughed.

Harry stared in disbelief at the two women. They had amused themselves with Lola's book? It soured him. They might not like the book, but at least Lola had tried. She damn sure didn't deserve their ridicule. "I don't find anything funny about a person striving toward her goal. I thought the book was clever," Harry said.

"But the dialogue, Harry! It was the *worst*," said Birta. "So stilted!"

"I'm sorry you didn't like it."

Birta blanched at the sound of Lola's voice; they all jerked around, none of them having noticed that she'd walked up to the picnic table.

Lola looked stunned. And *pissed*.

"I think it has promise, Lola," Cyrus said. "My offer still stands."

Lola flashed a thin smile at him. "Thank you. I can never express how much I appreciate it. I hope that doesn't sound stilted," she said, and shifted her attention to Birta. "Please. Go on," she said. "I don't want to interrupt your discussion of my horrible writing. Which would be the same writing you praised to my face, by the way."

Birta groaned. She stretched her arm out across the picnic table, as if reaching for Lola. "All right, darling, I did tell you I liked it. But I was trying to be encouraging."

Lola was shaking. One hand fisted at her side, and Harry had the impression she was working to keep from punching Birta in the mouth. "It was truly a pleasure getting to meet one of my favorite authors," she said. "But now I really wish I hadn't. I liked the idea of you better than the real you." She whirled around and strode away.

Melissa snorted and said, "Well *that* was awkward."

Harry glowered at Birta, not bothering to conceal his contempt. "What gives you the right to destroy someone's dream?"

Birta rolled her eyes. "Someone has to be honest with her, Harry. *You* were the one who wanted me to look at her book. *You* were the one who opened her up to criticism."

"There is a difference between constructive criticism and being a bitch," Harry said.

Birta gasped with anger and surged to her feet, bracing her hands against the picnic table as she leaned across it. "Don't you *dare* speak to me like that," she hissed.

"I'll do you one better," he said angrily. "I'll never speak to you again." He put his glass down onto the table and went after Lola. He hadn't gotten very far, however, before Melissa caught him, latching on to his arm. Harry tried to shake her off. "Not now, Lissa."

"Don't leave—"

"You were horrible back there," he snapped, jerking his arm from her hand. "You have a mean streak when you've had a couple of drinks, you know that?"

"I'm sorry!" she said, casting her arms wide. "I know I was horrible, but I can't help it, Harry. I'm just so *envious* of her." She pressed her fingertips to either side of her head and squeezed her eyes shut for a moment. "I feel like I'm competing for you, and I've never . . ." She sighed and dropped her hands. "I don't want to like her. I want to hate her, because she has you."

"She doesn't have me," Harry said impatiently. She wouldn't have him—she'd made that clear all week.

"Yes she does," Melissa said morosely. "You may not know it, but she does."

Harry scanned the upper deck. He couldn't see Lola any longer.

"Please, Harry," Melissa said, grabbing his hand. "I'm so sorry. I'm just going crazy with wanting you and needing you. I don't know how to get you back." She moved closer, slid one hand up his chest, around to the nape of his neck. "I would give anything if I could just go back and do it over, you know?"

"Okay," he said, and moved to take her hand from his neck, but before he could do it, she kissed him.

"Just give me another chance," she murmured.

Her kiss was as unsettling as the churning in his gut. There were many things he wanted to say to Melissa. But not here, not now. His only concern was finding Lola, and he pushed Melissa back. "I'll call you," he said, and walked away from her.

Twenty-seven

Lola wasn't hurt—she was *furious*.

She was furious with Birta for being such a raging bitch, and furious with herself for having allowed that to happen. She had to take ownership in it—she had pushed down her instincts about Birta so that she could "apprentice" in the hopes of some of the magic rubbing off on her.

Lola knew better than that. She knew that the only way anyone ever got ahead in this world was to work hard and pull themselves up, one rung at a time. Writers didn't sell books on the basis of who they knew—they sold them on the basis of a really good story.

She'd fled the party after that major disappointment—fortunately leaving before the magic hour when all the cabs disappeared—and had come home, flung off her dress and heels, yanked down her hair, and pulled on one of Harry's hoodies that just barely covered her ass. It was the closest thing at hand.

She was in the kitchen angrily making the dough for a batch of cookies when she heard Harry's truck in the drive. "Oh, hey," she said as he walked into the kitchen. As if nothing had happened. As if he'd just strolled in from work and she'd just written a dozen chapters.

He approached the kitchen cautiously, as well he should have, because Lola was certain she looked like a mad scientist. She was a mad woman, which was equally dangerous. "Lola? Are you okay?"

"Who, me?" Lola asked. "Sure! You mean that business at the Cantrells'?" She waved her hand at him. "No big deal. I figured out last week that Birta is an asshole."

He walked around the kitchen island.

"I'm okay!" she said, and moved just out of his reach. "Listen, not everyone is going to like my book. Can't please all the people all the time, you know," she chirped. "I'm making cookies. I need something really super sweet. When I'm really pissed off, I like to stuff my face." She pointed the spatula at him. "It's true. I'm not afraid to eat my emotions."

Harry reached for her again, and Lola threw up a hand. She was suddenly trembling; she could hardly hold on to the mixing bowl. "Don't touch me," she said, her voice rough. "Because if you touch me, I might disintegrate. I can't take your touch without all this *yearning*," she said, making a fist against her chest. "So please don't touch me, Harry, because I can't take it," she said, her voice shaking now.

Harry grabbed her then, pulling the bowl from her hand and putting it aside as he wrapped her in his embrace. He kissed her as if she were water and he a drowning man. His hands slid down her body, to her hips, holding her tightly to him. He felt so right, so hard and strong and virile against her, and Lola lost all control. All the feelings for him she'd tamped down suddenly exploded in her, and she was burning out of control, a five-alarm fire that nothing could douse.

He kissed her with as much fire as she kissed him, their tongues tangling, his hand cupping her face, stroking her hair. He spun her around, began marching her backward to the couch as she frantically undid the buttons of his shirt. They were wild for each other, their hands roaming, their bodies pressed hard to each other. He toppled her over the back of the couch, and they landed on the soft cushions, her knee between his legs, pushing against his hardness. He pressed his lips against her cheek, her eyes, and her mouth again . . . and then he paused.

"What? What is the hold up?" she asked impatiently, and pulled his head down to hers, dipping her tongue into his mouth. She was a fat little pig, spinning and roasting and basking in the flames of overwhelming desire for this man.

Harry moved, pulling Lola on top of him, casing her head with his hands so that he could kiss her deeply, then sliding his hands down, slipping under the sweatshirt, up her ribcage to her breasts. Her skin was blazing where he touched her. Lola wanted him inside her, but Harry wasn't moving fast enough. He kept looking at her. "What are you doing?" she asked frantically.

"*Looking* at you," he said, just as frantically.

"*Why?* We're kind of in the middle of something here."

He smiled. "You know why, you little lunatic. Because I want you. I want you so goddamn bad."

His admission, completely in lockstep with her own violent desire, turned Lola into a ravenous beast. She tried to continue their frantic lovemaking, but Harry paused again.

"*What?*" she asked impatiently.

"Look at me, Lola," he commanded. "I mean it. *Look* at me."

She could hardly catch her breath, but Harry had her pinned to the couch. So Lola looked at him. She looked directly into his eyes, and when she did, her heart began to jackhammer—she could see the raw want in his eyes. He truly *wanted* her, which made her yearning for him swell to the point of suffocating her. She lifted up on her elbows and kissed him, slowly and reverently, letting her emotions flow from her. She held nothing back. *Nothing.*

His clothing came off, and she was now wearing only a tiny bit of lace thong, which Harry promptly removed from her body. He twisted again, putting her on her back on that couch and moving on top of her.

Something had shifted in Lola: she could feel it, could feel the newness, the freshness of this thing between them emerging stronger and more beautiful than before.

She was impatient. She took him in hand and began to move, gazing up at him with fierce determination. He slid into her and Lola closed her eyes, sighing with relief. She felt herself fraying at the edges; the thread had been pulled, and she was rapidly untangling from all the confusion and old habits and fears of rejection.

Harry moved steadily, watching her, really seeing her, and Lola wasn't afraid of it. She began to move with him, urging him along, her hands tangling in his hair, her mouth dragging across his cheek, to his mouth. And then she was clutching him, her breath rising. He was hard and hot and he dug his fingers into her hips, lifting her up, pushing deeper until she cried out with release. He fell over the edge with her, gasping as the waves of fulfillment spilled over them.

Harry collapsed on top of her, breathing as hard as if he'd run up Juneberry Road.

Lola lazily twined her fingers in his hair. She didn't want it to be over. She traced a line down his spine, filled her hand with his bare hip. She kissed his cheek, then his neck. Harry tried to move himself off her chest, but apparently misjudged his place on the couch. The two of them tumbled off, landing on the rug. After a stunned moment, they both burst into laughter. Lola sat up, bracing her arms against his chest. "Hey," she said, pushing her hair from her face. "Which do you prefer? Cookies? Or skinny dipping?"

Harry caressed her arm as he smiled up at her. "Can I have both?"

"You can have anything you want," she said, and winked as she hopped up and walked into the kitchen to resume her baking.

In the nude.

◆ ◆ ◆

Sunday was possibly the most delightful day Lola had ever spent in her entire life.

She and Harry woke late, having spent half the night in the pool and in bed. They had a leisurely breakfast of pancakes, then sipped coffee as they dangled their legs in the pool, talking about everything and nothing.

Lola didn't ask Harry his plans, and he didn't ask her hers. They didn't talk about the night before. They didn't try to plot the future, they didn't try to dissect the last few weeks. They just existed together in that space of complete and utter compatibility and contentment.

Later, they munched Lola's batch of angry cookies while she worked on her book—Birta had ignited her determination—and Harry ran some numbers he wanted to think about before his meeting. Their phones rang with calls and beeped with text messages, but neither of them answered or looked at their screens. It quickly became clear to Lola that she was not the only one avoiding the outside world. It became so apparent, in fact, that she began to giggle every time one of their phones sounded.

In the afternoon they played a game of saying what they intended to do with the millions they hoped to make on books and bridges. Harry said he would buy a boat, maybe build a lake house in East Beach. Lola said she would put her mother in a better place and then open a bookstore. Harry said he would build a better place for her mother . . . maybe in Florida. Lola laughed and said that when her book was turned into a movie, she would thank him at the Oscars.

It was a whimsical day. They were like two little kids in a field of sunflowers.

Lola eventually returned to her work . . . or tried to. Harry kept distracting her. He put his hands on her shoulder and leaned over. "Who are you killing?" he asked.

"That's an interesting question," she said in all seriousness. "My girl met a pig on Match.com who dissed her. But when she goes to do the deed, he's gone, and she finds his mother in his apartment." She smiled devilishly. "His mother looks a lot like Birta Hoffman."

Harry laughed. And then he reached over her, closed her laptop, and put his hands on her breasts.

"You're going to keep me from being a literary success," she warned him as he nuzzled her neck.

"I'm hoping you can be a literary success tomorrow," he said, and pulled her to her feet, dancing her to a bedroom.

Yes, it was a wonderful, stupendous, beautiful, perfect summer day. Lola didn't allow herself to think about tomorrow, because for the space of one Sunday, she was going to pretend that this was forever.

But eventually, the spell had to break, and Harry was the one to do it. It began when Lola saw him looking at his phone, then responding to a text. She tried not to think about it. That could have been a text from anyone.

It could have been . . . but it wasn't.

Lola closed her laptop and busied herself making mushroom risotto.

When dinner was ready, they decided to eat outside.

"You're spoiling me rotten, Lola," Harry said. "It's delicious. I've probably gained ten pounds since I met you."

She looked at him. "I actually like to spoil you."

Harry looked up from his plate, surprised. "You do? Do you have anything else up your sleeve?"

She smiled. "Nope. I think you've seen it all."

Harry put his fork down. "Have I?"

The tone of his voice had changed. Lola immediately put her fork down, too, and bent her leg, propping her foot on the edge of her seat and wrapping her arms around her knee. Shielding herself. "Yep."

"There is nothing you want to say? Maybe discuss?"

Only everything. But as Lola was struggling to find the words and make herself walk out on the limb, she saw a range of emotions scud across Harry's face—sadness and hope. Weariness.

He reached for her hand. "You know, six months ago, I would have said that I knew exactly what I was doing. I would have said that I was completely certain about the woman in my life, about my career direction, about my decision to sell my apartment. Those were all pieces of the map I had drawn in my head of where I wanted to be and where I wanted to go. But things change, Lola. They changed when I met you."

She smiled dubiously. "You tried to kick me out when you met me."

Harry impatiently squeezed her hand. "You know what I mean. Everything changed—my feelings for Lissa. My confidence in my company. My entire direction in life became a big question mark. But I can look back on that now and see that it was a metamorphosis I needed. I was so sure of myself that I hadn't bothered to even *look* at myself. I have now, and I know what I want. I want this," he said, holding up their hands. "I want us. And I would really like to know what you want."

Lola didn't need a metamorphosis to know that she was falling in love with him. She wanted, more than anything, to *be* with him. She could hear Casey's voice: *Just say it, chickenshit.*

"Lola? What do you want?"

"I want . . . you to be happy," she said. "Whatever that means." She smiled. *Nothing is wrong, everything is fine! Take all the time you need to walk all over this.*

Harry stared at her. "What the hell does that mean?"

"It means that I want you to be sure of everything. I don't want you to wake up one day and wish you were with Melissa."

His face darkened and he dropped her hand. "Will you please stop thinking about Melissa? She's not your friend, she's not your concern."

"You were with her a long time—"

"I know how long I was with her!" he exploded, coming up out of his seat. "I want to know what *you want*," he said again.

Lola shrunk back in her chair. She was suddenly reminded of a school counselor she'd been forced to see when a teacher noted how disheveled she looked at school. The counselor had tried to pry information out of a ten-year-old Lola. She'd grown frustrated with Lola's evasive answers, then had said, *"Let me ask this another way. If you could have anything you wanted, what would it be?"*

"A house," Lola had said instantly. *"With a swing set. And maybe a bike we could share."*

The counselor had said, *"Well, that's not going to happen, sweetie, obviously. I can't get you a house or a swing set."*

"Lola?"

"I told you," she said.

He sighed. He looked down at the table, and locked his hands, ran them over his head. He gazed at her plaintively and said, "I don't know what has happened in your life that you can't express what you're feeling. But I'm sorry for you. I am so very sorry." He picked up the plates and went inside.

Their perfect Sunday came to a crashing end.

◆ ◆ ◆

Lola fretted half the night, tossing and turning in her bed, reliving that moment on the terrace. She was a coward and a fool. She had let her fears and insecurities loom over her like a beast, menacing everything she did. She couldn't live like this, she realized, like a scared little bird, always hopping back into her nest so that nothing could get her. That was the thing—there really was no danger except for the fear she'd allowed to live in her all these years.

She heard Harry in the kitchen at half past seven and got up. It took her a moment to find something to wear, and when she padded into the kitchen, she heard him on the phone.

"I'll see you around four, okay?" He was talking low, as if he was trying not to wake her. "Listen, I have to run. I'll explain when I see you—" There was an abrupt pause, and then he said, "Can it wait? Thanks. See you then." He clicked off.

Lola's heart began to beat wildly with panic. She knew without a doubt he was speaking to Melissa. She put her back to the wall, shoving her hands into her hair and squeezing against her head. What was she supposed to do? Had he given up on her so soon?

"Oh, you're up."

She jumped at the sound of his voice and whirled around. "I'm up."

Harry smiled fondly. He slipped his arm around her waist and shook his head. "What a mess," he said, and kissed her forehead. He let go of her and walked to the end of the kitchen counter where he began to stuff things into his pockets. "Okay, I'm out of here. I'm going to grab a coffee and do a little more work before my meeting."

"Sure, okay," she said. She was hugging herself, trying not to implode.

Harry smiled, but it was strangely distant. He'd given up. He began to walk for the door at the same moment her phone began to ring. "Harry?"

He turned back. "Yes?"

Lola's pulse began to pound in her ears. Her palms were damp—it was just like the night she met Birta and couldn't find her tongue. "Ah . . . I wanted to say something."

He looked suddenly hopeful and took a step toward her. "Okay," he said.

Lola's tongue felt thick. She swallowed. Her phone stopped ringing, then instantly started ringing again. She was distracted by it—she looked at the counter where it was buzzing.

"Don't answer it," he said.

The phone stopped ringing again. A moment later, it was buzzing with a text.

"What were you going to say, Lola?" he asked.

She opened her mouth. *I love you. I am falling in love, I love you, I don't know what I am, I just want to be with you. I'm telling you now before you go to Melissa. I'm standing up for me, I'm saying what I have to say, I am speaking my truth. I am not afraid.*

But her phone—the texts were coming one after another and she was suddenly filled with apprehension. She picked it up.

Mom seriously ill. Rushed to hospital. Come now.

"Oh my God," she said.

"What is it?"

"My mom," she said, and held up the phone so he could see the message.

Harry looked at the phone, then at her.

"I have to go," she said.

"Yes, of course. I'll give you a lift to the train station."

"No, no, you go on. I'll call Mallory. She'll get me there."

"Are you sure?" he asked uncertainly.

"I'm sure," she said. "She'll be happy to do it. Go, Harry. Don't worry about this. I'll, ah . . . I'll call you later." She turned back for her bedroom, but remembered something and whirled back around. "Good luck."

Harry hadn't moved. "Thanks," he said softly.

He remained standing there as Lola turned around and hurried to her room.

◆　◆　◆

Mallory was not happy with taking Lola to the train station. She insisted on letting her driver take her all the way to Long Island. "Seriously. It will give him something to do," she said. "Take all the time you need."

When Lola arrived at the hospital, her siblings were all gathered outside the same intensive care room. One of her mother's lungs had collapsed.

"We need to battle an infection that's cropped up, but I think she'll pull through," the doctor had said. "We're going to have to keep her a couple of nights."

"What are we going to do?" Kennedy asked. "I'm starting my new internship today. I have to show up."

Her four siblings looked at Lola. "Right," she said, sighing. "Let me run home and pick up a few things. I'll be back this afternoon to stay with her. Can anyone stay until I get back?"

"I will," said Casey gravely, raising her hand as if volunteering for a combat role.

Lola headed back to Lake Haven. When Mallory's driver turned into her drive, Lola asked, "Would you mind . . . I need to grab some stuff, but I'd really appreciate a ride to the Black Springs train station."

"Of course," he said. "I'll wait here."

She hopped out and hurried inside to collect her things.

She was in the laundry room, looking through a stack of clean clothing, when she heard voices on the drive. The front door squeaked open. *Harry.* God, she was glad he was here. She combed her fingers through her hair and stepped out of the laundry room with a smile.

But the man standing in the living room was not Harry. He started when he saw her, put his hands on his hips, and said, "Who the fuck are you?"

"Who are *you*?" she demanded. Her first ridiculous thought was that Zach Miller had forgotten about Harry and had loaned this house to some other dude.

"I'm Zach Miller," the man said. "I own this house. And you, whoever you are, are trespassing."

Twenty-eight

The meeting with Albert Cantrell and his construction manager had gone extremely well. Harry had hit it off with Bill Nelson, thank God—they were two men cut from the same cloth. Bill even seemed a little impressed with the work Harry had done to build his company thus far, proclaiming it smart. "Don't have a bridge guy lined up," Bill had said. "Let me see your response to the bid specs, and maybe we can work something out."

Harry left the Lakeside Bistro with more clarity and optimism than he'd felt in weeks. It was entirely possible that all his hard work was about to pay off.

Yep, Harry was certain again. He knew exactly what he wanted—at least what steps he wanted to take—and it included more than his own bridge design and construction company.

From East Beach, he drove to New York, parked at his parents' place, then Ubered downtown to meet Melissa.

She bounced out of her building with her tote bag slung over her shoulder, all smiles. God, but she was attractive. Men were noticing her as she jogged across the street in her heels to him. When she reached him, she put her arms around his neck and kissed his cheek like an old friend. "I'm so happy to see you!"

"Let's get a drink," he suggested.

"Sure!" She slipped her hand into his and chatted about work as they walked down the street to a bar he'd scoped out before. He liked it—it was quiet in here and he could say what he wanted to say without shouting.

Melissa settled on a bar stool and crossed her legs. She was facing him, her smile irrepressible. "I was so glad to hear from you, you have no idea. I thought you were really mad at me," she said, and then laughed as if that were impossible. Harry used to find that charming about her, the way she could deflect things that bothered him.

"I'm not mad," he said truthfully.

"Well you should be," she said with a laugh. "That was a *horrible* night. I had too much to drink, and you're right, I'm always awful when I drink. I'm going to quit," she said, and then, without any apparent sense of irony, said to the bartender, "A vodka martini, please."

Harry held up two fingers.

Melissa glanced sidelong at him. "Your dad has totally corrupted me with the martinis. Remember that Easter with the horrible snow? I think your dad went through three bottles of vodka that day." She giggled at the memory. Maybe she'd forgotten how frantic she'd been that they would be stuck with his drunk parents all day. She'd begged him to go outside to try to hail a cab in the middle of a blizzard.

Harry put his hand on her knee. "Lissa."

Her smile instantly faded. "Harry—"

"You have to accept the fact that this isn't going to work, you and me."

"Yes, it is," she said, and grabbed his hand in both of hers. "Of course it is. We can fix this."

Harry shook his head. "It's too late."

"Why?" she demanded. "Three months ago I was the love of your life! My God, Harry, we were just on a break! How can you not forgive me?"

"Forgive you?" He shook his head—she really didn't understand. "I forgive you Lissa, I forgave you a long time ago. This was never about that. You're right—three months ago I did believe you were the love of my life. And during this break, if that's what you want to call it, I realized . . . I didn't really love you like I thought I did."

Her mouth fell open with shock. And then her face turned ugly with rage. "How can you be so cruel?"

"I don't mean to be cruel, baby," he said, and cupped her chin. "I mean to be honest. It's hard to say this to you, because I do care about you, very much. But I have to be honest about my feelings. You were right—we have always wanted different things—"

"Don't give me that crap," she snapped, and pushed his hand away. "Why did you let me fawn over you for two weeks if you don't *love* me?"

"I told you we were over," he said, surprised. Did she really think he was lying about it?

She shoved his leg. "Is this because of your precious little Bambi?"

Harry's pulse jumped a notch. "No," he said coolly. "It has nothing to do with her. You and I are not a good match, Lissa. And I think you know it, too. In fact, even now, I'm not sure what it is you want. You couldn't wait to take your break. You couldn't wait to walk out of my life."

If looks could kill, Harry would be lying in a pool of blood right now. The bartender chose that inopportune moment to deliver the martinis. Melissa slowly stood up, took her drink in hand, and threw it at Harry. "Bastard," she said acidly. "You just want me to grovel."

"I don't want that," he said as he calmly wiped martini from his face.

"Fuck you," she said, and stormed out of the bar, slamming into a poor man who happened to have crossed her path.

The bartender silently handed Harry a towel.

Harry cleaned himself up as best he could, paid for the drinks, and left his untouched. He headed uptown to his parents' apartment.

His mother was in the kitchen when he let himself in. "Harry?" she asked, poking her head out the door. "What are you doing here?"

"Hi, Mom. I'm going to crash here, if you don't mind."

"Of course!" She came out of the kitchen and moved to kiss him, but wrinkled her nose. "Have you been drinking?"

"No," he said. "I had a run-in with a drink, though. I'm going to grab a shower, okay?"

Harry went through the motions of showering and dressing, but he felt like he was moving through a fog. He felt bad for Melissa, but it was a distant sort of sadness one feels for a friend. There was someone else on his mind. But if Lola couldn't express her feelings for him, then he would move on from there, too. He loved her—without a doubt, he loved her. But he didn't need a woman just to have one. What he wanted, more than anything, was for Lola to finally put herself first. That was the only way she would ever be able to be part of a healthy relationship. And if she couldn't do that, he wasn't going to stay. He wanted a partner, not a helpmate.

He desperately wanted to believe that she'd been on the verge of saying it this morning. But that family of hers kept the tether tight.

When he got out of the shower, he called Lola, but there was no answer. He didn't leave a message other than to ask her to call him, and tell her that he'd be staying overnight in the city.

Harry walked into the living room. His dad had come home, and as always, was happy to see his son. "How long are we going to have your company?"

"Just tonight," Harry said. "I'm headed back to East Beach tomorrow."

"Harry, come back to the city," his mother said with a playful pout. "We miss you terribly."

"I'm not that far away," Harry reminded her.

"You might as well be in Uganda as far as I am concerned. It's a horrible traffic jam out of the city."

Dosia stepped into the living room. "You eat dinner, Mr. Harry?"

"Of course," he said, and hugged her. "I wouldn't miss your cooking."

"No cooking. Take out," she said, and winked at him.

"So have you got any jobs lined up?" his dad asked.

"Not yet," Harry said. "But I've got a promising lead. If I get this bid, I really have a shot."

"Let's not speak of this bridge business tonight," his mother said wearily. "I just cringe at how much of your life you've wasted pursuing this notion. To think you had such a wonderful job. I wonder if Michaelson's will even take you back."

There was something strikingly familiar about his mother. It took him a moment, but Harry suddenly realized—she was as nasty to him as Birta had been to Lola.

"Did you see the Mets game?" his dad asked, cheerfully changing the subject as he'd trained himself to do all these years. When Mom started harping, Dad changed the subject.

They talked baseball for a while as father and sons will do when everything else requires too much emotion. His mother suffered in silence, her arms folded tightly across her body. But she couldn't stay silent for long. At dinner, she made the mistake of bringing up Melissa.

"Hazel said that you ran into Melissa recently," she said. "I hope you've realized your mistake there."

Harry's temples began to throb.

"She's perfect for you, Harry. Such a lovely young woman with a great job, a great future. Think how beautiful my grandchildren would be." She flashed a cool smile.

"Melissa and I are through, Mom," Harry said evenly. "We're never getting back together. I need you to accept it."

His mother didn't accept it. She put her fork down and glared at him. "I don't know where we went wrong, I honestly don't," she said. "You've had every advantage—great schools, great opportunities. You had a fabulous woman who would have been a devoted wife. You had a fantastic job that would have made you partner. And now, you're living in someone else's house, throwing your life away. And for what? For a couple of bridges?"

"Beth?" his father said, his voice light.

"*What?*"

"Shut up."

His mother shrieked, and Harry's gaze flew to his father. He had never heard him speak like that to his mother, not once.

But Dad was on a roll. "This fine young man," he said, pointing at Harry, "has set his sights on a goal. He has *goals*, Beth. He has dreams, and by God, he is pursuing them. I'll be damned if I am going to listen to you run him down for it one more *second*."

Harry's mother stared at her husband in shock. "How *dare* you, Jack!"

"No, Beth, how dare *you*. How can you not be bursting with pride? He is the man I wish I had the guts to be! For God's sake, let him live his life! Let him be his own man! Stop . . . *mothering* him to death!"

His mother's face crumbled. She grasped the table, and for a moment, Harry thought she might faint. He came partially out of his chair, but his mother abruptly pushed herself up out of her own chair, and with an acid glare at her husband, she stormed out of the room. They heard her sob just before they heard the slam of her bedroom door.

Harry turned a wide-eyed gaze to his dad.

His father shrugged. "She had it coming," he said, unapologetically. "Listen, Harry, don't do what I did. Don't marry for the sake of marrying. Don't take a job for the sake of the money. Keep doing what you're doing, son. I'm proud of you. Now, I better go and make sure she doesn't fling herself out the window." He stood up and paused next to Harry, put his hand on his shoulder and squeezed affectionately.

Harry stared down at his plate, amazed by what had just happened. "Mr. Harry? I make you a drink?" Dosia said from somewhere in the kitchen.

"A double, please," he said. "And make yourself one, Dosia. I'll join you in the kitchen."

◆ ◆ ◆

Harry tried to say good-bye to his mother the next morning, but she would not come out of her room. "She'll be fine," Dosia said. "Go now, Mr. Harry. Call her this week."

He attempted to get Lola on the phone again on the drive to East Beach, but again, she didn't answer. That was odd—he could understand that she hadn't answered yesterday. She'd probably been in Long Island all day. Had something happened? He hoped her mother was all right.

He was ruminating when he coasted down the drive of the lake house, and curious when he saw a Mercedes in the drive. Probably Mallory or one of her friends. At least it meant that Lola was here.

He parked, grabbed his bag, and walked into the lake house, expecting to find women on the terrace or in the pool. The door was not locked; he pushed it open, dropped his bag, and said, "Lola?"

"Where the fuck have you been?"

Zach's voice startled Harry; he gasped at the sight of his friend sitting on the couch, his arms spread out across the back of it. *Shit.* "Zach," he said.

"Yeah, *Zach.* Your friend, remember? The dude who lent you this awesome house when he shouldn't have? And you repay me by bringing some chick in here with you?"

Harry's heart suddenly began to race. "Where is she?"

"Fuck if I know. Why didn't you tell me about her?" Zach demanded, gaining his feet. "You just abuse my hospitality like that?"

"Where is she, Zach?" Harry said again. His heart was pounding in his chest now. "What did you say to her?"

"What did I *say*? I told her to get the hell out of my house."

Harry looked wildly about. Lola was gone? The kitchen was a mess, as usual. He stalked to the master bedroom and looked inside. The bed was unmade, and there were towels piled on the chair. But her clothes were picked up off the floor. He whirled around and stalked back to the living room. Her computer was gone, too.

Zach stood there with his legs braced apart and his arms folded over his chest.

"How did she leave? Did someone pick her up?"

Zach gaped at him. "Do I get *any* explanation for how you shit all over me? I don't know how she left, man! I kicked her out and I didn't take notes."

Harry couldn't say what came over him. Maybe it was because he'd realized that what he wanted from this life, above all else, was Lola Dunne. Whatever it was, he was moving before he realized it, flying over the back of the couch, grabbing for Zach.

"Get off me!" Zach shouted when Harry grabbed his lapels. "I had to hear about this from fucking Dobbs Harvey, Harry! He's on Sara's side, you dipshit! You've made a huge mess here. *Huge!*"

"Then talk to Sara!" Harry shouted, shoving Zach backward. "She gave this house to Lola. Not me."

"Yeah, well, looks like you've cozied up with Sara's side, too."

Harry rolled his eyes and pushed past Zach. He walked back to his room and began to stuff his belongings into a duffel, his papers and computer into a briefcase.

Zach followed him. "What are you doing?" he asked. "Come on, man, you don't have to go. You have to help me figure out how to spin this."

"I have to find Lola," Harry said tightly.

Zach grabbed his shoulder and tried to force him around, but Harry shoved him off.

"Jesus!" Zach said. "What is the matter with you?"

Harry pushed past Zach with as many of his things as he could carry and walked out. He threw them in the back of the truck, then rubbed his face, thinking. How would he find her?

Twenty-nine

Lola's neck hurt. She'd been sleeping on Casey's futon for the last three nights trying to figure out what she was going to do next. So far, no solutions had come to her. She leaned her head against the subway train's grimy window and closed her eyes. *What an awful week it had been.*

The first thing Lola had had to do after Zach kicked her out was to explain to Mallory what had happened. Mallory's driver, who apparently never had anything to do, was suddenly in high demand that afternoon and had explained to Mallory when she called for him that he was helping Lola move.

"Move?" Lola had heard her shout over the phone. "Come and get me before you take her anywhere!"

On the way to the train station, Lola had told Mallory the truth. "I lied," she said. "I don't really know Zach Miller. I know Sara Miller."

"What?" Mallory shouted. "Tell me everything and don't leave out a single detail."

Lola told Mallory the story of how she'd come to be in the lake house on their way to the train station. Mallory kept gasping and saying things like *"Get out!"*

When Lola had finished her story, Mallory had looked confused. "But . . . what about Harry?"

That was the million-dollar question, wasn't it?

Lola had been on the train to Brooklyn when she'd realized she'd left her phone at the lake house. Worse, she couldn't remember Harry's number. If it was possible for her day to get any blacker, it did in that moment.

The next person Lola had had to explain her situation to was Casey, who came stomping out of her apartment building to help Lola gather her things from the cab she'd taken from Grand Central. "I don't understand!" Casey said. "You were putting yourself out there!" She said it as if mystified by how someone could put themselves "out there" and not succeed. "You have to call Harry, you know. You can't leave that twisting in the wind."

"I forgot my phone. It's in Zach's house," Lola had said morosely.

"Oh my *God*, it's like you intentionally sabotage yourself!" Casey had shouted angrily.

Casey was right too damn much of the time.

Lola knew where Harry's parents lived—that much she remembered. But in between her mother's hospitalization and that nagging idea that she knew Harry had intended to meet Melissa that day, she hadn't yet gone uptown to knock on that door. Why was he going to meet Melissa?

In the gritty part of Long Island where Lola's mother lived, Lola got off the train and walked the four blocks to the home, where her mother had been moved just this morning.

Lola could hear her mother ranting about something as she walked down the hall to her room. "Mom?" She poked her head into the room her mother shared with poor Mrs. Porelli.

"Well, look what the cat drug in," her mother sneered. "I don't know what you're doing out there, Lola, but I don't need perverts coming here."

"What's that supposed to mean?" Lola asked, sighing, and dropped her backpack on a chair.

"That man come looking for you," her mother said, waving her hand.

What was her mother confused about now? "What man?"

"Some man says he's been to the hospital with you before. Says he's looking for you."

Lola's heart spasmed and then stopped. It just *stopped*. And yet, somehow, she managed to drag enough breath to say, "Harry?"

"I don't know what the hell his name is! I just know he come in here asking if I knew where you were. I said I don't have a clue, that no one cares about me out here. And then he asked for Casey. You know what kind of man that is? Can't have one sister, he'll take another?"

"Mom!" Lola cried. She was going to hyperventilate or pass out, whichever came first. Harry had been *here*? How did he even know where *here* was? "What did you tell him?"

"I told him I ain't telling no pervert where my daughters are. And he left."

Lola choked down a sob and sank onto the end of her mother's bed. "He left?"

"Are you deaf? Course he left. I'm not putting up with that shit."

Her heart was lamely beating again, but without conviction. It wanted to die. "Did he say what he wanted?"

"No! I wouldn't've cared if he did!"

"Oh, Mom," Lola said sadly. "What have you done?"

"Like it or not, missy, I'm your mother. Course I'm going to watch out for you if you're too dumb to do it yourself."

Lola's heart skipped and found its determination, fueled by ire. "Oh, yeah, thanks," she snapped. "Here's the thing, Mom—we don't need you to protect us now. We're adults, the danger is behind us. We needed you to protect us *then*."

Her mother's eyes widened with surprise. "You better not be speaking to me like that, Lola Elizabeth Dunne."

"Maybe I should have spoken to you like that a long time ago," Lola said dispassionately. "Maybe I should have learned to speak my heart a very long time ago instead of always hiding it from you and the authorities and anyone else who I feared would hurt us."

"That's a load of bullshit," her mother said.

"No, Mom, it's not. All my life, I have been careful not to say the wrong thing, not to give off any hint of despair because I was so afraid someone would come and take us away. And now, as an adult, I can't say what I feel. I never told you how hard you made our lives. I never told Will how angry I was with him. I never told Harry—" She caught herself.

"Never told Harry what?" her mother asked, peering at her.

"That I love him," Lola said. "Happy now?"

Her mother laughed.

◆　◆　◆

Lola dragged herself home, her emotional beatdown now complete. She was so numb she couldn't think. She was going to take a shower, put on something nice, and go to the Westbrooks' apartment with the hope of getting a message to Harry. And if she somehow managed to see him again—he'd probably run like the wind after talking to her mother—Lola would say what she'd meant to say to him Monday morning. She would say what she'd wanted to say for a few weeks now. And she would pray with all her might that it was not too late.

She used the spare key to get into Casey's apartment. It was dark; Casey wasn't home from work yet. Lola went into Casey's room and fell face down onto her bed and into a deep, morose sleep.

She thought she was dreaming when she heard Casey talking loudly. It took her a moment to rouse herself from sleep and sit up. It was no dream—Casey was shouting into the intercom to the front door.

"Please let me up."

Lola gasped. *Harry!*

"No!"

Lola shot off the bed and ran into the living room. Casey was standing in front of the intercom with her hands on her hips. She gestured for Lola to go back into the bedroom.

"Casey, please. Is she up there?"

Casey looked at Lola and lifted her shoulders.

"Yes," Lola said.

Casey frowned. She pressed the intercom button. "It depends," she said, looking at Lola. "It depends on what she is going to say to you."

"What the hell are you doing?" Lola cried, and raced for the intercom. But Casey blocked it, pushing her sister back. "You have to do it, Lola. You have to say what you feel for this guy or I am going to kill you. I've read your book, so I know how to do it."

"Will you butt out?" Lola said angrily, trying to push past her.

"No! I'm not going to sit back and watch you ruin your life with all these damn phobias!"

Lola pushed Casey, who banged into the coatrack she had at the door. Casey looked as if she was going to haul off and hit her, but they were both startled by a knock at the door. Casey whirled around and looked out the peephole. *"It's him!"* she hissed.

"I know you're in there, Lola," Harry said through the door.

Lola pushed Casey aside and threw open the door.

"How did you get in?" Casey asked angrily from behind Lola.

"Some guy coming out held the door open for me," he said, and braced his arm against the door frame and glared at Lola. "For God's sake, woman, where have you been? Why haven't you answered your phone?"

"Because she forgot it at your friend's house," Casey said.

"What?" Harry said, looking annoyed.

"Okay, all right, I can take it from here," Lola said, gesturing for Casey to back off. "It's true. In the mad rush of being kicked out of the lake house, I left my phone behind. I haven't had a chance to replace it because my mother was in the hospital. How did you find me?" Lola demanded.

"Your mother," he said. "I left her my number."

"She didn't tell me that!" Lola said irritably. "My mother *called* you?"

"May I come in?" Harry asked as two women passed by behind him. "I'll tell you everything."

Lola stepped back to let him in.

"Our mother *called* you?" Casey echoed incredulously when he'd shut the door.

"Yep. She cussed me out and then told me where to find you. Lola, I am so sorry Zach kicked you out. I wish I'd been there—I would have sorted it out with him."

"I don't think so," Lola snorted. "He's threatening to sue me, just so you know. And of course I haven't told Sara yet because I left my phone behind. She's going to be furious. Oh, and I don't have a place to live. My mother *called* you?"

"She called me. Because I was pretty adamant that I needed to talk to you," he said, stepping closer to her. "Look, I need to get something off my chest—"

"Lola!" Casey said frantically. "Don't let him—"

"All right, everyone wait a minute!" Lola shouted, throwing up her hands. "Casey, go in your bedroom, give us a minute here. Harry, sit down."

Harry didn't sit. He shoved his hands in his pockets. "I'll hear what you have to say standing up."

"Okay, fine," she said. "First, I want to say I wish I wasn't such a chickenshit. I know that about myself, and no matter how hard I try not to be, it keeps happening. I just have this irrational fear of disappointment. But from here on out, I am only speaking my truths, okay?"

"Your what?"

"It's from her counseling," Casey said.

Lola jerked around. "Casey! Bedroom!"

"Fine," Casey said, slinking out. "I'm just trying to help."

Lola turned back to Harry. "So here is my truth, Harry. I have fallen in love with you," she said. "Yes, it's true! I want to be with you every day. I would do anything for you, absolutely anything. I've been completely despondent without you. I *love* you . . . but you have to love me, too," she said, pointing at him. "If this is just an experiment for you, or you aren't entirely certain, or if you were meeting Melissa for a reason, then you need to go build your bridges and leave me alone. Do you get it? Do you understand? No more friends with benefits. I'm *in*. I'm in one hundred percent, in over my head, and you know what I want? I want you."

Harry nodded. He ran a hand over his hair. "I went to see Melissa to tell her to stop hoping, that it was never going to happen. That I love someone else."

That warm honey feeling was Lola's heart melting. "You did?"

Harry slowly sank to his knees.

"What are you doing?" Lola asked, confused.

"I have been waiting for you to say it, Lola. I have been waiting for you to admit you love me. Because I love you, too, more than I thought was possible to love someone. I want you, too, all or nothing . . . but I knew I couldn't have that if you couldn't even tell me how you felt. I had to hear you say it before I could even think of proposing to you."

"Before you *what*?" Casey shouted from the bedroom.

"Lola Dunne, will you marry me?" he asked.

The floor seemed to shift under Lola's feet. "Are you *crazy*?"

"Crazy for you, you little lunatic. I realize this is all spur of the moment, seeing as how I was pretty sure I would never see you again. I don't have a ring, and honestly, I can't afford one right now. But I've always gone after what I've wanted, Lola. I've always been very sure of myself. When everyone around me told me I was wrong, I knew what I was doing was right. And then I met you, and suddenly, everything was upside down and I'd never been so uncertain in my life . . . until I realized that I wasn't confused. Actually, I've never had so much clarity in my life. I never knew what I truly wanted until you rose up out of that pool, Lola, and I want *you*. I *love* you. And I want to marry you."

"He's crazy!" Casey shouted. "But ohmigod, if you don't say yes, I'll hurt you," she added, suddenly appearing next to Lola.

Lola's heart was racing. This couldn't be happening; it was too good, too perfect. But the thing she was feeling in her chest was sheer joy. Harry was right in something he'd once said—she never would have known how utterly joyful and beautiful this moment could be had she not been so terribly disappointed before.

Harry winced. "God, don't say no," he said. "I've never actually proposed to anyone in my life. It's you or nothing, Lola Dunne."

"What are you doing?" Casey cried, and chucked Lola in the back.

Lola stumbled, catching herself on his shoulders. She smiled. She sank down on her knees in front of him. "Yes, Harry Westbrook. *Yes*, I will marry you. I love you, Handsome Harry! I love you, I love you." She threw her arms around his neck. "But maybe we save getting married until we've had a chance to know each other a little longer?"

"Not making any promises," he said, and kissed her neck, toppling over with her onto the rug and landing on a pair of Casey's shoes.

"Not my Stuart Weitzmans!" Casey cried, and tried to pull them out from underneath Harry, which caused her to trip and end up next to them on the floor. "This is ridiculous," she said.

Lola laughed. She laughed with the gaiety of a little girl who never had much opportunity to laugh. Until now.

Epilogue

Lola's book, *Apartment 3C*, was a modest success. The reviews said the writing was "engaging" and that she was a "debut author to watch" . . . but the sales were not exactly what the publisher had hoped. Still, all was not lost—her publisher wanted a second book. "Maybe something a little more upbeat," her editor suggested.

"Don't listen to her," Cyrus warned Lola. "You write what you want to write. We'll sell it. I believe in you, Lola."

Lola was grateful for his confidence in her and had been working on an idea about three college girls who kill a professor who slept with one of them. Cyrus sounded a little uncertain when she told him, but said, "Write it. We'll go from there."

Harry won the bid for only one of the three bridges in the toll road project, but it was enough to get him a leg up. He won two other contracts after that, both of them small jobs, but big enough that they were helping him build the resume he needed.

After the dustup with Zach and Sara died down, the lake house was sold to a Wall Street banker. Zach and Harry were friends again. Sara moved to Los Angeles.

Harry and Lola's income was modest, so they rented a two-bedroom cottage from the East Beach Lake Cottages. Their front porch overlooked the lake, and even though times were lean, they were really quite happy.

Lola wrote in the mornings, then worked part-time in Mallory's candy shop in the afternoons. She loved cooking for Harry who, unlike Will, appreciated her skills. He boasted that he'd gained ten pounds in the year they'd been together, although Lola couldn't see where he'd put it.

They spent Sundays with his parents, and once a month they made the trip out to Long Island to see her mother. Neither of them could take more than that. Her mother's health continued to deteriorate, but her acid tongue remained very much intact. "I don't know why you want to get married," she'd said to Lola. "You'll probably end up divorced again."

"No, she won't," Harry said. "And you should be more supportive."

"Don't tell me what I ought to be, mister," her mother said, coughing violently with her anger. But Lola thought her mother really liked Harry.

Her siblings certainly did. It occurred to her one day that they'd stopped calling her and had started calling for Harry. "Is Harry there? I have a question about my car," Ty would say. Or, "Is Harry home? I need some advice about this guy," Casey would say. Lola wasn't bothered by it—she was happy that they loved Harry, too.

Harry's mother, on the other hand, did not like Lola. She was still mourning the loss of Melissa. Lola knew this because Mrs. Westbrook would say to her, "Melissa was such a lovely girl."

"Your mom is never going to come around," Lola warned Harry one evening as they drove back to Lake Haven. "You're going to have to choose between your mother and me."

He laughed. "No contest."

"You better mean me," she said. Harry took her hand, a big grin on his face.

One night, Lola was in bed, a book propped on her knees, a bowl of popcorn on the bed beside her. She heard Harry's truck on the drive, heard his boots on the steps of the porch. He walked into the bedroom, a dirty mess of flannel and denim and sweat.

Lola grinned. "Hey, there, Hardhat Harry. I left some King Ranch chicken in the fridge for you."

Harry didn't say anything. He walked deeper into the room and dropped his hard hat.

Lola looked at the hat, then at him. "Are you all right?"

"Yep," he said, and pulled his shirt over his head. "Something extraordinary happened."

He looked so serious, that Lola's heart began to race. "What happened?" she asked, and pushed herself up, her book falling off her lap. "Did someone die?"

"No. Remember that project in Maryland I told you about?"

"Yes, the two overpasses. Oh no," she said, and smiled sadly. "Did it go to someone else?"

Harry laughed. "Oh ye of little faith. No, it went to me. I got the first draw against the funds today."

"That's wonderful!" she exclaimed, clapping her hands. "Congratulations!"

"But that's not the extraordinary news." He walked over to the bed and sank down on one knee beside her. "Lola, do you still love me?"

"Pretty much," she said airily. "Why, did you do something?"

"Do you still want to marry me?"

"Of course. Do you still want to marry me?"

"Does this answer your question?" He reached into his pocket and pulled out a ring, holding it up to her. It was incredible—a diamond the size of the nail on her little finger, glittering in the lamplight.

Lola's eyes widened with shock. "Harry, are you insane? We don't have the money for a ring!"

"I didn't buy it."

She gasped. "What the hell have you done, Harry Westbrook?" she demanded, guessing that he had traded his pickup or some foolish thing for it.

Harry laughed and took her hand, sliding the ring onto her finger. "Look at that, a perfect fit."

Lola held her hand up to admire it. "Is it real?"

"Of course it is, you little lunatic. It belonged to my grandmother."

Lola stared at him. "What?"

"The extraordinary thing is that my mother gave it to me. She asked me to come into the city today. She said it was time I made an honest woman of you."

"No she didn't," Lola scoffed. Mrs. Westbrook despised her.

But Harry nodded.

"*Your* mother said that? She hates me!"

"Apparently she doesn't," he said, grinning. "She finally gets how much I love you, Lola. And I do. I love you so much," he said, and kissed her knuckles. "You're the best thing that ever happened to me."

"Oh, Harry," she said. "I love you, too. More than life." She couldn't imagine how this man had come into her life, had made her open up, had coaxed her into walking out on that limb. But he had, and she would love him with all her heart as long as she lived. "I love you," she said again, and leaned down to kiss him.

Harry came up, gathering her in his arms, and rolling with her on the bed. The popcorn spilled beneath his weight.

"What is that?" he asked as he kissed her. "What's that sound?"

"Popcorn," she whispered, and rolled on top of him, pushing popcorn out of the way, kissing him. "Don't worry, I'll make another batch."

Harry chuckled against her lips. "You're a little lunatic, you know that? But you're my lunatic."

Truer words had never been spoken, because Lola was absolutely crazy for her Handsome Harry.

If you enjoyed this book, connect with Julia London online!

Read all about Julia and her books: http://julialondon.com/

Like Julia on Facebook: https://www.facebook.com/JuliaLondon

Sign up for the newsletter: https://www.julialondon.com/newsletter

Follow Julia on Twitter: https://twitter.com/JuliaFLondon

Read about Julia on Goodreads: http://www.goodreads.com/JuliaLondon

About the Author

Julia London is the *New York Times*, *USA Today*, and *Publishers Weekly* bestselling author of more than thirty romance novels. Her historical titles include the popular Desperate Debutantes series, the Secrets of Hadley Green series, and the Cabot Sisters series; her contemporary works include the Lake Haven, Pine River, and Cedar Springs series. She has won the RT Bookclub Award for Best Historical Romance and has been a six-time finalist for the prestigious RITA Award for excellence in romantic fiction. She lives in Austin, Texas.